the gravely put-upon, Alexia Maccon rolled herself out of bed and picked up her nightgown from where it lay, a puddle of frills and lace, on the stone floor.

It was one of her husband's wedding gifts to her. Or more probably gifts to *him,* as it was made of a soft French silk and had scandalously few pleats. It was quite fashion-forward and daringly French, and Alexia rather liked it. Conall rather liked taking it off her. Which was how it had ended up on the floor. They had negotiated a temporal relationship with the nightgown; most of the time she was able to wear it only out of the bed. He could be very persuasive when he put his mind, and other parts of his anatomy, to it. Lady Maccon figured she would have to get used to sleeping in the altogether. Although there was that niggling worry that the house might catch fire and cause her to dash about starkers in full view of all. The worry was receding slowly, for she lived with a pack of werewolves and was acclimatizing to their constant nudity—by necessity if not preference. There was, currently, far more hairy masculinity in her life than any Englishwoman should really have to put up with on a monthly basis. That said, half the pack was away fighting in northern India; someday there would be even more full-moon maleness. She thought of her husband; him she had to deal with on a *daily* basis.

Praise for *Soulless*:

"Carriger debuts brilliantly with a blend of victorian romance, screwball comedy of manners and alternate history . . ."   —*Publishers Weekly* (Starred Review)

BY GAIL CARRIGER

The Parasol Protectorate

Soulless

Changeless

Blameless

CHANGELESS

The Parasol Protectorate: Book the Second

GAIL CARRIGER

orbit

www.orbitbooks.net

corriged

This book is a work of fiction. Names, characters, places, and incidents are the product of the author's imagination or are used fictitiously. Any resemblance to actual events, locales, or persons, living or dead, is coincidental.

If you purchase this book without a cover you should be aware that this book may have been stolen property and reported as "unsold and destroyed" to the publisher. In such case neither the author nor the publisher has received any payment for this "stripped book."

Orbit
Hachette Book Group
237 Park Avenue
New York, NY 10017
Visit our website at www.orbitbooks.net

Orbit is an imprint of Hachette Book Group. The Orbit name and logo are trademarks of Little, Brown Book Group Limited.

Printed in the United States of America

First Orbit edition: April 2010

10 9 8 7 6 5 4

Acknowledgments

With grateful thanks to the three least-appreciated and hardest-working proselytizers of the written word: independent bookstores, librarians, and teachers.

CHANGELESS

CHAPTER ONE

Wherein Things Disappear, Alexia Gets Testy Over Tents, and Ivy Has an Announcement

They are what?"

Lord Conall Maccon, Earl of Woolsey, was yelling. Loudly. This was to be expected from Lord Maccon, who was generally a loud sort of gentleman—the ear-bleeding combination of lung capacity and a large barrel chest.

Alexia Maccon, Lady Woolsey, muhjah to the queen, Britain's secret preternatural weapon extraordinaire, blinked awake from a deep and delicious sleep.

"Wasn't me," she immediately said, without having the barest hint of an idea as to what her husband was carrying on about. Of course, it usually *was* her, but it would not do to fess up right away, regardless of whatever it was that had his britches in a bunch this time. Alexia screwed her eyes shut and squirmed farther into the warmth of down-stuffed blankets. Couldn't they argue about it later?

"What do you mean *gone*?" The bed shook slightly with the sheer volume behind Lord Maccon's yell. The amazing thing was that he wasn't nearly as loud as he could be when he really put his lungs into it.

"Well, I certainly did not tell them to go," denied Alexia into her pillow. She wondered who "they" were. Then she came about to the realization, taking a fluffy-cottony sort of pathway to get there, that he wasn't yelling at her but at someone else. In their bedroom.

Oh dear.

Unless he was yelling at himself.

Oh *dear.*

"What, *all* of them?"

Alexia's scientific side wondered idly at the power of sound waves—hadn't she heard of a recent Royal Society pamphlet on the subject?

"All at once?"

Lady Maccon sighed, rolled toward the hollering, and cracked one eyelid. Her husband's large naked back filled her field of vision. To see any more, she'd have to lever herself upright. Since that would probably expose her to more cold air, she declined to lever. She did, however, observe that the sun was barely down. What was Conall doing awake and aloud so freakishly early? For, while her husband roaring was not uncommon, its occurrence in the wee hours of late afternoon was. Inhuman decency dictated that even Woolsey Castle's Alpha werewolf remain quiet at this time of day.

"How wide of a radius, exactly? It canna have extended this far."

Oh dear, his Scottish accent had put in an appearance. That never bode well for anyone.

"All over London? No? *Just* the entire Thames embankment and city center. That is simply not possible."

This time Lady Maccon managed to discern a mild murmuring response to her husband's latest holler. Well, she consoled herself, at least he hadn't gone entirely potty. But who would dare attempt to rustle up Lord Maccon in his private quarters at such an abysmal hour? She tried once more to see over his back. *Why* did he have to be so substantial?

She levered.

Alexia Maccon was known as a lady of regal bearing and not much more. Society generally considered her looks too swarthy to give much credence despite her rank. Alexia, herself, had always believed good posture was her last best hope and was proud to have acquired the "regal bearing" epithet. This morning, however, blankets and pillows thwarted her; she could only flounder gracelessly up to her elbows, her backbone as limp as a noodle.

All that her Herculean effort revealed was a hint of wispy silver and a vaguely human form: Formerly Merriway.

"Mummer murmur," said Formerly Merriway, straining for full apparition in the not-quite darkness. She was a polite ghost, relatively young and well preserved, and still entirely sane.

"Oh, for goodness' sake." Lord Maccon seemed to be getting only more irritated. Lady Maccon knew that particular tone of voice well—it was usually directed at her. "But there is nothing on this Earth that can *do* that."

Formerly Merriway said something else.

"Well, have they consulted all the daylight agents?"

Alexia strained to hear. Already gifted with a low, sweet voice, the ghost was difficult to understand when she intentionally dampened her tone. Formerly Merriway might have said, "Yes, and they have no idea either."

The ghost seemed frightened, which caused Alexia more concern than Lord Maccon's irritation (which was sadly frequent). Little could frighten the already dead, with the possible exception of a preternatural. And even Alexia, soulless, was only dangerous under very specific circumstances.

"What, no idea at all? Right." The earl tossed his blankets aside and climbed out of bed.

Formerly Merriway gasped and shimmered about, presenting her transparent back to the completely naked man.

Alexia appreciated the courtesy, even if Lord Maccon did not. Polite to the core was poor little Merriway. Or what was left of her core. Lady Maccon, on the other hand, was not so reticent. Her husband had a decidedly fine backside, if she did say so herself. And she had said so, to her scandalized friend Miss Ivy Hisselpenny, on more than one occasion. It may be far too early to be awake, but it was never too early to admire something of that caliber. The artistically pleasing body part drifted out of view as her husband strode toward his dressing chamber.

"Where is Lyall?" he barked.

Lady Maccon tried to go back to sleep.

"What! Lyall's gone too? Is *everyone* going to disappear on me? No, I did not send him. . . ." A pause. "Oh yes, you are perfectly correct, I did. The pack was"—

blub blub blub—"coming in at"—*blub, blub*—"station."
Splash. "Shouldn't he have returned by now?"

Her husband was obviously washing, as periodically
his bellowing was interrupted by soggy noises. Alexia
strained to hear Tunstell's voice. Without his valet, her
louder half was bound to look quite disastrously disheveled. It was never a good idea to let the earl dress unsu-
pervised.

"Right, well, send a claviger for him posthaste."

At which point, Formerly Merriway's spectral form
vanished from view.

Conall reappeared in Alexia's line of sight and gathered up his gold pocket watch from the bedside table.
"Of course, they will take it as an insult, but nothing to
be done about it."

Ha, she had been right. He was, in fact, not dressed at
all but was wearing only a cloak. *No Tunstell then.*

The earl seemed to remember his wife for the first
time.

Alexia counterfeited sleep.

Conall shook Alexia gently, admiring both the tousled
mound of inky hair and the artfully feigned disinterest.
When his shaking became insistent, she blinked long
lashes at him.

"Ah, good evening, my dear."

Alexia glared at her husband out of slightly red-rimmed
brown eyes. This early evening tomfoolery wouldn't be
so horrible if he had not kept her up half the day. Not that
those particular exertions had been unpleasant, simply
exuberant and lengthy.

"What are you about, husband?" she inquired, her
voice laced buttery-smooth with suspicion.

"All apologies, my dear."

Lady Maccon absolutely hated it when her husband called her his "dear." It meant he was up to something but was not going to tell her about it.

"I must run off to the office early tonight. Some important BUR business has cropped up." From the cloak and the fact that his canines were showing, Alexia surmised that he literally meant run, in wolf form. Whatever was going on must need urgent attention, indeed. Lord Maccon usually preferred to arrive at BUR in carriage, comfort, and style, not fur.

"Has it?" muttered Alexia.

The earl began to tuck the blankets about his wife. His large hands were unexpectedly gentle. Touching his preternatural spouse, his canines disappeared. In that brief moment, he was mortal.

"Are you meeting with the Shadow Council tonight?" he asked.

Alexia considered. Was it Thursday? "Yes."

"You are in for an interesting conference," advised the earl, goading her.

Alexia sat up, undoing all of his nice tucking. "What? Why?" The blankets fell, revealing that Lady Maccon's endowments were considerable and not fabricated through fashionable artifice such as stuffed corset or too-tight stays. Despite nightly familiarity with this fact, Lord Maccon was prone to dragging her onto secluded balconies at balls in order to check and "make certain" this remained the case.

"I *am* sorry for waking you so early, my dear." There was that dreaded phrase again. "I promise I shall make it up to you in the morning." He waggled his eyebrows at her lasciviously and leaned down for a long and thorough kiss.

Lady Maccon sputtered and pushed at his large chest ineffectually.

"Conall, *what* is going on?"

But her irritating werewolf of a husband was already away and out of the room.

"Pack!" His holler resounded through the hallway. At least this time he had made a pretense of seeing to her comfort by shutting the door first.

Alexia and Conall Maccon's bedroom took up the whole of one of the highest towers Woolsey had to offer, which, admittedly, was more of a dignified pimple off the top of one wall. Despite this comparative isolation, the earl's bellow could be heard throughout most of the massive building, even down to the back parlor, where his clavigers were taking their tea.

The Woolsey clavigers worked hard about their various duties during the day, looking after slumbering werewolf charges and taking care of daylight pack business. For most, tea was a brief and necessary respite before they were called to their other nonpack work. As packs tended to favor boldly creative companions, and Woolsey was close to London, more than a few of its clavigers were actively engaged in West End theatricals. Despite the lure of Aldershot pudding, Madeira cake, and gunpowder black tea, their lord's yodel had them up and moving as fast as could be desired.

The entire house suddenly became a hubbub of activity: carriages and men on horseback came and went, clattering on the stone cobbles of the forecourt; doors slammed; voices called back and forth. It sounded like the dirigible disembarkation green in Hyde Park.

Emitting that heaviest of sighs that denotes the gravely put-upon, Alexia Maccon rolled herself out of bed and picked up her nightgown from where it lay, a puddle of frills and lace, on the stone floor. It was one of her husband's wedding gifts to her. Or more probably gifts to *him*, as it was made of a soft French silk and had scandalously few pleats. It was quite fashion-forward and daringly French, and Alexia rather liked it. Conall rather liked taking it off her. Which was how it had ended up on the floor. They had negotiated a temporal relationship with the nightgown; most of the time, she was able to wear it only out of the bed. He could be very persuasive when he put his mind, and other parts of his anatomy, to it. Lady Maccon figured she would have to get used to sleeping in the altogether. Although there was that niggling worry that the house might catch fire and cause her to dash about starkers in full view of all. The worry was receding slowly, for she lived with a pack of werewolves and was acclimatizing to their constant nudity—by necessity if not preference. There was, currently, far more hairy masculinity in her life than any Englishwoman should really have to put up with on a monthly basis. That said, half the pack was away fighting in northern India; someday there would be even more full-moon maleness. She thought of her husband; him she had to deal with on a *daily* basis.

A timid knock sounded, followed by a long pause. Then the door to the bedchamber was pushed slowly open, and a heart-shaped face paired with dark blond hair and enormous violet eyes peered in. The eyes were apprehensive. The maid to whom they belonged had learned, to her abject mortification, to give her master and mistress extra time before disturbing them in the bedchamber. One could never predict Lord Maccon's amorous moods, but one could certainly predict his temper if they were interrupted.

Noting his absence with obvious relief, the maid entered carrying a basin of hot water and a warm white towel over one arm. She curtsied gracefully to Alexia. She wore a modish, if somber, gray dress with a crisp white apron pinned over it. Alexia knew, though others did not, that the high white collar about her slender neck disguised multiple bite marks. As if being a former vampire drone in a werewolf household were not shocking enough, the maid then opened her mouth and proved that she was also, quite reprehensibly, French.

"Good evening, madame."

Alexia smiled. "Good evening, Angelique."

The new Lady Maccon, barely three months in, had already established her taste as quite daring, her table as incomparable, and her style as trendsetting. And while it was not generally known among the ton that she sat on the Shadow Council, she was observed to be on friendly terms with Queen Victoria. Couple that with a temperamental werewolf husband of considerable property and social standing, and her eccentricities—such as carrying a parasol at night and retaining an overly pretty French maid—were overlooked by high society.

Angelique placed the basin and a towel on Alexia's dressing table and disappeared once more. She reappeared a polite ten minutes later with a cup of tea, whisked away the used towel and dirty water, and returned with a determined look and an air of quiet authority. Usually, there was a minor contest of wills when dressing Lady Maccon, but recent praise in the society column of the *Lady's Pictorial* had bolstered Alexia's faith in Angelique's decisions à la toilette.

"Very well, you harridan," said Lady Maccon to the silent girl. "What am I wearing tonight?"

Angelique made her selection from the wardrobe: a military-inspired tea-colored affair trimmed in chocolate brown velvet and large brass buttons. It was very smart and appropriate to a business meeting of the Shadow Council.

"You will have to leave off the silk scarf," said Alexia, her token protest. "I shall need to show neck tonight." She did not explain that bite marks were monitored by the palace guards. Angelique was not one of those who knew Alexia Maccon sat as muhjah. She may be Alexia's personal maid, but she was still French, and despite Floote's feeling on the matter, the domestic staff didn't have to know *everything*.

Angelique acquiesced without protest and put Lady Maccon's hair up simply, complementing the severity of the dress. Only a few loops and tendrils peeked out from under a small lace cap. Then Alexia made good her escape, aflutter with curiosity over her husband's early departure.

There was no one to ask. No one waited at the dinner table; clavigers and pack alike had vanished along with the earl. The house was empty but for the servants. Alexia turned her concentrated interest on them, but they scattered about their various tasks with the ease of three months' practice.

The Woolsey butler, Rumpet, refused, with an air of affronted dignity, to answer her questions. Even Floote claimed to have been in the library all afternoon and overheard nothing.

"Floote, truly, you simply *must* be acquainted with what has transpired. I depend upon you to know what is going on! You always do."

Floote gave her a look that made her feel about seven years of age. Despite graduating from butler to personal secretary, Floote had never quite lost his severe aura of butlerness.

He handed Alexia her leather dispatch case. "I reviewed the documents from last Sunday's meeting."

"Well, what is your opinion?" Floote had been with Alexia's father before her, and, despite Alessandro Tarabotti's rather outrageous reputation (or perhaps because of it), Floote had learned *things*. Alexia was finding herself, as muhjah, more and more reliant upon his opinion, if only to confirm her own.

Floote considered. "My concern is with the deregulation clause, madam. I suspect that it is too soon to release the scientists on their own recognizance."

"Mmm, that was my assessment as well. I shall recommend against that particular clause. Thank you, Floote."

The elderly man turned to go.

"Oh, and, Floote."

He turned back, resigned.

"Something substantial has happened to overset my husband. I suspect research in the library may be called for when I return tonight. Best to clear your schedule."

"Very good, madam," said Floote with a little bow. He glided off to summon her a carriage.

Alexia finished her repast, gathered up her dispatch case, her latest parasol, and her long woolen coat, and wandered out the front door.

Only to discover exactly where everyone had gone—outside onto the sweeping front lawn that led up to the cobbled courtyard of the castle. They had managed to multiply themselves, don attire of a military persuasion, and, for some reason known only to their tiny little werewolf brains, proceed to engage in setting up a considerable number of large canvas tents. This involved the latest in government-issue self-expanding steam poles, boiled in large copper pots like so much metal pasta. Each one started out the size of a spyglass before the heat caused it to suddenly expand with a popping noise. As was the general military protocol, it took far more soldiers than it ought to stand around watching the poles boil, and when one expanded, a cheer erupted forth. The pole was grasped between a set of leather potholders and taken off to a tent.

Lady Maccon lost her temper. "What *are* you all doing out here?"

No one looked at her or acknowledged her presence.

Alexia threw her head back and yelled, *"Tunstell!"* She had not quite the lung capacity to match that of her massive husband, but neither was she built on the delicate-flower end of the feminine spectrum. Alexia's father's ancestors had once conquered an empire, and it was when Lady Maccon yelled that people realized how that was accomplished.

Tunstell came bouncing over, a handsome, if gangly, ginger fellow with a perpetual grin and a certain carelessness of manner that most found endearing and everybody else found exasperating.

"Tunstell," Alexia said calmly and reasonably, she thought, "*why* are there tents on my front lawn?"

Tunstell, Lord Maccon's valet and chief among the clavigers, looked about in his chipper way, as if to say that he had not noticed anything amiss and was now delighted to find that they had company. Tunstell was always chirpy. It was his greatest character flaw. He was also one of the few residents of Woolsey Castle who managed to remain entirely unfazed by, or possibly unaware of, either Lord or Lady Maccon's wrath. This was his second-greatest character flaw.

"He didn't warn you?" The claviger's freckled face was flushed with exertion from helping to raise one of the tents.

"No, *he* most certainly did not." Alexia tapped the silver tip of her parasol on the front stoop.

Tunstell grinned. "Well, my lady, the rest of the pack has returned." He flipped both hands at the canvas-ridden chaos before her, waggling his fingers dramatically. Tunstell was an actor of some note—everything he did was dramatic.

"Tunstell," said Alexia carefully, as though to a dim child, "this would indicate that my husband possessed a very, very big pack. There are no werewolf Alphas in England who can boast a pack of such proportions."

"Oh, well, the rest of the pack brought the rest of the regiment with them," explained Tunstell in a conspiratorial way, as though he and Alexia were partners engaged in the most delightful lark.

"I believe it is customary for the pack and fellow officers of a given regiment to separate upon returning home.

So that, well, one doesn't wake up to find hundreds of soldiers camping on one's lawn."

"Well, Woolsey has always done things a little differently. Having the biggest pack in England, we're the only ones who split the pack for military service, so we keep the Coldsteam Guards together for a few weeks when we get home. Builds solidarity." Tunstell gestured expansively once more, his fine white hands weaving about in the air, and nodded enthusiastically.

"And does this solidarity have to occur on Woolsey's front lawn?" *Tap tap tap* went the parasol. The Bureau of Unnatural Registry (BUR) was experimenting with new weaponry of late. At the disbanding of the Hypocras Club several months previous, a small compressed steam unit had been discovered. It apparently heated continually until it burst. Lord Maccon had shown it to his wife. It made a ticking noise just prior to explosion, rather like that of Alexia's parasol at this precise moment. Tunstell was unaware of this correlation or he might have proceeded with greater caution. On the other hand, being Tunstell, he might not.

"Yes, isn't it jolly?" crowed Tunstell.

"But why?" *Tap tap tap.*

"It is where we have always camped," said a new voice, apparently belonging to someone equally unfamiliar with the ticking, exploding steam device.

Lady Maccon whirled to glare at the man who dared to interrupt her midrant. The gentleman in question was both tall and broad, although not quite to her husband's scale. Lord Maccon was Scottish-big; this gentleman was only English-big—there was a distinct difference. Also, unlike the earl, who periodically bumped into things as though his form were larger than his perception of it, this man seemed entirely comfortable with his size. He wore full officer formals and knew he looked good in them. His boots were spit-shined, his blond hair coiffed high, and he boasted an accent that very carefully was no accent at all. Alexia knew the type: education, money, and blue blood.

She gritted her teeth. "Oh, it is, is it? Well, not anymore." She turned back to Tunstell. "We are hosting a dinner party the evening after next. Have them remove those tents immediately."

"Unacceptable," said the large blond gentleman, moving closer. Alexia began to believe that he was no gentleman, despite his accent and immaculate appearance. She also noticed that he had the most cutting blue eyes, icy and intense.

Tunstell, a look of worry behind his cheery grin, seemed unable to decide whom to obey.

Alexia ignored the newcomer. "If they must camp here, move them around to the back."

Tunstell turned to do her bidding but was stopped by the stranger, who put a large white-gloved hand on his shoulder.

"But this is preposterous." The man's perfect teeth snapped at Lady Maccon. "The regiment has always taken up residence in the forecourt. It is far more convenient than the grounds."

"Now," said Alexia to Tunstell, still ignoring the intruder. Imagine talking to her in such a tone of voice, and they hadn't yet been introduced.

Tunstell, less cheerful than she had ever seen him, was looking back and forth between her and the stranger.

Any moment now, he might place his hand upon his head and enact a swoon of confusion.

"Stay precisely where you are, Tunstell," instructed the stranger.

"Who the devil are you?" Alexia asked, the man's cavalier interference irritating her into using actual profanity.

"Major Channing Channing of the Chesterfield Channings."

Alexia gawked. No wonder he was so very full of himself. One would have to be, laboring all one's life under a name like that.

"Well, Major Channing, I shall ask you not to interfere with the running of the household. It is *my* domain."

"Ah, you are the new housekeeper? I was not informed that Lady Maccon had made any such drastic changes."

Alexia was not surprised by this assumption. She was very well aware of the fact that she was not of the appearance others patently expected of a Lady Maccon, being too Italian, too old, and too, frankly, ample. She was going to correct his error before further embarrassment ensued, but he did not provide her with the opportunity. Clearly Channing Channing of the Chesterfield Channings enjoyed the cadence of his own voice.

"Don't you worry your pretty little head about our camping arrangements. I assure you, neither his lordship nor her ladyship will take you to task." The ladyship in question flushed at his presumption. "You simply let us get on with our business and return to your duties."

"I can assure you," said Alexia, "everything that occurs in or around Woolsey Castle concerns me."

Channing Channing of the Chesterfield Channings

smiled his perfect smile and twinkled his blue eyes in a way Alexia was certain he believed to be alluring. "Now, really, neither of us has time for this, do we? Just you scamper off and get about your daily chores, and we shall see about a bit of a reward later for your obedience."

Was that a leer? Alexia actually thought it might be. "Are you philandering with me, sir?" She was imprudently startled into asking.

"Would you like me to be?" he replied, grin widening.

Well, that certainly settled that. *This* was no gentleman.

"Uh-oh," said Tunstell very softly, backing away slightly.

"What a nauseating thought," said Lady Maccon.

"Oh, I don't know," said Major Channing, moving in closer, "a fiery Italian thing like you, with a nice figure and not too old, might have a few lively nights left. I always did fancy a bit of the foreign."

Alexia, who was only half Italian, and that only by birth, having been raised English to the bone, could not decide which part of that sentence offended her most. She sputtered.

The repulsive Channing person looked like he might actually try to touch her.

Alexia hauled off and hit him, hard, with her parasol, right on the top of his head.

Everyone in the courtyard stopped what they were about and turned to look at the statuesque lady currently engaged in whacking their third in command, Woolsey Pack Gamma, commander of the Coldsteam Guards abroad, with a parasol.

The major's eyes shifted to an even icier blue and

black about the rim of each iris, and two of his perfect white teeth turned pointed.

Werewolf, was he? Well, Alexia Maccon's parasol was tipped with silver for a reason. She walloped him again, this time making certain the tip touched his skin. At the same time, she rediscovered her powers of speech.

"How dare you! You impudent"—*whack*—"arrogant"—*whack*—"overbearing"—*whack*—"unobservant dog!" *Whack, whack.* Normally Alexia wasn't given to such language or unadulterated violence, but circumstances seemed to warrant it. He was a werewolf and, without her touching him and canceling out his supernatural abilities, practically impossible to damage. Thus, she felt justified in clobbering him a couple of times for discipline's sake.

Major Channing, shocked by a physical attack from an apparently defenseless housekeeper, shielded his head and then grabbed the parasol, using it to yank her toward him. Alexia lost her grip, and Major Channing stumbled back in possession of the accessory. He looked like he wanted to hit her back with it, which could have done Alexia some real damage, as she had no supernatural healing abilities at all. But instead, he tossed the parasol aside and made as if to slap her.

Which was when Tunstell leaped onto his back. The redhead wrapped long arms and legs about the major, trapping Channing's limbs at his sides.

The assembled newcomers gasped in horror. For a claviger to attack a member of the pack was unheard of and was grounds for instant expulsion. However, those of the pack and their companion clavigers who knew who

Alexia was all dropped whatever they were doing and rushed forward to assist.

Major Channing shook Tunstell off and backhanded him hard across the face. The strike sent Tunstell to the ground easily. The claviger gave a loud groan and collapsed.

Alexia gave the blond blackguard a glare of wrath and bent to check on the fallen redhead. His eyes were closed, but he appeared to be breathing. She stood and said calmly, "I would stop this now, if I were you, Mr. Channing." She dropped the "major" out of contempt.

"I should say not," said the man, unbuttoning his uniform and stripping off his white gloves. "Now you both need discipline."

In the next second, he began to change. In polite company, this would have been shocking, but most everyone there had witnessed the event before. Over the decades since pack integration, the military had become as comfortable with werewolf change as they were with profanity. But to change in front of a lady, even if one did think she was a housekeeper? Murmurs of alarm rippled through the crowd.

Alexia was also surprised. It was only just nightfall, and it was nowhere near full moon. Which meant this man was older and more experienced than his brash behavior indicated. He was also darn good at the change, polished in its execution despite what her husband had once described as the worst pain a man could stand and still live. Alexia had seen youngsters of the pack writhe and whimper, but Major Channing shifted smoothly from human to wolf. Skin, bone, and fur rearranged itself, resulting in one of the most beautiful wolves Alexia had ever seen: large and almost pure white, with icy blue eyes. He shook off the remains of his clothing and circled slowly about her.

Alexia braced herself. One touch from her and he would be human again, but that was no guarantee of safety. Even mortal, he would still be bigger and stronger than she, and Alexia was without her parasol.

Just as the huge white wolf charged forward, a new wolf leaped in front of Alexia and Tunstell, teeth bared. The newcomer was considerably smaller than Major Channing, with sandy fur frosted black about the head and neck, pale yellow eyes, and an almost foxlike face.

There was an awful thud of fur-covered flesh, and the two scrabbled against one another, claws and teeth ripping. The white wolf was bigger, but it presently became clear that the smaller wolf possessed greater speed and cunning. He used the other's size against him. In a matter of moments, the smaller wolf had twisted about and taken a clean firm death grip on Major Channing's throat.

Quick as it had started, the fight ended. The white wolf flopped instantly down, rolling to present his belly in submission to his diminutive opponent.

Alexia heard a groan and dragged her eyes away from the fight to see that Tunstell was now sitting upright and blinking blearily. He was bleeding copiously from the nose but otherwise appeared merely dazed. Alexia passed him a handkerchief and bent to look for her parasol. She used it as an excuse not to watch as the two werewolves changed back into human form.

She did peek. What hot-blooded woman wouldn't? Major Channing was all muscle, longer and leaner than her husband but, honesty compelled her to admit, not at all unsightly. What surprised her was the small sandy-haired man of indeterminate age standing calmly next to him. She would never have accused *Professor Lyall* of gratuitous musculature. But there he was, assuredly fit. What profession had Lyall had before he became a werewolf? Alexia wondered, not for the first time. A couple of clavigers appeared with long cloaks and covered over the object of Lady Maccon's speculation.

"What the hell is going on?" Major Channing spat as soon as his jaw had sufficiently returned to human form. He turned to glare at the urbane man standing quietly next to him.

"I did not challenge *you*. You know I would never challenge you. We settled that years ago. This was a perfectly acceptable matter of pack discipline. Misbehaving clavigers must be tamed."

"Unless, of course, one of them is no claviger," said Professor Randolph Lyall, long-suffering Beta of the Woolsey Pack.

The blond man looked nervous. His face lost most of its arrogance. Alexia thought he was considerably more attractive that way.

Professor Lyall sighed. "Major Channing, Woolsey Pack Gamma, allow me to introduce you to Lady Alexia Maccon, curse-breaker, and your new Alpha female."

Alexia disliked the term *curse-breaker;* it sounded terribly sportsmanlike, as though she were about to engage in a protracted bout of unremitting cricket. Since some werewolves still considered their immortality a curse, she supposed it was an odd kind of accolade, praise that she could stave off the bestiality of full moon. To be called curse-breaker was certainly more complimentary than *soul-sucker.* Trust the vampires to come up with a term that implied an even more crass kind of sport than cricket—if such a thing could be conceived.

Alexia found her parasol and stood. "I could say it was a pleasure to meet you, Major Channing, but I would not wish to perjure myself so early in the evening."

"Well, confound it," said Major Channing, glaring first at Lyall and then at everyone else around him, "why didn't any of you *tell* me?"

Alexia did feel a little guilty at that. She had let her temper get the better of her. But really, he hadn't given her time to introduce herself.

"I take it you were not informed of my appearance, then?" Alexia asked, prepared to chalk another thing up onto the board of her husband's mistakes for the night. He was going to get a ruddy earful when he got home.

Major Channing said, "Well, no, not precisely. I mean, yes, we had a short missive a couple months back, but the description was not . . . you understand . . . and I thought you would be . . ."

Alexia hefted her parasol thoughtfully.

Channing backpedaled rapidly. ". . . less Italian," he said finally.

"And my dear husband did not warn you of the truth of it when you arrived?" Alexia was looking more thoughtful than angry. Perhaps Major Channing was not so bad. After all, she, too, had been surprised at Lord Maccon's choosing *her* to wed.

Major Channing looked irritated at that. "We have not yet seen him, my lady. Or this faux pas might have been avoided."

"I do not know about that." Lady Maccon shrugged.

"He is prone to exaggerating my virtues. His descriptions of me are generally a tad unrealistic."

Major Channing dialed his charm back up to the highest setting—Lady Maccon could practically see the gears crunching and the steam spiraling off his body. "Oh, I doubt that, my lady." Unfortunately for the Gamma, who did genuinely recognize Alexia's appeal, Alexia chose to take offense.

She went cold, her brown eyes hard and her generous mouth compressed into a straight line.

He hurriedly switched the subject, turning to Professor Lyall. "Why was our venerated leader not at the station to meet us? I had some fairly urgent business to discuss with him."

Lyall shrugged. There was an air about him that suggested the major not push this particular subject. It was the nature of a Gamma to criticize, but equally common was a Beta's support, no matter how rude the Alpha's actions. "Urgent BUR matters," was all he answered.

"Yes, well, my business might also be urgent," snapped Major Channing. "Hard to know, especially when he is unavailable to see to the needs of the pack."

"What exactly happened?" Professor Lyall's tone implied that whatever this urgent business, it was probably Major Channing's fault.

"The pack and I experienced something unusual on board ship." Major Channing clearly felt that if the Beta could be cagey, so could he. He turned pointedly to Alexia. "A pleasure to make your acquaintance, Lady Maccon. I apologize for the dust-up. Ignorance is no excuse; I assure you I am well aware of that. Nevertheless,

I shall endeavor to make it up to you to the best of my poor abilities."

"Apologize to Tunstell," replied Lady Maccon.

That was a blow: the pack Gamma, third in command, apologizing to a lowly claviger. Major Channing sucked in his breath but did exactly as he was told. He made a pretty speech to the redhead, who looked progressively more and more embarrassed as it rattled on, terribly conscious of his Gamma's humiliation. By the end, Tunstell was so flushed his freckles had disappeared entirely behind the red. After which Major Channing disappeared in a huff.

"Where is he going?" wondered Lady Maccon.

"Most likely to move the regiment's camping arrangements to the back of the house. It will have to wait a short while, my lady, for the tent poles to cool."

"Ah." Alexia grinned. "I win."

Professor Lyall sighed, looked briefly up toward the moon, and said as though appealing to a higher deity, "Alphas."

"So"—Alexia gave him an inquiring look—"would you mind explaining Channing Channing of the Chesterfield Channings to me? He does not seem like a man my husband would choose to run with his pack."

Professor Lyall tilted his head to one side. "I am not privy to his lordship's feelings on the gentleman, but regardless of Lord Maccon's preferences, Channing was inherited along with Woolsey. As was I. Conall had no choice. And, quite frankly, the major is not so bad. A good soldier to have guarding one's back in a battle, and that is the honest truth. Try not to be too put off by his manner. He has always behaved himself in the capacity of Gamma, a decent third in command, despite disliking both Lord Maccon and myself."

"Why? I mean, why you? I can perfectly comprehend not liking my husband. *I* dislike him intensely most of the time."

Professor Lyall stifled a chuckle. "I am given to understand that he does not approve of spelling one's name with two *ll*'s. He finds it inexcusably Welsh. I suspect he may be quite taken with you, however."

Alexia twirled her parasol, embarrassed. "Pity's sake, was he being honest under all that syrupy charm?" She wondered what it was about her physique or personality that only large werewolves seemed to find her alluring. And would it be possible to change that quality?

Professor Lyall shrugged. "I should steer well clear of him in that arena, if I were you."

"Why?"

Lyall struggled for the polite way of putting it and then finally settled on the indelicate truth. "Major Channing likes his woman feisty, to be sure, but that is because he likes"—a delicate pause—"refining them."

Alexia wrinkled her nose. She sensed the indelicate underpinning to Professor Lyall's comment. She would have to research it later, confident that her father's library would provide. Alessandro Tarabotti, preternatural, had lived a racy life and passed on to his daughter a collection of books, some of them with terribly wicked sketches, which attested to his raciness. Alexia had those books to thank for the fact that some of her husband's more innovative desires did not provoke her into fainting fits on a regular basis.

Professor Lyall merely shrugged. "Some women like that kind of thing."

"And some women like needlepoint," replied Alexia, resolving to think no more on her husband's problematic Gamma. "And some women like extraordinarily ugly hats." This comment was sparked by the fact that she had just caught sight of her dear friend, Miss Ivy Hisselpenny, disembarking from a hackney at the end of Woolsey's long entranceway.

Miss Hisselpenny was a long way away, but there was no doubt it was her—no one else would dare sport such a hat. It was a mind-numbing purple, trimmed in bright green, with three high feathers emerging from what looked to be an entire fruit basket arranged about the crown. Fake grapes spilled down and over one side, dangling almost to Ivy's pert little chin.

"Fiddlesticks," said Lady Maccon to Professor Lyall. "Am I ever going to make it to my meeting?"

Lyall took that as a hint and turned to go. Unless, of course, he was fleeing from the hat. His mistress stopped him.

"I truly do appreciate your unexpected intervention just now. I did not think he would actually attack."

Professor Lyall looked at his Alpha's mate thoughtfully. It was a rare unguarded look, his face free of its customary glassicals, his mild hazel eyes puzzled. "Why unexpected? Didn't you think I was capable of defending you in Conall's place?"

Lady Maccon shook her head. It was true she had never had much confidence in the physical abilities of her husband's Beta, with his slight frame and professorial ways. Lord Maccon was massive and treelike; Professor Lyall was built more on the shrub scale. But that wasn't what she had meant. "Oh no, unexpected because

I had assumed you would be with my husband tonight, if this BUR problem is so very bad."

Professor Lyall nodded.

Lady Maccon tried one last time. "I don't suppose it was the arrival of the regiment that had my husband in a dither?"

"No. He knew the regiment was due in; he sent me to meet them at the station."

"Oh, he did, did he? And he did not see fit to inform me?"

Lyall, realizing he might have just gotten his Alpha into some very hot water indeed, dissembled. "I believe he was under the impression you knew. It was the dewan who ordered the military recall. Withdrawal papers came through the Shadow Council several months ago."

Alexia frowned. She remembered vaguely the potentate arguing vociferously with the dewan on this subject at the beginning of her stint as muhjah. The dewan had won, since the strength of Queen Victoria's regiments and the building of her empire was dependent upon her alliance with the packs. The vampires held controlling interest in the East India Company and its mercenary troops, of course, but this had been a matter for the regulars and so the werewolves. Still, Lady Maccon had not realized the results of that decision would end up encamping on her doorstep.

"Don't they have a proper barracks somewhere they should be shambling off to?"

"Yes, but it is tradition for them all to stay here for several weeks while the pack re-forms—before the daylight soldiers head homeward."

Lady Maccon watched Ivy wend her way through the

chaos of military tents and baggage. She moved with such purpose it was as though she walked with exclamation marks. Hydrodine engines emitted small puffs of yellow smoke at her as she passed and compressed expansion tent stakes hissed as they were pulled prematurely from the ground. All were now being taken back down and moved around the side of the house and into Woolsey's extensive grounds.

"Have I mentioned recently how much I dislike tradition?" Alexia said, and then panicked. "Are we expected to feed them all?"

The grape bunches bobbed in time with Ivy's rapidly mincing footsteps. She did not even pause to investigate the disarray. She was clearly *in a hurry,* which meant Ivy had *news of note*.

"Rumpet knows what to do. Don't concern yourself," advised Professor Lyall.

"You really cannot tell me what is going on? He was up so very early, and Formerly Merriway was definitely involved."

"Who, Rumpet?"

That earned the Beta a look of profound disgust.

"Lord Maccon did not inform me of the particulars," Professor Lyall admitted.

Lady Maccon frowned. "And Formerly Merriway won't. You know how she gets, all-over nervous and floaty."

Ivy attained the steps to the front door.

As she neared, Professor Lyall said hastily, "If you will excuse me, my lady, I should be getting on."

He bowed to Miss Hisselpenny and vanished around the corner of the house after Major Channing.

Ivy curtsied to the departing werewolf, a strawberry on a long silk stem wiggling about in front of her left ear. She didn't take offense at Lyall leaving so precipitously. Instead, she trotted up to the stoop, blithely ignoring Alexia's dispatch case and waiting carriage, certain in the knowledge that her news was far more important than whatever affair was causing her friend to depart forthwith.

"Alexia, did you know there is an entire regiment decamping on your front lawn?"

Lady Maccon sighed. "Really, Ivy, I would never have noticed."

Miss Hisselpenny ignored the sarcasm. "I have the most splendid *news*. Should we go in for tea?"

"Ivy, I have business in town, and I am already late." Lady Maccon refrained from mentioning that business was with Queen Victoria. Ivy knew nothing of her preternatural state, nor her political position, and Alexia thought it best to keep her friend ignorant. Ivy was particularly adept at being ignorant but could cause extensive havoc with the smallest scrap of information.

"But, *Alexia,* this is very important gossip!" The grapes vibrated in agitation.

"Oh, have the winter shawls from Paris come into the shops?"

Ivy tossed her head in frustration. "Alexia, must you be so tiresome?"

Lady Maccon could barely tear her eyes off of the hat. "Then, please, do not keep it to yourself one moment longer. Pray tell me at once." Anything to get her dearest friend gone posthaste. Really, Ivy could be too inconvenient.

"Why is there a regiment on your lawn?" Miss Hisselpenny persisted.

"Werewolf business." Lady Maccon dismissed it in the manner calculated to most efficiently throw Ivy off the scent. Miss Hisselpenny had never quite accustomed herself to werewolves, even after her best friend had the temerity to marry one. They were not exactly commonplace, and she had never had to cope with their brand of gruffness and sudden nudity. She simply couldn't seem to acclimatize to it the way Alexia had. So she preferred, in typical Ivy fashion, to forget they existed.

"Ivy," said Lady Maccon, "what exactly *are* you doing here?"

"Oh, Alexia, I am terribly sorry for descending upon you so unexpectedly! I hadn't the time to send round a card, but I simply had to come and tell you as soon as it was decided." She opened her eyes wide and flipped both hands toward her head. "*I* am engaged."

CHAPTER TWO

A Plague of Humanization

Lord Conall Maccon was a very large man who made for an exceedingly large wolf. He was bigger than any natural wolf could ever hope to be and less rangy, with too much muscle and not enough lank. No passerby would be in any doubt, had they seen him, that he was a supernatural creature. That said, those few people traveling the cold winter road on this particular early evening could not see him. Lord Maccon was moving fast, and he boasted a dark brindled pelt so that, but for his yellow eyes, he faded almost completely into the shadows. On more than one occasion, his wife had called him handsome in his wolf form, yet she had never called him so as a human. He would have to ask her about that. Conall ruminated a moment; then again, perhaps he would not.

Such were the mundane thoughts that passed through a werewolf's head as he ran the country lanes toward London. Woolsey Castle was some distance away from the metropolis, just north of Barking, a good two hours by carriage or dirigible and a little less on four legs. Time passed and eventually wet grass, neat hedgerows, and startled bunnies gave way to muddy streets, stone walls, and disinterested alley cats.

The earl found himself enjoying the run a good deal less when, just after entering the city proper, right around Fairfoot Road, he abruptly and completely lost his wolf form. It was the most astonishing thing—one moment he was dashing along on four paws, and the next his bones were crunching, his fur retreating, and his knees crashing down upon the cobbles. It left him, shivering and panting, naked in the road.

"Great ghosts!" exclaimed the aggrieved nobleman.

Never had he experienced the like. Even when his gloriously frustrating wife used her preternatural touch to force him back into humanity, it was not so sudden. She generally gave him some warning. Well, a little warning. Well, a yell or two.

He looked about, worried. But Alexia was nowhere near, and he was pretty darn certain he had managed to leave her safe, if fuming, back at the castle. There were no other preternaturals registered for the greater London area. What, then, had just happened?

He looked to his knees, which were bleeding slightly and quite definitely not healing. Werewolves were supernatural: such minor scrapes ought to be closing up right before his eyes. Instead they leaked his slow old blood onto the muddy stones.

Lord Maccon tried to change back, reaching for that place from which he drove his body to split its biological nature. Nothing. He tried for his Anubis Form, the Alpha's ace, with the head of the wolf and the body of a man. Still nothing. Which left him sitting on Fairfoot Road, completely unclothed, and deeply confused.

Struck with the spirit of investigation, he backtracked a short way. He tried for Anubis Form, changing just his head into that of a wolf, an Alpha trick that was faster than full shift. It worked but left him in a conundrum: dally about as a wolf, or press on to the office naked? He changed his head back.

Normally, when there was a chance he might have to change publicly, the earl carried a cloak in his mouth. But he had thought to make it safely to the BUR offices and into the cloakroom there before decency became necessary. Now he regretted such careless confidence. Formerly Merriway had been right—something was terribly wrong in London, and that apart from the fact that he was currently lollygagging about starkers inside it. It would appear that it was not only the ghosts who were being affected. Werewolves, too, were undergoing alteration. He gave a tight smile and retreated hurriedly behind a pile of crates. He would lay good money that the vampires weren't growing any feeding fangs tonight either— at least not the ones living near the Thames. Countess Nadasdy, queen of the Westminster hive, must be positively frantic. Which, he realized with a grimace, meant he was likely to get the unparalleled pleasure of a visit from Lord Ambrose later that evening. It was going to be a long night.

The Bureau of Unnatural Registry was not situated, as many a confused tourist expected, in the vicinity of Whitehall. It was in a small, unassuming Georgian building just off Fleet Street, near the *Times* offices. Lord Maccon had made the switch ten years ago, when he discovered that it was the press, not the government, that generally had a handle on what was truly transpiring around the city—political or otherwise. This particular evening, he had cause to regret his decision, as he now had to make his way through the commercial district as well as several crowded thoroughfares in order to get to his office.

He almost managed the trek without being seen, skulking through the grubby streets and around the mud-spattered corners—London's finest back alleys. It was quite the feat, as the streets were crawling with soldiers. Fortunately, they were intent on celebrating their recent return to London and not his large white form. But he was spotted by the most unexpected individual, near St. Bride, the unfragrant scent of Fleet Street in the air.

A toff of the highest water, dressed to the nines in a lovely cut-front jacket and stunning lemon-yellow cravat tied in the Osbaldeston style, materialized out of the darkness behind a brewing pub, where no toff had a right to be. The man doffed his top hat amiably at the naked werewolf.

"Why, I do declare, if it isn't Lord Maccon. How *do* you do? Fancy, aren't we a tad underdressed for an evening's stroll?" The voice was mildly familiar and laced with amusement.

"Biffy," said the earl on a growl.

"And how is your lovely wife?" Biffy was a drone of reputation, and his vampire master, Lord Akeldama, was a dear friend of Alexia's. Much to Lord Maccon's annoyance. So, come to think of it, was Biffy. Last time the drone had visited Woolsey Castle with a message from his master, he and Alexia had spent hours discussing the latest hairstyles out of Paris. His wife had a penchant for gentlemen of the frivolous persuasion. Conall paused to deduce what that said about his own character.

"Hang my lovely wife," he answered. "Get into that tavern there and wrestle me up a coat of some kind, would you?"

Biffy arched an eyebrow at him. "You know, I would offer you my coat, but it's a swallowtail, hardly useful, and would never fit that colossal frame of yours anyway." He gave the earl a long, appraising look. "Well, well, isn't my master going to be all of a crumble for not having seen this?"

"Your impossible patron has seen me naked already."

Biffy tapped his bottom lip with a fingertip and looked intrigued.

"Oh for goodness' sake, you were there," said Lord Maccon, annoyed.

Biffy only smiled.

"A cloak." A pause, then the added grumble of, "Please!"

Biffy vanished and returned with alacrity, bearing an oilskin greatcoat of ill design and briny smell but that was at least large enough to cover the earl's indignities.

The Alpha shrugged it on and then glared at the still-smiling drone. "I smell like parboiled seaweed."

"Navy's in town."

"So, what do you know of this madness?" Biffy might be a pink, and his vampire master even more so, but Lord Akeldama was also London's main busybody, and he ran his ring of impeccably clad informants so efficiently it put anything the government could muster to shame.

"Eight regiments came into port yesterday: the Black

Scotts, Northumberland, the Coldsteam Guards—"
Biffy was pointedly obtuse.

Lord Maccon interrupted him. "Not that—the mass exorcism."

"Mmm, *that*. That is why I was waiting for you."

"Of course you were," sighed Lord Maccon.

Biffy stopped smiling. "Shall we walk, my lord?"
He took up position next to the werewolf, who was no werewolf at all anymore, and they strode together toward Fleet Street. The earl's bare feet made no noise on the cobbles.

"What!" The amazed exclamation emanated from not one, but two sources: Alexia *and* the heretofore forgotten Tunstell. The claviger had sat down behind the corner of the stoop to nurse the results of Major Channing's discipline.

Upon hearing Miss Hisselpenny's news, however, the gangly actor reappeared. He was sporting a large red mark about the right eye, which was destined to darken in a most colorful manner, and was pinching his nose to stanch the flow of blood. Both Alexia's handkerchief and his own cravat appeared much the worse for the experience.

"Engaged, Miss Hisselpenny?" In addition to his disheveled aspect, Tunstell was looking quite tragic, in a Shakespearean comedy kind of way. From behind the handkerchief, his eyes were wide in distress. Tunstell had been mighty taken with Miss Hisselpenny ever since they danced together at Lord and Lady Maccon's wedding, but they had not been allowed to mingle socially since. Miss Hisselpenny was a lady of consequence, and

Tunstell was but a lowly claviger and an actor to boot. Alexia had not comprehended the extent of his attachment. Or perhaps the attachment meant more now that it was no longer possible.

"To whom?" Lady Maccon asked the obvious question.

Ivy ignored her and dashed to Tunstell's side.

"You are injured!" she gasped, bunches of grapes and silk strawberries bobbing about. She pulled out her own minuscule handkerchief, embroidered with small clusters of cherries, and dabbed at his face unhelpfully.

"A mere scratch, Miss Hisselpenny, I assure you," said Tunstell, looking pleased by her ministrations, as ineffectual as they may be.

"But you are bleeding, simply gouts and gouts of it," insisted Ivy.

"Not to worry, not to worry, the business end of a fist will do that to a person, you know."

Ivy gasped. "Fisticuffs! Oh, how *perfectly* horrid! Poor Mr. Tunstell." Ivy petted an unbloodied corner of the man's cheek with her white-gloved hand.

Poor Mr. Tunstell did not seem to mind, if this was the result. "Oh, please, do not trouble yourself so," he said, leaning into her caress. "My, what an enchanting hat, Miss Hisselpenny, so"—he hesitated, searching for the right word—"fruity."

Ivy blushed beet red at that. "Oh, do you like it? I bought it specially."

That did it. "Ivy," said Alexia sharply, bringing her friend back around to the important business at hand. "To whom have you gotten yourself engaged, exactly?"

Miss Hisselpenny snapped back to the present, drifting away from the alluring Mr. Tunstell. "His name is

Captain Featherstonehaugh, and he has just returned with the Northumberling Fusilli, all the way from Inja."

"You mean the Northumberland Fusiliers."

"Is that not what I just said?" Ivy was all big-eyed innocence and excitement.

The dewan's army reshuffling clearly involved far more regiments than Alexia had thought. She would have to find out what the queen and her commanders were about at the Shadow Council meeting.

The meeting she was now inexcusably late for.

Miss Hisselpenny continued. "It is not a bad match, although Mama would have preferred a major at the very least. But you know"—she lowered her voice to almost a whisper—"I haven't really the luxury of choice at my age."

Tunstell looked quite put out upon hearing that. He thought Miss Hisselpenny a grand catch, older than he to be sure, but imagine her having to settle on a mere captain. He opened his mouth to say so but showed unexpected restraint upon receipt of a high-stakes glare from his mistress.

"Tunstell," instructed Lady Maccon, "go away and be useful. Ivy, felicitations on your impending nuptials, but I really must be off. I have an important meeting, for which I am now late."

Ivy was watching Tunstell's retreating back. "Of course, Captain Featherstonehaugh was not exactly what I had hoped for. He is quite the military man, you understand, very stoic. That kind of thing would seem to suit you, Alexia, but _I_ had hoped for a man with the soul of a bard."

Alexia threw her hands up into the air. "_He_ is a claviger. You know what that means? Someday, relatively soon, he will petition for metamorphosis and then probably die in the attempt. Even if he came through intact, he would then be a werewolf. You don't even *like* werewolves."

Ivy gave her an even-wider-eyed look as if butter wouldn't melt in her mouth. The grapes bobbed. "He could always leave before that."

"To be what? A professional actor? Living on a penny a day and the approbation of a fickle public?"

Ivy sniffed. "Who says we are discussing Mr. Tunstell?"

Alexia was driven to distraction. "Get into the carriage, Ivy. I shall take you back to town."

Miss Hisselpenny nattered on about her impending marriage and its companion apparel, invitation list, and comestibles for the entirety of the two-hour ride into London. Not much was said, however, about the prospective groom. Alexia was made to realize, during the course of that drive, that he apparently was of little consequence to the proceedings. She watched her friend climb down and trot inside the Hisselpenny's modest town house with a slight pang of concern. What was Ivy doing? But with no time at the moment to worry over Miss Hisselpenny's *situation,* Lady Maccon directed the driver on to Buckingham.

The guards were expecting her. Lady Maccon was always at the palace two hours after dark on Sundays and Thursdays without fail. And she was one of the most unproblematic of the queen's regular visitors, being the least high-and-mighty, for all her forthright tone and pointed opinions. After the first two weeks, she had even gone to the trouble of learning all of their names. It was the little things that made someone grand. The ton were suspicious of Lord Maccon's choice, but the military was rather pleased with it. They welcomed straightforward talk, even from a female.

"You are late, Lady Maccon," said one, checking her neck for bite marks and her dispatch case for illegal steam devices.

"Don't I know it, Lieutenant Funtington, don't I know it," replied the lady.

"Well, we shan't keep you. Go on in, my lady."

Lady Maccon gave him a tight smile and went.

The dewan and the potentate were already waiting for her. Queen Victoria was not. The queen usually arrived nearer to midnight, after presiding over her family and supper, and stayed only to hear the results of their debate and formulate any final decisions.

"I cannot apologize enough for having kept you both," said Alexia. "I had unexpected squatters on my front lawn and an equally unexpected engagement to handle this evening. No excuses, I know, but those are my reasons."

"Well, there you have it," snarled the dewan, "The affairs of the British Empire must wait on squatters and your good graces." Landed as the Earl of Upper Slaughter but without any real country seat, the dewan was one of the few werewolves in England who could give the Earl of Woolsey a fight for his fur and had had occasion to prove it. He was almost as big as Conall Maccon but slightly older-looking, with dark hair, a wide face, and deep-set eyes. He ought to have been handsome, except that his mouth was a little too full, the cleft in his chin a little too pronounced, and his mustache and muttonchops astonishingly assertive.

Alexia had spent long hours wondering over that mustache. Werewolves did not grow hair, as they did not age. Where had it come from? Had he always had it? For how many centuries had his poor abused upper lip labored under the burden of such vegetation?

Tonight, however, she ignored both him and his facial protuberances. "So," she said, sitting down and placing the dispatch case on the table next to her, "shall we on to business?"

"By all means," replied the potentate, his voice honeyed and cool. "Are you feeling well this evening, muhjah?"

Alexia was surprised by the question. "Quite."

The vampire member of the Shadow Council was the more dangerous of the two. He had age on his side and much less to prove than the dewan. Also, while the dewan made a show of disliking Lady Maccon for form's sake, Alexia knew for a fact that the potentate actually loathed her. He had registered an official complaint in writing on the occasion of her marriage to the Woolsey Pack Alpha and the same again when Queen Victoria brought her in to sit on the Shadow Council. Alexia had never discerned exactly why. But he had the support of the hives in this as in most things, which made him far more powerful than the dewan, for whom pack loyalty seemed wobbly.

"No stomach ailments?"

Alexia gave the vampire a suspicious look. "No, none. Could we get on?"

Generally, the Shadow Council administered supernatural interaction with the Crown. While BUR handled enforcement, the Shadow Council dealt with legislative issues, political and military guidance, and the occasional sticky-residue snafu. During Alexia's few months on board, discussions had ranged from hive authorization in the African provinces, to military code covering the death of an Alpha overseas, to neck-exposure mandates in public museums. They had not yet had a genuine crisis to deal with. This, Alexia felt, was going to be interesting.

She snapped open the lid of her dispatch case and extracted her harmonic auditory resonance disruptor, a spiky little apparatus that looked exactly like two tuning forks sticking out of a crystal. She tapped one fork with her finger, waited a moment, and then tapped the other. The two produced a discordant, low-pitched humming noise, amplified by the crystal that would prevent their conversation from being overheard. She placed the device carefully in the middle of the massive meeting table. The sound was annoying, but they had all learned to deal with it. Even inside the security of Buckingham Palace, one could never be too careful.

"What, exactly, has happened in London this evening? Whatever it was had my husband up scandalously early, just after sunset, and my local ghost informant in a positive fluster." Lady Maccon removed her favorite little notebook and a stylographic pen imported from the Americas.

"You do not know, muhjah?" sneered the dewan.

"Of course I know. I am simply wasting everyone's time by inquiring, for my own amusement." Alexia was sarcastic to the last.

"Neither of us look any different to you this evening?" The potentate steepled his long fingers together on the tabletop, pure white and snakelike against the dark mahogany, and looked at her out of beautiful, deep-set green eyes.

"Why are you humoring her? Obviously she *must* have something to do with it." The dewan stood and began to pace about the room—his customary restless state during most of their meetings.

Alexia pulled her favorite glassicals out of her dispatch case and put them on. They were properly called *monocular cross-magnification lenses with spectral modifier attachment,* but everyone was calling them *glassicals* these days, even Professor Lyall. Alexia's were made of gold, inset with decorative onyx around the side that did not boast multiple lenses and a liquid suspension. The many small knobs and dials were also made of onyx, but the expensive touches did not stop them from looking ridiculous. All glassicals looked ridiculous: the unfortunate progeny of an illicit union between a pair of binoculars and opera glasses.

Her right eye became hideously magnified out of all proportion as she twiddled one dial, homing in on the potentate's face. Fine even features, dark eyebrows, and green eyes—the face seemed totally normal, natural even. The skin looked healthy, not so pale. The potentate gave a little smile, all his teeth in perfect boxlike order. Remarkable.

There would be the problem. No fangs.

Lady Maccon stood and went to stand in front of the dewan, stopping him in his impatient movements. She trained the glassicals upon his face, focusing on the eyes:

plain old brown. No yellow about the iris, no hidden quality of open-field or hunter instincts.

In silence, thinking hard, she sat back down. Carefully, she removed the glassicals and put them away.

"Well?"

"Am I to understand you are both laboring under a state, that is, afflicted with, um"—she groped for the correct way of putting it—"that is, infected by . . . normality?"

The dewan gave her a disgusted look. Lady Maccon made a note in her little journal.

"Astonishing. And how many of the supernatural set are also contaminated into being mortal?" she asked, stylographic pen poised.

"Every vampire and werewolf in London central." The potentate was incurably calm.

Alexia was truly stunned. If all of them were no longer supernatural, that meant that any or all of them could be killed. She wondered, as a preternatural, if she was being affected. She went introspective for a moment. She felt like herself—difficult to tell, though.

"What's the geographical extent of those disabled?" she asked.

"It seems to be concentrated around the Thames embankment area, extending in from the docklands."

"And if you leave the affected zone, do you return to your supernatural state?" the scientific side of Alexia instantly wanted to know.

"Excellent inquiry." The dewan disappeared out the door, presumably to send a runner to find out the answer to that question. Normally they would have had a ghost agent handle such a job. Where was she?

"And the ghosts?" Lady Maccon asked, frowning.

"That is how we know the extent of the afflicted area. Not a single ghost tethered in that zone has appeared since sundown. Every one has vanished. Exorcised." The potentate was watching her closely. He, of course, would assume Alexia had something to do with this. Only one creature had the inherent power to exorcise ghosts, as unpleasant a job as it was, and that creature was a preternatural. Alexia was the only preternatural in the London locale.

"Gods," breathed Lady Maccon. "How many ghosts lost were in the Crown's employ?"

"Six worked for us; four worked for BUR. Of the remaining specters, eight were in the poltergeist stage, so no one misses them, and eighteen were at the end stages of disanimus." The potentate tossed a pile of paperwork in Alexia's direction. She flipped through the stack, looking at the details.

The dewan came back into the room. "We will know your answer within the hour." He resumed his pacing.

"In case you are curious, gentlemen, I spent the entire day asleep at Woolsey Castle. My husband can attest to that fact, as we do not maintain separate bedrooms." Alexia blushed slightly but felt her honor demanded she stand up for herself.

"Of course he can," said the vampire who currently was no vampire at all but a natural human. For the first time in hundreds of years. He must be absolutely shaking in those hugely expensive Hessian boots of his. To face mortality after so very long. Not to mention the fact that one of the hives was in the afflicted zone—which meant a queen was in danger. Vampires, even roves like the potentate, would do almost anything to protect a queen.

"You mean, your werewolf husband who sleeps daylight solid. And whom I highly doubt you touch while you sleep?"

"Of course I do not." Alexia was taken aback that he need ask. Staying in contact with Conall all night, every night, would cause him to age, and while she abhorred the idea of growing old without him, she wasn't about to inflict mortality on him. He would also grow facial hair and come over more than usually scruffy of a morning.

"So you admit you could have snuck out of the house?" The dewan stopped pacing and glared at her.

Lady Maccon made a clucking noise of denial. "Have you met my staff? If Rumpet didn't stop me, Floote would, not to mention Angelique running about fussing over my hair. Sneaking out, I am sorry to say, is a thing of my past. But you are welcome to blame me if you are too lazy to try and figure out what is really going on here."

The potentate, of all people, seemed a little more convinced. Perhaps it was simply that he did not want to believe she had access to such an ability.

Alexia continued. "I mean, really, how could one preternatural, however powerful, affect an entire area of the city? I have to touch you in order to force your humanity. I have to touch a dead body in order to exorcise its ghost. I could not possibly manage to be in all those places at once. Besides which, I am not touching you right now, am I? And you are both mortal."

"So what are we dealing with? A whole pack of preternaturals?" That was the dewan. He was prone to thinking in numbers, the consequence of an overabundance of military training.

The potentate shook his head. "I have seen BUR's records. There are not enough preternaturals in all of England to exorcise so many ghosts at once. There are probably not enough in the civilized world."

Alexia wondered *how* he had seen such records. She would have to tell her husband about that. Then she returned her attention to the business at hand. "Is there anything more powerful than a preternatural?"

The not-vampire shook his head again. "Not in this particular way. Vampire edict tells us that soul-suckers are the second most deadly creatures on the planet. But it also says that the most deadly of all is no leech, but a different kind of parasite. This cannot be the work of one of them."

Lady Maccon scribbled this down in her book. She was intrigued and a little put out. "Worse than us soul-suckers? Is that possible? And here I was thinking myself a member of the most hated set. And what do you call *them*?"

The potentate ignored this question. "That will teach you to get full of yourself."

Alexia would have pressed the issue but suspected that line of questioning would be ignored. "So this must be the result of a weapon, a scientific apparatus. That is the only possible explanation."

"Or we could take that ridiculous man Darwin's theories to heart and postulate a newly evolved species of preternatural."

Alexia nodded. She had her reservations about Darwin and his prattle on origins, but there might be some little merit to his ideas.

The dewan, however, pooh-poohed the idea. Were-wolves were, largely, of a much less scientific bent than vampires, except where advances in weaponry were concerned. "I am more sympathetic to the muhjah on this point if nothing else. If she isn't doing it herself, then it must be some newfangled contrivance of technical origin."

"We *are* living in the Age of Invention," agreed the potentate.

The dewan looked thoughtful. "The Templars have finally managed to unify Italy and declare themselves Infallible; perhaps they are turning their attention outward once more?"

"You think this may herald a second Inquisition?" The potentate blanched. He could do that now.

The dewan shrugged.

"There is no point in wild speculation," said the ever-practical Lady Maccon. "Nothing suggests that the Templars are involved."

"You are Italian," grumbled the dewan.

"Oh, fiddlesticks, is everything in this meeting going to come back around to my being my father's daughter? My hair is curly too—could that somehow be involved? I am the product of my birth, and there is nothing I can change about that, or believe you me, I might have opted for a smaller nose. Let us simply agree that the most likely explanation for this kind of wide-scale preternatural effect is a weapon of some kind." She turned to the potentate. "You are *positive* you have never heard of this kind of thing happening before?"

He frowned and rubbed at the crease between his green eyes with the tip of one white finger. It was an oddly human gesture. "I will consult the edict keepers on the subject, but, no, I do not think so."

Alexia looked to the dewan. He shook his head.

"So the question is, what could someone hope to gain by this?"

Her supernatural colleagues looked at her blankly.

A tap came on the closed door. The dewan went to answer it. He spoke softly for a moment through the crack and then returned with an expression transformed from scared to bemused.

"The effects would appear to be negated just outside the afflicted zone we discussed earlier. Werewolves, at least, revert back to fully supernatural. The ghosts, of course, cannot relocate to take advantage of this fact. And I cannot speak for the vampires."

What he did not say was that what changed werewolves was also likely to change vampires—they were more alike than either race preferred to admit.

"I shall look into this myself, personally, as soon as our meeting is concluded," said the potentate, but he was clearly relieved. It had to be a product of his human condition; normally his emotions were not so obvious.

The dewan sneered at him. "You will be able to move that endangered queen of yours, should you deem it necessary."

"Do we have any further business to address?" asked the potentate, ignoring the comment.

Alexia reached forward to tap at the harmonic auditory resonance disruptor with the butt end of her stylographic pen, getting it vibrating once more. Then she looked to the dewan. "Why have so many regiments returned home recently?"

"Indeed, I had noticed something of an overabundance of the military roaming the streets as I left my house this evening." The potentate looked curious.

The dewan shrugged, trying for casualness and failing. "Blame Cardwell and his blasted reforms."

Alexia sniffed pointedly. She approved of the reforms, far more humane to cut out flogging and change enlistment tactics. But the dewan was an old-timer; he liked his soldiers disciplined, poor, and mildly bloody.

He continued as though she hadn't sniffed. "We had that steamer in from West Africa several months ago crying that the Ashantis were giving us hell. The Secretary of War pulled everyone we could spare out of the east and back here for rotation."

"Do we still have that many troops in India? I thought the region was pacified."

"Not hardly. But we have the numbers to pull several regiments out and leave the East India Company and its mercenaries to take the brunt of it. The empire should stay sound. The duke wants proper regiments with werewolf attachments down in West Africa, and I can't say I blame him. It's a nasty business down there. These incoming regiments you see around London are to reconfigure as two separate battalions and ship back out within a month. It's causing a moon's worth of mess. Most had to be routed through Egypt in order to get back here fast enough, and I still don't know how we are going to stretch to fill the orders. Still, they're here now, clogging up the London taverns. Best get them fighting again right quick."

He rounded on Lady Maccon. "Which reminds me.

Get your husband to keep his ruddy packs under control, would you?"

"Packs? There was only the one last time I checked, and let me inform you, it is not my husband who has to discipline them. Constantly."

The dewan grinned, causing his massive mustache to wiggle. "I am guessing you met Major Channing?" There were just few enough werewolves in England that, as Alexia had come to learn, they all seemed to know one another. And gracious did they enjoy a good gossip.

"You would be guessing correctly." Lady Maccon made a sour face.

"Well, I was referring to the earl's other pack, the Highland one, Kingair," said the dewan. "They were running with the Black Watch regiment, and there's been a bit of a dust-up. I thought your husband might stick a paw in."

Lady Maccon frowned. "I doubt it."

"Lost their Alpha out there, the Kingair Pack, you do realize? Niall something-or-other, a full colonel, nasty business. The pack was ambushed during high noon, when they were at their weakest and couldn't change shape. Threw the whole regiment over for a while there. Losing a ranking officer like that, werewolf Alpha or not, caused quite a fuss."

Alexia's frown deepened. "No, I was not aware." She wondered if her husband knew of this. She tapped her lip with the back of her pen. It was highly unusual for a former Alpha to survive the loss of his pack, and she had never managed to extract from Conall the whys and wherefores of his abandonment of the Highlands. But Alexia was pretty darn certain that a leadership void placed him under some sort of obligation to his former pack, even if it had been decades.

The discussion moved on to speculation as to who might be responsible for the weapon: various not-as-secret-as-they-wanted societies, foreign nations, or factions within the government. Lady Maccon was convinced it was Hypocras Club style scientists and held firm on her stance over deregulation. This frustrated the potentate, who wanted the surviving Hypocras Club members released to his tender mercies. The dewan sided with the muhjah. He wasn't particularly interested in scientific research of this kind, but he wasn't about to see it fall wholly into vampire hands. This derailed the conversation onto distribution of Hypocras goods. Alexia suggested they go to BUR, and despite her husband's charge of the institution, the potentate agreed so long as a vampire agent was attached.

By the time Queen Victoria arrived to confer with her council, they had come to several decisions. They informed her of the plague of humanization and their theory that it was some kind of secret weapon. The queen was appropriately worried. She knew perfectly well that the strength of her empire rested on the backs of her vampire advisors and her werewolf fighters. If they were at risk, so was Britain. She was particularly insistent that Alexia look into the mystery. After all, exorcism was supposed to be under the muhjah's jurisdiction.

Since she would have gone out of her way to investigate regardless, Lady Maccon was happy to have official sanction. She left the Shadow Council meeting with a feeling of unexpected accomplishment. She desperately wanted to pigeonhole her husband in his BUR den, but, knowing that would only end in a row, she headed home to Floote and the library instead.

Lady Alexia Maccon's father's collection of books, normally an excellent, or at least distracting, source of information, proved a disappointment on the matter of large-scale negation of the supernatural. Nor did it have anything to say on the potentate's tantalizing comment concerning a threat to vampires worse than soul-suckers. After hours of flipping through the worn leather-covered books, ancient scrolls, and personal journals, Lady Maccon and Floote had uncovered absolutely nothing. There were no further notes in her little leather book and no further insight into the mystery.

Floote's silence was eloquent.

Alexia nibbled a light breakfast of toast with potted ham and kippered salmon and went to bed just before dawn, defeated and frustrated.

She was awakened in the early morning by her husband, in an entirely dissimilar state of frustration. His big rough hands were insistent, and she was not unwilling to awaken thus, especially as she had some very pressing questions that needed answers. Still, it was daylight, and most respectable supernatural folk ought to be asleep. Fortunately, Conall Maccon was a strong enough Alpha to be awake several days running without the ill effects younger members of a pack would sustain from such solar contamination.

His approach was unique this time. He was squirming his way up under the covers from the foot of the bed toward where she lay. Alexia's newly opened eyes met the ludicrous sight of an enormous lump of bedclothes, swaying back and forth like some sort of encumbered jellyfish, laboring toward her. She was lying on her side, and his chest hair tickled the backs of her legs. He was lifting up her nightgown as he went. A little kiss whiskered just behind one knee, and Alexia jerked her leg in reaction. It tickled something dreadful.

She flipped the blankets and glared down at him. "What are you doing, you ridiculous man? You are acting like some sort of deranged mole."

"Being stealthy, my little terror. Do I not *seem* stealthy?" He spoke with mock affront.

"Why?"

He looked a little bashful, which was a categorically absurd expression for an enormous Scotsman to wear. "I was after the romanticism of an undercover approach, wife. The BUR agent mystique. Even if this BUR agent is disgracefully late home."

His wife propped herself up on one elbow and raised both eyebrows, clearly trying to suppress laughter but still look intimidating.

"No?"

The eyebrows went, if possible, higher.

"Humor me."

Alexia swallowed down a bubble of mirth and pretended a gravity suitable to a Lady Maccon. "If you insist, husband." She placed a hand to her heart and sank back into the pillows with a sigh of the type she imagined emitted by the heroine of a Rosa Carey novel.

Lord Maccon's eyes were halfway between caramel and yellow, and he smelled of open fields. Alexia wondered if he had traveled home in wolf form.

"Husband, we must talk."

"Aye, but later," he muttered. He began hiking her nightgown up farther, turning his attention to less ticklish but no-less-sensitive areas of her body.

"I loathe this article of clothing." He pulled the offending garment off and tossed it to its customary repose on the floor.

Lady Maccon went almost cross-eyed in her attempt to watch him as he moved predatorily the rest of the way up her body.

"You purchased it." She squirmed down to bring herself in greater contact with his body, her excuse being that it was cold and he had yet to replace the covers.

"So I did. Remind me to stick to parasols from now on."

His tawny eyes turned almost completely yellow; they tended to do that at this stage in the proceedings. Alexia loved it. Before she could protest, had she thought to, he swooped in for a full, all-absorbing kiss of the kind that, when they were standing, tended to make her knees go wobbly.

But they were not standing, and Alexia was now fully awake and unwilling to give in to the persuasions of her knees, her husband's mouth, or any other area of the body for that matter.

"Husband, I am very angry with you." She panted slightly as she made the accusation and tried to remember why.

He bit down softly at the meaty place between her shoulder and neck. Alexia let out a small moan.

"What have I done this time?" he paused to ask before continuing with his oral expedition about her body: her husband, the intrepid explorer.

Alexia writhed, attempting to get away.

But her movements only caused him to groan and become more insistent.

"You left me with an entire regiment encamping on my front lawn," she finally remembered to accuse.

"Mmm." Warm kisses littered her torso.

"And there was a certain Major Channing Channing of the Chesterfield Channings to boot."

He husband left off his nibbling to say, "You make him sound like some sort of disease."

"You *have* met him, I assume?"

The earl snorted softly and then began kissing her again, moving down toward her stomach.

"You knew they were coming, and you did not see fit to inform me."

He sighed, a puff of breath across her bare belly. "Lyall."

Alexia pinched his shoulder. He returned his amorous attentions to her lower body. "Yes! Lyall had to introduce me to my own pack. I've never met the soldier element before. Remember?"

"I am given to understand, from my Beta, that you handled a particularly hard situation perfectly adequately," he said between kisses and little licks. "Care to handle something else hard?"

Alexia thought maybe she might care to. After all, why should she be the only one panting? She pulled him up for a proper kiss and reached downward.

"And what about this mass exorcism in London? You did not see fit to tell me about that either?" she grumbled, squeezing softly.

"Um, well, that . . ." He huffed against her hair. Persuasive mouth. Mutter mutter. ". . . ended." He nibbled her neck, his attentions becoming even more insistent.

"Wait," Alexia squeaked. "Were we not having a conversation?"

"I believe *you* were having a conversation," replied Conall before remembering there was only one surefire way to shut his wife up. He bent forward and sealed her mouth with his.

CHAPTER THREE

Hat Shopping and Other Difficulties

Alexia lay staring thoughtfully up at the ceiling, feeling about as wet and as limp as a half-cooked omelet. Suddenly she stiffened. "*What* did you say had ended?"

A soft snore greeted her question. Unlike vampires, werewolves did not appear dead during the day. They simply slept very, very heavily.

Well, not *this* werewolf. Not if Lady Maccon had anything to say about it. She poked her husband hard in the ribs with a thumb.

It might have been the poke or it might have been the preternatural contact, but he awoke with a soft snuffle.

"What ended?"

With his wife's imperious face peering down at him, Lord Maccon took a moment to wonder why he had thought to crave such a woman in his life. Alexia bent over and nibbled at his chest. Ah, yes, initiative and ingenuity.

The nibbles stopped. "Well?"

And manipulation.

His bleary tawny eyes narrowed. "Does that brain of yours never stop?"

Alexia gave him an arch, "Well, yes." She looked at the angle of the sunlight creeping in around the edge of one heavy velvet drape. "You do seem to be able to give it pause for a good two hours or so."

"Was that all? What do you say, Lady Maccon—shall we try for three?"

Alexia batted at him without any real annoyance. "Aren't you supposed to be too old for this kind of continuous exercise?"

"What a thing to say, my love," snorted the earl, offended. "I am only just over two hundred, a veritable cub in the woods."

But Lady Maccon was not to be so easily distracted a second time. "So, what ended?"

He sighed. "That strange mass preternatural effect ceased at about three a.m. this morning. Everyone who should have returned to supernatural normal did, except for the ghosts. Any ghost tethered in the Thames embankment area seems to have been permanently exorcised. We brought in a volunteer ghost with a body about an hour after normality returned. He remained perfectly fine and tethered, so any new ghosts should establish in the area without difficulty, but all the old ones are gone for good."

"So that is it? Crisis averted?" Lady Maccon was disappointed. She must remember to jot this all down in her little investigation notebook.

"Oh, I think not. This isn't something that can be swept under the proverbial carpet. We must determine what exactly occurred. Everyone knows of the incident, even the daylight folk. Although they are, admittedly, much less upset about it than the supernatural set. Everybody wants to know what happened."

"Including Queen Victoria," interjected Alexia.

"I lost several excellent ghost agents in that mass exorcism. So did the Crown. I also had office visits from the *Times,* the *Nightly Aethograph,* and the *Evening Leader,* not to mention a very angry Lord Ambrose."

"My poor darling." Lady Maccon petted his head sympathetically. The earl hated dealing with the press, and he could barely tolerate being in the same room as Lord Ambrose. "I take it Countess Nadasdy was in a tizzy over the matter."

"To say nothing of the rest of her hive. After all, it has been thousands of years since a queen was in such danger."

Alexia sniffed. "It probably did them all some good." It was no secret she bore little love for and had absolutely no trust in the Westminster Hive queen. Lady Maccon and Countess Nadasdy were carefully polite to each other. The countess *always* invited Lord and Lady Maccon to her rare and coveted soirees, and Lord and Lady Maccon pointedly *always* attended.

"You know, Lord Ambrose had the audacity to threaten me? Me!" The earl was practically growling. "As though it were my fault!"

"I would have suspected he thought it was mine," suggested his wife.

Lord Maccon became even more angry. "Aye, well, he and his whole hive are deuced ignorant arses, and their opinion is of little consequence."

"Husband, language please. Besides, the potentate and the dewan felt the same."

"Did they threaten you?" The earl reared upright and grumbled several dockside phrases.

His wife interrupted his tirade by saying, "I completely see their point."

"What?"

"Be reasonable, Conall. I am the only soulless in this area, and so far as anyone knows, only preternaturals have this kind of effect on supernaturals. It is a logical causal leap to take."

"Except that we both know it was not you."

"Exactly! So who was it? Or what was it? What really did happen? I am certain you have some theory or other."

At that her husband chuckled. He had, after all, attached himself to a woman without a soul. He should not be surprised by her consistent pragmatism. Amazed by how quickly his wife could improve his mood by simply being herself, he said, "You first, woman."

Alexia tugged him down to lie next to her and pillowed her head in the crook between his chest and shoulder. "The Shadow Council has informed the queen that we believe it to be a newly developed scientific weapon of some kind."

"Do you agree?" His voice was a rumble under her ear.

"It is a possibility in this modern age, but it is only, at best, a working hypothesis. It might be that Darwin is right, and we have attained a new age of preternatural evolution. It might be that the Templars are somehow involved. It might be that we are missing something vital."

She directed a sharp glare at her silent spouse. "Well, what has BUR uncovered?"

Alexia had a private theory that this was part of her role as muhjah. Queen Victoria had taken an unexpectedly favorable interest in seeing Alexia Tarabotti married to Conall Maccon, prior to Alexia's assumption of the post. Lady Maccon often wondered if that wasn't a wish to see greater lines of communication open between BUR and the Shadow Council. Although, Queen Victoria probably did not think such communication would take place quite so carnally.

"How much do you know about Ancient Egypt, wife?" Conall dislodged her and leaned up on one arm, idly rubbing the curve of her side with his free hand.

Alexia tucked a pillow under her head and shrugged. Her father's library included a large collection of papyrus scrolls. He had had some fondness for Egypt, but Alexia had always been more interested in the classical world. There was something unfortunately fierce and passionate about the Nile and its environs. She was much too practical for Arabic with its flowery scrawl when Latin, with all its mathematic precision, made for such an attractive alternative.

Lord Maccon pursed his lips. "It was ours, you know? The werewolves'. Way back, four thousand years or more, lunar calendar and everything. Long before the daylight folk built up Greece and before the vampires extruded Rome, we werewolves had Egypt. You have seen how I can keep my body and turn only my head into wolf shape?"

"The thing that only true Alphas can do?" Alexia remembered it well from the one time she had seen him do it. It was unsettling and mildly revolting.

He nodded. "To the present day, we still call it the Anubis Form. Howlers say that, for a time, we were worshipped as gods in Ancient Egypt. And that was our downfall. For there are legends of a disease, a massive epidemic that struck only the supernatural: the God-Breaker Plague, a pestilence of unmaking. They say it swept the Nile clean of blood and bite, of werewolves and vampires alike, all of them dying as mortals within the space of a generation, and no metamorphosis came again to the Nile for a thousand years."

"And now?"

"Now in all of Egypt, there exists just one hive, near Alexandria, as north as it can get and still be delta. They represent what remains of the Ptolemy Hive. Just that one, and it came in with the Greeks, and is only six vampires strong. A few mangy packs roam the desert far up the Nile, way to the south. But they say the plague still dwells in the Valley of the Kings, and no supernatural has ever practiced any form of archaeology. It is our one forbidden science, even now."

Alexia processed this information. "So you believe we may be facing down an epidemic? A disease like this God-Breaker Plague?"

"It is possible."

"Then why would it simply disappear?"

Conall rubbed his face with his large callused hand. "I do not know. Werewolf legends are kept in the oral tradition, from howler to howler. We have no written edicts. Thus, they shift through time. It is possible the plague of the past was not so bad as we remember or that they simply did not know to leave the area. Or it is possible that what we have now is some completely new form of the disease."

Alexia shrugged. "It is at least as good a theory as our weapon hypothesis. I suppose there is only one way to find out."

"The queen has placed you on the case, then?" The earl never liked the idea of Alexia undertaking field operations. When he first recommended her for the job of muhjah, he thought it a nice, safe political position, full of paperwork and tabletop debate. It had been so long since England had a muhjah, few remembered what the preternatural advisor to the queen actually did. She was indeed meant to legislatively balance out the potentate's vampire agenda and the dewan's military obsession. But she was also meant to take on the role of mobile information gatherer, since preternaturals were confined by neither place nor pack. Lord Maccon had been spitting angry when he found out the truth of it. Werewolves, by and large, loathed espionage as dishonorable—the vampire's game. He'd even accused Alexia of being a kind of drone to Queen Victoria. Alexia had retaliated by wearing her most voluminous nightgown for a whole week.

"Can you think of someone better suited?"

"But, wife, this could become quite dangerous, if it is a weapon. If there is malice behind the action."

Lady Maccon let out a huff of disgust. "For everyone but *me*. I am the only one who would not be adversely affected, and, so far as I can tell, I seem to be essentially unchanged. Well, me and one other type of person. Which reminds me—the potentate said something interesting this evening."

"Really. What an astonishingly unusual occurrence."

"He said that according to the edicts, there exists a creature worse than a soul-sucker. Or perhaps it *used* to exist. You would not know anything about this, would you, husband?" She watched Conall's face quite closely.

There was a flicker of genuine surprise in his tawny eyes. In this, at least, he appeared to have no ready answer carefully prepared.

"I have never heard talk of such a thing. But then again, we are different in our perceptions, the vampires and the werewolves. We see you as a curse-breaker, not a soul-sucker and, as such, not so bad. So for werewolves, there are many things worse than you. For the vampires? There are ancient myths from the dawn of time that tell of a horror native to both day and night. The werewolves call this the *skin-stealer*. But it is only a myth."

Alexia nodded.

A hand began gently stroking the curve of her side.

"Are we done talking now?" the earl asked plaintively.

Alexia gave in to his demanding touch, but only, of course, because he sounded so pathetic. It had nothing, whatsoever, to do with her own quickening heartbeat.

She entirely failed to remember to tell Conall about his former pack's now-dead Alpha.

Alexia awakened slightly later than usual to find her husband already gone. She expected to encounter him at the supper table so was not overly troubled. Her mind already plotting investigations, she did not bother to protest the outfit her maid chose, replying only with, "That should do well enough, dear," to Angelique's suggestion of the pale blue silk walking dress trimmed in white lace.

The maid was astonished by her acquiescence, but her surprise was not sufficient to affect her efficiency. She had her mistress smartly dressed, if a tad too de mode for Alexia's normal preferences, and down at the dining table in a scant half hour—a noteworthy accomplishment by anyone's standards.

Everyone else was already seated at the supper table. In this particular case, "everyone else" included the pack, both residents and returnees, half the clavigers, and the insufferable Major Channing—about thirty or so. "Everyone else" did not, however, appear to include the master of the house. Lord Maccon made for a tangibly large absence, even in such a crowd.

Sans husband, Lady Maccon plonked herself down next to Professor Lyall. She gave him a little half-smile as a partial greeting. The Beta had not yet commenced his meal, preferring to begin with a hot cup of tea and the evening paper.

Startled by her sudden appearance, the rest of the table scrambled to stand politely as she joined them. Alexia waved them back to their seats, and they returned with much clattering. Only Professor Lyall managed a smooth stand, slight bow, and reseat with the consummate grace of a dancer. And all that without losing his place in his newspaper.

Lady Maccon quickly served herself some haricot of veal and several apple fritters and began eating so the others about the table could stop fussing and continue with their own meals. Really, sometimes it was simply too vexatious to be a lady living with two dozen gentlemen. Not to mention the hundreds now encamped on the Woolsey grounds.

After only a moment to allow her husband's Beta to acclimatize to her presence, Lady Maccon struck. "Very well, Professor Lyall, I shall bite: where has he gone now?"

The urbane werewolf said only, "Brussels sprouts?"

Lady Maccon declined in horror. She enjoyed most foods, but brussels sprouts were nothing more than underdeveloped cabbages.

Professor Lyall said, crinkling his paper, "*Shersky and Droop* are offering the most interesting new gadget for sale, just here. It is a particularly advanced form of teakettle, designed for air travel, to be mounted on the sides of dirigibles. It harnesses the wind via this small whirligig contraption that generates enough energy to boil water." He pointed out the advertisement to Alexia, who was distracted despite herself.

"Really? How fascinating. And so very useful for those more frequent dirigible travelers. I wonder if . . ." She trailed off and gave him a suspicious look. "Professor Lyall, you are trying to persuade me away from the point. Where has my husband gone?"

The Beta put down the now-useless newspaper and dished himself a fine piece of fried sole from a silver platter. "Lord Maccon left at the crack of dusk."

"That was not what I asked."

On the far side of Lyall, Major Channing chuckled softly into his soup.

Alexia glared at him and then turned a sharp look onto the defenseless Tunstell, seated at the other side of the table among the clavigers. If Lyall would not talk, perhaps Tunstell would. The redhead met her glare with wide eyes and quickly stuffed his face with a large mouthful of veal, trying to look as if he knew absolutely nothing.

"At least tell me if he was dressed properly?"

Tunstell chewed slowly. Very slowly.

Lady Maccon turned back to Professor Lyall, who was calmly slicing into his sole. Lyall was one of the few werewolves she had met who actively preferred fish to meat.

"Did he head off to Claret's?" she asked, thinking the earl might have business at his club before work.

Professor Lyall shook his head.

"I see. Are we to play at guessing games, then?"

The Beta sighed softly through his nose and finished his bite of sole. He put down his knife and fork with great precision on the side of his plate and then dabbed, unnecessarily, at his mouth with the corner of his serviette.

Lady Maccon waited patiently, nibbling at her own dinner. After Professor Lyall had put the damask serviette back into his lap and shoved his spectacles up his nose, she said, "Well?"

"He had a message this morning. I'm not privy to the particulars. He then swore a blue streak and set off northward."

"Northward to where, exactly?"

Professor Lyall sighed. "I believe he has gone to Scotland."

"He did *what*?"

"And he did not take Tunstell with him." Professor Lyall stated the obvious in clear annoyance, pointing to the redhead who was looking ever more guilty and ever more eager to continue chewing rather than participate in the conversation.

Lady Maccon worried at that information. Why should Conall take Tunstell? "Is he in danger? Shouldn't you have gone with him, then?"

Lyall snorted. "Yes. Picture the state of his cravat without a valet to tie him in." The Beta, always the height of understated elegance, winced in imagined horror.

Alexia privately agreed with this.

"Could not take me," muttered the Tunstell in question. "Had to go in wolf form. Trains are down, what with the engineer's strike. Not that I should mind going; my play's finished its run, and I've never seen Scotland." There was a note of petulance in his tone.

Hemming, one of the resident pack members, slapped Tunstell hard on the shoulder. "Respect," he growled without looking up from his meal.

"Where, precisely, has my husband taken himself off to in Scotland?" Lady Maccon pressed for details.

"The southern part of the Highlands, as I understand it," replied the Beta.

Alexia recovered her poise. What little she had. Which admittedly wasn't generally considered much. The southern Highland area was the vicinity of Conall's previous abode. She thought she understood at last. "I take it he found out about his former pack's Alpha being killed?"

Now it was Major Channing's turn to be surprised. The blond man practically spat out his mouthful of fritter. "How did *you* know that?"

Alexia looked up from her cup of tea. "I know many things."

Major Channing's pretty mouth twisted at that.

Professor Lyall said, "His lordship did say something about dealing with an embarrassing family emergency."

"Am I not family?" wondered Lady Maccon.

To which Lyall muttered under his breath, "And often embarrassing."

"Careful there, Professor. Only one person is allowed to say insulting things about me to my face, and you are certainly not large enough to be he."

Lyall actually blushed. "All apologies, *mistress*. I forgot my tongue." He emphasized her title and pulled his cravat down to show his neck ever so slightly.

"*We* are all his family! And he simply left us." Major Channing seemed to be even more annoyed by Alexia's husband's departure than she was. "Pity he didn't talk to me beforehand. I might have given him reason to stay."

Alexia turned hard brown eyes on Woolsey's Gamma. "Oh yes?"

But Major Channing was busy puzzling over something else. "Of course, he might have known, or at least guessed. What *did* they get up to those months without an Alpha to guide them?"

"I don't know," pressed Alexia, although his talk was clearly not directed at her. "Why don't *you* tell *me* what you were going to tell him?"

Major Channing started and managed to look both guilty and angry at the same time. Everyone's attention was on him.

"Yes," came Lyall's soft voice, "why don't you?" There was steel there, behind the studied indifference.

"Oh, it is nothing much. Only that, while we were on the boat and for the entirety of the journey over the Mediterranean and through the straits, none of us could change into wolf form. Six regiments with four packs, and we all grew beards. Basically, we were mortal the whole time. Once we left the ship and traveled some ways toward Woolsey, we suddenly became our old supernatural selves once more."

"That is very interesting given recent occurrences, and you didn't manage to tell my husband?"

"He never had time for me." Channing seemed angrier than she was.

"You took that as a slight and did not make him listen? That is not only stupid but could prove dangerous." Now Alexia was getting angry. "Is someone a little jealous?"

Major Channing slammed his palm down on the table, rattling the dishes. "We have only *just* arrived back after six years abroad, and *our* illustrious Alpha takes off, leaving his pack to go and see to the business of another!" The major practically spat the words out in his self-righteousness.

"Yup," said Hemming from nearby, "definitely jealous."

Major Channing pointed a threatening finger at him. He had wide, elegant hands, but they were callused and rough, making Alexia wonder what backcountry he had fought to tame in the years before he became a werewolf. "Take greater caution with your words, runt. I outrank you."

Hemming tilted his head, exposing his throat in acknowledgment of the threat's validity, and then proceeded to finish his supper and keep his opinions to himself.

Tunstell and the rest of the clavigers watched the conversation with wide-eyed interest. Having the entire pack home was a novel experience for them. The Cold-steam Guards had been stationed in India long enough for most of the Woolsey clavigers to have never met the full pack.

Lady Maccon decided she had had enough of Major Channing for one evening. With this new information, it was even more urgent she head into town, and so she rose from her chair and called for the carriage.

"Back into London again this evening, my lady?" wondered Floote, appearing in the hallway with her mantle and hat.

"Unfortunately, yes." His lady was looking perturbed.

"Will you be needing the dispatch case?"

"Not tonight, Floote. I am not going as muhjah. Best to remain as innocuous-looking as possible."

Floote's silence was eloquent, as so many of Floote's silences were. What his beloved mistress made up for in brains she lacked in subtlety; she was about as innocuous as one of Ivy Hisselpenny's hats.

Alexia rolled her eyes at him. "Yes, well, I take your point, but there is something I am missing about last night's incident. And now we know that whatever it was came into town with the regiments. I simply must see if I can catch Lord Akeldama. What BUR did not uncover, his boys will have."

Floote looked slightly perturbed by this. One eyelid fluttered almost imperceptibly. Alexia would never have noticed had she not labored under twenty-six years of acquaintance with the man. What it meant was that he did not entirely approve of her fraternization with the most outlandish of London's vampire roves.

"Do not alarm yourself, Floote. I shall take prodigious care. Pity I do not have a legitimate excuse for going into town tonight, though. People will remark upon my break from the normal schedule."

A timid feminine voice said, "My lady, I may be able to assist with that."

Alexia looked up with a smile. Female voices were rare about Woolsey Castle, but this was one of the few commonly heard ones. As ghosts went, Formerly Merriway was an amenable one, and Alexia had grown fond of her over the last few months. Even if she was timid.

"Good evening, Formerly Merriway. How are you tonight?"

"Still holding myself together, mistress," replied the ghost, appearing as nothing more than a shimmery grayish mist in the brightness of the gas-lit hallway. The front hall was at the farthest end of her tether, so it was difficult for her to solidify. It also meant her body must be located somewhere in the upper portion of Woolsey Castle, probably walled in somewhere, a fact Alexia preferred not to think about and hoped fervently never to smell.

"I have a personal message to deliver to you, my lady."

"From my impossible husband?" It was a safe guess, as Lord Maccon was the only one who would employ a ghost rather than some sensible means of communication, like perhaps waking up his own wife and talking to her before he left for once.

The ghostly form swayed a bit up and down, Formerly Merriway's version of a nod. "From his lordship, yes."

"Well?" barked Alexia.

Formerly Merriway skittered back slightly. Despite copious promises from Alexia that she was not going to wander about the castle looking to lay hands on Merriway's corpse, the ghost could not get over her fear of the preternatural. She persisted in seeing imminent exorcism behind every threatening attitude Alexia took, which, given Alexia's character, made for a constant state of nervousness.

Alexia sighed and modified her tone. "What was his message to me, Formerly Merriway, please?" She used the hall mirror to pin on her hat, careful not to upset Angelique's hairdo. It perched far to the back of the head in an entirely useless manner, but as the sun was not out, Alexia supposed she did not have to mind the lack of shade.

"You are to go hat shopping," said Formerly Merriway, quite unexpectedly.

Alexia wrinkled her forehead and pulled on her gloves. "I am, am I?"

Formerly Merriway gave her bobbing nod once again. "He recommends a newly opened establishment on Regent Street called Chapeau de Poupe. He emphasized that you should visit it without delay."

Lord Maccon rarely took an interest in his own attire. Lady Maccon could hardly believe he would suddenly take an interest in hers.

She said only, "Ah, well, I was just thinking how I did not like this hat. Not that I really require a new one."

"Well, I certainly know someone who does," said Floote with unexpected feeling from just behind her shoulder.

"Yes, Floote, I *am* sorry you had to see those grapes yesterday," Alexia apologized. Poor Floote had very delicate sensibilities.

"Suffering comes unto us all," quoth Floote sagely. Then he handed over a blue and white lace parasol and saw her down the steps and into the waiting carriage.

"To the Hisselpenny town residence," he instructed the driver, "posthaste."

"Oh, Floote." Lady Maccon stuck her head out the window as the carriage wheeled off down the drive. "Cancel tomorrow's dinner party, would you? Since my husband has chosen to absent himself, there is simply no point."

Floote tipped his head at the retreating carriage in acknowledgment and went to see to the details.

Alexia felt justified in turning up on Ivy's doorstep without announcement, as Ivy had done that very thing to her the evening before.

Miss Ivy Hisselpenny was sitting listlessly in the front parlor of the Hisselpennys' modest town address, receiving visitors. She was delighted to see Alexia, however unexpected. The whole Hisselpenny household was generally elated to receive Lady Maccon; never had they thought Ivy's odd little relationship with bluestocking spinster Alexia Tarabotti would flower into such a social coup de grace.

Lady Maccon swept in to find Mrs. Hisslepenny and her clacking knitting needles, keeping wordless vigil to her daughter's endless chatter.

"Oh, Alexia! Tremendous."

"And a good evening to you too, Ivy. How are you tonight?"

This was rather an imprudent question to ask Miss Hisselpenny, as Miss Hisselpenny was prone to telling one the answer—in excruciating detail.

"Would you believe? The announcement of my engagement to Captain Featherstonehaugh was in the *Times* this morning, and practically *no one* has called all day! I have received only twenty-four visitors, and when Bernice got engaged last month, she had twenty-seven! Shabby, I call it, perfectly shabby. Although, I suppose you would make it twenty-five, dearest Alexia."

"Ivy," said Alexia without further shilly-shallying, "why bother to lay about here awaiting insult? You clearly require some diversion. And I am in just the humor to provide it. For I do believe you are in dire need of a new hat. You and I should go shopping for one."

"Right this very instant?"

"Yes, immediately. I hear there is a divine new shop just opened on Regent Street. Shall we give it our patronage?"

"Oh." Ivy's cheeks pinkened in delight. "The Chapeau de Poupe? It is supposed to be very daring, indeed. Some ladies of my acquaintance have even referred to it as *fast*." A little gasp at that word emitted from Ivy's perennially quiet mama, but that good lady did not offer any comment to companion her inhalation, so Ivy continued. "You know, only the most forward ladies frequent that establishment. The actress Mabel Dair is supposed to stop in regularly. And the proprietress is said to be quite the scandal herself."

Everything about her friend's outraged tone told Alexia that Ivy was dying to visit Chapeau de Poupe.

"Well, it sounds like just the place to find something a little more unusual for the winter season, and as a newly engaged lady, you do realize you simply must have a new hat."

"Must I?"

"Trust me, my dearest Ivy, you most definitely must."

"Well, Ivy dear," said Mrs. Hisselpenny in a soft voice, setting down her knitting and looking up. "You should go and change. It would not do to keep Lady Maccon waiting on such a generous offer."

Ivy, pressed most firmly into doing something she wished to do more than anything else in the world, trotted upstairs with only a few more token protests.

"You will try to help her, won't you, Lady Maccon?" Mrs. Hisselpenny's eyes were quite desperate over her once-again clicking needles.

Alexia thought she understood the question. "You are also worried about this sudden engagement?"

"Oh no, Captain Featherstonehaugh is quite a suitable match. No, I was referring to Ivy's headwear preferences."

Alexia swallowed down a smile, keeping her face perfectly serious. "Of course. I shall do my very best, for queen and country."

The Hisselpennys' manservant appeared with a welcome tea tray. Lady Maccon sipped a freshly brewed cup in profound relief. All in all, it had been quite the trying evening thus far. With Ivy and hats in her future, it was only likely to get worse. Tea was a medicinal necessity at this juncture. Thank goodness Mrs. Hisselpenny had thought to provide.

Lady Maccon resorted to painfully pleasant discussion of the weather for a quarter of an hour. None too soon, Ivy reappeared in a walking dress of orange taffeta ruffled to within an inch of its life, and a champagne brocade overjacket, paired with a particularly noteworthy flowerpot hat. The hat was, not unexpectedly, decorated with a herd of silk mums and here and there a tiny feather bee on the end of a piece of wire.

Alexia forbore to look at the hat, thanked Mrs. Hisselpenny for the tea, and hustled Ivy into the Woolsey carriage. Around them, London's night society was coming to life, gas lights being lit, elegantly dressed couples hailing cabs, here and there a reeling group of rowdy young blunts. Alexia directed her driver to proceed on to Regent Street, and they arrived in short order at Chapeau de Poupe.

At first Alexia was at a loss as to why her husband wanted her to visit Chapeau de Poupe. So she did what any young lady of good breeding would do. She shopped.

"Are you certain you wish to go hat shopping with me, Alexia?" asked Ivy as they pushed in through the wrought-iron door. "Your taste in hats is not mine."

"I should most profoundly hope not," replied Lady Maccon with real feeling, looking at the flower-covered monstrosity atop her friend's sweet round little face and glossy black curls.

The shop proved to be as reported. It was exceptionally modern in appearance, all light airy muslin drapes, with soft peach and sage striped walls and bronze furniture with clean lines and matched cushions.

"Ahooo," said Ivy, looking about with wide eyes. "Isn't this simply too French?"

There were a few hats on tables and on wall hooks, but most were hanging from little gold chains suspended from the ceiling. They fell to different heights so that one had to brush through the hats to get around the shop, and they swayed slightly, like some alien vegetation. And such hats—caps of embroidered batiste with Mechlin lace, Italian straw shepherdesses, faille capotes, velvet toques that put Ivy's flowerpot to shame, and outrageous pifferaro bonnets—dangled everywhere.

Ivy was immediately entranced by the ugliest of the bunch: a canary-yellow felt toque trimmed with black currants, black velvet ribbon, and a pair of green feathers that looked like antennae off to one side.

"Oh, not that one!" said both Alexia and another voice at the same time when Ivy reached to pull it off the wall.

Ivy's hand dropped to her side, and both she and Lady Maccon turned to see the most remarkable-looking woman emerging from a curtained back room.

Alexia thought, without envy, that this was quite probably the most beautiful female she had ever seen. She had a lovely small mouth, large green eyes, prominent cheekbones, and dimples when she smiled, which she was doing now. Normally Alexia objected to dimples, but they seemed to suit this woman. Perhaps because they were offset by her thin angular frame and the fact that she had her brown hair cut unfashionably short, like a man's.

Ivy gasped upon seeing her.

This was not because of the hair. Or, not entirely because of it. This was because the woman was also dressed head to shiny boots in perfect and impeccable style—for a man. Jacket, pants, and waistcoat were all to the height of fashion. A top hat perched upon that scandalously short hair, and her burgundy cravat was tied into a silken waterfall. Still, there was no pretense at hiding her femininity. Her voice, when she spoke, was low and melodic, but definitely that of a woman.

Alexia picked up a pair of burnt umber kid gloves from a display basket. They were as soft as butter to the touch, and she looked at them to stop herself from staring at the woman.

"I am Madame Lefoux. Welcome to Chapeau de Poupe. How may I serve you fine ladies?" She had the hint of a French accent, but only the barest hint, utterly unlike Angelique, who could never seem to handle the "th" sound.

Ivy and Alexia curtsied with a little tilt to their heads, the latest fashion in curtsies, designed to show that the neck was unbitten. One wouldn't want to be thought a drone without the benefit of vampiric protection. Madame Lefoux did the same, although it was impossible to tell if her neck was bitten under that skillfully tied cravat. Alexia noted with interest that she wore two cravat pins: one of silver and one of wood. Madame Lefoux might keep night hours, but she was cautious about it.

Lady Maccon said, "My friend Miss Hisselpenny has recently become engaged and is in dire need of a new hat." She did not introduce herself, not yet. Lady Maccon was a name best kept in reserve.

Madame Lefoux took in Ivy's copious flowers and feather bees. "Yes, this is quite evident. Do walk this way, Miss Hisselpenny. I believe I have something over here that would perfectly suit that dress."

Ivy dutifully trotted after the strangely clad woman. She gave Alexia a look over her shoulder that said, as clearly as if she had the gumption to say it aloud, *what the deuce is she wearing?*

Alexia wandered over to the offensive yellow toque she and Madame Lefoux had so hastily warned Ivy off of. It completely contrasted with the general sophisticated tenor set by the other hats. Almost as though it wasn't meant to be purchased.

As the extraordinary patroness seemed to be thoroughly distracted by Ivy (well, who wouldn't be?), Alexia used the handle of her parasol to gently lift the toque and peek underneath. It was at that precise moment she deduced why it was her husband had sent her to Chapeau de Poupe.

There was a hidden knob, disguised as a hook, secreted under the hideous hat. Alexia quickly replaced the hat and turned away to begin innocently wandering about the shop, pretending interest in various accessories. She began to notice that there were other little hints as to a second nature for Chapeau de Poupe: scrape marks on the floor near a wall that *seemed* to have no door and several gas lights that were not lit. Alexia would wager good money that they were not lights at all.

Lady Maccon would not have thought to be curious, of course, had her husband not been so insistent she visit the establishment. The rest of the shop was quite unsuspicious, being the height of la mode, with hats appealing

enough to hold even *her* unstylish awareness. But with
the scrapes and the hidden knob, Alexia became curious,
both about the shop and its owner. Lady Maccon might
be soulless, but the liveliness of her mind was never in
question.

She wandered over to where Madame Lefoux had actually persuaded Miss Hisselpenny to don a becoming
little straw bonnet with upturned front, decorated about
the crown with a few classy cream flowers and one grace-
ful blue feather.

"Ivy, that looks remarkably well on you," she praised.

"Thank you, Alexia, but don't you find it a tad reserved? I'm not convinced it quite suits."

Lady Maccon and Madame Lefoux exchanged a
look.

"No, I do not. It is nothing like that horrible yellow
thing at the back you insisted on at first. I went to take a
closer look, you know, and it really is quite ghastly."

Madame Lefoux glanced at Alexia, her beautiful face
suddenly sharp and her dimples gone.

Alexia smiled, all teeth and not nicely. One couldn't
live around werewolves and not pick up a few of their
mannerisms. "It cannot possibly be your design?" she
said mildly to the proprietress.

"The work of an apprentice, I do assure you," replied
Madame Lefoux with a tiny French shrug. She put a new
hat onto Ivy's head, one with a few more flowers.

Miss Hisselpenny preened.

"Are there any more . . . like it?" wondered Alexia,
still talking about the ugly yellow hat.

"Well, there is that riding hat." The proprietress's
voice was wary.

Lady Maccon nodded. Madame Lefoux was naming the hat nearest to the scrape marks Alexia had observed on the floor. They understood one another.

There came a pause in conversation while Ivy expressed interest in a frosted pink confection with feather toggles. Alexia spun her closed parasol between two gloved hands.

"You seem to be having problems with some of your gas lighting as well," said Alexia, all mildness and sugar.

"Indeed." A flicker of firm acknowledgment crossed Madame Lefoux's face at that. "And, of course, there is the door handle. But you know how it goes—there are always kinks to work out after opening a new establishment."

Lady Maccon cursed herself. The door handle—how had she missed that? She wandered over casually, leaning on her parasol to look down at it.

Ivy, all insensible of the underpinnings to their conversation, went on to try the next hat.

The handle on the inside of the front door was far larger than it ought to be and seemed to be comprised of a complicated series of cogs and bolts, far more security than any ordinary hat shop required.

Alexia wondered if Madame Lefoux was a French spy.

"Well," Ivy was telling Madame Lefoux in a chatty manner when Alexia rejoined them, "Alexia always says my taste is abysmal, but I can hardly see how she has much ground. Her choices are so often banal."

"I lack imagination," admitted Alexia. "Which is why I keep a highly creative French maid."

Madame Lefoux looked mildly interested at that. Her dimples showed in a little half-smile.

"And the eccentricity of carrying a parasol even at night? I take it I am being honored by a visit from Lady Maccon?"

"Alexia," Miss Hisselpenny asked, scandalized, "you never introduced yourself?"

"Well I—" Alexia was grappling for an excuse, when . . .

Boom!

And the world about them exploded into darkness.

CHAPTER FOUR

_____

The Proper Use of Parasols

An enormous noise shook the structure around them. All of the hats on the ends of their long chains swung about violently. Ivy let out the most milk-curdling scream. Someone else yelled, rather soberly by comparison. The gas lighting went out, and the shop descended into darkness.

It took a moment for Lady Maccon to realize that the explosion had not, in fact, been intended to kill _her_. Given her experiences over the past year, this was a novel change of pace. But it also made her wonder if the explosion had been intended to kill someone else.

"Ivy?" Alexia asked the darkness.

Silence.

"Madame Lefoux?"

Further silence.

Alexia crouched down, as much as her corset would allow, and felt about, willing her eyes to acclimatize to the black. She felt taffeta: the ruffles attached to Ivy's prone form.

Alexia's heart sank.

She patted Ivy all about for injury, but Miss Hisselpenny seemed unscathed. Light puffs of breath hit the back of Lady Maccon's hand when she passed it under Ivy's nose, and there was a pulse—shallow but solid. Apparently, Miss Hisselpenny had simply fainted.

"Ivy!" she hissed.

Nothing.

"Ivy, please!"

Miss Hisselpenny shifted slightly and murmured, "Yes, Mr. Tunstell?" under her breath.

Oh dear, thought Alexia. What a terribly unsuitable match, and Ivy already engaged to someone else. Lady Maccon had no idea that things had progressed so far as to involve *murmurings* in times of distress. Then she felt a stab of pity. Better to let Ivy have her dreams while she could.

So Lady Maccon left her friend as she lay and did not reach for the smelling salts.

Madame Lefoux, on the other hand, was nowhere to be found. She had apparently vanished into the blackness. Perhaps seeking the source of the explosion. Or perhaps being the source of the explosion.

Alexia could guess as to where the Frenchwoman had disappeared. Her eyes now partly adjusted to the gloom, she made her way along the wall toward the back of the shop, where the scrape marks were located.

She felt all about the wallpaper for a switch or a knob of some kind, finally finding a lever hidden under a glove display box. She pressed it sharply down, and a door swung open before her, nearly cracking her on the nose.

Lady Maccon managed to determine that it was no

room or passageway but a large shaft with several cables down the middle and two guide rails on the side. She craned her head inside and looked up, hanging on to the doorjamb. What appeared to be a steam-powered windlass occupied the whole of the top of the shaft. She found a cord to one side of the doorway that, when pulled upon, engaged the windlass. With many puffs of steam and some creaking and groaning, a boxy cage appeared from out of the shaft depths. Alexia was familiar with the concept—an ascension room. She'd had previous dealings with a less sophisticated version at the Hypocras Club. She had found that they did not suit her stomach, but she stepped into the cage regardless, closing the grate behind her, and turned a crank on one side to lower the contraption.

The cage bumped when it hit the ground, causing Alexia to stumble violently up against the side. Parasol held defensively before her as though it were a cricket bat, she opened the grate and stepped out into an illuminated underground passageway.

The lighting mechanism was like nothing Lady Maccon had ever seen. It must be some kind of gas, but it appeared as an orange tinted mist inside glass tubing set along the ceiling. The mist swirled about within its confines, causing the illumination to be patchy and faint in odd, shifting patterns. *Light cast as clouds,* thought Alexia fancifully.

At the end of the passage was an open doorway, out of which spilled a mass of brighter orange light and three voices raised in anger. As she neared, Alexia realized the passage must traverse directly underneath Regent Street. She also realized the voices were arguing in French.

Alexia had a good grasp of the modern languages, so she followed the gist of the conversation without difficulty.

"What could possibly have possessed you?" Madame Lefoux was asking, her voice still smooth despite her annoyance.

The entranceway appeared to service a laboratory of some kind, although it was nothing like those Alexia had seen at the Hypocras Club or the Royal Society. It had more the look of an apparatus factory, with massive machine components and other gadgetry.

"Well, you see, I could not for the life of me get the boiler running."

Alexia peeked into the room. It was huge and in a complete and utter muddle. Containers had been knocked off tables, glass had shattered, and thousands of tiny gears were scattered across the dirt floor. A jumble of cords and wire coils lay on the ground along with the hat stand they had once been hanging on. There was black soot everywhere, coating both those tubes, gears, and springs that had not fallen and the larger pieces of machinery. Outside the blast zone, things were also in disarray. A pair of glassicals lay atop a pile of research books. Large diagrams drawn in black pencil on stiff yellow paper were pinned haphazardly to the walls. It was clear that some accident had disrupted matters, but it was equally clear the place had been untidy well before the unfortunate event.

It was noisy, as many of those mechanisms and gadgets not affected by the blast were running. Steam puffed out in little gasps and whistles, gears clanked, metal chain links clicked, and valves squealed. Such a cacophony of noises as only the great factories of the north might make. But it wasn't an invasive noise, more a symphony in engineering.

Partly hidden behind the piles, Madame Lefoux stood, hands on angular trouser-clad hips, legs wide like a man, glaring down at some species of grubby child. The urchin came complete with grease-smeared face, filthy hands, and jaunty tilt to his newsboy cap. He was clearly in a hot spot of bother but seemed less apologetic than excited about his inadvertent pyrotechnics.

"So, what did you do, Quesnel?"

"I just soaked a bit of rag in ether and tossed it into the flame. Ether catches fire, no?"

"Oh, for goodness sake, Quesnel. Don't you ever listen?" This came from a new voice, a ghost, who was making a show of sitting sidesaddle on an overturned barrel. She was a very solid-looking specter, which meant her dead body must be relatively close and well preserved. Regent Street was well north of the exorcised zone, so she would have escaped last night's incident undead. If the ghost's speech was anything to go by, her body must have traveled over from France, or she had died in London an immigrant. Her face was sharply defined, her visage that of a handsome older woman who resembled Madame Lefoux. Her arms were crossed over her chest in annoyance.

"Ether!" shrieked Madame Lefoux.

"Well, yes," said the ragamuffin.

"Ether is explosive, you little . . ." After which followed a stream of unpleasant words, which still managed to sound pleasant in Madame Lefoux's mellow voice.

"Ah," replied the boy with a shameless grin. "But it did make a fantastic bang."

Alexia could not help herself; she let out a little giggle.

All three gasped and looked over at her.

Lady Maccon straightened up, brushed her blue silk walking dress smooth, and entered the cavernous room, swinging her parasol back and forth.

"Ah," said Madame Lefoux, switching back to her impeccable English. "Welcome to my contrivance chamber, Lady Maccon."

"You are a woman of many talents, Madame Lefoux, an inventor as well as a milliner?"

Madame Lefoux inclined her head. "As you see, the two more often cross paths than one would think. I should have realized you would deduce the function of the windlass engine and the location of my laboratory, Lady Maccon."

"Oh," replied Alexia. "Why should you have?"

The Frenchwoman dimpled at her and bent to retrieve a fallen vial of some silvery liquid, which had managed to escape Quesnel's explosion unbroken. "Your husband informed me that you were clever. And prone to interfering overmuch."

"That sounds like something he would say." Alexia made her way through the shambles, lifting her skirts delicately to keep them from getting caught on fragments of glass. Now that she could see them closer up, the gadgets lying about Madame Lefoux's contrivance chamber were amazing. There seemed to be an entire assembly line of glassicals in midconstruction and a massive apparatus that looked to be composed of the innards of several steam engines welded to a galvanometer, a carriage wheel, and a wicker chicken.

Alexia, tripping only once over a large valve, completed her trek across the room and nodded politely to the child and the ghost.

"How do you do? Lady Maccon, at your service."

The scrap of a boy grinned at her, made an elaborate bow, and said, "Quesnel Lefoux."

Alexia gave him an expressionless look. "So, *did* you get the boiler started?"

Quesnel blushed. "Not exactly. But I did get a fire started. That should count for something, don't you feel?" His English was superb.

Madame Lefoux cast her hands heavenward.

"Indubitably," agreed Lady Maccon, endearing herself to the child for all time.

The ghost introduced herself as Formerly Beatrice Lefoux.

Alexia nodded to her politely, which surprised the ghost. The undead were often subjected to rudeness from the fully alive. But Lady Maccon always stood on formality.

"My impossible son and my noncorporeal aunt," explained Madame Lefoux, looking at Alexia as though she expected something.

Lady Maccon filed away the fact that they all had the same last name. Had Madame Lefoux not married the child's father? How very salacious. But Quesnel did not look at all like his mother. She need not have claimed him. He was a towheaded, pointy-chinned little creature with the most enormous violet eyes and not a dimple in sight.

The lady inventor said to her family, "This is Alexia Maccon, Lady Woolsey. She is also muhjah to the queen."

"Ah, my husband saw fit to tell you that little fact, did he?" Alexia was surprised. Not many knew about her political position, and, as with her preternatural state, both she and her husband preferred to keep it that way: Conall, because it kept his wife out of danger; Alexia, because it caused most individuals, supernatural or otherwise, to come over all funny about soullessness.

The ghost of Beatrice Lefoux interrupted them. "You are ze muhjah? Niece, you allow an exorcist into ze vicinity of my body? Uncaring, thoughtless child! You are ze worse than your son." Her accent was far more pronounced than her niece's. She moved violently away from Alexia, floating back and upward off the barrel upon which she had pretended to sit. As though Alexia could *do* anything damaging to her spirit. Silly creature.

Lady Maccon frowned, realizing that the aunt's presence eliminated Madame Lefoux as a suspect in the case of the mass exorcism. She could not have invented a weapon that acted like a preternatural, not here, not if her aunt's spirit resided in the contrivance chamber.

"Aunt, do not get so emotional. Lady Maccon can only kill you if she touches your body, and only I know where that is kept."

Alexia wrinkled her nose. "Please do not agitate yourself so, Formerly Lefoux. I prefer not to perform exorcisms in any event: decomposing flesh is very squishy." She shuddered delicately.

"Oh, well, thank you for that," sneered the ghost.

"Ew!" said Quesnel, fascinated. "Have you conducted simply masses of them?"

Alexia narrowed her eyes at him in a way she hoped was mysterious and cunning, and then turned back to his mother. "So, in what capacity did my husband see fit to inform you of my nature and my position?"

Madame Lefoux was leaning back slightly, a faint look of amusement on her lovely face. "What could your ladyship possibly mean?"

"Was he in attendance upon you as Alpha, as earl, or as the head of BUR investigations?"

Madame Lefoux dimpled once more at that. "Ah, yes, the many faces of Conall Maccon."

Alexia bridled at the Frenchwoman's use of Conall's first name. "And how long, exactly, have you known my husband?" Abnormal dress was one thing, but loose morals were an entirely different matter.

"Calm yourself, my lady. My interest in your husband is purely professional. He and I know each other through BUR transactions, but he visited me here a month ago as the earl and your husband. He wished me to make you a special gift."

"A gift?"

"Indeed."

"Well, where is it?"

Madame Lefoux looked to her son. "Scat, you. Go find the cleaning mechanicals, hot water, and soap. Listen to your former great-aunt; she will tell you what can take water immersion and what will need to be cleaned and repaired by some other means. You have a very long night ahead of you."

"But, *Maman,* I simply wanted to see what would happen!"

"So, now you see. What happens is it makes your *maman* angry and gets you nights and nights of cleaning as punishment."

"Aw, *Maman!*"

"Right this very minute, Quesnel."

Quesnel sighed loudly and scampered off with a "nice to meet you" directed over his shoulder at Lady Maccon.

"That will teach him to run experiments without some valid hypothesis. Go after him, please, Beatrice, and keep him away for at least a quarter of an hour while I finish my business with Lady Maccon."

"Fraternizing with a preternatural! You run a far more dangerous game than I did in my day, niece," grumbled the ghost, but she dispersed easily enough, presumably after the boy.

"Pleasure to make your acquaintance, Formerly Lefoux," said Alexia defiantly to the now-empty air.

"Please do not concern yourself with her attitude. Even when alive, my aunt was difficult. Brilliant, but difficult. An inventor like me, you see, but less socially indoctrinated, I am afraid."

Lady Maccon smiled. "I have met many such scientists, and most of them could not claim brilliance as an excuse. That is not to say they didn't claim it, of course, just that . . ." She trailed off. She was babbling. She wasn't certain why, but something about the beautiful, strangely dressed Frenchwoman made Alexia nervous.

"So." The inventor moved closer to her. Madame Lefoux smelled of vanilla and mechanical oil. "We find ourselves alone. It is a genuine pleasure to meet you, Lady Maccon. The last time I was in the company of a preternatural, I was but a small child. And, of course, he was nowhere near as striking as you."

"Well, uh, thank you." Alexia was a little taken aback by the compliment.

The inventor took her hand gently. "Not at all."

The skin of the inventor's palm was callused. Lady Maccon could feel the roughness even through her gloves. At the contact, Alexia experienced certain slight palpitations that had, heretofore, been associated only with the opposite sex and, more specifically, her husband. Not much truly shocked Alexia. This did.

As soon as was seemly, she withdrew her hand, blushing furiously under her tan. Considering it a rude betrayal by her own body, Alexia ignored the phenomenon and grappled ineffectually for a moment, trying to remember the direction of her inquiry and the reason they were now alone together. Which was? Ah, yes, at her *husband's* insistence.

"I believe you may have something for me," she said at long last.

Madame Lefoux doffed her top hat in acknowledgment. "Indeed I do. One moment, please." With a sly smile, she moved off to one side of the lab and rummaged about for a moment in a large steamer trunk. Eventually, she emerged with a long skinny wooden box.

Lady Maccon held her breath in anticipation.

Madame Lefoux carried it over and flipped open the lid.

Inside was a not-very-prepossessing parasol of outlandish shape and indifferent style. Its shade was slate gray in color, edged in embroidered lace, with a thick cream ruffle trim. It had a peculiarly long spike at its tip, decorated with two egg-sized metal globules, like seed-pods, one near the fabric and another closer to the tip. Its ribs were oversized, making it bulky and umbrella-like, and its shaft was extremely long, ending in a chubby, knobby, richly decorated handle. The handle looked like something that might top an ancient Egyptian column, carved with lotus flowers—or a very enthusiastic pine-apple. The parasol's parts were entirely of brass, in what looked to be variable alloys, giving it a wide-ranging coloration.

"Well, Conall's taste strikes again," commented Alexia, whose own taste, while not particularly imaginative or sophisticated, at least did not tend toward the bizarre.

Madame Lefoux dimpled. "I did my best, given the carrying capacity."

Alexia was intrigued. "May I?"

The inventor offered her the box.

Lady Maccon lifted out the monstrosity. "It's heavier than it looks."

"That is one of the reasons I made it so very long. I thought it might serve double as a walking stick. Then you would not have to carry it everywhere."

Alexia tested it. The height was ideal for just that. "Is it likely to be something I must carry everywhere?"

"I believe your esteemed husband would prefer it so."

Alexia demurred. It leaned heavily toward the ugly end of the parasol spectrum. Many of her favorite day dresses would clash most horribly with all that brass and gray, not to mention the decorative elements.

"Also, of course, it had to be tough enough to serve as a defensive weapon."

"A sensible precaution, given my proclivities." Lady Maccon had destroyed more than one parasol through the application of it against someone else's skull.

"Would you like to learn its anthroscopy?" Madame Lefoux became gleeful as she made the offer.

"It has anthroscopy? Is that healthy?"

"Why, certainly. Do you believe I would design an object so ugly without sufficient cause?"

Alexia passed her the heavy accessory. "By all means."

Madame Lefoux took hold of the handle, allowing Alexia to maintain a grip on the top spire. Upon closer examination, Alexia realized the tip had a tiny hydraulic hinge affixed to one side.

"When you press here"—Madame Lefoux indicated one of the lotus petals on the shaft just below the large handle—"that tip opens and emits a poisoned dart equipped with a numbing agent. And if you twist the handle so . . ."

Alexia gasped as, just above where she gripped the end, two wickedly sharp spikes flipped out, one of silver and one of wood.

"I did notice your cravat pins," Lady Maccon said.

Madame Lefoux chuckled, touching them delicately with her free hand. "Oh, they are more than simply cravat pins."

"Of that I have no doubt. Does the parasol do anything else?"

Madame Lefoux winked at her. "Ah, that is just the

beginning. In this, you understand, Lady Maccon, I am an artist."

Alexia licked her bottom lip. "I am certainly beginning to comprehend that fact. And here I thought only your hats were exceptional."

The Frenchwoman blushed slightly, the color visible even in the orange light. "Pull this lotus petal here, and so."

Every noise in the lab fell silent. All the whirring, clanking, and puffs of steam that had faded into the background as ambient sound became suddenly noticeable by way of their absence.

"What?" Alexia looked about. All was still.

And then, moments later, the mechanisms started up once more.

"What happened?" she asked, looking in awe down at the parasol.

"The nodule here"—the inventor pointed to the egg attachment near the shade section of the parasol—"emitted a magnetic disruption field. It will affect any metal of the iron, nickel, or cobalt family, including steel. If you need to seize up a steam engine for any reason, this will probably do the trick, but only for a brief amount of time."

"Remarkable!"

Again the Frenchwoman blushed. "The disruption field is not of my own invention, but I did make it substantially smaller than Babbage's original design." She continued on. "The ruffles contain various hidden pockets and are fluffy enough to disguise small objects." She reached inside the wide ruffle and pulled out a little vial.

"Poison?" asked Lady Maccon, tilting her head to one side.

"Certainly not. Something far more important: perfume. We cannot very well have you fighting crime unscented, now, can we?"

"Oh." Alexia nodded gravely. After all, Madame Lefoux *was* French. "Certainly not."

Madame Lefoux pushed the shade up, revealing that the parasol was of an old-fashioned pagoda shape. "You can also turn it thus"—she flipped the parasol around so that the shade was pointing the wrong direction—"and twist and press here." She pointed to a small nodule just above the magnetic disruption emitter, in which a tiny dial was set. "I have designed it to be quite difficult to operate, to prevent any unfortunate accidents. The rib caps of the parasol will open and emit a fine mist. At one click, these three will emit a mixture of *lapis lunearis* and water. At two clicks, the other three ribs will emit *lapis solaris* diluted in sulfuric acid. Make certain that you, and anyone you care about, stay well out of the blast area and upwind. Although the *lunearis* will cause only mild skin irritation, the *solaris* is toxic and will kill humans as well as disabling vampires." With a sudden grin, the scientist added, "Only werewolves are resistant. The *lunearis* is, of course, for them. A direct spray should render the species in question helpless and gravely ill for several days. Three clicks and both will emit at once."

"Quite outstanding, madame." Alexia was suitably impressed. "I did not know there were any poisons capable of disabling either species."

Madame Lefoux said mildly, "I once had access to a partial copy of the Templar's Amended Rule."

Lady Maccon's mouth dropped. "You what?"

The Frenchwoman elucidated no further.

Alexia took the parasol, turning it about in her hands reverently. "I shall have to change over half my wardrobe to match it, of course. But I suspect it will be worth it."

Madame Lefoux dimpled in pleasure. "It *will* also keep the sun at bay."

Lady Maccon snorted in amusement. "As to the cost, has my husband dealt with the necessities?"

The Frenchwoman held up a small hand. "Oh, I am well aware that Woolsey can see to the expense. And I have had dealings with your pack before."

Alexia smiled. "Professor Lyall?"

"Mainly. He is a curious man. One wonders, sometimes, as to his motivations."

"He is not a man."

"Just so."

"And you?"

"I, too, am not a man. I simply enjoy dressing like one," replied Madame Lefoux, purposefully choosing to misinterpret Alexia's question.

"So you say," replied Lady Maccon. Then she frowned, remembering something Ivy had said about the new hat shop: that actresses like Mabel Dair were known to frequent it. "You are dealing with the hives as well as the packs."

"And why would you say that?"

"Miss Hisselpenny mentioned that Miss Dair visited your establishment. She is drone to the Westminster Hive."

The Frenchwoman turned away, busying herself with tidying the laboratory. "I provide to those who can afford my services."

"Does that include loners and roves? Have you catered to, for example, Lord Akeldama's taste?"

"I have not yet had the pleasure," replied the inventor.

Alexia noted that the Frenchwoman did not say that she had not *heard* of him.

Lady Maccon decided to meddle. "Ah, this is a grave lapse! It ought to be rectified immediately. Would you be free for tea later this evening, say around midnight? I shall consult with the gentleman in question and see if he is available."

Madame Lefoux looked curious but wary. "I believe I could arrange to get away. How very kind of you, Lady Maccon."

Alexia inclined her head in grand-dame fashion, feeling silly. "I shall send around a card with the address, if he is amenable." She wanted to meet with Lord Akeldama alone first.

Just then, a new noise made itself heard through the hubbub of machinery, a querulous, high-pitched, "Alexia?"

Lady Maccon whirled about. "Oh dear, Ivy! She has not made her way down here, has she? I believe I closed the door to the ascension chamber behind me."

Madame Lefoux looked unperturbed. "Oh, do not concern yourself. It is only her voice. I have an auditory capture and dispersal amplifier funneling sounds in from the shop." She pointed to where a trumpet-shaped object was cabled to the ceiling. Lady Maccon had thought it some kind of gramophone. But Ivy's voice emanated from it, as clearly as if she were in the laboratory with them. Astonishing.

"Perhaps we should return to the shop and attend her," suggested the inventor.

Alexia, clutching her new parasol to her ample bosom like a newborn child, nodded.

They did so, to find that the gas lighting was up and running once more. And that, under the bright lights of the empty shop, Miss Hisselpenny was still reposing on the floor, but now seated upright and looking pale and confused.

"What happened?" she demanded as Lady Maccon and Madame Lefoux approached.

"There was a loud bang, and you fainted," replied Alexia. "Really, Ivy, if you did not lace your corset so tight, you would not be so prone to the vapors. It is reputed to be terribly bad for your health."

Miss Hisselpenny gasped at the mention of *underclothing* in a public hat shop. "Please, Alexia, do not spout such radical folderol. Next thing, you will want me to engage in dress reform!"

Lady Maccon rolled her eyes. The very idea: *Ivy* in bloomers!

"What have you got there?" Miss Hisselpenny asked, focusing on the parasol Lady Maccon clasped to her chest.

Alexia crouched down to show the parasol to her friend.

"Why, Alexia, that is quite beautiful. It does not reflect your customary taste at all," approved Miss Hisselpenny with glee.

Trust Ivy to like the hideous thing for its looks.

Miss Hisselpenny glanced eagerly up at the Frenchwoman. "I should like one just like it, in perhaps a nice lemon yellow with black and white stripes. Would you have such an item to hand?"

Alexia giggled at Madame Lefoux's shocked expression.

"I should think not," the inventor croaked out finally, having cleared her throat twice. "Should I"—she winced slightly—"order you one?"

"Please do."

Alexia stood and said softly in French, "Perhaps without the additional garnishing."

"Mmm," replied Madame Lefoux.

A little bell chimed cheerfully as someone new wandered into the shop. Miss Hisselpenny struggled to rise from her undignified lounge upon the floor.

The newcomer approached them, parting the forest of dangling hats and, upon seeing Ivy's plight, leaped to her aid.

"Why, Miss Hisselpenny, are you unwell? Let me offer my most humble services."

"Tunstell," interjected Alexia, glaring at the young man. "What are *you* doing *here*?"

The redheaded claviger ignored her, cooing over Miss Hisselpenny solicitously.

Ivy attained her feet and clutched at his arm, leaning against his side weakly and looking up at him out of big dark eyes.

Tunstell seemed to be taking a long, leisurely swim in those eyes, like some sort of gormless guppy.

Actors, the lot of them. Alexia poked at his bottom, nicely packaged in some excessively tight britches, with the tip of her new parasol. "Tunstell, explain your presence at once."

Tunstell jumped slightly and looked at her in a mal-treated manner.

"I have a message from Professor Lyall," he said, as though she were somehow to blame for this.

Lady Maccon did not ask how Lyall had known she would be at Chapeau de Poupe. The ways of her husband's Beta were often mysterious and better left unquestioned.

"Well?"

Tunstell was staring once more into Miss Hisselpenny's eyes.

Alexia tapped the parasol on the wooden floor, enjoying the metallic clicking noise it made. "The message."

"He requests for you to visit with him at BUR as a matter of some urgency," said Tunstell without looking at her.

A matter of urgency was pack code for activation of Lady Maccon as muhjah. Lyall had some information for the Crown. Alexia nodded. "In that case, Ivy, you would not mind if I left you under Tunstell's care while you complete your shopping? He will see you safely off. Won't you, Tunstell?"

"It would be my very great pleasure." Tunstell beamed.

"Oh, I believe that would suit adequately," breathed Ivy, smiling back.

Lady Maccon wondered if she had ever been so foolish over Lord Maccon. Then she recalled that her affection generally took the form of threats and verbal barbs. She gave herself a pat on the back for avoiding sentimentality.

The inventor-cum-milliner walked her to the front door.

"I shall send a card around presently when I determine Lord Akeldama's availability. He should be at home, but you never can tell with roves. This summons from Professor Lyall cannot possibly take long." Alexia looked back at Tunstell and Ivy, engaged in an overly familiar tête-à-tête. "Please, do try to prevent Miss Hisselpenny from purchasing anything too hideous, and see that Tunstell puts her into a hackney but does not get into it himself."

"I shall do my level best, Lady Maccon," replied Madame Lefoux with an abbreviated bow—so short as to be almost rude. Then, in a quick-fire movement, she caught one of Alexia's hands with her own. "It was a great pleasure to meet you at last, my lady." Her grip was firm and sure. Of course, lifting and building all that machinery below street level would give anyone a certain degree of musculature, even the rail-thin woman before her. The inventor's fingers caressed Alexia's wrist just above the perfect fit of her gloves, so quickly that Alexia was not certain the action had occurred. There was that faint scent of vanilla mixed with gear oil once more. Then Madame Lefoux smiled, dropped Alexia's hand, and turned back into the shop, disappearing among the swinging jungle of fashionable headgear.

Professor Lyall and Lord Maccon shared an office at BUR headquarters, on Fleet Street, but it was always considerably cleaner whenever the earl was not in residence. Lady Alexia Maccon breezed in, swinging her new parasol proudly and hoping Lyall would ask about it. But Professor Lyall was mightily distracted behind a pile of paperwork and a stack of metal scrolls with acid-etched notes upon them. He stood, bowed, and sat back down again as a matter of course rather than courtesy. Whatever had occurred was clearly occupying all of his considerable attention. His glassicals were perched upon his head, mussing his coiffure. Was it possible that his cravat could be minutely askew?

"Are you well, Professor Lyall?" Alexia asked, quite worried by the cravat.

"I am in perfect health, thank you for asking, Lady Maccon. It is your husband who concerns me, and I have no way to get through to him at present."

"Yes," said the earl's wife, deadpan, "I daily face a similar dilemma, frequently when he and I are in conversation. What has he gone and done now?"

Professor Lyall smiled slightly. "Oh no, nothing like that. It is simply that the plague of humanization has struck again, moving northward as far as Farthinghoe."

Alexia frowned at this new information. "Curious. It is on the move, is it?"

"And heading in the same direction as Lord Maccon. Though slightly ahead of him."

"And he doesn't know that, does he?"

Lyall shook his head.

"That family matter, it's the dead Alpha, isn't it?"

Lyall ignored this and said, "Don't know quite how it's moving so fast. The trains have been down since yesterday—strike. Trust the daylight folk to become inefficient at a time like this."

"By coach, perhaps?"

"Could be. It seems to be moving quickly. I should like to make the earl aware of this information, but there is no way to contact him until he arrives at the Glasgow offices. Not to mention Channing's blather about the boat ride over. This thing is mobile and Conall doesn't know that."

"You think he might overtake it?"

The Beta shook his head again. "Not at the rate it is moving. Lord Maccon is fast, but he said he was not going to push this run. If it keeps traveling north at the rate I predict, it will hit Scotland several days before he does. I have sent a note to our agents in the north, but I thought you should know as well, as muhjah."

Alexia nodded.

"Will you inform the other members of the Shadow Council?"

Lady Maccon frowned at that. "I do not think that is entirely wise just yet. I think it might wait until our next meeting. You should file a report, of course, but I shall not go out of my way to tell the potentate and the dewan."

The Beta nodded and did not inquire as to her reasons.

"Very well, Professor Lyall. If there is nothing else, I should be off. I have need of Lord Akeldama's council."

Professor Lyall gave her an unreadable look. "Well, I suppose someone must. Good evening, Lady Maccon."

Alexia left without ever having shown Professor Lyall her new parasol.

CHAPTER FIVE

Lord Akeldama's Latest

L ord Akeldama was indeed in residence and willing to receive Alexia. Despite the rudeness of her unannounced visit, he seemed genuinely pleased to see her. It was difficult to tell through the vampire's self-consciously frivolous mannerisms, but Alexia thought she detected real warmth beneath the flatterings and flutterings.

The ancient vampire sashayed forward to greet her, both arms extended, dressed in his version of the "casual gentleman at home." For most men of means and taste, this meant a smoking jacket, opera scarf, long trousers, and soft-soled derbies. For Lord Akeldama, this meant that the jacket was of pristine white silk with black embroidered birds of some lean oriental persuasion splashed about, the scarf a bright peacock-patterned teal, the trousers the latest in tight-fitting black jacquard, and the shoes cut in a flashy wingtip style with a black and white spectator coloration that was held by many to be rather vulgar.

"My *darling* Alexia. How fortuitous. I have just received delivery of the most divine new *plaything*. You *must* take a gander and give me your expert opinion!" Lord Akeldama addressed Lady Maccon by her given name and had done so since the night they met. And yet, Alexia realized for the first time as she took his hands in a firm grip, she had no idea what his was.

At the preternatural contact, Lord Akeldama turned from supernaturally beautiful, his skin ice white and his blond hair shining gold, to the merely pretty young man he had once been before his metamorphosis.

Lady Maccon kissed him softly on both cheeks, as though he were a child. "And how are you this evening, my lord?"

He leaned against her, momentarily calm in his fully human state, before resuming his animated chatter. "Perfectly *splendid,* my little tea biscuit, perfectly *splendid.* There is a mystery waffling about London town, and I am immersed in the thick of it. You know how I do so dearly *love* a mystery." He kissed her back, a loud smack to the forehead, and then released her hands to curl his arm affectionately with hers.

"And it has certainly been all abuzz around my humble little abode since the excitement of yesterday." He led her into said abode, which was anything but humble. It had an extravagant arched and frescoed hallway with marble busts of pagan gods. "I suppose, *you* know *all* about it, you high-powered political *daffodil,* you."

Alexia loved Lord Akeldama's drawing room, not that she could tolerate it in her own house, but it was a nice place to visit. It was quite old-fashioned in appearance, white and gilded gold like something from a French painting of pre-Napoleonic times.

The vampire unceremoniously ejected a fat calico from her slumbering possession of a gold brocade love seat with tasseled trim and settled gracefully into her place. Lady Maccon seated herself in an armchair nearby, one that felt deliciously thronelike.

"Well, my creamy *pudding* cup, Biffy told me *the* most attractive little story last night." Lord Akeldama's ethereal face was intent under its unnecessary coating of white powder and pink blush. "Quite the bedtime romance."

Lady Maccon was not certain she wanted to hear this story. "Oh, uh, did he? Where is Biffy, by the way? Is he about?"

Lord Akeldama fiddled with his gold monocle. The glass was, of course, plain. Like all vampires, he had perfect vision. "La, the troublesome boy is causing mischief somewhere not too far away, I am certain. He is in a bit of a kerfuffle over a necktie, but never mind that; you must permit me to tell you what he saw yester eve."

Lady Maccon forestalled him. "Before you do, my lord, might we send round an invitation to a new acquaintance I have made? I should very much like the two of you to know one another."

That stalled Lord Akeldama. "*Really,* my darling little kumquat, how thoughtful. Who is he?"

"*She* is one Madame Lefoux."

Lord Akeldama smiled slightly at that. "I did hear you had been hat shopping recently."

Alexia gasped. "How did you know that? Oh, how vexatious! Do you mean to say that you are already acquainted with the lady? Madame Lefoux indicated nothing to that effect."

"You can hardly expect *me* to reveal *my* sources, snow drop. As to the rest, I do not know her; I merely know *of* her, and I should enjoy meeting her socially very much indeed. I hear she affects masculine garb! I shall send a card directly." He reached to pull a small bell rope. "So, do tell: *what* did you purchase from the *scandalous* Frenchwoman, my little clementine?"

Alexia showed him the parasol.

Lord Akeldama was alarmed by its appearance. "Oh dear, it is rather"—he cleared his throat—"*loud,* is it not?"

Alexia thought that rich coming from a man wearing black and white wingtip shoes and a teal scarf. She said only, "Yes, but it does the most delicious things." She was about to explain further when a polite knock interrupted them, and Biffy trotted into the room.

"You rang?" Biffy was an agreeable young blunt with stylish proclivities and prodigious physical charms who always seemed to turn up when least expected and most wanted. Had he not been born into wealth and status, he might have made for an excellent butler. He was Lord Akeldama's favorite drone, although the vampire would never confess openly to having favorites any more than he would wear the same waistcoat two days running. Alexia had to admit there was something special about Biffy. He was certainly a dab hand with the curling iron, better at hair arrangements than even the otherwise unparalleled Angelique.

"Biffy, my *dove,* dash round to that scrumptious new hat shop on Regent Street and collect the proprietress for a bit of a hobnob, would you, darling? There's a good fellow. She should be expecting something of the kind."

Biffy smiled. "Certainly, my lord. Good evening, Lady Maccon. Is this arrangement of your making? You know the master here has been dying to meet Madame Lefoux ever since she opened that shop, with no excuse to do so for an age."

"Biffy!" hissed Lord Akeldama.

"Well, you have," replied Biffy truculently.

"Off with you, you impossible infant, and keep that *lovely* mouth shut."

Biffy bowed shortly and tripped lightly out, lifting his hat and gloves from a nearby side table as he went.

"That young whippersnapper will be the death of me. However, he has an *admirable* knack for being in the right place at the right time. Yesterday evening, for example, he was outside the Pickled Crumpet, that *horrible* little pub near St. Bride, known for a preponderance of military and blood whores. Not his normal watering hole by *any* means. And you will *never* guess whom he encountered skulking about the back alleyway, just behind the pub."

Lady Maccon sighed. "My husband?"

Lord Akeldama was crestfallen. "He told you."

"No, it simply seems like the exact kind of place where my husband would be skulking."

"Well, let *me* tell *you,* my petunia blossom! Biffy says that he was in a perfectly indelicate condition, trying to make his way toward Fleet Street."

"Inebriated?" Lady Maccon was doubtful. Generally speaking, werewolves were not prone to intoxication. Their constitutions did not allow for it. Besides which, that simply was not *like* her husband.

"Oh no. The poor dear had encountered that *disas-*

trous malady ravaging the downtown area and found himself entirely human and unclothed quite suddenly in the heart of London."

Lord Akeldama's eyes were twinkling.

Lady Maccon could not help herself; she began to laugh. "No wonder he did not tell me about the incident. Poor thing."

"Not that Biffy complained about the spectacle."

"Well, who would?" Alexia had to give credit where it was due, and her husband did have quite the splendid physique. "That is interesting, though. It means that one does not have to be present when this antisupernatural blight attacks. One can wander into the infected area and be struck down."

"You think it is a *disease* of some kind, do you, my little pumpernickel?"

Lady Maccon cocked her head to one side. "I do not know with any certainty what it may be. What do you think it is?"

Lord Akeldama rang a different bell rope for tea. "I believe it to be a weapon of some kind," he said, unusually blunt.

"You have heard of something like it before?" Lady Maccon sat up straight, intent on her friend. Lord Akeldama was a very old vampire. There were rumors he was older even than Countess Nadasdy, and everyone knew she was five hundred or more.

The vampire tossed his queue of long blond hair back off his shoulder. "No, I have not. But it does not have the *feel* of a sickness about it, and my experience with the Hypocras Club has taught me not to underestimate modern scientists and their vulgar technological *dabblings*."

Lady Maccon nodded. "I agree, and so does the rest of the Shadow Council. BUR is holding out that it is a disease, but I am leaning in favor of a newly fashioned weapon. Have your boys found out anything of significance?"

Lord Akeldama puffed out his cheeks. He did not like open acknowledgment that his collection of apparently decorative and inconsequential drones, possessed of high family connection and little evident sense, were in fact consummate spies. He resigned himself to Alexia, and, via Alexia, to Lord Maccon and BUR, knowing of his activities, but he did not like them mentioned openly.

"Not as much as I had hoped. Although one of the ships, the *Spanker,* transporting multiple regiments and associated packs, was said to be afflicted by a *human condition* the *entire* passage home."

"Yes, Major Channing mentioned something of the kind. Although the Woolsey Pack had returned to supernatural normalcy by the time they reached the castle."

"And what do *we* think of Major Channing?"

"*We* try *not* to think on that repulsive individual at all."

Lord Akeldama laughed, and a handsome young butler entered with the tea tray. "You know, I once tried to recruit him, decades ago."

"Did you really?" Lady Maccon could not countenance the idea; for one thing, she did not believe Major Channing leaned in Lord Akeldama's direction, although there were rumors about military men.

"He was a *splendid* sculptor before he turned. Did you know? We all knew he had a good chance of having excess soul; vampires and werewolves were vying to be his patron. Such a sweet young talented thing."

"We *are* discussing the same Major Channing, are we not?"

"He rebuffed *me* and went into soldiering, thought it more *romantic*. Eventually, he was converted to the fuzzy side of the supernatural during the Napoleonic war."

Alexia was not clear on what to make of this information. So she returned to the original topic. "If it is a weapon, I must find where it has gone. Lyall said it was headed north, and we believe it to be going by coach. The question is, where, and who is carrying it?"

"And *what* exactly is it?" added the vampire, pouring the tea. Lady Maccon took hers with milk and a little sugar. He took his with a dash of blood and a squeeze of lemon.

"Well, if Professor Lyall claims it is heading northward, then northward it is. Your husband's Beta is *never* wrong." There was an odd tone in Lord Akeldama's voice. Alexia looked at him sharply. He added only, "When?"

"Just before I came here."

"No, no, primrose. I mean, when did *it* begin to move northward?" He passed a small plate of some excellent biscuits, declining the comestibles himself.

Lady Maccon did some quick calculations. "Seems like it would have had to depart London late yesterday evening or early this morning."

"Just as the humanization in London stopped?"

"Precisely."

"So what we need to know is what regiments, or packs, or individuals came in on the *Spanker,* then proceeded north yesterday morning."

Lady Maccon had a sinking feeling all fingers were about to point in one particular direction. "I place great confidence in the fact that Professor Lyall is already hunting down just that information."

"But you already have a good idea of who the perpetrators might be, don't you, my little *periwinkle*?" Lord Akeldama stopped relaxing back into the love seat and tilted forward to peer at her through his monocle.

Lady Maccon sighed. "Call it instinct."

The vampire smiled, showing his two long fangs, pointed and strikingly lethal. "Ah, yes, your preternatural ancestors were hunters for generations, *sugardrop*." Delicacy did not permit him to remind her that they hunted vampires.

"Oh no, not that kind of instinct."

"Oh?"

"Perhaps instead I should say 'wifely intuition.'"

"Ah." Lord Akeldama's smile widened. "You believe your oversized husband to be connected to the weapon?"

Lady Maccon frowned and nibbled a biscuit. "No, not exactly, but where my dear spouse goes . . ." She trailed off.

"You think this whole thing may be connected to his visiting Scotland?"

Alexia sipped her tea and remained silent.

"You think this has something to do with the Kingair Pack losing their Alpha?"

Alexia started. She did not realize that little fact was common knowledge. How *did* Lord Akeldama come by his information so quickly? It was really remarkable. If only the Crown could be so efficient. Or BUR for that matter.

"A pack without an Alpha can behave badly, but on this kind of scale? You think—"

Lady Maccon interrupted her friend. "*I think* Lady Maccon may suddenly feel quite oppressed by the dirty London air. I think Lady Maccon may have need of a vacation. Perhaps to the north? I hear Scotland is lovely this time of year."

"Are you barmy? Scotland is wholly *abysmal* this time of year."

"Indeed, why would one wish to travel there, especially with the trains down?" This was a new voice, tinged with a very faint French accent.

Madame Lefoux had not forgone her men's garb, although she had formalized it for visiting, changing her colorful cravat for one of white lawn and her brown top hat for a black one.

"Lady Maccon fancies herself in need of air," replied Lord Akeldama, rising and going forward to greet his new guest. "Madame Lefoux, I presume?"

Alexia blushed at not having jumped in to make proper introductions, but the other two seemed to have matters well in hand.

"How do you do? Lord Akeldama? A pleasure to make your acquaintance at last. I have heard much of your charms." The inventor gave the vampire's startling black and white shoes and smoking jacket an intent look.

"And I yours," replied the vampire, casting an equally critical eye to the inventor's stylish masculine garb.

Alexia noted a certain undercurrent of wariness,

as though they were two vultures circling the same carcass.

"Well, there is no accounting for taste," said the Frenchwoman softly. Lord Akeldama appeared about to take offense, but the lady added, turning slightly to the side, "Scotland, Lady Maccon, are you certain?"

A flash of wary approval crossed the vampire's face at that. "Do sit," he offered. "You smell divine by the way. Vanilla? A lovely scent. And so very *feminine*."

Was that a return jibe? wondered Alexia.

Madame Lefoux accepted a cup of tea and sat on another little settee, next to the relocated calico cat. The cat clearly believed Madame Lefoux was there to provide chin scratches. Madame Lefoux provided.

"Scotland," replied Lady Maccon firmly. "By dirigible, I think. I shall make the arrangements directly and depart tomorrow."

"You shall find that difficult. Giffard's is not open to nighttime clientele."

Lady Maccon nodded her understanding. Dirigibles catered to daylight folk, *not* the supernatural set. Vampires could not ride them, as they flew too high out of territory range. Ghosts were usually inconveniently tethered. And werewolves did not like to float—prone to terrible airsickness, her husband had explained the first and only time she intimated interest in such a mode of transport.

"Tomorrow afternoon," she amended, "but let us talk of more pleasant things. Lord Akeldama, are you interested in hearing about some of Madame Lefoux's inventions?"

"Indeed."

Madame Lefoux described several of her more recent devices. Despite his old-fashioned house, Lord Akeldama was fascinated with modern technological developments.

"Alexia has shown me her new parasol. You do *impressive* work. You are not seeking a patron?" he asked after some quarter of an hour's talk, clearly impressed with the Frenchwoman's intelligence, if nothing else.

Understanding fully the unspoken code, the inventor shook her head. Given Madame Lefoux's appearance and skills, Alexia was in no doubt she had received offers of a similar nature in the past. "Thank you kindly, my lord. You do me particular favor, as I know you prefer male drones. But I am happily situated and of independent means, with no wish to bid for immortality."

Lady Maccon followed this interchange with interest. So Lord Akeldama thought Madame Lefoux had excess soul, did he? Well, if her aunt had turned into a ghost, excess soul might run in the family. She was about to ask an impolitic question when Lord Akeldama rose, rubbing his long white hands together.

"Well, my little *buttercups*."

Uh-oh, Alexia winced in sympathy. Madame Lefoux had achieved Akeldama-appellative status. They would now have to suffer together.

"Would you *charming* blossoms like to see my newest acquisition? Quite the beauty!"

Alexia and Madame Lefoux exchanged a look, put down their teacups, and rose to follow him with no argument.

Lord Akeldama led them out into the arched and gilded hallway and up several sets of increasingly elaborate staircases. Eventually they attained the top of the town house, entering what should have been the attic. It proved, instead, to have been made over into an elaborate room hung with medieval tapestries and filled with an enormous box, large enough to house two horses. It was raised up off the floor via a complex system of springs and was quilted in a thick fabric to prevent ambient noise from reaching its interior. The box, itself, comprised two small rooms filled with machinery. The first, Lord Akeldama described as the transmitting room, and the second the receiving room.

Alexia had never seen such a thing before.

Madame Lefoux had. "Why, Lord Akeldama, such an expense! You have purchased an aethographic transmitter!" She looked about the crowded interior of the first room with enthusiastic appreciation. Her dimples were in danger of reappearing. "She's beautiful." The inventor ran reverent hands over the many dials and switches that controlled the transmitting room's tangled gadgetry.

Lady Maccon frowned. "The queen is reputed to own one. I understand she was urged to acquire it as a replacement for the telegraph, shortly after the telegraph proved itself an entirely unviable method of communication."

Lord Akeldama shook his blond head sadly. "I was *vastly* disappointed to read of the report of that failure. I had such hopes for the telegraph." There'd been a noted gap in long-distance communication ever since, with the scientific community scrabbling to invent something that was more compatible with highly magnetic aetheromagnetic gasses.

"The aethographor is a wireless communication apparatus, so it does not suffer from such severe disruption to the electromagnetic currents as the telegraph," Lord Akeldama explained.

Lady Maccon narrowed her eyes at him. "I *have* read of the new technology. I simply had not thought to *see* it so soon." As a matter of course, Alexia had been angling for an invitation to see the queen's aethographor for over a fortnight, with little success. There was some delicacy to its function that would not allow it to be interrupted during operation. She had also tried, unsuccessfully, to visit BUR's aethographor. She knew that they had one at the London offices, because she saw rolls of etched metal lying about. Her husband had been utterly impossible about it. "Wife," he had finally stated in abject frustration, "I canna interrupt business simply to satisfy your curiosity." Unfortunately for Alexia, since they had come into government possession, both aethographors had been in constant operation.

Lord Akeldama picked up an etched metal roll, flattened it out, and slotted it into a special frame. "You put the message for transfer, so, and activate the aetheric convector."

Madame Lefoux, looking about with avid interest, interrupted him mid-explanation. "You would, of course, first have to input an outgoing crystalline valve frequensor, just here." She pointed to the control board, then started. "Where is the resonator cradle?"

"Aha!" crowed the vampire, apparently thrilled she had noticed this flaw. "This is the latest and greatest design, *squash blossom.* It does not operate via *crystalline* compatibility protocol!"

Madame Lefoux looked to Lady Maccon. "Squash

blossom," she mouthed silently, her expression half offended, half amused.

Alexia shrugged.

"Usually," explained Lord Akeldama to Alexia, misinterpreting the shrug, "the transmitting component of the aethographor requires the installation of a specific valve, depending on the message's intended destination. You see, a companion valve must also be installed in the other party's receiving room. Only with both in place can a message transfer from point A to point B. The problem is, of course, that exact times must be agreed upon beforehand by both parties, and each must possess the appropriate valve. The queen has an entire library of valves linked to different aethographors dotted all about the empire."

Madame Lefoux was frowning. "And yet your device has none? It is not very useful, Lord Akeldama, to transmit a message into the aether with no one at the other end to receive it."

"Aha!" The vampire pranced about the tiny room in his ridiculous shoes, looking far too pleased with himself. "*My* aetheric transponder does not need one! I have had it installed with the latest in frequency transmitters so that I can tune to whatever aetheromagnetic setting is desired. All I need is to know the crystalline valve's orientation on the receiving end. And to receive all I need is the right time, a good scan, and someone who has my codes. Sometimes I can even pick up messages intended for *other* aethographors." He frowned a moment. "Story of my life, if you think about it."

"Good Lord." Madame Lefoux was obviously impressed. "I had no idea such technology even existed. I knew they were working on it, of course, but not that it had finally been built. Impressive. May we witness it in action?"

The vampire shook his head. "I have no messages to go out at the present time and am not expecting any incoming."

Madame Lefoux looked crestfallen.

"So what happens, exactly?" asked Lady Maccon, who was still looking closely at the equipment.

Lord Akeldama was all too delighted to explain. "Ever notice that the metal paper has a faint grid on it?"

Alexia switched her attention to a scroll of metal Lord Akeldama handed her. The surface was, indeed, divided into a standardized grid. "One letter per square?" she hypothesized.

Lord Akeldama nodded and explained further. "The metal is exposed to a chemical wash that causes the etched letters to burn through. Then two needles pass over each grid square, one on top and the other on the bottom. They spark whenever they are exposed to one another through the letters. *This* causes an aether wave that is bounced off the upper aethersphere and, in the absence of solar interference, *transmits globally*." His gesturing throughout became wilder and wilder, and on the last phrase, he did a little pirouette.

"Astounding." Lady Maccon was impressed, both with the technology and Lord Akeldama's ebullience.

He paused, recovering his equanimity, then continued with the explanation. "Only a receiving room tuned to the appropriate frequency will be able to pick up the message. Come with me."

He led them into the receiving room section of the aethographor.

"Receivers, mounted on the roof *directly* above us, pick up the signals. A skilled operator is required to tune out ambient noise and amplify the signal. The message then displays there"—he gestured, hands waving about like flippers, at two pieces of glass with black particulate sandwiched between and a magnet mounted to a small hydraulic arm hovering above—"one letter at a time."

"So someone must be in residence to read and record each letter?"

"And they must do so utterly silently," added Madame Lefoux, examining the delicacy of the mounts.

"And they must be ready in an instant, for the message destroys itself as it goes," Lord Akeldama added.

"Now I comprehend the reason for the noise-proof room and the attic location. This is clearly a most delicate device." Lady Maccon wondered if *she* could operate such an apparatus. "You have, indeed, made an impressive acquisition."

Lord Akeldama grinned.

Alexia gave him a sly look. "So what precisely *is* your compatibility protocol, Lord Akeldama?"

The vampire pretended offense, looking coquettishly up at the ceiling of the box. "Really, Alexia, what a thing to ask on your *very* first showing."

Lady Maccon only smiled.

Lord Akeldama sidled over and slotted her a little slip of paper upon which was written a series of numbers. "I have reserved the eleven o'clock time slot especially for you, my dear, and will begin monitoring all frequencies at that time starting a week from today." He bustled off and reappeared with a faceted crystalline valve. "And here is this, tuned to my frequency, just in case the apparatus you employ is less progressive than my own."

Alexia tucked the little slip of paper and the crystalline valve into one of the hidden pockets of her new parasol. "Does any other private residence own one?" she wondered.

"Difficult to know," replied Lord Akeldama. "The receiver *must* be mounted upon the roof, so one could conceivably hire a dirigible for air reconnaissance and float about looking for them, but I hardly think that an efficient approach. They are very dear, and there are few private individuals who could see to the expense. The Crown, of course, has two, but others? I only have the list of official compatibility protocols: that is a little under one hundred aethographors dotted about the empire."

Reluctantly, Alexia realized that time was getting on, and if she intended to leave for Scotland, she had much to do in the space of one night. For one thing, she would have to send round to the queen to alert her to the fact that her muhjah would be missing meetings of the Shadow Council for the next few weeks.

She made her excuses to Lord Akeldama. Madame Lefoux did the same, so that the two ladies found themselves exiting his residence at the same time. They paused to take leave of one another on the stoop.

"Do you really propose to float to Scotland tomorrow?" inquired the Frenchwoman, buttoning her fine gray kid gloves.

"I think it best I go after my husband."

"Should you travel alone?"

"Oh, I shall take Angelique."

Madame Lefoux started slightly at the name. "A Frenchwoman? Who is that?"

"My maid, inherited from the Westminster Hive. She is a dab hand with the curling iron."

"I am certain she is, if she was once under Countess Nadasdy," replied the inventor with a kind of studied casualness.

Alexia felt there was some kind of double meaning to the comment.

Madame Lefoux did not give her the chance for further inquiry, as she nodded her good-bye, climbed into a waiting hackney, and was gone before Lady Maccon had time to say more than a polite good night.

Professor Randolph Lyall was impatient, but no one would ever guess it to look at him. Partly, of course, because currently he looked like a slightly seedy and very hairy dog, skulking about the bins in the alley next to Lord Akeldama's town house.

How much time, he was wondering, *could possibly be required to take tea with a vampire?* A good deal, apparently, if Lord Akeldama and Lady Maccon were involved. Between the two of them, they could talk all four legs off a donkey. He had encountered them in full steam on only one memorable occasion and ever since had avoided the experience assiduously. Madame Lefoux had been a surprise addition to the party, although she probably was not adding much to the conversation. It was odd to see her out of her shop and paying a social call. He made a mental note: this was something his Alpha should know about. Not that he had orders to watch the inventor. But Madame Lefoux *was* a dangerous person to know.

He shifted about, nose to the wind. Some strange new scent on the air.

Then he noticed the vampires. Two of them, lurking in the shadows well away from Lord Akeldama's house. Any closer and the effete vampire would sense their alien presence, larvae not of his line in his territory. So, what were they there for? What were they about?

Lyall lowered his tail between his legs and slunk a quick circle behind them, coming at them from down-wind. Of course, vampires had nowhere near as fine a sense of smell as werewolves but they had better hearing.

He crept in close, trying to be as silent as possible.

Neither of the vampires were BUR agents, that was for certain. Unless Lyall missed his guess, these were Westminster's get.

They did not appear to be doing anything but simply watching.

"Fangs!" said one of them finally. "How bloody long can it take to have tea? Especially if one of them ain't drinking it?"

Professor Lyall wished he had brought his gun. Difficult to carry, though, in one's mouth.

"Remember, he wants it done stealthy; we are simply checking. Don't want to go at it with the werewolves over nothing. You know . . ."

Lyall, who did *not* know, wanted to very badly, but the vampire, most unhelpfully, did not continue.

"I think he's paranoid."

"Ours is not to question, but I believe the mistress agrees with you. Doesn't stop her from humoring—"

The other vampire suddenly held up a hand, cutting his companion off.

Lady Maccon and Madame Lefoux emerged from Lord Akeldama's town house and made their good-byes on the stoop. Madame Lefoux swung herself up into a cab, and Lady Maccon was left alone, looking thoughtful on the front steps.

The two vampires moved forward toward her. Lyall did not know what they intended, but he guessed it was probably not good. It certainly was not worth risking his Alpha's wrath to find out. Quick as a flash, he slithered underneath one of the vampires, tripping him up, in the next movement lunging for the other, teeth snapping hard around anklebone. The first vampire, reacting rapidly, jumped so fast to one side as to be almost impossible to follow, at least for normal sight. Lyall, of course, was not normal.

He leaped, meeting the vampire halfway, lupine body slamming into the man's side, throwing him off. The second vampire lunged toward him, grabbing for his tail.

The entire scuffle took place in almost complete silence, only the sound of snapping jaws marking the activity.

It gave Lady Maccon just enough time, although she did not know she needed it, to climb into the Woolsey carriage and set off down the street.

The two vampires both stilled as soon as the vehicle was out of sight.

"Well, that's a sticky wicket," said one.

"Werewolves," said the other in disgust. He spat at Lyall, who paced, hackles raised, between them, forestalling any idea of pursuit. Lyall paused to sniff delicately at the wad of spit—eau de Westminster Hive.

"Really," said the first to Lyall, "we weren't going to harm one hair of that swarthy Italian head. We simply had a little test in mind. No one would have even known."

The other elbowed him, hard. "Hush you, that's Professor Lyall, that is. Lord Maccon's Beta. The less he knows about anything, the better."

With that, the two doffed their hats at the still growling, still bristling wolf in front of them and, turning, took off at a leisurely pace toward Bond Street.

Professor Lyall would have followed, but he decided on more precautionary measures and set a brisk trot to follow Alexia and ensure she arrived home safely.

Lady Maccon caught Professor Lyall when he came in, just before dawn. He looked exhausted, his already lean face pinched and drawn.

"Ah, Lady Maccon, you have waited up for me? How kind."

She searched for the sarcasm in his words, but if it was there, it was cleverly disguised. He was good. Alexia often wondered if Professor Lyall had been an actor before metamorphosis and somehow managed to hold on to his creativity despite sacrificing most of his soul for immortality. He was so very skilled at doing, and being, what was expected.

He confirmed her suspicions. Whatever it was that had caused the wide-scale lack of supernatural was definitely heading north. BUR had determined that the hour of London's return to supernatural normal correlated with the departure of the Kingair Pack toward Scotland. He was not surprised that Lady Maccon had arrived at the same conclusion.

He was, however, decidedly against the idea that she should go trailing after.

"Well, who else should go? I, at least, will remain entirely unaffected by the affliction."

Professor Lyall glared at her. "*No one* should go after it. The earl is perfectly capable of handling the situation, even if he doesn't yet know he has two problems to deal with. You seem to have failed to realize we all wandered around undamaged for centuries before you appeared in our lives."

"Yes, but look what a mess you have made of things prior to my arrival." Lady Maccon was not to be dissuaded from her chosen course of action. "Someone has to tell Conall that Kingair is to blame."

"If none of them are changing, he'll find out as soon as he arrives. His lordship would not like you following him."

"His lordship can eat my fat—" Lady Maccon paused, thought the better of her crass words, and said, "—does not have to like it. Nor do you. The fact remains that this morning Floote will secure for me passage on the afternoon's dirigible to Glasgow. His lordship can take it up with me when I arrive."

Professor Lyall had no doubt that his poor Alpha would do just that and be similarly humbled. Still, he would not give in so easily. "You shall have to take Tunstell with you, at the very least. The lad has been pining to visit the north ever since his lordship left, and he will be able to keep an eye on you."

Lady Maccon was truculent. "I do not need him. Have you seen my new parasol?"

Lyall had seen the purchase order and been suitably

impressed, but he was no fool. "A woman, even a married woman, cannot float without proper escort. It is simply not done. You and I are both well aware of that fact."

Lady Maccon frowned. He was right, bother it. She sighed and figured that at least Tunstell was a pushover.

"Oh, very well, if you insist," she conceded with ill grace.

The intrepid Beta, older than most werewolves still living in the greater London environs—Lord Maccon and the dewan included—did the only thing he could under the circumstances. Pulled his cravat aside to expose his neck, gave a little bow, and took himself off to bed without another word, leaving Lady Maccon in possession of the field.

Her ladyship sent the hovering Floote to rouse poor Tunstell from his bed and give him the unexpected news that he would be departing for Scotland. The claviger, who had only just climbed into bed, having spent the better part of the night looking at ladies' hats, wondered a tad about the sanity of his mistress.

Just after sunrise, having gotten very little sleep, Lady Maccon commenced packing. Or, it should be said more precisely that Lady Maccon commenced arguing with Angelique over what should be packed. She was interrupted by a visit from the only person on the planet capable of consistently routing her in verbal skirmishes.

Floote brought up the message.

"Good gracious, what on earth is *she* doing here? And at such an early hour!" Alexia put the calling card back down on the little silver tray; checked her appearance, which was only just passable for receiving; and wondered if she should take the time to change. Should one risk keeping a caller waiting or face criticism for being dressed in attire unbecoming to a lady of rank? She chose the latter, deciding to get the encounter over and done with as quickly as possible.

The woman waiting for her in the front parlor was a diminutive blond with a rosy complexion that owed more to artifice than nature, wearing a visiting dress of pink and white stripes that would better suit a lady half her age.

"Mama," said Lady Maccon, presenting her cheek for the halfhearted kiss her mother wafted in her direction.

"Oh, Alexia," cried Mrs. Loontwill, as though she had not seen her eldest in years. "I am quite overset with the most nervous misery; such a to-do is afoot. I require your immediate assistance."

Lady Maccon was dumbfounded—a state that did not afflict her often. Firstly, her mother had not insulted her appearance. Secondly, her mother actually seemed to be seeking her help in some matter. *Her* help.

"Mama, do sit. You are quite discombobulated. I shall order tea." She gestured to a chair, and Mrs. Loontwill sank into it gratefully. "Rumpet," Alexia addressed the hovering butler, "tea, please. Or would you prefer sherry, Mama?"

"Oh, I am not *that* overset."

"Tea, Rumpet."

"However, the situation *is* very dire. Such poopitations of the heart as you would not *believe*."

"Palpitations," corrected her daughter softly.

Mrs. Loontwill relaxed slightly, and then all of a sudden sat up straight as a poker, looking wildly about.

"Alexia, none of your husband's *associates* are in residence, are they?"

This was her mother's delicate way of referring to the pack.

"Mama, it is full daylight. They are all in residence, but they are also all abed. I, myself, have been up most of the night." She said this last as a subtle hint, but her mother existed well beyond subtlety.

"Well, you *would* marry into the supernatural set. Not that I am complaining about your catch, my dear, far from it." Mrs. Loontwill puffed up her chest like a pink-striped quail. "My daughter, Lady Maccon."

It was a constant source of amazement to Alexia that the only thing she had ever done in her entire life that pleased her mama was marry a werewolf.

"Mama, I really have a great deal to accomplish this morning. And you indicated you were visiting regarding a matter of some considerable urgency. What has happened?"

"Well, you see, it is your sisters."

"You finally comprehend what intolerable little ninnies they both are?"

"Alexia!"

"What about them, Mama?" Lady Maccon was wary. It wasn't that she did not love her sisters; it was simply that she did not *like* them very much. They were half sisters to be precise: Misses Loontwills the pair of them, while Alexia had been a Miss Tarabotti before her marriage. They were as blond, as silly, and as nonpreternatural as their pink-striped mama.

"They are in the most terrible argument at the moment."

"Evylin and Felicity are fighting? How surprising." The sarcasm was entirely lost on Mrs. Loontwill.

"I know! But I speak nothing but truth. You must comprehend perfectly my distress at this. You see, Evylin has become engaged. Not a catch quite up to your standards, of course—we cannot expect lightning to strike twice—but a tolerable match. The gentleman is not supernatural, thank heavens; one irregular in-law is more than enough. Regardless, Felicity cannot countenance the fact that her younger sister will marry before her. She is being perfectly beastly over the whole thing. So Evylin suggested, and I agree, that perhaps she needs to get out of London for a spell. So I suggested, and Mr. Loontwill agreed, that a trip to the countryside would be just the thing to brighten up her spirits. So I have brought her here, to you."

Lady Maccon did not quite follow. "You have brought Evylin?"

"No, dear, no. Do pay attention! I have brought Felicity." Mrs. Loontwill produced a ruffled fan and began waggling it about violently.

"What, here?"

"Now you are being purposefully dull-witted," accused her mother, prodding her with the fan.

"I am?" Where *was* Rumpet with the tea? Lady Maccon was in desperate need. Her mother often caused that kind of reaction.

"I have brought her here to stay with you, of course."

"What! For how long?"

"As long as is required."

"But, what?"

"I am certain you could use the company of family,"

insisted her mother. She took a moment to glance about the parlor, a cluttered but friendly room, full of books and large pieces of leather furnishing. "And this place could certainly benefit from additional feminine influence. There is not a single doily in sight."

"Wait . . ."

"She has packed for a two-week stay, but, you understand, as I have a wedding to arrange, she may need to remain at Woolsey longer. In which case, you will have to go shopping."

"Now wait just a moment—" Alexia's voice rose in aggravation.

"Good, that is settled, then."

Alexia was left gaping like a fish.

Mrs. Loontwill stood, apparently recovered from her palpitations. "I shall go fetch her from the carriage, shall I?"

Lady Maccon trailed her mother out of the parlor and down the front steps to find Felicity, surrounded by a prodigious amount of baggage, on her front lawn.

Without further ado, Mrs. Loontwill kissed both of her daughters on the cheek, climbed back into the carriage, and departed in a whirl of lavender perfume and pink stripes.

Lady Maccon looked her sister over, still in shock. Felicity was dressed in the latest of velvet long coats, white with a red front, hundreds of tiny black buttons running up it, and a long white skirt with red and black bows. Her blond hair was up, and her hat was perched back on her head in just the kind of precarious manner Angelique would approve of most.

"Well," Lady Maccon said brusquely, "I guess you had best come in."

Felicity looked about at her bags and then maneuvered delicately around them and swept up the front steps and into the house.

"Rumpet, would you please?" Lady Maccon, left behind with the luggage, indicated the massive pile with her chin.

Rumpet nodded.

Lady Maccon stopped him as he passed. "Do not bother to see them unpacked, Rumpet. Not just yet. We shall see if we can arrange this differently."

The butler nodded. "Very good, my lady."

Lady Maccon followed her sister into the house.

Felicity had found her way into the front parlor and was pouring herself some of the tea. Without asking. She glanced up when Lady Maccon entered. "I do declare, you are looking rather puffy about the face, sister. Have you gained weight since I saw you last? You know, I do so worry about your health."

Alexia refrained from commenting that the only worry Felicity felt was over next season's gloves. She sat down across from her sister, folded her arms ostentatiously over her ample chest, and glared. "Out with it. Why would you possibly allow yourself to be foisted off on me?"

Felicity cocked her head to one side, sipped her tea, and demurred. "Well, your complexion seems to have improved. One might even mistake you for an English-woman. That is nice. I should never have believed it had I not seen it for myself."

Pale skin had been popular in England since vampires officially emerged into, and took over, much of the higher ranks. But Alexia had her father's Italian skin and no interest in fighting its inclinations merely to look like one of the undead. "Felicity," she said sharply.

Felicity looked to one side and tutted in annoyance. "Well, if I must. Let me simply say it has become desirable for me to absent myself from London for a short while. Evylin is being overly smug. You know how she gets if she has something and she knows you want it."

"The truth, Felicity."

Felicity glanced about as though looking for some clue or hint, and then said finally, "I was under the impression that the regiment was in residence here at Woolsey."

Ah, thought Alexia, so that was what was going on. "Oh, you were, were you?"

"Well, yes, I was. Are they?"

Lady Maccon narrowed her eyes. "They are encamped around the back."

Felicity immediately stood, brushing down her skirts and plumping her curls.

"Oh no, you don't. Sit right back down there, young lady." Alexia took great satisfaction in treating her sister as though she were an infant. "There is no point; you simply cannot stay with me."

"Why ever not?"

"Because I am not stopping here. I have business in Scotland, and I depart this afternoon. I cannot very well leave you at Woolsey alone and without a chaperone, especially as the regiment *is* in residence. Simply think how that would look."

"But why Scotland? I should hate to have to go to Scotland. It is such a barbaric place. It is *practically*

Ireland!" Felicity was clearly perturbed at this disruption in her carefully wrought plans.

Alexia came up with the most Felicity-safe reason for traveling that she could think of, off of the top of her head. "My husband is in Scotland on pack business. I am to join him there."

"Well, piffle!" exclaimed Felicity, sitting back down with a *whump*. "What a frightful bother. Why do you always have to be so inconvenient, Alexia? Can you not think of *me* and my needs for a change?"

Lady Maccon interrupted what looked to be a long diatribe. "I am confident your suffering is quite beyond all description. Shall I call for the Woolsey carriage so you can at least travel back to town in style?"

Felicity looked glum. "It cannot be countenanced, Alexia. Mama will have your head if you send me back now. You know how impossible she can be about these things."

Lady Maccon did know. But what was to be done?

Felicity sucked on her teeth. "I suppose I shall simply have to accompany you to Scotland. It will be a terrible bore, of course, and you know how I hate traveling, but I shall bear it with grace." Felicity looked oddly cheered by this idea.

Lady Maccon blanched. "Oh no, absolutely not." A week or more in her sister's company and she would go categorically bonkers.

"I think the idea has merit." Felicity grinned. "I could instruct you on the subject of appearance." She gave Alexia a sweeping up-and-down look. "It is clear you are in need of expert guidance. Now, if I were Lady Maccon, I should not choose such somber attire."

Lady Maccon rubbed at her face. It would make for a good cover story, removing her deranged sister from London for a desperately needed airing. Felicity was just self-involved enough not to notice or remark upon any of Alexia's muhjah activities. Plus, it would give Angelique someone else to fuss over for a change.

That decided matters.

"Very well. I hope you are prepared to travel by air. We are catching a dirigible this afternoon."

Felicity looked uncharacteristically unsure of herself. "Well, if I must, I must. But I am certain I did not pack the correct bonnet for air travel."

"Cooee!" A voice reverberated down the hallway outside the open parlor door. "Anyone home?" it rang forth, singsong.

"Now what?" wondered Lady Maccon, fervently hoping she would not miss float-off. She did not want to delay her travel, particularly now that she must keep the regiment and Felicity separated.

A head appeared around the edge of the doorjamb. The head was wearing a hat comprised almost entirely of red feathers, all standing straight upright, and a few tiny puffy white ones, looking like nothing so much as an overly excited duster with a case of the pox.

"Ivy," stated Alexia, wondering if her dear friend was perhaps secretly the leader of a Silly Hat Liberation Society.

"Oh, Alexia! I let myself in. I do not know where Rumpet has taken himself off to, but I saw the parlor door open, so I deduced you must be awake, and I thought I ought to tell you . . ." She trailed off upon realizing Alexia was not alone.

"Why, Miss Hisselpenny," purred Felicity, "what are *you* doing *here*?"

"Miss Loontwill! How do you do?" Ivy blinked at Alexia's sister in utter surprise. "I might ask you the same question."

"Alexia and I are taking a trip to Scotland this afternoon."

The feather duster trembled in confusion. "You are?" Ivy looked rather hurt that Alexia would not see fit to inform her of such a trip. And that Alexia would choose Felicity as a companion, when Ivy knew how much Alexia loathed her sister.

"By dirigible."

Miss Hisselpenny nodded sagely. "So much more sensible. Rail is such an undignified way to travel. All that rapid racing about. Floating has so much more gravitas."

"It was decided at the last minute," said Lady Maccon, "both the trip and Felicity joining me. There has been some domestic difficulty at the Loontwills'. Frankly, Felicity is jealous that Evy is getting married." There was no way Lady Maccon would allow her sister to seize control of a conversation at the expense of her dear friend's feelings. It was one thing to put up with Felicity's jibes herself and another to witness them turned upon defenseless Miss Hisselpenny.

"What a lovely hat," Felicity said to Ivy snidely.

Lady Maccon ignored her sister. "I am sorry, Ivy. I would have invited you. You know I would, but my mother insisted, and you know how utterly impossible *she* can be."

Miss Hisselpenny nodded, looking gloomy. She came fully into the room and sat down. Her dress was subdued for Ivy: a simple walking gown of white with red polka dots, boasting only one row of red ruffles and fewer than six bows—although the ruffles were very puffy, and the bows were very large.

"I am assured floating is terribly unsafe, even so," added Felicity, "Us two women traveling alone. Don't you think you should ask several members of the regiment to accompany—?"

"No, I most certainly should not!" replied Lady Maccon sharply. "But I do believe Professor Lyall will insist upon Tunstell joining us as escort."

Felicity pouted. "Not that horrible redheaded thespian chap? He is so fearfully jolly. Must he come? Could we not get some nice soldier instead?"

Miss Hisselpenny quite bristled upon hearing Tunstell disparaged. "Why, Miss Loontwill, how bold you are with your opinions of young men you should know nothing of. I'll thank you not to cast windles and dispersions about like that."

"At least I am smart enough to have an opinion," snapped Felicity back.

Oh dear, thought Alexia, *here we go.* She wondered what a "windle" was.

"Oh," Miss Hisselpenny gasped. "I certainly do have an opinion about Mr. Tunstell. He is a brave and kindly gentleman in every way."

Felicity gave Ivy an assessing look. "And now here I sit, Miss Hisselpenny, thinking it is *you* who is probably overly familiar with the gentleman in question."

Ivy blushed as red as her hat.

Alexia cleared her throat. Ivy should not have been so bold as to reveal her feelings openly to one such as

Felicity, but Felicity was behaving like a veritable harpy. If this was a window into her behavior of late, no wonder Mrs. Loontwill wanted her out of the house.

"Stop it, both of you."

Miss Hisselpenny turned big, beseeching eyes upon her friend. "Alexia, are you certain you cannot see your way to allowing me to accompany you as well? I have never been in a dirigible, and I should so very much like to see Scotland."

In truth, Ivy was vastly afraid of floating and had never before showed any interest in geography outside of London. Even inside London, her geographic concerns centered heavily on Bond Street and Oxford Circus, for obvious pecuniary reasons. Alexia Maccon would have to be a fool not to realize that Ivy's interest lay in Tunstell's presence.

"Only if you believe your mother and your *fiancé* can spare you," said Lady Maccon, emphasizing that last in the hopes that it might remind Ivy of her prior commitment and force her to see reason.

Miss Hisselpenny's eyes shone. "Oh, thank you, Alexia!"

And there went the reason. Felicity looked as though she had just been forced to swallow a live eel.

Lady Maccon sighed. Well, if she must have Felicity as companion, she could do worse than to have Miss Hisselpenny along as well. "Oh dear," she said. "Am I suddenly organizing the Lady's Dirigible Invitational?"

Felicity gave her an inscrutable look and Ivy beamed.

"I shall just head back to town to obtain Mama's permission and to pack. What time do we float?"

Lady Maccon told her. And Ivy was off and out the front door, never having told Alexia why she had jaunted all the way out to Woolsey Castle in the first place.

"I shudder to think what that woman will choose as headgear for floating," said Felicity.

CHAPTER SIX

The Lady's Dirigible Invitational

Alexia could see it all in the society papers:
Lady Maccon boarded the Giffard Long-Distance Airship, Standard Passenger Class Transport Model, accompanied by an unusually large entourage. She was followed up the gangplank by her sister, Felicity Loontwill, dressed in a pink traveling dress with white ruffled sleeves, and Miss Ivy Hisselpenny, in a yellow carriage dress with matching hat. The hat had an excessive veil, such as those sported by adventurers entering bug-infested jungles, but otherwise the two young ladies made for perfectly appropriate companions. The party was outfitted with the latest in air-travel goggles, earmuffs, and several other fashionable mechanical accessories designed to facilitate the most pleasant of dirigible experiences.

Lady Maccon was also accompanied by her French maid and a gentleman escort. There was some question as to the appropriateness of the gentleman, a ginger fellow who might have trod the boards on more than one occasion. It was thought odd that Lady Maccon was seen off by her personal secretary, a former butler, but the presence of her mother more than made up for this gaffe. Lady Maccon is one of London's premiere eccentrics; these things must be taken in stride.

The lady herself wore a floating dress of the latest design, with tape-down skirt straps, weighted hem, a bustle of alternating ruffles of teal and black designed to flutter becomingly in the aether breezes, and a tightly fitted bodice. There were teal-velvet-trimmed goggles about her neck and a matching top hat with an appropriately modest veil and drop-down teal velvet earmuffs tied securely to her head. More than a few of the ladies walking through Hyde Park that afternoon stopped to wonder as to the maker of her dress, and a certain matron of low scruples plotted openly to hire away Lady Maccon's excellent maid. True, Lady Maccon carried a garish foreign-looking parasol in one hand and a red leather dispatch case in the other, neither of which matched her outfit, but one must be excused one's luggage when traveling. All in all, Hyde Park's afternoon perambulators reported favorably on the elegant departure of one of the season's most talked-about brides.

Lady Maccon thought they must look like a parade of stuffed pigeons and found it typical of London society that what pleased them annoyed her. Ivy and Felicity would not leave off bickering, Tunstell was revoltingly bouncy, and Floote had refused to accompany them to Scotland on the grounds that he might be suffocated by an overabundance of bustle. Alexia was just thinking it was going to be a long and tedious journey when an impeccably dressed young gentleman hove into view. The leader of their procession, a frazzled ship's steward trying to steer them to their respective rooms, paused in the narrow passageway to allow the gentleman to pass.

Instead, the gentleman stopped and doffed his hat at the parade of newcomers. The smell of vanilla and mechanical oil tickled Lady Maccon's nose.

"Why," said Alexia in startlement, "Madame Lefoux! What on Earth are *you* doing *here*?"

Just then, the dirigible jerked against its tethers as the massive steam engine that drove it through the aether rumbled into life. Madame Lefoux stumbled forward against Lady Maccon and then righted herself. Alexia felt that the Frenchwoman had taken a good deal longer to do so than was necessary.

"Clearly we are not 'on Earth' for much longer, Lady Maccon," said the inventor, dimpling. "I thought, after our conversation, that I, too, would enjoy visiting Scotland."

Alexia frowned. To travel so soon after opening a brand-new shop, not to mention leaving both her son and her ghostly aunt behind, seemed unwarranted. Clearly the inventor must be a spy of some kind. She would have to keep her guard up around the Frenchwoman, which was sad, as Alexia rather enjoyed the inventor's company. It was a rare thing for Lady Maccon to encounter a woman more independent and eccentric than herself.

Alexia introduced Madame Lefoux to the rest of her party, and the Frenchwoman was unflaggingly polite to all, although there might have been a slight wince upon seeing Ivy's eyeball-searing ensemble.

The same could not be said of Alexia's entourage. Tunstell and Ivy bowed and curtsied, but Felicity openly snubbed the woman, clearly taken aback by her abnormal attire.

Angelique, too, seemed uncomfortable, although the maid did curtsy as required by someone in her position. Well, Angelique had very decided opinions on proper attire. She probably did not approve of a woman dressing as a man.

Madame Lefoux gave Angelique a long and hard look, almost predatory. Lady Maccon assumed it had something to do with both of them being French, and her suspicions were confirmed when Madame Lefoux hissed something at Angelique in a rapid-fire undertone in her native tongue, too fast for Alexia to follow.

Angelique did not respond, turning her lovely little nose up slightly and pretending to be busy fluffing the ruffles on Lady Maccon's dress.

Madame Lefoux bade them all farewell.

"Angelique," Lady Maccon addressed her servant thoughtfully, "what was that?"

"It waz nothing of import, my lady."

Lady Maccon decided the matter might wait for a later time and followed the steward into her cabin.

She did not remain inside for long, as she wished to explore the ship and be on deck to witness float-off. She had waited years to float the skies, having followed the development of airship technology detailed in the Royal Society papers from a very young age. To be on board a dirigible at last was a joy not to be dampened by French mannerisms.

Once the last of the passengers had boarded and been shown to their respective cabins, the crew cast off the rope tethers, and the great balloon hoisted them slowly into the sky.

Lady Maccon gasped to see the world retreating below them, people disappearing into the landscape, landscape disappearing into a patchwork quilt, and final, irrevocable proof that the world was, indeed, round.

Once they floated through normal air and were high up into the aether, a young man, dangerously perched at the very back of the engines, spun up the propeller, and, with steam emitting in great puffs of white out the back and sides of the tank, the dirigible floated forward in a northerly direction. There came a slight jolt as it caught the aetheromagnetic current and picked up speed, going faster than it looked like it ought to be able to go, with its portly boatlike passenger decks dangling below the massive almond-shaped canvas balloon.

Miss Hisselpenny, who had joined Lady Maccon on deck, recovered from her own awe and began singing. Ivy had a good little voice, untrained but sweet. "Ye'll take the high road," she sang, "and I'll take the low road, and I'll be in Scotland afore ye."

Lady Maccon grinned at her friend but did not join her. She knew the song. Who didn't? It had been a forerunner in Giffard's dirigible travel marketing campaign. But Alexia's was a voice meant for commanding battles, not singing, as anyone who ever heard her sing took great pains to remind her.

Lady Maccon found the whole experience invigorating. The air up high was colder and somehow fresher than that of London or the countryside. She felt strangely comforted by it, as though this were her element. It must be the aether, she supposed, replete with its gaseous mix of aetheromagnetic particles.

However, she liked it far less the next morning when she awoke with a queasy stomach and a feeling of floating inside as well as out.

"Air travel takes some over like that, my lady," said the steward, adding by way of explanation, "derangement of the digestive components." He sent round one of the ship's hostesses with a tincture of mint and ginger. Very little put Alexia off her food, and with the help of the tincture, she recovered a measure of her appetite by midday. Part of the queasiness, she supposed, was the fact that she was readjusting her routine to that of daylight folk, after spending months conducting her business mainly at night.

Felicity only noticed that Alexia was getting new color in her cheeks.

"Of course, not just anyone looks good in a sun hat. But I do believe, Alexia, that you ought to make that sacrifice. If you are wise, you will take my advice in this matter. I know sun hats are not often worn these days, but I think someone of your unfortunate propensities might be excused the old-fashioned nature of the accessory. And why do you go gadding about with that parasol at all times of day and yet never use it?"

"You are sounding more and more like our mama," replied Lady Maccon.

Ivy, who was flitting from one railing to the other, cooing over the view, gasped at the cutting nature of such a statement.

Felicity was about to respond in kind when Tunstell appeared, entirely distracting her. She'd deduced Ivy and

Tunstell's regard for one another and thus was now committed to securing Tunstell's affection for herself, for no other reason than to show Ivy that she could.

"Oh, Mr. Tunstell, how lovely of you to join us." Felicity batted her eyelashes.

Tunstell reddened slightly and bobbed his head at the ladies. "Miss Loontwill. Lady Maccon." A pause. "And how do you feel today, Lady Maccon?"

"The airsickness fades by luncheon."

"How terribly convenient of it," remarked Felicity. "You might hope it would hold on a trifle longer given your inclination toward robustness and obvious affection for food."

Lady Maccon did not rise to the bait. "It would be better if the luncheons were not so consistently subpar." All food on board the dirigible appeared to favor the bland and steamed approach. Even the much-lauded high tea had been disappointing.

Felicity carefully knocked her gloves off the little table next to the deck chair in which she lounged.

"Oh, how careless of me. Mr. Tunstell, would you mind?"

The claviger stepped forward and bent to retrieve them for her.

Felicity shifted quickly and angled herself in such a way that Tunstell was now bending over her legs, practically facedown in the skirts of her green dress. It was a rather intimate arrangement, and, of course, Ivy came bouncing around the corner of the deck right at that very moment.

"Oh!" said Ivy, somewhat deflated in her bounciness.

Tunstell straightened, handing Felicity her gloves. Felicity took them from him slowly, allowing her fingers to trail over his hand.

Ivy's countenance looked remarkably similar to that of a bilious poodle.

Lady Maccon wondered that her sister had not gotten herself into trouble before now, with such behavior. When had Felicity turned into such a hardened little flirt?

Tunstell bowed to Ivy. "Miss Hisselpenny. How do you do?"

"Mr. Tunstell, please do not let my presence disturb you."

Lady Maccon stood up, ostentatiously fixing the ear flaps of her flying hat. Really, it was too vexing: Felicity overly bold, Ivy engaged to another, and poor Tunstell stuck making puppy eyes at the both of them in his confusion.

Tunstell went to bow over Miss Hisselpenny's hand. The dirigible encountered turbulence in the aether and lurched, causing Ivy and Tunstell to blunder into one another. Tunstell caught at her arm, helping her to stay upright while Ivy blushed like an overripe strawberry, her eyes downcast.

Alexia decided she needed a brisk walk on the forward deck.

Usually uninhabited, the forward deck was the windiest the dirigible had to offer. Both ladies and gentlemen tended to give it a miss, as it upset the hair something dreadful, but Alexia had no such qualms, even knowing she would earn a heavily accented chiding from Angelique upon her return. She turned the muffs down about her ears, donned her goggles, grabbed her parasol, and sallied forth.

The forward deck was, however, already occupied.

Madame Lefoux, dressed as impeccably and as inappropriately as always, stood next to that very same Angelique at the rails to one side, looking down over the patchwork of the British landscape spread below them like some sort of ill-designed and asymmetrical quilt. The two were whispering to each other heatedly.

Lady Maccon cursed the wind of air travel, for it carried their words away before reaching her, and she would have dearly loved to know what was being said. She thought of her dispatch case. Had Floote packed any listening mechanicals?

Deciding there was nothing else for it but a direct frontal attack, Alexia moved as quietly as possible across the deck, hoping to catch some part of the conversation before they noticed her presence. She was in luck.

". . . assume proper responsibility," Madame Lefoux was saying in French.

"Cannot happen, not yet." Angelique moved closer to the other woman, placing small, pleading hands on the inventor's arm. "Please do not ask it of me."

"Better happen soon or I'll tell. You know I will." Madame Lefoux tossed her head, top hat tilting dangerously but staying in place, as it was tied on for travel. She shrugged off the blond woman's grip.

"Soon, I promise." Angelique pressed herself against the inventor's side and nested her head on the other woman's shoulder.

Again Madame Lefoux shrugged her off. "Games, Angelique. Games and fancying up a lady's hair. That is all you have now, isn't it?"

"It is better than selling hats."

Madame Lefoux rounded on the maid at that, gripping the woman's chin in her hand, one set of goggle-covered eyes meeting another. "Did she really kick you out?" Her tone was both vicious and disbelieving.

Lady Maccon was close enough by then to meet her maid's big violet eyes behind the plain brass goggles when the girl looked away. Angelique started at the appearance of her mistress, and her eyes filled with tears. With a little sob, she cast herself at Lady Maccon so that Alexia had no choice but to catch her.

Alexia was disturbed. Even though she was French, Angelique was rarely given to displays of emotion. Angelique composed herself, hurriedly withdrew from her mistress's arms, bobbed a curtsy, and rushed away.

Alexia had liked Madame Lefoux, but she could hardly condone her distressing the domestic staff. "The vampires rejected her, you know. It is a sensitive subject. She does not like to talk about the hive giving her up to me."

"I wager she doesn't."

Lady Maccon bristled. "Any more than you would tell me the real reason you are on board this dirigible." The Frenchwoman would have to learn: a pack protected its own. Alexia might only be pack by proxy, but Angelique was still in its service.

Green eyes met her brown ones for a long moment. Two sets of goggles were no impediment, but Lady Maccon could not interpret that expression. Then the inventor reached up and stroked the back of her hand down the side of Alexia's face. Alexia wondered why the French were so much more physically affectionate than the English.

"Did you and my maid have some kind of *association* in the past, Madame Lefoux?" Alexia asked, not responding to the touch, although it made her face feel hot even in the cold aether wind.

The inventor dimpled. "We did once, but I assure you I am currently free of all such entanglements." Was she being purposefully obtuse? She moved closer.

Alexia, always blunt, cocked her head to one side and asked, "Who are you working for, Madame Lefoux? The French government? The Templars?"

The inventor backed away slightly, strangely upset by the question. "You misconstrue my presence here, Lady Maccon. I assure you, I work only for myself."

"I would not trust her if I were you, my lady," said Angelique, fixing Alexia's hair before supper that evening. The maid was ironing it straight with a specially provided steam iron, much to both their disgust. Straight and loose was Ivy's idea. Miss Hisselpenny had insisted Alexia be the one to try the fancy iron invention out, because Alexia was married and could suffer the burden of risky hair.

"Is there something I should know, Angelique?" Lady Maccon asked gently. The maid so rarely offered up an opinion that was not fashion related.

Angelique paused in her ministrations, her hand fluttering a moment about her face as only the French could flutter. "Only zat I knew her before I became drone, in Paris."

"And?"

"And we did not part with ze friendly terms. A matter, how do you say, personal."

"Then I would not dream of prying further," replied Alexia, dearly wishing to pry.

"She did not say anything about me to you, my lady?" the maid asked. Her hand went up to stroke the high collar about her neck.

"Nothing of consequence," replied Lady Maccon.

Angelique did not look convinced. "You do not trust me, do you, my lady?"

Alexia looked up in surprise, meeting Angelique's eyes in the looking glass. "You were drone to a rove, but you also served the Westminster Hive. *Trust* is a strong word, Angelique. I trust that you will do my hair to the height of fashion and that your taste should govern my own disinterest in the matter. But you cannot ask me for more than that."

Angelique nodded. "I see. So it iz not something Genevieve said?"

"Genevieve?"

"Madame Lefoux."

"No. Should it be?"

Angelique lowered her eyes and shook her head.

"You will tell me nothing more about your previous relationship?"

Angelique remained silent but her face seemed to indicate that she thought this inquiry excessively personal.

Lady Maccon excused her maid and went to find her little leather journal, the better to collect her thoughts and make a few notations. If she suspected Madame Lefoux of being a spy, she ought to jot this down, along with her reasoning. Part of the purpose of the notebook was to leave adequate record should anything untoward happen to her. She had commenced the practice upon assuming her position as muhjah, though she used the journal for personal notes, not state secrets. Her father's journals had proved helpful on more than one occasion. She would like to think her own might be of equal assistance to future generations. Although probably not in quite the same way as Alessandro Tarabotti's. She didn't go in for recording *that* type of information.

The stylographic pen was where she had left it, on the nightstand, but her notebook had vanished. She checked all about—under the bed, behind the furniture—but could find it nowhere. With a sinking feeling, she went looking for her dispatch case.

A knock came at her door, and before she could come up with some excuse to keep the visitor at bay, Ivy trotted into the room. She looked flushed and nervous, her hat of the day a floof of black lace draped over masses of dark side curls, the earmuffs underneath only visible because Ivy was tugging at them.

Alexia paused in her hunt. "Ivy, what is wrong? You look like a perturbed terrier with an ear mite problem."

Miss Hisselpenny cast herself dramatically facedown on Alexia's small bed, clearly in some emotional distress. She mumbled into the pillow. Her voice was suspiciously high.

"Ivy, what is wrong with your voice? Have you been up in engineering, on the Squeak Deck?" Since the dirigible maintained buoyancy through the application of helium, it was a legitimate assumption for any vocal abnormalities.

"No," squeaked Ivy. "Well, maybe for a short while."

Lady Maccon stifled a laugh. Really, it was too absurd-sounding. "Who were you up there with?" she inquired archly, although she could very well hazard a guess.

"No one," squeak, squeak. "Well, in actuality, I mean to say, I might have been with . . . uh . . . Mr. Tunstell."

Lady Maccon snickered. "I wager he sounded pretty funny too."

"A slight leak occurred while we were up there. But there was grave need for a small moment of privacy."

"How romantic."

"Really, Alexia, this is no time for levity! I am all aquiver, facing a ghastly emotional crisis, and you issue forth nothing more than scads of unwanted jocularity."

Lady Maccon composed her features and tried to look like she was not amused at her friend's expense, annoyed at her friend's appearance, nor still glancing about her room in search of the missing dispatch case. "Let me hazard a guess. Tunstell has professed his undying love?"

"Yes," Ivy wailed, "and I am engaged to another!" On the word *engaged,* she finally stopped squeaking.

"Ah, yes, the mysterious Captain Featherstonehaugh. And let us not forget that, even if you were not affianced, Tunstell is an entirely unsuitable match. Ivy, he makes his living as a *thespian.*"

Ivy groaned. "I know! In addition, he is your husband's *valet!* Oh, it is all so messily plebeian." Ivy rolled over on the bed, the back of her wrist pressed to her forehead. She kept her eyes tightly shut. Lady Maccon wondered if Miss Hisselpenny did not have a possible future career on the stage herself.

"Which also makes him a claviger. Well, well, well, you have got yourself into a pretty pickle." Lady Maccon tried to sound sympathetic.

"Oh, but, Alexia, I am quite fearfully afraid that I might just possibly, maybe a little itty-bitty bit, love him back."

"Shouldn't you be certain of a thing like that?"

"I do not know. Should I be? How does one determine one's own state of enamorment?"

Lady Maccon snickered. "I am hardly one to elucidate. It took me ages to realize I had feelings for Conall beyond abhorrence, and quite frankly, I am still not certain that feeling does not persist unto this very moment."

Ivy was taken aback. "Surely you jest?"

Alexia cast her mind back to the last time she had engaged in a protracted encounter with her husband. There had been a good deal of moaning at the time, if memory served. "Well, he has his uses."

"But, Alexia, what do *I* do?"

At that moment, Lady Maccon spotted her missing dispatch case. Someone had shoved it in the corner between the wardrobe and the door to the washroom. Alexia was quite certain that was not where she had left it.

"Aha, how did you get there?" she said to the missing accoutrement, and went to retrieve it.

Ivy, eyes still shut, pondered this question. "I have no idea how I allowed myself into such an untenable position. You must help me, Alexia. This is a *cataplasm* of epic proportions!"

"Too true," agreed Lady Maccon, considering the state of her beloved dispatch case. Someone had tried to break open the catch. Whomever it was must have been disturbed in the act, or they would have stolen the case as well as her notebook. Her little leather journal would fit inside a vest or under a skirt, but the dispatch case would not. The villain must have left it behind as a result. Lady Maccon considered possible suspects. The ship's domestic staff had access to her rooms, of course, and Angelique. But, really, given the state of the locks on board, it could have been anyone.

"He kissed me," Miss Hisselpenny keened.

"Ah, well, that *is* something like." Alexia decided nothing more could be determined from the dispatch case, at least not with Ivy still in the room. She went to sit next to her friend's prostrate form. "Did you enjoy kissing him?"

Ivy said nothing.

"Did you enjoy kissing Captain Featherstonehaugh?"

"Alexia, the very idea. We are only engaged, not married!"

"So you have not kissed the good captain?"

Ivy shook her head in an excess of embarrassment.

"Well, then, what about Tunstell?"

Miss Hisselpenny flushed even redder. Now she looked like a spaniel with a sunburn. "Well, maybe, just a little."

"And?"

Miss Hisselpenny opened her eyes, still blushing furiously, and looked at her married friend. "Is one supposed to enjoy kissing?" she practically whispered.

"I believe it is generally thought to be a pleasant pastime. You read novels, do you not?" replied Lady Maccon, trying desperately to keep a straight face.

"Do you enjoy doing . . . *that* with Lord Maccon?"

Lady Maccon did not hesitate, credit where it was due and all. "Unreservedly."

"Oh, well, I thought it was a little"—Ivy paused—"damp."

Lady Maccon cocked her head to one side. "Well, you must understand, my husband has considerable experience in these matters. He is hundreds of years older than I."

"And that does not trouble you?"

"My dear, he will live hundreds of years longer than I as well. One must come to terms with these things if one fraternizes with the supernatural set. I admit it is hard, knowing we will not grow old together. But if you choose Tunstell, you may eventually have to face the same concerns. Then again, your time together could be cut short, as he may not survive metamorphosis."

"Is that likely to occur soon?"

Lady Maccon knew very little about this aspect of pack dynamics. So she only shrugged.

Ivy sighed, a long, drawn-out exhalation that seemed to encompass all the problems of the empire. "It is all too much to think about. My head is positively awhirl. I simply do not know what to do. Don't you see? Don't you comprehend my cacophony?"

"You mean catastrophe?"

Ivy ignored her. "Do I throw over Captain Featherstonehaugh, and his five hundred a year, for Mr. Tunstell and his unstable"—she shuddered—"working-class station? Or do I continue with my engagement?"

"You could always marry your captain and pursue a dalliance with Tunstell on the side."

Miss Hisselpenny gasped, sitting fully upright in her outrage at such a proposal. "Alexia, how could you even *think* such a thing, let alone suggest it aloud!"

"Well, yes, of course, those damp kisses *would* have to improve."

Ivy threw a pillow at her friend. "Really!"

Lady Maccon, it must be admitted, gave little further thought to her dear friend's dilemma. She transferred all the most delicate documents and important smaller instruments and devices out of her dispatch case and into the pockets of her parasol. Since she was already known as an eccentric parasol-carrier, no one remarked upon its continued presence at her side, even well after dark.

Dinner was a strained affair, stiff with tension and suspicion. Worse, the food was horrible. True, Alexia had very high standards, but the fare continued to be ghastly. Everything—meat, vegetables, even pudding—appeared to have been steamed into flaccid colorless submission, with no sauce, or even salt, to bolster the flavor. It was like eating a wet handkerchief.

Felicity, who had the palate of a country goat and tucked in without pause to anything laid before her, noticed that Alexia was only picking at her food. "Nice to see you are finally taking measures, sister."

Lady Maccon, lost in thought, replied with an unguarded, "Measures?"

"Well, I am terribly concerned for your health. One simply should not weigh so much at your age."

Lady Maccon poked at a sagging carrot and wondered if anyone would miss her dear sister were she to be oh-so-gently tipped over the rail of the upper deck.

Madame Lefoux glanced up. She gave Alexia an appraising look. "I think Lady Maccon appears in fine health."

"I think you are being fooled by her unfashionable robustness," said Felicity.

Madame Lefoux continued as though Felicity hadn't spoken. "You, on the other hand, Miss Loontwill, are looking a touch insipid."

Felicity gasped.

Alexia wished, yet again, that Madame Lefoux were not so clearly a spy. She would be a good egg otherwise. Was it she who had tried to get into the dispatch case?

Tunstell came wandering in, full of excuses for his tardiness, and took his seat between Felicity and Ivy.

"How nice of you to join us," commented Felicity.

Tunstell looked embarrassed. "Have I missed the first course?"

Alexia examined the steamed offering before her. "You can have mine if you like. I find my appetite sorely taxed these days."

She passed the graying mass over to Tunstell, who looked at it doubtfully but began eating.

Madame Lefoux continued talking to Felicity. "I have an interesting little invention in my rooms, Miss Loontwill, excellent for enlivening the facial muscles and imparting a rosy hue to the cheeks. You are welcome to try it sometime." There was a slight dimpling at that, suggesting this invention was either sticky or painful.

"I would not think, with your propensities, that you would be concerned with feminine appearances," shot back Felicity, glaring at the woman's vest and dinner jacket.

"Oh, I assure you, they concern me greatly." The Frenchwoman looked at Alexia.

Lady Maccon decided Madame Lefoux reminded her

a little bit of Professor Lyall, only prettier and less vulpine. She looked to her sister. "Felicity, I seem to have misplaced my leather travel journal. You have not seen it anywhere, have you?"

The second course was presented. It looked only slightly more appetizing than the first: some unidentifiable grayish meat in a white sauce, boiled potatoes, and soggy dinner rolls. Alexia waved it all away in disgust.

"Oh dear, sister, you have not taken up writing, have you?" Felicity pretended shock. "Quite frankly, all of that reading is outside of enough. I had thought that being married would cure you of such an unwise inclination. I never read if I can help it. It is terribly bad for the eyes. And it causes one's forehead to wrinkle most horribly, just there." She pointed between her eyebrows and then said pityingly to Lady Maccon, "Oh, I see you do not have to worry about *that* anymore, Alexia."

Lady Maccon sighed. "Oh, pack it in, Felicity, do."

Madame Lefoux hid a smile.

Miss Hisselpenny said suddenly in a loud and highly distressed voice, "Mr. Tunstell? Oh! Mr. Tunstell, are you quite all right?"

Tunstell was leaning forward over his plate, his face gone pale and drawn.

"Is it the food?" wondered Lady Maccon. "Because if it is, I entirely understand your feelings on the subject. I shall have a conversation with the cook."

Tunstell looked up at her. His freckles were standing out and his eyes watering. "I feel most unwell," he said distinctly before lurching to his feet and stumbling out the door.

Alexia looked after him for a moment with her mouth

agape, then glared suspiciously down at the food set before them. She stood. "If you will excuse me, I think I had best check on Tunstell. No, Ivy, you stay here." She grabbed her parasol and followed the claviger.

She found him on the nearest observation deck, collapsed on his side against a far rail, clutching at his stomach.

Alexia marched up to him. "Did this come over you quite suddenly?"

Tunstell nodded, clearly unable to speak.

There came a faint smell of vanilla, and Madame Lefoux's voice behind them said, "Poison."

CHAPTER SEVEN

Problematic Octopuses
and Airship Mountaineering

Randolph Lyall was old, for a werewolf. Something on the order of three hundred or so. He had long since stopped counting. And through all that time, he had played this little game of chess with local vampires: they moved their pawns and he moved his. He'd been changed shortly before King Henry absorbed supernaturals legally into the British government, so he'd never known the Dark Ages, not personally. But he, like every other supernatural on the British Isles, worked hard to keep them from returning. Funny how such a simple objective could so easily become adulterated by politics and new technology. Of course, he could simply march up to the Westminster Hive and *ask* them what they were about. But they would no more tell him than he would tell them Lord Maccon had BUR agents watching the hive twenty-four hours a day.

Lyall reached his destination in far less time than it

would have taken by carriage. He changed into human form in a dark alley, throwing the cloak he'd carried in his mouth about his naked body. Not precisely dress appropriate for paying a social visit, but he was confident his host would understand. This *was* business. Then again, one never could tell with vampires. They had, after all, dominated the fashion world for decades as a kind of indirect campaign against werewolves and the uncivilized state shifting shape required.

He reached forward and pulled the bell rope on the door in front of him.

A handsome young footman opened it.

"Professor Lyall," said Professor Lyall, "to see Lord Akeldama."

The young man gave the werewolf a very long look. "Well, well. You will not mind, sir, if I ask you to wait on the stoop while I inform the master of your presence?"

Vampires were odd about invitations. Professor Lyall shook his head.

The footman disappeared, and a moment later, Lord Akeldama opened the door in his stead.

They had met before, of course, but Lyall had never yet had occasion to visit the vampire at home. The decoration was—he discerned as he peered into the glittering interior—very loud.

"Professor Lyall." Lord Akeldama gave him an appraising look through a beautiful gold monocle. He was dressed for the theater, and one pinky pointed out as he lowered the viewing device. "And *alone*. To what do I owe this honor?"

"I have a proposition for you."

Lord Akeldama looked the werewolf up and down

once more; his blond eyebrows, darkened by artificial means, rose in surprise. "Why, Professor Lyall, how *charming*. I think you had best come inside."

Without looking up at Madame Lefoux, Alexia asked, "Is there anything built into my parasol to counteract poison?"

The inventor shook her head. "The parasol was designed as an offensive device. Had I known we would need an apothecary's kit, I would have added that feature."

Lady Maccon crouched down over Tunstell's supine form. "Run to the steward and see if he has an emetic on board, syrup of ipecac or white vitriol."

"At once," said the inventor, and dashed off.

Lady Maccon envied Madame Lefoux the masculine attire. Her own skirts were getting caught about her legs as she tried to tend to the afflicted claviger. His face was paper white, freckles stark against it, and there was a sheen of sweat on his forehead dampening his red hair.

"Oh no, he is suffering so. Will he recover soon?" Miss Hisselpenny had defied Alexia's order and tracked them down to the observation deck. She, too, crouched over Tunstell, her skirts spilling about her like a great over-iced meringue. She patted uselessly at one of Tunstell's hands, which were clenched over his stomach.

Alexia ignored her. "Tunstell, you must try to purge yourself." She made her voice as authoritative as possible, disguising her worry and fear with gruffness.

"Alexia!" Miss Hisselpenny was appalled. "Imagine suggesting such a thing. How undignified! Poor Mr. Tunstell."

"He must eject the contents of his stomach before the toxin enters his system any further."

"Do not be a ninnyhammer, Alexia," replied Ivy with a forced laugh. "It is just a bit of food poisoning."

Tunstell groaned but did not move.

"Ivy, and I mean this with the kindest and best of intentions, bugger off."

Miss Hisselpenny gasped and stood up, scandalized. But at least she was out of the way.

Alexia helped Tunstell to turn over so he was on his knees. She pointed a finger over the side of the dirigible autocratically. She made her voice as low and as tough as possible. "Tunstell, this is your Alpha speaking. Do as I tell you. You must regurgitate now." Never in all her time had Alexia supposed she would someday be ordering someone to throw up their supper.

But the command in her voice seemed to get through to the claviger. Tunstell stuck his head under the rail and over the side of the dirigible and tried to retch.

"I can't," he said finally.

"You must try harder."

"Regurgitation is an involuntary action. You cannot simply order me to do it," replied Tunstell in a small voice.

"I most certainly can. Besides which, you are an actor."

Tunstell grimaced. "I've never had cause to vomit onstage."

"Well, if you do this, you shall know how if you need to in the future."

Tunstell tried again. Nothing.

Madame Lefoux returned clutching a bottle of ipecac.

Alexia made Tunstell take a large gulp.

"Ivy, run and fetch a glass of water," she ordered her friend, mostly to get her out of the way.

In moments, the emetic took effect. As unsavory as the supper had been to eat, it was even less pleasant going the other direction. Lady Maccon tried not to look or listen.

By the time Ivy returned with a goblet of water, the worst was over.

Alexia made Tunstell drink the entirety of the glass. They waited a full quarter of an hour more while his color returned, and he was finally able to attain an upright position.

Ivy was in a flutter over the whole incident, agitating about the recovering man with such vigor that Madame Lefoux was driven to desperate measures. She extracted a small flask from her waistcoat pocket.

"Have a little nip of this, my dear. Calm your nerves." She handed it to Ivy.

Ivy nipped, blinked a couple times, nipped again, and then graduated from frantic to loopy. "Why, that *burns* all the way down!"

"Let's get Tunstell to his room." Alexia hoisted the redhead to his feet.

With Ivy walking backward before them and weaving side to side like an iced tea cake with delusions of shepherding, Lady Maccon and Madame Lefoux managed to get Tunstell to his rooms and onto bed.

By the time all the excitement had ended, Lady Maccon found she had lost her appetite entirely. Nevertheless, appearances must be kept up, so she returned to the dining cabin with Ivy and Madame Lefoux. She was in a mental quandary: why on earth, or in aether for that matter, would someone try to kill Tunstell?

Ivy walked into one or two walls on their way back.

"What did you give her?" Alexia hissed to the inventor.

"Just a bit of cognac." Madame Lefoux's dimples flashed.

"Very effective stuff."

The rest of the meal passed without incident, if one ignored Ivy's evident inebriation, which occasioned two spills and one bout of hysterical giggling. Alexia was about to rise and excuse herself when Madame Lefoux, who had been silent throughout most of the postpurge meal, spoke to her.

"Do you think you might take a little turn with me about the ship before bed, Lady Maccon? I should like a private word," she asked politely, dimples safely stored away.

Not entirely surprised, Alexia acquiesced, and the two left Felicity to sort out after-dinner activities on her own.

As soon as they were alone, the inventor got straight to the point. "I do not think the poison was meant for Tunstell."

"No?"

"No. I believe it was meant for you, secreted in the first dish that you turned away and Tunstell consumed in your stead."

"Ah, yes, I recall. You may be right."

"What a strange temperament you have, Lady Maccon, to accept near-death so easily as that." Madame Lefoux tilted her head to one side.

"Well, the whole episode does make far more sense that way."

"It does?"

"Why, yes. I cannot imagine Tunstell has many enemies, but people are always trying to exterminate me." Lady Maccon was relieved and strangely comfortable with this revelation, as though things were not right with the universe unless someone was actively trying to kill her.

"Do you have a suspect?" the inventor wanted to know.

"Aside from you?" Lady Maccon shot back.

"Ah."

The Frenchwoman turned away, but not before Alexia spotted a little tinge of hurt in her eyes. Either she was a good actress or she was not guilty.

"I am sorry to offend," said Lady Maccon, not sorry in the least. She followed the inventor over to the rail, leaning on it next to her. The two women stared out into the evening aether.

"I am not upset that you think me capable of poison, Lady Maccon. I am offended you should think I would be so ham-handed with it. Had I wished you dead, I have had ample opportunity and access to numerous techniques far less clumsy than the one employed this evening." She pulled a gold watch out of the pocket of her vest and pressed a little catch on the back. A small injection needle sprang out of the bottom.

Alexia did not ask what was in the needle.

Madame Lefoux folded it back in and tucked the watch away once more.

Alexia took a long assessing look at the amount and

type of jewelry the Frenchwoman wore. Her two cravat pins were in place, one wood, one silver. And there was another chain leading to her other vest pocket. A different kind of watch, or some other gadget, perhaps? The buttoner pin seemed suddenly suspicious, as did the metal cigar case tucked into the band of her top hat. Come to think on it, Alexia had never seen the woman smoke a cigar.

"True," said Alexia, "but the primitive nature of the attempt could be to throw me off the scent."

"You are of a suspicious inclination, are you not, Lady Maccon?" The Frenchwoman still did not look at her but seemed to find the cold night sky infinitely fascinating.

Lady Maccon came over philosophical. "Possibly that has something to do with having no soul. I prefer to think of it as pragmatism rather than paranoia."

Madame Lefoux laughed. She turned toward Alexia, dimples back.

And just like that, something solid hit Alexia hard across the back at exactly the correct angle to tilt her forward and over the railing. She tumbled, ass over teakettle, right over the edge of the deck. She felt herself falling, and screaming, scrabbling with both hands for purchase on the side of the dirigible. Why was the darn thing so smooth? The carrier body of the dirigible was shaped like a huge duck, and the observation deck was at its fattest point. In falling down, she was also falling away.

There was a horrible long moment when Alexia *knew* all was lost. She knew that all her future held in store was the long cold rush of aether and then air followed by a sad, wet thud. And then she was stopped with an abrupt jerk and flipped upside down, her head crashing hard into the side of the ship. The reinforced metal hem of her dress, designed to keep her copious skirts from floating about in the aether breezes, had wrapped fast around a spur that stuck out of the side of the ship two decks down, part of the docking mechanism.

She hung, suspended, her back against the ship's side. Carefully, cautiously, she twisted, climbing her own body with her hands, seeking out the spur of metal, until she could wrap her arms around it. She reflected that this was probably the first and last time in her life she would have cause to value the ridiculous fashions society foisted upon her sex. She realized she was still screaming and stopped, slightly embarrassed with herself. Her mind became a blur of worries. Could she trust in the security of the little metal spur to which she now clung? Was Madame Lefoux safe? Had her parasol fallen over the edge with her?

She took several calming breaths and assessed the situation: *not dead yet, but not precisely safe either.* "Ha-looo," she called out. "Anyone? A little assistance if you would be so kind."

The cold aether rushed past her, wrapping a loving chill about her legs, which were protected now only by her underdrawers and were unused to such exposure. No one answered her call.

Only then did she realize that, despite the fact that she had stopped screaming, the screaming had not stopped. Above her, she could see the figure of Madame Lefoux struggling against a cloaked opponent against the white backdrop of the blimp. Whoever had pushed Alexia over the edge obviously intended Madame Lefoux to follow. But the inventor was putting up a good deal of fight. She was struggling valiantly, arms pinwheeling, top hat tilting frantically from side to side.

"Help!" Alexia cried, hoping someone might hear her above the racket.

The struggling continued. First Madame Lefoux, then the covert enemy, leaned back over the railing, only to twist aside at the last moment and fight on. Then Madame Lefoux jerked away, fumbling with something. There came the sound of a loud burst of compressed air. The whole dirigible jerked suddenly to one side.

Alexia's grip loosened. She was distracted from the battle above by her own, more pressing, danger as she tried to reestablish her purchase on the helpful little spur.

The sound of forced air rang forth again, and the cloaked villain vanished from sight, leaving Madame Lefoux slumped back against the railing above. The dirigible lurched again, and Alexia let out a little *eep* of distress.

"Halloo! Madame Lefoux, a little assistance if you please!" she yelled up at the top of her voice. She had cause to appreciate her lung capacity and the vocal practice that living with a confrontational husband and a pack of unruly werewolves had given her.

Madame Lefoux turned and looked down. "Why, Lady Maccon! I was convinced you had fallen to your death! How wonderful that you are still alive."

Alexia could barely make out what the Frenchwoman was saying. The inventor's normally melodic voice was high and tinny, a helium-afflicted squeak. The inflation apparatus for the blimp must have developed a severe leak to be affecting voices all the way down to the observation deck.

"Well, I am not going to be here much longer," yelled back Alexia.

The top hat nodded agreement. "Hold on, Lady Maccon, I shall fetch crewmen to collect you directly."

"What?" yelled Alexia. "I cannot make you out at all. You have come over all squeaky."

Madame Lefoux's top hat and associated head disappeared from view.

Alexia entertained herself by concentrating on holding on as hard as she could and yelling a bit more for form's sake. She was indebted to those few puffy clouds floating below her, for they obscured the distant ground. She did not want to know exactly how far she had to fall.

Eventually, a small porthole window popped open near one of her booted feet. A familiar ugly hat stuck out the tiny hole. The face wearing the hat tilted up and back and witnessed Alexia's indecorous position.

"Why, Alexia Maccon, what *are* you doing? You appear to be dangling." The voice was a little slurred. Ivy was clearly still laboring under the effects of Madame Lefoux's cognac. "How undignified of you. Stop it at once!"

"Ivy. Assist me, would you?"

"I hardly see what I can do," replied Miss Hisselpenny. "Really, Alexia, what could have possessed you to attach yourself to the side of the ship in such a juvenile fashion? It is positively barnacle-like."

"Oh, for goodness' sake, Ivy, it is not like I intended to end up this way." Ivy tended toward dense, it was true, but alcohol evidently caused her to attain new heights of fatheadedness.

"Oh? Well, then. But honestly, Alexia, I do not mean to be boorish, but do you realize that your underdrawers are exposed to the night air, not to mention the public view?"

"Ivy, I am hanging on for dear life to the side of a floating dirigible, leagues up in the aether. Even you must admit there are some instances wherein protocol should be relaxed."

"But why?"

"Ivy, I fell, obviously."

Miss Hisselpenny blinked bleary dark eyes at her friend. "Oh, deary me, Alexia. Are you actually in real danger? Oh no!" Her head retreated.

Alexia wondered what it said about her character that Ivy had genuinely believed she would intentionally go climbing about the side of a floating dirigible.

Some sort of silky material was shoved out the window and up at her.

"What is that?"

"Why, my second-best cloak."

Lady Maccon gritted her teeth.

"Ivy, did you miss the part where I am hanging, an inch from death? Do get help."

The cloak vanished, and Miss Hisselpenny's head reappeared. "As bad as that, is it?"

The dirigible lurched, and Alexia swayed to one side with a squeal of alarm.

Ivy fainted, or possibly passed out from the alcohol.

As was to be expected, it was Madame Lefoux who provided the rescue in the end. Mere moments after Ivy vanished from view, a long rope ladder flopped down next to Alexia. She was able, with some difficulty, to transfer her grip from the metal spur to the ladder and climb up. The steward, several worried crewmembers, and Madame Lefoux stood anxiously awaiting her ascent.

Strangely, once Lady Maccon had attained the deck, her legs no longer seemed to function as nature intended. She slid gracelessly onto the wooden deck.

"I think I might reside here for a moment," she said after her third attempt to rise resulted only in wobbly knees and bones akin to jellyfish tentacles.

The steward, an immaculate if portly man dressed in a uniform of yellow canvas and fur, hovered about her in great concern, wringing his hands. He was clearly most upset that such a thing as a Lady of Quality falling off his craft had occurred. What would the company say if word got out? "Is there anything I can get you, Lady Maccon? Some tea perhaps, or something a little stronger?"

"Tea, I think, would be quite the restorative," replied Alexia, mostly to get him to stop hovering about like a worried canary.

Madame Lefoux crouched down next to her. Yet another reason to envy the Frenchwoman her mode of dress. "Are you certain you are in good health, my lady?" Her squeaky voice had gone, the helium leak having apparently been fixed while Lady Maccon was rescued.

"I am finding myself less delighted by the height and notion of floating than I was at the onset of our journey," replied Alexia. "But never mind that. Quickly now, before the steward returns, what happened after I fell? Did you see the attacker's face, ascertain his purpose or intention?" She left off the "Were you in cahoots?" part of that question.

Madame Lefoux shook her head, looking serious. "The miscreant wore a mask and a long cloak; I could not even say with certainty if it was a male or a female. I do apologize. We struggled for a time, and eventually I managed to disentangle myself and get off a shot with the dart emitter. The first one missed and cut a hole through one of the dirigible helium ports, but the second caught our enemy a glancing blow to the side. Apparently that was sufficient to instill fear, for the attacker took flight and managed to escape mostly unharmed."

"Bollix," swore Lady Maccon succinctly. It was one of her husband's favorite words, and she would normally never deign to use it, but current circumstances seemed to warrant its application. "And there are far too many crew and passengers on board to stage an inquest, even if I did not want to keep my preternatural state and role as muhjah a comparative secret."

The Frenchwoman nodded.

"Well, I think I may be able to stand now."

Madame Lefoux bent to help her up.

"Did I lose my parasol in the fall?"

The inventor dimpled. "No, it tumbled to the floor of the observation deck. I believe it is still there. Shall I have one of the hands bring it to your room?"

"Please."

Madame Lefoux signaled to a nearby deckhand and sent him off to find the missing accessory.

Lady Maccon was feeling a little dizzy and was annoyed with herself for it. She had been through worse during the preceding summer and saw no reason to come over weak and floppy due to a mere dabbling with gravity. She allowed the inventor to assist her to her room but refused to call Angelique.

She sat gratefully down on her bed. "A little sleep and I shall be right as rain tomorrow."

The Frenchwoman nodded and bent over her solicitously. "You are certain you do not need assistance to disrobe? I would be happy to help in your maid's stead."

Alexia blushed at the offer. Had she been wrong to doubt the inventor? Madame Lefoux did seem to be quite the best sort of ally to have. And, despite her masculine attire, she smelled amazing, like vanilla custard. Would it be so awful if this woman were to become a friend?

Then she noticed that the cravat around Madame Lefoux's neck was stained on one side with a small amount of blood.

"You were injured while fighting off the attacker and said nothing!" she accused, worried. "Here, let me see." Before the inventor could stop her, Lady Maccon pulled her down to sit on the bed and began untying the long length of Egyptian cotton wound about Madame Lefoux's elegant neck.

"It is of little consequence," the Frenchwoman asserted, blushing.

Lady Maccon ignored all protestations and tossed the cravat to the floor—it was ruined anyway. Then, with gentle fingers, she leaned in close to check the woman's neck. The wound appeared to be nothing more than a scratch, already clotted.

"It looks quite shallow," she said in relief.

"There, you see?" Self-consciously, Madame Lefoux shifted away from her.

Alexia caught a glimpse of something else upon the woman's neck. Something that the cravat had kept hidden: near the nape, partly covered by a few short curls of hair. Lady Maccon craned her head about to see what it might be.

A mark of some kind, dark against the woman's fine white skin, was inked in careful black lines. Alexia brushed the hair aside in a soft caress, startling the Frenchwoman, and leaned in, overcome with curiosity.

It was a tattoo of an octopus.

Lady Maccon frowned, oblivious to the fact that her hand still lay softly against the other woman's skin. Where had she seen that image before? Abruptly, she remembered. Her hand twitched, and only through sheer strength of character did she stop herself from jerking away in horror. She had seen that octopus depicted in brass over and over again, all about the Hypocras Club just after Dr. Siemons kidnapped her.

An awkward silence ensued. "Are you certain you are quite well, Madame Lefoux?" she inquired finally, for lack of anything better to say.

Misinterpreting her continued physical contact, the lady inventor twisted to face her, their noses practically touching. Madame Lefoux slid her hand up Alexia's arm.

Lady Maccon had read that Frenchwomen were much more physically affectionate than British women in their friendship, but there was something unbearably personal in the touch. And no matter how good she smelled and how helpful she had been, there was that octopus mark to consider. Madame Lefoux could not be trusted. The fight could have been staged. She could have an associate on board. She could still be a spy, intent on procuring the muhjah's dispatch case through any possible means. Alexia pulled away from the caressing hand.

At the withdrawal, the inventor stood. "I shall excuse myself. We could probably both use some rest."

Breakfast the next morning saw everyone back about their regular routine, bruises, bonnets, and all. Miss Hisselpenny forbore to mention Alexia's clumsy attempt at scaling Mt. Dirigible out of mortification over her dear friend's exposed underpinnings. Madame Lefoux was impeccably, if incorrectly, dressed and unflaggingly polite, with no comment on the previous evening's aerial escapade. She inquired kindly after Tunstell's health, to which Alexia responded favorably. Felicity was horrible and snide, but then Felicity had been a repulsive earwig ever since she first grew a vocabulary. It was as though nothing untoward had occurred at all.

Lady Maccon only nibbled at her food, not from any concern that there would be another attempted poisoning, but because she was still feeling slightly airsick. She was looking forward to having solid, unpretentious ground under her feet once more.

"What are your plans for the day, Lady Maccon?" inquired Madame Lefoux when all other pleasantries were exhausted.

"I envision an exhausting day of lying about in a deck chair, broken up with small but thrilling strolls about the ship."

"Capital plan," replied Felicity.

"Yes, sister, but I was going to sit in that deck chair

with a book, not a supercilious expression and a hand mirror," shot back Alexia.

Felicity only smiled. "At least I possess a face worth looking at for extended periods of time."

Madame Lefoux turned to Ivy. "Are they always like this?"

Miss Hisselpenny had been staring dreamily off into space. "What? Oh, them, yes, as long as I've know them. Which is a dog's age now. I mean to say, Alexia and I have been friends for quite these four years. Imagine that."

The inventor took a bite of steamed egg and did not respond.

Lady Maccon realized she was exposing herself to ridicule by bickering with her sibling.

"Madame Lefoux, what did you do before you came to London? You resided in Paris, I understand? Did you have a *hat shop* there too?"

"No, but my aunt did. I worked with her. She taught me everything I know."

"Everything?"

"Oh yes, *everything*."

"A remarkable woman, your aunt."

"You have no idea."

"Must be the excess soul."

"Oh." Ivy was intrigued. "Did your aunt come over all phantomy after death?"

Madame Lefoux nodded.

"How nice for you." Ivy smiled her congratulations.

"I suspect *I* will be a ghost in the end," said Felicity, preening. "I am the type to have extra soul. Don't you all agree? Mama says I am remarkably creative for someone who does not play or sing or draw."

Alexia bit her tongue. Felicity was about as likely to have excess soul as a hassock. She turned the conversation forcibly back to the inventor. "What made you leave your home country?"

"My aunt died, and I came over here looking for something precious that had been stolen from me."

"Oh, really? Did you find it?"

"Yes, but only to come to the understanding that it was never mine to begin with."

"How tragic for you," sympathized Ivy. "I had just such a thing happen with a hat once."

"It matters little. It had changed beyond all recognition by the time I located it."

"How mysterious and cryptic you are." Lady Maccon was intrigued.

"It is not entirely my story to tell and others may be injured in the telling if I am not careful."

Felicity yawned ostentatiously. She was little interested in anything not directly connected to herself. "Well, this is all very fascinating, but I am off to change for the day."

Miss Hisselpenny rose as well. "I believe I shall go check on Mr. Tunstell, to ascertain if he has been provided with an adequate breakfast."

"Highly unlikely—none of us were," said Alexia, whose delight in the imminent end to their voyage was encouraged by the idea of eating food that was not bland and steamed into submission.

They parted ways, and Alexia was about to pursue her highly strenuous plans for the day when she realized that if Ivy had gone to check on Tunstell, the two would be isolated together, and that was *not a good idea*. So she hightailed it after her friend toward the claviger's cabin.

She found Miss Hisselpenny and Tunstell engaged in what both probably thought was an impassioned embrace. Their lips were, in fact, touching, but nothing else was, and Ivy's greatest concern throughout the kiss seemed to be keeping her hat in place. The hat was of a masculine shape but decorated with the most enormous bow of purple and green plaid.

"Well," said Lady Maccon loudly, interrupting the couple, "I see you have recovered with startling alacrity from your illness, Tunstell."

Miss Hisselpenny and the claviger jumped apart. Both turned red with mortification, though it must be admitted that Tunstell, being a redhead, was far more efficient at this.

"Oh dear, Alexia," exclaimed Ivy, leaping back. She made for the door as rapidly as the strapped-down floating skirts of her travel dress would allow.

"Oh no, Miss Hisselpenny, please, come back!" Tunstell cried, and then, shockingly, "Ivy!"

But the lady in question was gone.

Alexia gave the ginger-haired young man a hard look. "What are you up to, Tunstell?"

"Oh, Lady Maccon, I am unreservedly in love with her. That black hair, that sweet disposition, those capital hats."

Well goodness, thought Alexia, *he really must be in love if he likes the hats.* She sighed and said, "But, really, Tunstell, be serious. Miss Hisselpenny cannot possibly have a future with you. Even if you were not up for metamorphosis presently, you are an *actor,* with no substantial prospects of any kind."

Tunstell donned a tragic-hero expression, one she had seen more than once in his portrayal of Porccigliano in the West End production of *Death in a Bathtub.* "True love will overcome all obstacles."

"Oh bosh. Be reasonable, Tunstell. This is no Shakespearian melodrama; this is the 1870s. Marriage is a practical matter. It must be treated as such."

"But you and Lord Maccon married for love."

Lady Maccon sighed. "And how do you figure that?"

"No one else would put up with him."

Alexia grinned. "By which you mean that no one else would put up with me."

Tunstell judiciously ignored that statement.

Lady Maccon explained. "Conall is the Earl of Woolsey and as such is permitted the eccentricity of a highly inappropriate wife. You are not. And *that* is a situation unlikely to alter in the future."

Tunstell still looked starry-eyed and unrelenting.

Lady Maccon sighed. "Very well, I see you are unmoved. I shall go determine how Ivy is coping."

Miss Hisselpenny was coping by engaging in a protracted bout of hysteria in one corner of the observation deck.

"Oh, Alexia, what am I to do? I am overcome with the injustice of it all."

Lady Maccon replied with a suggestion. "Seek the assistance of an ugly-hat-addiction specialist this very instant?"

"You are horrible. Be serious, Alexia. You must recognize that this is a travesty of unfairness!"

"How is that?" Lady Maccon did not follow.

"I love him so very much. As Romeo did Jugurtha, as Pyramid did Thirsty, as—"

"Oh, please, no need to elaborate further," interjected Alexia, wincing.

"But what would my family *say* to such a union?"

"They would say that your hats had leaked into you head," muttered Alexia, unheard under her breath.

Ivy continued wailing. "What would they *do*? I should have to break off my engagement with Captain Featherstonehaugh. He would be so *very* upset." She paused, and then gasped in horror. "There would have to be a *printed* retraction!"

"Ivy, I do not think that is the best course of action, throwing Captain Featherstonehaugh over. Not that I have met the man, mind you. But to go from a sensible, income-earning military man to *an actor*? I am very much afraid, Ivy, that it would be generally regarded as reprehensible and even indicative of"—she paused for dramatic effect—"*loose morals*."

Miss Hisselpenny let out an audible gasp and stopped crying. "You truly believe so?"

Lady Maccon went in for the kill. "Even, dare I say it, *fastness*?"

Ivy gasped again. "Oh no, Alexia, say not so. Truly? To be thought such a thing. How absolutely grisly. Oh what a pickle I am in. I suppose I shall have to throw over Mr. Tunstell."

"To be fair," admitted Lady Maccon, "Tunstell has confessed openly to appreciating your choice of headgear. You may very well be giving up on true love."

"I know. Is that not simply the worst thing you have *ever* heard, *ever*?"

Lady Maccon nodded, all seriousness. "Yes."

Ivy sighed, looking forlorn. To distract her, Alexia asked casually, "You did not perchance *hear* anything unusual last night after supper, did you?"

"No, I did not."

Alexia was relieved. She did not want to explain to Ivy the fight on the observation deck.

"Wait, come to think on it, yes," Ivy corrected herself, twisting a coil of black hair about one finger.

Uh-oh. "What was that?"

"You know, it was a most peculiar thing—just before I drifted off to sleep, I heard someone yelling in French."

Now that *was* interesting, "What did they say?"

"Do not be absurd, Alexia. You know perfectly well I do not speak French. Such a nasty slippery sort of language."

Lady Maccon considered.

"It could have been Madame Lefoux talking in her sleep," Ivy suggested. "You know she has the cabin next to mine?"

"I suppose that is possible." Alexia was not convinced.

Ivy took a deep breath. "Well, I should get on with it, then."

"On with what?"

"Throwing over poor Mr. Tunstell, possibly the love of my life." Ivy was looking nearly as tragic as the young man had moments earlier.

Alexia nodded. "Yes, I think you better had."

Tunstell, in grand thespian fashion, did not take Miss Hisselpenny's rejection well. He staged a spectacular bout of depression and then sank into a deep sulk for the rest of the day. Overwrought, Ivy came pleading to Alexia. "But he has been so very dour. And for a whole three hours. Could I not relent, just a little? He may never recover from this kind of heartache."

To which Alexia replied, "Give it more time, my dear Ivy. I think you will find he may recuperate eventually."

Madame Lefoux came up at that moment. Seeing Miss Hisselpenny's crestfallen face, she inquired, "Has something untoward occurred?"

Ivy let out a pathetic little sob and buried her face in a rose-silk handkerchief.

Alexia said in a hushed voice, "Miss Hisselpenny has had to reject Mr. Tunstell. She is most overwrought."

Madame Lefoux's face took on an appropriately somber cast. "Oh, Miss Hisselpenny, I am sorry. How ghastly for you."

Ivy waved the wet handkerchief, as much as to say, *words cannot possibly articulate my profound distress.* Then, because Ivy never settled for meaningful gestures when verbal embellishments could compound the effect, she said, "Words cannot possibly articulate my profound distress."

Alexia patted her friend's shoulder. Then she turned to the Frenchwoman. "Madame Lefoux, might I beg a small word in private?"

"I am always at your disposal, Lady Maccon. For *any-thing.*" Alexia failed to examine the possible meaning of that "anything."

The two women moved out of Miss Hisselpenny's earshot over to a secluded corner of the relaxation deck, out of the ever-present aether breezes. To Alexia, these felt faintly tingly, almost like charged particles, but friendlier. She imagined the aether gasses as a cloud of fireflies swarming close to her skin and then flitting off as the dirigible rode one strong current and passed through others. It was not unpleasant but could be distracting.

"I understand you got into an argument late last night, after our little escapade." Lady Maccon did not sugarcoat her words.

Madame Lefoux puffed out her lips. "I might have yelled at the steward for his negligence. He did take an inexcusably long time to get that rope ladder."

"The argument was in French."

Madame Lefoux made no response to that.

Lady Maccon switched tactics. "Why are you following me to Scotland?"

"Are you convinced it is you, my dear Lady Maccon, that I am following?"

"I hardly think you have also developed a sudden passion for my husband's valet."

"No, you would be correct in that."

"So?"

"So, I am no danger to you or yours, Lady Maccon. I wish you could believe that. But I cannot tell you more."

"Not good enough. You are asking me to trust you without reason."

The Frenchwoman sighed. "You soulless are so very logical and practical, it can be maddening."

"So my husband is prone to complaining. You have met a preternatural before, I take it?" If she could not convince the inventor to explain her presence, perhaps she could learn more about the mysterious woman's past.

"Once, a very long time ago. I suppose I could tell you about it."

"Well?"

"I met him with my aunt. I was perhaps eight years old. He was a friend of my father's—a very good friend, I was given to believe. Formerly Beatrice is the ghost of my father's sister. My father himself was a bit of a bounder. I am not exactly legitimate. When I was dumped on his doorstep, he gave me to Aunt Beatrice and died shortly thereafter. I remember a man coming to see him after that, only to find that I was all that was left. The man gave me a present of honey candy and was sad to learn of my father's death."

"He was the preternatural?" Despite herself, Lady Maccon was intrigued.

"Yes, and I believe they were once very close."

"And?"

"You understand my meaning: very close?"

Lady Maccon nodded. "I fully comprehend. I am, after all, a friend of Lord Akeldama's."

Madame Lefoux nodded. "The man who visited was your father."

Alexia's mouth fell open. Not because of this insight into her father's preferences. She knew his taste to run to both the exotic and the eclectic. From reading his journals, she guessed him to be, at best, an opportunist in matters of the flesh. No, she gasped because it was such an odd coincidence, to find out that this woman, not so much older than herself, had once met her father. Had known what he was like—alive.

"I never knew him. He left before I was born," Lady Maccon said before she could stop herself.

"He was handsome but stiff. I remember believing that all Italian men would be like him: cold. I could not have been more wrong, of course, but he made an impression."

Lady Maccon nodded. "So I have been given to understand by others. Thank you for telling me."

Madame Lefoux switched topics abruptly. "We should continue to keep the full details of the incident last night a secret from your companions."

"No point in worrying the others, but I shall have to tell my husband after we land."

"Of course."

The two women parted at that; Lady Maccon was left wondering. She knew why *she* wanted to keep the scuffle a secret, but why did Madame Lefoux?

CHAPTER EIGHT

Castle Kingair

They landed just before sunset on a patch of green near the Glasgow train station. The dirigible came to rest as lightly as a butterfly on an egg, if the butterfly were to stumble a bit and list heavily to one side and the egg to take on the peculiar characteristics of Scotland in winter: more soggy and more gray than one would think possible.

Alexia disembarked with pomp and circumstance similar to her embarkation. She spearheaded a parade of bustle-swaying ladies, like so many fabric snails, onto firm (well, truthfully, rather squishy) land. The bustles were particularly prevalent due to the general relief at being able to wear a proper one once more and to pack the floating skirts away. The snails were followed by Tunstell, laden with a quantity of hatboxes and other package; four stewards with various trunks; and Lady Maccon's French maid.

No one, thought Alexia smugly, could accuse her of traveling without the dignity due to the Earl of Woolsey's wife. She might gad about town alone or in the care of only one unwed young lady, but clearly she *traveled* in company. Unfortunately, the effect of her arrival was undermined by the fact that the ground persisted in reeling about under her, causing Lady Maccon to tilt to one side and take an abrupt seat atop one of her trunks.

She dismissed Tunstell's concern by sending him away to hire an appropriate conveyance to take them into the countryside.

Ivy wandered about the green to stretch her legs and look for wildflowers. Felicity came to stand next to Alexia and began immediately to carry on about the horrible weather.

"Why must it be so gray? Such a greeny sort of gray goes so badly with the complexion. And it is so awful to travel by coach anywhere in such weather. Must we go by coach?"

"Well," said Lady Maccon, driven to annoyance, "this *is* the north. Do stop being silly about it."

Her sister continued to complain, and Alexia watched out of the corner of her eye as Tunstell veered near to Ivy on his way across the landing green and hissed something in her ear. Ivy said something back, an excess of emotion coloring the sharp movements of her head. Tunstell's back straightened and he turned away to walk on.

Ivy came to sit next to Alexia, trembling lightly.

"I do not know what I *ever* saw in that man." Miss Hisselpenny was clearly overwrought.

"Oh dear, has something come between the lovebirds? Is there trouble afoot?" said Felicity.

When no one answered her, she trotted after the rapidly departing claviger. "Oh, Mr. Tunstell? Would you like some company?"

Lady Maccon looked to Ivy. "Am I to understand that Tunstell did not take your rejection well?" she inquired, trying not to sound as weak as she felt. She was still dizzy, and the ground seemed quite taken with shifting about like a nervous squid.

"Well, no, not as such. When I . . ." Ivy started and then broke off, her attention diverted by an exceedingly large dog charging in their direction. "Mercy me, what is that?"

The immense dog resolved into being, in actuality, a very large wolf, with a wad of fabric wrapped about its neck. Its fur was a dark brown color brindled gold and cream, and its eyes were pale yellow.

Upon reaching them, the wolf gave Miss Hisselpenny a polite little nod and then put its head in Lady Maccon's lap.

"Ah, husband," said Alexia, scratching him behind the ears, "I figured you would find me, but not so quickly as this."

The Earl of Woolsey lolled his long pink tongue at his wife good-naturedly and tilted his head in Miss Hisselpenny's direction.

"Yes, of course," replied Alexia to the unspoken suggestion. She turned to her friend. "Ivy, my dear, I suggest you look away at this juncture."

"Why?" wondered Miss Hisselpenny.

"Many find a werewolf's shape change rather unsettling and—"

"Oh, I am certain I should not be at all disconcerted," interrupted Miss Hisselpenny.

Lady Maccon was not convinced. Ivy was, circumstances had shown, prone to fainting. She continued her explanation. "*And* Conall will not be clothed when the transformative event has completed."

"Oh!" Miss Hisselpenny put a hand to her mouth in alarm. "Of course." She turned quickly away.

Still, one could not help but hear, even if one did not look: that slushy crunchy noise of bones breaking and reforming. It was similar to the echoing sound that dismembering a dead chicken for the stew pot makes in a large kitchen. Alexia saw Ivy shudder.

Werewolf change was never pleasant. That was one of the reasons pack members still referred to it as a curse, despite the fact that, in the modern age of enlightenment and free will, clavigers *chose* metamorphosis. The change comprised a good deal of biological rearranging. This, like rearranging one's parlor furniture for a party, involved a transition from tidy to very messy to tidy once more. And, as with any redecoration, there was a moment in the middle where it seemed impossible that everything could possibly go back together harmoniously. In the case of werewolves, this moment involved fur retreating to become hair, bones fracturing and mending into new configurations, and flesh and muscle sliding about on top of or underneath the two. Alexia had seen her husband change many times, and every time she found it both vulgar and scientifically fascinating.

Conall Maccon, Earl of Woolsey, was considered proficient at the change. No one could beat out Professor Lyall for sheer elegance, of course, but at least the earl was fast, efficient, and made none of those horribly pugilistic grunting noises the younger cubs were prone to emitting.

In mere moments, he stood before his wife: a big man, without being fat. Alexia had commented once that, given his love of food, he probably would have become portly had he aged as normal humans did. Luckily, he had elected for metamorphosis sometime in his midthirties and so had never gone to seed. Instead he remained forever a well-muscled mountain of a man who needed the shoulders of his coats tailored, his boots specially ordered, and near constant reminding that he must duck through doorways.

He turned eyes, only a few shades darker than they had been in wolf form, to his wife.

Lady Maccon stood to help him pull on his cloak but sat back down before she could do so. She was still not steady on her feet.

Lord Maccon immediately stopped shaking out the garment in question and knelt, naked, before her.

"What's wrong?" he practically yelled.

"What?" Ivy turned to see what was going on, caught a glimpse of the earl's naked backside, squeaked, and turned back away, fanning herself with one gloved hand.

"Do not fuss, Conall. You are upsetting Ivy," grumbled Lady Maccon.

"Miss Hisselpenny is always upset over something. *You* are a different matter. You don't *do* these kinds of things, wife. You are not that feminine."

"Well, I like that!" Lady Maccon took offense.

"You understand my meaning perfectly. Stop trying to distract me. What's wrong?" He drew entirely the wrong conclusion. "You're sickening! Is that why you've come, to tell me you're ill?" He looked like he wanted to shake her but did not dare.

Alexia looked straight into his worried eyes and said slowly and carefully, "I am perfectly fine. It is simply taking a little time for me to get my land legs back. You know how it can be after a long air or sea journey."

The earl looked vastly relieved. "Not a very good floater, my love, as it turned out?"

Lady Maccon gave her husband a reproachful look and replied petulantly, "No, not so very good at the floating. No." Then she changed the subject. "But, really, Conall, you know I welcome the spectacle, but poor Ivy! Put your cloak on, do."

The earl grinned, straightened under her appreciative eye, and wrapped his long cloak about his body.

"How did you know I was here?" Alexia asked as soon as he was decent.

"The lewd display has ended, Miss Hisselpenny. You are safe," Lord Maccon informed Ivy, settling his massive frame next to his wife. The trunk creaked at the added weight.

Lady Maccon snuggled against her husband's side happily.

"Simply knew," he grumbled, wrapping one long, fabric-shrouded arm about her and hauling her closer against him. "This landing patch is just off my route to Kingair. I caught your scent about an hour ago and saw the dirigible coming in for a landing. Figured I had better come see what was going on. Now you, wife. What are you doing in Scotland? With Miss Hisselpenny no less."

"Well, I had to bring some kind of companion. Society would not very well condone my floating across the length of England by myself."

"Mmm." Lord Maccon glanced over, eyes heavy-lidded, at the still-nervous Ivy. She had not yet reconciled herself to talking with an earl dressed only in a cloak so was standing a little distance off with her back to them.

"Give her a bit more recuperation time," advised Alexia. "Ivy's sensitive, and you are such a shock to the system, even fully dressed."

The earl grinned. "Praise, wife? How unusual from you. Nice to know I still have the capacity to unsettle others, even at my age. But stop trying to avoid the subject. Why *are* you here?"

"Why, darling"—Lady Maccon batted her eyelashes at him—"I was coming to Scotland to see *you* of course. I missed you so."

"Ah, wife, how romantic of you," he replied, not believing a word of it. He looked down at her fondly. Not as far down as he would have had to on most women, mind you. His Alexia was rather strapping. He preferred her that way. Undersized women reminded him of yippy dogs.

He rumbled softly, "Lying minx."

She leaned in. "It will have to wait until later, when others cannot overhear," she whispered against his ear.

"Mmm." He turned in toward her and kissed her lips, warm and adamant.

"Ahem." Ivy cleared her throat.

Lord Maccon took his time breaking off the kiss.

"Husband," said Lady Maccon, her eyes dancing. "You remember Miss Hisselpenny?"

Conall gave his wife *a look,* and then stood and bowed.

As though he and the nonsensical Miss Hisselpenny had not formed a lasting acquaintance these three months since his marriage.

"Good evening, Miss Hisselpenny. How do you do?"

Ivy curtsied. "Lord Maccon, how unexpected. You were notified of our arrival time?"

"No."

"Then how?"

"It is a werewolf machination, Ivy," explained Alexia. "Do not trouble yourself."

Ivy did not.

Lady Maccon said to her husband carefully, "I also have my sister and Tunstell accompanying me. And Angelique, of course."

"I see, an unexpected wife and reinforcements. Are we anticipating a battle of some kind, my dear?"

"If I were, I should only have to set the enemy against the sharp barbs of Felicity's tongue to rout them thoroughly. The size of my traveling party is, however, entirely unintentional."

Miss Hisselpenny acted a bit guilty at that statement.

Lord Maccon gave his wife a look of profound disbelief.

Alexia went on. "Felicity and Tunstell are procuring transportation as we speak."

"How thoughtful of you, to bring me my valet."

"Your valet has been a resounding nuisance."

Miss Hisselpenny gasped.

Lord Maccon shrugged. "He usually is. There is an art to irritation that only few of us can achieve."

Lady Maccon said, "That must be how werewolves select personalities for metamorphosis. Regardless, Tunstell was required. Professor Lyall insisted upon a male escort, and as we were traveling by dirigible, we could not bring a member of the pack."

"Better not to anyway, seeing as this is someone else's territory."

A polite clearing of the throat occurred at that juncture, and the Maccons turned about to find Madame Lefoux hovering nearby.

"Ah, yes," said Lady Maccon. "Madame Lefoux was also on board the dirigible with us. Quite *unexpectedly*." She emphasized the last word for her husband's benefit so that he might understand her concern over the inventor's presence. "I believe you and my husband are already acquainted, Madame Lefoux?"

Madame Lefoux nodded. "How do you do, Lord Maccon?"

The earl bowed slightly and then shook Madame Lefoux's hand, as he would a man. Lord Maccon's opinion appeared to be that if Madame Lefoux dressed as a male, she should be treated as such. Interesting approach. Or perhaps he knew something Alexia did not.

Lady Maccon said to her husband, "Thank you for the lovely parasol, by the way. I shall put it to good use."

"I never doubted that. I am a little surprised you have not already."

"Who says I have not?"

"That's my sweet, biddable little wife."

Ivy said, surprised, "Oh, but Alexia is not sweet."

Lady Maccon only grinned.

The earl seemed genuinely pleased to see the Frenchwoman. "Delighted, Madame Lefoux. You have business in Glasgow?"

The inventor inclined her head.

"I don't suppose I could persuade you to visit Kingair? I just heard in town that the pack is experiencing some technical difficulties with its aethographic transmitter, newly purchased, secondhand."

"Good Lord, husband. Does everyone have one but us?" his wife wanted to know.

The earl turned sharp eyes on her. "Why? Who else acquired one recently?"

"Lord Akeldama, of all people, and he has the latest model. Would you be very cross if I said I rather covet one myself?"

Lord Maccon reflected upon the state of his life wherein he had somehow gained a spouse who could not give a pig's foot for the latest dresses out of Paris but who whined about not owning an aethographic transmitter. Well, at least the two were comparable obsessions so far as expense was concerned.

"Well, my little bluestocking bride, someone has a birthday coming up."

Alexia's eyes shone. "Oh, splendid!"

Lord Maccon kissed her softly on the forehead and then turned back to Madame Lefoux. "Well, can I persuade you to stop over at Kingair for a few days and ascertain if there is anything you can do to help?"

Alexia pinched her husband in annoyance. When would he learn to ask her about these things first?

Lord Maccon captured his wife's hand in one big paw and shook his head ever so slightly at her.

The inventor frowned, a little crease in her creamy forehead. Then, as though the crease had never been, the dimples appeared, and she accepted the invitation.

Alexia managed only a brief, private word with her husband as they piled their luggage into two hired carriages.

"Channing says the werewolves couldn't change all the boat ride over."

Her husband blinked at her, startled. "Really?"

"Oh, and Lyall says the plague is moving northward. He thinks it beat us to Scotland."

Lord Maccon frowned. "He thinks it's something to do with the Kingair Pack, doesn't he?"

Alexia nodded.

Strangely, her husband grinned. "Good, that gives me an excuse."

"Excuse for what?"

"Showing up on their doorstep; they'd never let me in otherwise."

"What?" Alexia hissed at him. "Why?" But they were interrupted by Tunstell's return and unparalleled excitement at seeing Lord Maccon.

The rented carriages rattled down the track to Kingair in ever-growing darkness. Alexia was bound to either silence or inanities by the presence of Ivy and Madame Lefoux in their carriage. It was too dark and rainy to see much outside the window, a fact that upset Ivy.

"I did so want to *see* the Highlands," said Miss Hisselpenny. As though there would be some sort of line, drawn on the ground, that indicated transition from one part of Scotland to the next. Miss Hisselpenny had already commented that Scotland looked a lot like England, in a tone of voice that suggested this a grave error on the landscape's part.

Inexplicably tired, Alexia dozed, her cheek resting on her husband's large shoulder.

Felicity, Tunstell, and Angelique rode in the other carriage, emerging with an air of chummy gaiety that confused Alexia and tormented Ivy. Felicity was flirting shamelessly, and Tunstell was doing nothing to dissuade her. But the sight of Castle Kingair dampened everyone's spirits. As if to compound matters, as soon as they and all their luggage had alighted and the carriages trundled off, the rain began to descend in earnest.

Castle Kingair was like something out of a Gothic novel. Its foundation was a huge rock that jutted out over a dark lake. It put Woolsey Castle to shame. There was the feel of real age about the place, and Alexia would bet good money that it was a drafty, miserably old-fashioned creature on the inside.

First, however, it appeared that they would have to get past a drafty, miserably old-fashioned creature on the outside.

"Ah," said Lord Maccon upon seeing the reception committee of one, standing, arms crossed, outside the castle front gates. "Gird your loins, my dear."

His wife looked up at him, her wet hair falling from its fancy arrangement. "I do not think you should be discussing my loins just now, husband," she said in a sprightly manner.

Miss Hisselpenny, Felicity, and Madame Lefoux came to stand next to them, shivering in the rain, while Tunstell and Angelique began organizing the baggage.

"Who is that?" Ivy wanted to know.

The personage stood shrouded in a long, shapeless

plaid cloak, face shadowed under a beaten coachman's hat of oiled leather that had seen better days and barely survived them.

"One might well ask instead, *what* is that?" corrected Felicity, her nose wrinkled in disgust, her parasol raised ineffectually against the deluge.

The woman—for upon closer inspection, the personage did appear to be, to some slight degree, of the female persuasion—did not move forward to greet them. Nor did she offer them shelter. She simply stood and glared. And her glaring was most definitely centered on Lord Maccon.

They approached cautiously.

"You're nae welcome here, Conall Maccon, you ken!" she yelled, long before they were within any reasonable conversational distance. "Hie yourself back away now afore you be fighting all what's left of this here pack."

Under the shade of the hat, she appeared to be of middling years, handsome but not pretty, with strong features and coarse thick hair, tending toward gray. She boasted the general battle-ax demeanor of an especially strict governess. This was the kind of woman who took her tea black, smoked cigars after midnight, played a mean game of cribbage, and kept a bevy of repulsive little dogs.

Alexia liked her immediately.

The woman shouldered a rifle with consummate skill and pointed it at Lord Maccon.

Alexia liked her less.

"And dinna be thinking you can change on me. Pack's

been free of yon werewolf's curse for months, since we started out across the sea."

"Which would be why I'm here, Sidheag." Lord Maccon continued to advance. He was a good liar, her husband, thought Lady Maccon proudly.

"You be doubting these bullets be silver?"

"What matters that, if I'm as mortal as you?"

"Och, you always were a sharp one with the tongue."

"We have come to help, Sidheag."

"Who's been saying we need help? You're na wanted here. Hie yourself off Kingair territory, the lot of ye."

Lord Maccon sighed heavily. "This is BUR business, and your pack's behavior has called me down on you, willing or nae. I'm not here as Woolsey Alpha. I am not even here as mediator for your Alpha gap. I am here as sundowner. What did you expect?"

The woman flinched away, but she also put down the gun. "Aye. I see it now to rights. 'Tis na that you care what happens to the pack—*your* old pack. You're simply here touting queen's will. Turn-tail coward, that's what you are, Conall Maccon, and naught more."

Lord Maccon had almost reached her by now. Only Lady Maccon still trailed behind him. The rest had stopped at the sight of the woman's gun. Alexia glanced back over her shoulder to see Ivy and Felicity huddled near Tunstell, who had a small pistol pointed steadily at the woman. Madame Lefoux stood next to him, her wrist held at just such an angle to suggest some more exotic form of firearm was concealed but enabled just inside the sleeve of her greatcoat.

Lady Maccon, parasol at the ready, moved toward her husband and the strange woman. He was speaking in a low voice so that the party behind them could not hear through the rain. "What did they get up to overseas, Sidheag? What mess did you get into over there after Niall died?"

"What do you care? You up and abandoned us."

"I had no choice." Conall's voice was weary with remembered arguments.

"Bollix to that, Conall Maccon. 'Tis a cop-out, well and truly, and we both be knowing it. You fixing the mess you left behind these twenty years gone, now that you're back?"

Alexia looked at her husband, curious. Perhaps she would get the answer to something she'd always wondered about. Why would an Alpha abdicate one pack, only to seek out and fight to rule another?

The earl remained silent.

The woman pushed the worn old hat back off her head to look up at Lord Maccon. She was tall, almost as tall as he, so she did not have to look up far. She was no slight thing either. There was muscle rolling about noticeably under that massive cloak. Alexia was suitably impressed.

The woman's eyes were a terribly familiar tawny brown color.

Lord Maccon said, "Let us inside out of this muck and I will think about it."

"Pah!" spat the woman. Then she marched up the beaten stone path toward the keep.

Lady Maccon looked to her husband. "Interesting lady."

"Dinna you start," he growled at her. He turned back to the rest of their party. "That is about as much of an invitation as we're likely to receive around these parts. Come on inside. Leave the luggage. Sidheag will send a man out to get it."

"And you are convinced she will not simply toss it all into the lake, Lord Maccon?" wondered Felicity, clutching her reticule protectively.

Lord Maccon snorted. "No guarantees."

Lady Maccon immediately left his side and retrieved her dispatch case from the mound of luggage.

"Does this thing work as an umbrella?" she asked Madame Lefoux on her way back, waving the parasol.

The inventor looked sheepish. "I forgot that part."

Alexia sighed and squinted up into the rain. "Capital. Here I stand, about to meet the dreaded in-laws looking like nothing so much as a drowned rat."

"Be fair, sister," contradicted Felicity. "You look like a drowned toucan."

And with that, the little band entered Castle Kingair.

It was just as drafty and old-fashioned on the inside as its appearance would suggest from the outside. *Neglected* was too fine a term for it. The carpets were gray-green, threadbare relics from the time of King George; the chandelier in the entranceway supported *candles,* of all ridiculous forms of lighting; and there were actual medieval tapestries hanging against the walls. Alexia, who was fastidious, ran one gloved finger along the banister railing and tutted at the dust.

The Sidheag woman caught her at it.

"Na up to yon high-falutin' London standards, young miss?"

"Uh-oh," said Ivy.

"Not up to standards of common household decency," shot back Alexia. "I heard the Scots were barbarians, but this"—she brushed her fingers together, releasing a small cloud of gray powder—"is ridiculous."

"I'm na stopping you from heading back out into the rain."

Lady Maccon cocked her head to one side. "Yes, but would you stop me from dusting? Or do you have a particular attachment to grime?"

The woman chuckled at that.

Lord Maccon said, "Sidheag, this is my wife, Alexia Maccon. Wife, this is Sidheag Maccon, Lady Kingair. My great-great-great-granddaughter."

Alexia was surprised. Her guess would have been a grand-niece of some kind, not a direct descendent. Her husband had been married before he changed? Now *why* hadn't he told her that?

"But," objected Miss Hisselpenny, "she looks older than Alexia." A pause. "She looks older than you, Lord Maccon."

"I would not try to understand, if I were you, dear," consoled Madame Lefoux with a slight dimpling at Ivy's distress.

"I am just about forty," replied Lady Kingair, unabashed at stating her age before strangers and in polite company. Really, this part of the country was just as primitive as Floote had said. Lady Maccon shuddered delicately and adjusted her grip on her parasol, prepared for anything.

Sidheag Maccon looked pointedly at the earl. "Nigh on too old."

Felicity wrinkled her nose. "Ew, this is simply too revoltingly peculiar. Why did you *have* to involve yourself in the supernatural set, Alexia?"

Lady Maccon merely gave her sister an arch look.

Felicity answered her own question. "Oh yes, I remember now—no one else would have you."

Alexia ignored that and looked with interest at her husband. "You never told me you had a family *before* you became a werewolf."

Lord Maccon shrugged. "You never asked." He turned to introduce the rest of the party. "Miss Hisselpenny, my wife's companion. Miss Loontwill, my wife's sister. Tunstell, my primary claviger. And Madame Lefoux, who would be happy to examine your broken aethographor."

Lady Kingair started. "How did you ken that we . . . ? Never mind. You always were uncanny with the knowing. You being BUR has na improved that to anyone else's comfort. Weel, that's one welcome guest. Delighted to meet ye, Madame Lefoux. I have, of course, heard of your work. We've a claviger who's familiar with your theories, a bit o' an amateur inventor himself."

Then the Scotswoman looked at her great-great-great-grandfather. "I'm supposing you'd as lief see the rest o' the pack?"

Lord Maccon inclined his head.

The Lady of Kingair reached off to the side of the darkened stairwell and clanged a bell hidden there. It made a noise halfway between a moo and a steam engine coming to an abrupt halt, and suddenly the hallway was filled with large men, most of them in skirts.

"Good heavens," exclaimed Felicity, "what *are* they wearing?"

"Kilts," explained Alexia, amused at her sister's discomfort.

"Skirts," replied Felicity, deeply offended, "and short ones at that, as though they were opera dancers."

Alexia swallowed a giggle. Now there was a funny image.

Miss Hisselpenny did not seem to know where to look. Finally she settled on staring up at the candelabra in abject terror. "Alexia," she hissed to her friend, "there are knees positively everywhere. What do I do?"

Alexia's attention was on the faces of the men around her, not their unmentionable leg areas. There seemed to be an equal mix of disgust and delight at seeing Lord Maccon.

The earl introduced her to those he knew. The Kingair Pack Beta, nominally in charge, was one of the unhappy ones, while the Gamma was one of those pleased to see Conall. The remaining four members fell two for and two against and ranged themselves to stand accordingly, as though at any moment fisticuffs might spontaneously break out. Kingair was smaller than the Woolsey Pack, and less unified. Alexia wondered what kind of man the post-Conall Alpha had been, to lead this contentious lot.

Then, with unseemly haste, Lord Maccon grabbed the surly Beta, who responded in a halfhearted manner to the name of Dubh, and dragged him off into a private parlor, leaving Alexia to mitigate the tense social atmosphere he left behind.

Lady Maccon was equal to the task. No one of her stalwart character, required since birth to supervise first Mrs. Loontwill and later two equally improbable sisters, was unprepared for even such trying circumstances as large, kilted werewolves en masse.

"We heard about you," said the Gamma, whose name sounded like something slippery to do with bogs. "Knew the old laird had suckered himself to a curse-breaker." He paced about Alexia slowly in a circle as though examining her for flaws. It felt very doglike to Alexia. She was prepared to jump back if he cocked a leg.

Luckily, his statement was misconstrued by both Ivy and Felicity. Alexia was not *known* as a preternatural to either of them and she preferred to keep it that way. Both young ladies seemed to assume that the phrase *curse-breaker* was some queer Scottish term for wife.

Felicity said, sneering at the enormous man in front of her, "Really, can you not speak English?"

Lady Maccon said quickly, ignoring her sister, "You have the upper hand on me. I know nothing of you." They were all so very large. She was not used to feeling diminutive.

The Gamma's broad face went pinched at that. "Over a century he was master o' this pack and he na mentioned us to ye?"

"Could be *me* he does not want to know you, rather than you he does not want to talk about," offered Alexia.

The werewolf gave her a long, assessing look. "I'm thinking 'tis that he never brought us up, did he?"

Sidheag interrupted them. "Enough gossip. We'll show you to your rooms. Lads, go grab in the extras—blasted English canna travel light."

The upstairs bedrooms and guest accommodations seemed no better off than the rest of the castle, muted in color and dank in smell. The room given to Lord and

Lady Maccon was tidy enough but musty, with decorations of brownish red some hundred years or so outdated. There was a large bed, two small wardrobes, a dressing table for Alexia, and a dressing chamber for her husband. The color scheme and general appearance reminded Lady Maccon of nothing so much as a damp, malcontented squirrel.

She checked about the chamber for a safe place to secrete her dispatch case, with little success. There seemed nowhere acceptably discreet, so she trundled three doors down to where Miss Hisselpenny was billeted.

As she passed one of the other chambers, she heard Felicity say, in a breathy voice, "Oh, Mr. Tunstell, shall I be safe in the room right next to yours, do you think?"

Seconds later, she witnessed Tunstell, panic in every freckle, emerge from Felicity's room and dive into the refuge of his small valet accommodations just off of Conall's dressing chamber.

Ivy was busy unpacking her trunk when Alexia tapped politely on her door and wandered in.

"Oh, thank heavens, Alexia. I was just pondering, do you think there might be ghosts in this place? Or worse, poltergeists? Please do not think I am at all bigoted against the supernatural set, but I simply cannot withstand an overabundance of ghosts, especially not those at the final stage of disanimus. I heard they get all over funny in the head and go wafting about losing bits of their noncorporeal selves. One rounds a corner of some perfectly respectable passageway only to find a disembodied eyebrow floating halfway between ceiling and potted palm." Miss Hisselpenny shuddered as she carefully stacked her twelve hatboxes next to the wardrobe.

Alexia thought back to what her husband had said. If the werewolves here could not change, then the plague of humanization must be infecting Castle Kingair. The castle would have been completely exorcised.

"I have a funny feeling, Ivy," she said with confidence, "that ghosts will definitely not be frequenting this locale."

Ivy looked unconvinced. "But, Alexia, really you must admit to the fact that this building seems like the kind of place that *ought* to have ghosts."

Lady Maccon clicked her tongue in exasperation. "Oh, Ivy, do not be ridiculous. Appearances have nothing to do with it; you know that. Only in Gothic novels are ghosts linked so, and we both know how utterly fanciful fiction has become recently. Authors never *do* get the supernatural correct. I mean to say, the last one I read essentially claimed metamorphosis had to do with *magic,* when everyone knows there are perfectly valid scientific and medical explanations for excess soul. Why, just the other day, I read that—"

Miss Hisselpenny interrupted her hastily before she could go on. "Yes, well, no need to overset me with blue-stocking explanations and Royal Society papers. I shall take your word for it. What time did Lady Kingair say supper was to commence?"

"Nine, I believe."

Another look of panic suffused her friend's face. "Will they be serving"—she gulped—"haggis, do you think?"

Lady Maccon made a face. "Surely not for our first meal. But best prepare yourself; one never knows." Con-all had described the disastrous foodstuff, with unwarranted delight, during their carriage ride in. The ladies were living in mortal terror as a result.

Ivy sighed. "Very well. We had better get dressed, then. Would my periwinkle taffeta be appropriate for the occasion?"

"For the haggis?"

"No, silly, for dinner."

"Does it have a matched hat?"

Miss Hisselpenny looked up from tidying her stack of hatboxes with a disgusted expression. "Alexia, do not talk such folderol. It is a *dinner* gown."

"Then I think it will serve very well. May I ask you a favor? I have a gift for my husband in this case. Do you think I might conceal it in your room for the time being so he does not accidentally uncover it? I wish it to be a surprise."

Miss Hisselpenny's eyes shone. "Oh, really! How lovely and wifely of you. I should never have pegged you for a romantic."

Lady Maccon winced.

"What is it?"

Alexia grappled with her brain for an appropriate answer. What would one possibly buy for a man and then hide in a dispatch case? "Uh. Socks."

Miss Hisselpenny was crushed. "Only socks? I hardly think socks cry out for secrecy."

"They are lucky, special socks."

Miss Hisselpenny saw no apparent illogicality in that and carefully tucked Lady Maccon's dispatch case behind her stack of hatboxes.

"I may need to access it from time to time," said Alexia.

Miss Hisselpenny was bemused. "Why?"

"To, uh, check on the condition of the, uh, socks."

"Alexia, are you feeling quite the thing?"

Lady Maccon instantly spoke, in order to throw Miss Hisselpenny off the scent. "Did you know, I just passed Tunstell leaving Felicity's rooms."

Ivy gasped. "No!" She immediately began furiously arranging her accessories for dinner, tossing gloves, jewelry, and lacy hair cap on top of the dress already laid out upon the bed.

"Alexia, I do not mean to be at all rude. But I really do believe your sister may be an actual nincompoop."

"Oh, that is perfectly all right, Ivy dear. I cannot stomach her myself," replied Lady Maccon. And then, because she felt guilty for having told her about Tunstell, "Would you like to borrow Angelique this evening to do up your hair? The rain's ruined mine beyond all repair I'm afraid, so it would be a wasted effort."

"Oh, really? Thank you, that would be lovely." Ivy perked up immediately.

With that, Lady Maccon retreated to her own room to dress.

"Angelique?" The maid was busy unpacking when Lady Maccon reentered her bedroom.

"I have told Ivy she may have you for her hair this evening. Not a thing could possibly be done to help mine at this point." Alexia's dark locks were a mass of frizzy curls in reaction to the unpleasant Scottish climate. "I shall simply pop on one of those horrible lace matron's caps you are always trying to get me to wear."

"Yez, my lady." The maid bobbed a curtsy and went to do as she was bid. She paused in the doorway, looking back at her mistress. "Please, my lady, why is Madame Lefoux still with us?"

"You really do not like her, do you, Angelique?"

A quintessentially French shrug met that statement.

"It was my husband's idea, I am afraid to say. I do not trust her either, mind you. But you know how Conall gets. Apparently, Kingair has a malfunctioning aethographic transmitter. I know, you might well look surprised. Who would have thought a backwater place like this could possess anything so modern? Apparently they do, and it has been having difficulties. Secondhand goods, I understand. Well, what do you expect? Anyhow, Conall brought Madame Lefoux along to give it the old once-over. Nothing I could do to stop him."

Angelique looked blank at that and bobbed a quick curtsy, and went off to see to Ivy.

Alexia ruminated over the outfit the maid had selected for her to wear. And then, because she really could not count on her own sense of style to do any better, put it on.

Her husband came in just as she was struggling to fasten the buttons up the back of the bodice.

"Oh, good, there you are. Do this up for me, would you, please?"

Entirely ignoring her command, Lord Maccon strode over to her in three quick steps and buried his face in the side of her neck.

Lady Maccon emitted an exasperated sigh but at the same time swiveled around to wrap her arms about his neck.

"Well, that is very helpful, darling. You do realize we are due for—"

He kissed her.

When breathing eventually became a necessity, he said, "Well, wife, been wanting to do that the entire carriage ride here." He moved his large hands down to her posterior and hoisted her against his big, firm body.

"And here I thought you were thinking about politics most of the ride; you sported such a terrible frown," replied his wife with a grin.

"Well, that too. I *can* do two things at once. For example, right now I am talking to you and also devising a means by which to extract you from this gown."

"Husband, you cannot take it off of me. I just put it on."

He seemed disinclined to agree with that statement, instead putting a concerted effort into undoing all her careful work and shoving the dress aside.

"Did you really like the parasol I gave you?" he asked, sweetly hesitant, drifting his fingertips up over her now-bare shoulders and upper back.

"Oh, Conall, such a lovely gift, with magnetic disruption field generator, poison darts, and everything. So very thoughtful. I was delighted to find I had not lost it during the fall."

The fingers stopped drifting abruptly. "Fall? What fall?"

Lady Maccon knew that burgeoning roar well. She squirmed against him in an effort to distract him. "Uh," she hedged.

Lord Maccon pushed her slightly away, holding her by the shoulders.

She patted him as best she could on the chest. "Oh, it was nothing, dear—simply a little tumble."

"Little tumble! Little tumble off of what, wife?"

Alexia looked down and away and tried to mumble. Since she had a naturally assertive voice, this did not work at all well. "A dirigible."

"A dirigible." Lord Maccon's tone was hard and flat. "And did that dirigible happen to be floating in the air at the time?"

"Umm, well, possibly, not quite air . . . more in the region of, well, aether . . ."

A hard glare.

Alexia hung her head and peeked at him through her eyelashes.

Lord Maccon steered his wife, as though she were an unwieldy rowboat, backward toward the bed and forced her to sit down upon it. Then he flopped down next to her.

"Start at the beginning."

"You mean the evening I woke up to find you had taken yourself off to Scotland without even speaking to me about it?"

Lord Maccon sighed. "It was a serious family matter."

"And what am I, a nodding acquaintance?"

Conall actually had the grace to look slightly shamefaced at that. "You must allow me some little time to get used to having a wife."

"You mean you did not acclimatize to it the last time you were wed?"

He frowned at her. "*That* was a long time ago."

"I certainly hope so."

"Before I changed. And it was a matter of duty. In those days, one simply didna turn werewolf without leaving an heir behind. I was to be laird; I could not possibly become supernatural without first ensuring the prosperity of the clan."

Alexia was not inclined to let him off lightly for keeping her in the dark on this matter, even if she perfectly understood his reasons. "I gathered as much by the fact that you seem to have produced a child. What I question is the fact that, for some reason, you elected not to tell me you still had living descendants."

Lord Maccon snorted, grabbing his wife's hand and caressing her wrist with his callused thumbs. "You met Sidheag. Would you want to claim her as a relation?"

Alexia sighed and leaned against his broad shoulder. "She seems like a fine, upstanding woman."

"What she is is an impossible grouch."

Lady Maccon smiled into her husband's shoulder. "Well, there can be no doubt as to which side of the family she gets that from." She switched tactics. "Are you going to tell me anything substantial about this previous family of yours? Who was your wife? How many children did you have? Am I likely to encounter any other Maccons of import scattered about?" She stood, continuing about her preparations for dinner, trying not to show how much she cared about his answers. This was one aspect of being married to an immortal she had not figured into her equation. Of course, she knew he had taken previous lovers; at two centuries, she would be concerned if he had not, and she had almost nightly reason to be grateful for his experience. But previous wives? This she had not considered.

He lay back on the bed, folding his arms behind his head, looking at her out of predatory eyes. There was no denying it—impossible man her husband, but also a terribly sexy beast.

"Are *you* going to tell me about falling off the dirigible?" he countered.

Alexia fastened earrings to her ears. "Are *you* going to tell *me* why you hightailed it off to Scotland without your valet, leaving me to deal with Major Channing at the supper table, Ivy hat shopping, and half of London still recovering from a severe bout of humanization? Not to mention the fact that I had to travel the length of England *all by myself.*"

They heard Miss Hisselpenny squealing in the hallway and then a chatter of other voices, Felicity perhaps, and Tunstell.

Lord Maccon, still lounging poetically upon the bed, sniffed.

"Very well, travel the length of England accompanied by Ivy and my sister, which is very possibly worse—and still your fault."

The earl rose, came over, and buttoned up the back of her dress. Alexia was only mildly disappointed. They were running late for dinner, and she was starving.

"Why are you here, wife?" he asked bluntly.

Lady Maccon leaned back, exasperated. They were getting nowhere with this conversation. "Conall, answer me this: have you been able to change since we arrived at Kingair?"

Lord Maccon frowned. "I had not thought to try."

She gave him an aggrieved look via the mirror, and he let go of her and stepped back. She watched him, his busy hands stilled. Nothing happened.

He shook his head and came back. "Not possible. It feels a little as though I am in contact with you and trying for my wolf form. Not difficult, or even elusive, simply unavailable. That part of me, the werewolf part, has vanished."

She turned to him. "I came because I am muhjah, and this changelessness is connected to the Kingair Pack. I saw you sneak away and talk to the Beta. None of this pack has been able to shift in months, have they? For how long exactly has this been going on? Since boarding the *Spanker* and traveling home? Or before? Where did they find the weapon? India? Egypt? Or is it a plague they have brought back? What happened to them overseas?"

Lord Maccon looked at his wife in the looking glass, his big hands on her shoulders. "They willna tell me. I am no longer Alpha here. They owe me no explanation."

"But you are BUR's chief sundowner."

"This is Scotland; BUR's authority is weak here. Besides, these people were my pack for generations. I may have no wish to lead them anymore, but I do not want to kill any of them either. They know that. I simply want to know what is happening here."

"You and I both, my love," replied his wife. "You don't mind if I wish to question your brethren on the matter?"

"I dinna see how you will make over any better than I." Conall was doubtful. "They do not know you are muhjah, and you'd be wise to keep it that way. Queen Victoria isna so loved in this part of the world."

"I'll be discreet." Her husband's eyebrows reached for the sky at that. "Very well, as discreet as possible for me."

"It canna hurt," he said, and then thought better of it. This was Alexia, after all. "So long as you refrain from using that parasol."

His lady wife grinned maliciously. "I shall be direct, but not that direct."

"Why do I doubt you? Well, watch out for Dubh; he can be difficult."

"Not up to Professor Lyall's caliber as a Beta, shall we say?"

"Um, that's not for me to say. Dubh was never my Beta, not even my Gamma."

That *was* interesting news. "But this Niall, the one who was killed in battle over seas, he wasn't your Beta either?"

"Na. Mine died," he replied shortly, in a tone of voice that said he did not want to discuss the matter further. "Your turn. This dirigible fall, wife?"

Alexia stood, finished with her ablutions. "Someone else is on the scent: a spy of some kind or some other agent, a member of the Hypocras Club, perhaps. While Madame Lefoux and I were strolling the observation deck, someone tried to push us over the side. I fell and Madame Lefoux fought off whomever it was. I managed to stay my fall and climbed to safety. It was nothing, really, except that I nearly lost the parasol. And I am no longer partial to dirigible travel."

"I should think not. Well, wife, try not to get yourself killed for at least a few days?"

"Are you going to tell me the real reason you came back to Scotland? Do not think you have thrown me off the scent so easily."

"I never doubted you, my sweet demure little Alexia."

Lady Maccon gave him her best, most fierce, battle-ax expression, and they went down to dinner.

CHAPTER NINE

In Which Meringues Are Annihilated

Lady Maccon wore a dinner gown of black with white pleated trim and white satin ribbon about the neck and sleeves. It would have cast her in a suitably subdued and dignified tone except that, due to the protracted argument with her husband, she had entirely forgotten to stuff her hair under a cap. Her dark tresses rioted about her head, only partially confined by the morning's updo, a heaven of frizz and feathering. Lord Maccon adored it. He thought she looked like some exotic gypsy and wondered if she might be amenable to donning gold earrings and dancing topless about their room in a loose red skirt. Everyone else was outraged—imagine the wife of an earl appearing at dinner with frizzy hair. Even in Scotland such things were simply not done.

The rest of the company was already at dinner when they arrived. Ivy had rejected the blue gown for a more excitable puce monstrosity, with multiple poufs of ruffles like so many taffeta puffballs, and a wide belt of bright crimson tied in an enormous bow above the bustle. Felicity had chosen an uncharacteristic white and pale green lace affair, which made her look deceptively demure.

Conversation was already in flow. Madame Lefoux was in deep consult with one of the Kingair clavigers, a bespectacled young man with high-arched eyebrows that gave him a perpetual expression of equal parts panic and curiosity. They appeared to be ruminating on the malfunction of the aethographor and formulating plans to investigate it after the meal.

Kingair's Beta, Gamma, and four other pack members all looked glum and uninterested in the world about them, but spoke comfortably enough to Ivy and Felicity on the inanities of life, such as the appalling Scottish weather and the appalling Scottish food. Both of which the ladies made a show of liking more than was the case and the gentlemen a show of liking less.

Lady Kingair was in a fine fettle, waxing sharp and grumpy at the head of the table. She paused in the act of waving austere hands at the footmen to glower at her distant grandfather and his new wife for their unpardonable tardiness.

Lord Maccon hesitated upon entering the room, as though unsure of where to sit. The last time he'd been in residence he would have sat at the foot of the table, a spot now ostentatiously vacant. As a guest in his old home, his precedence was unknown. An earl would sit in one chair, a family member in another, and a BUR representative in still another. There was a cast to his expression that said eating with his former pack at all was burden enough. What had they done, Alexia wondered, to earn his disgust and his neglect? Or was it something he had done?

Lady Kingair noticed the hesitation. "Canna choose?

Is that not just like you? May as well take Alpha position, Gramps, naught else for it."

The Kingair Beta paused in his discussion with Felicity (aye, Scotland was terribly green) and looked up at this.

"He's na Alpha here! Have you run mad?"

The woman stood. "Shut your meat trap, Dubh. Someone's gotta fight challengers, and you'd go belly-up to the first man capable of Anubis Form."

"I'm not a coward!"

"Tell that to Niall."

"I had his back. He missed the signs and the scent. Shoulda known they'd ambush."

Conversation deteriorated at that point. Even Madame Lefoux and Mr. Querulous Brows paused in their pursuit of scientific superiority as tension spread about the supper table. Miss Loontwill stopped flirting with Mr. Tunstell. Mr. Tunstell stopped glancing hopefully in Miss Hisselpenny's direction.

In a desperate bid to reestablish civilized talk and decorum, Miss Hisselpenny said, quite loudly, "I see they are bringing in the fish course. What a pleasant surprise. I do so love fish. Don't you Mr., uh, Dubh. It is so very, um, salty."

The Beta sat back down at that, bemused. Alexia sympathized. What could one say to such a statement? The gentleman, for he still was such despite a hot temper and lupine inclinations, replied to Ivy, as required by the standards of common decency, with a, "I, too, am mighty fond of fish, Miss Hisselpenny."

Some more daring scientific philosophers claimed that the manners of the modern age had partly developed in order to keep werewolves calm and well behaved in public. Essentially, the theory was that etiquette somehow turned high society into a kind of pack. Alexia had never given it much credence, but seeing Ivy, through the mere application of fish-riddled inanities, tame a man like that was quite remarkable. Perhaps there was something to the hypothesis after all.

"What is your very favorite kind?" persisted Miss Hisselpenny breathily. "The pink, the white, or the bigger sort of grayish fishes?"

Lady Maccon exchanged a look with her husband and tried not to laugh. She took her own seat on his left-hand side, and with that, the fish in question was served and dinner continued.

"I like fish," chirruped Tunstell.

Felicity drew his attention immediately back to herself. "Really, Mr. Tunstell? What is your preferred breed?"

"Well"—Tunstell hesitated—"you know, the um, ones that"—he made a swooping motion with both hands—"uh, swim."

"Wife," murmured the earl, "what is your sister up to?"

"She only wants Tunstell because Ivy does."

"Why should Miss Hisselpenny have any interest whatsoever in my actor-cum-valet?"

"Exactly!" replied his lady wife enthusiastically. "I am glad we are in agreement on this matter: a most unsuitable match."

"Women," said her still-perplexed husband, reaching over and serving himself a portion of fish—the white kind.

The conversation never did improve much after that.

Alexia was too far away from Madame Lefoux and her scientifically inclined dinner companion to engage in any intellectual conversation, much to her regret. Not that she could have contributed: they had moved on to magnetic aether transmogrification, which was far beyond her own cursory knowledge. Nevertheless, it verbally surpassed her end of the table. Her husband concentrated on eating as though he had not fed in several days, which he probably hadn't. Lady Kingair seemed incapable of multisyllabic sentences that were not crass or dictatorial in tone, and Ivy kept up a constant flow of fish-related commentary to a degree Alexia would never have countenanced had she been the intended target. The problem being, of course, that Miss Hisselpenny knew nothing on the subject of fish—a vital fact that seemed to have escaped her notice.

Finally, in desperation, Alexia grasped the conversational reins and inquired rather casually as to how the pack was enjoying its vacation from the werewolf curse.

Lord Maccon rolled his eyes heavenward. Hardly had he supposed even his indomitable wife would confront the pack so directly, en masse, and over dinner. He thought she would at least approach members individually. But then, subtlety never had been her style.

Lady Maccon's comment interrupted even Miss Hisselpenny's talk of fish. "Oh dear, have you become afflicted too?" said the young lady, glancing sympathetically around the table at the six werewolves present. "I had heard members of the supernatural set were, well, indisposed, last week. My aunt said that all the vampires took to their hives, and most of the drones were called in. She was supposed to see a concert, but it was canceled

due to the absence of a pianist belonging to the Westminster Hive. All of London was on its ear. Really, there
are not all that many of"—she paused, having talked
herself into a corner—"well, you know, the *supernatural persuasion* in London, but there certainly is a *fuss*
when they cannot leave their homes. Of course, we knew
werewolves must be affected, too, but Alexia never said
anything to me about it, did you, Alexia? Why, I even
saw you, just the next day, and you said not a word on the
subject. Was Woolsey unaffected?"

Lady Maccon did not bother to respond. Instead, she
turned sharp brown eyes upon the Kingair Pack sitting
about the table. Six large, guilty-looking Scotsman who
apparently had nothing to say for themselves.

The pack exchanged glances. Of course, they assumed
Lord Maccon would have told his wife they were unable
to change, but they did think it a tad injudicious of her,
not to say overly direct, to bring the subject up publicly
at supper.

Finally, the Gamma said awkwardly, "It has been an
interesting few months. Of course, Dubh and myself have
been supernatural long enough to safely experience daylight with few of the, uh, associated difficulties, at least
during new moon. But the others have rather enjoyed
their vacation."

"I've only been a werewolf for a few decades, but I
hadna realized how much I missed the sun," commented
one of the younger pack members, speaking for the first
time.

"Lachlan's been singing again—hard to be mad about
that."

"But now it's beginning to annoy," added a third. "The humanity, not the singing," he added hastily.

The first grinned. "Yeah, imagine, at first we missed the light; now we miss the curse. Once one is accustomed to being a wolf part of the time, it is hard to be denied it."

The Beta gave them all a warning look.

"Being mortal is so inconvenient," complained a third, ignoring the Beta.

"These days, even the tiniest of cuts take forever to heal. And one is so verra weak without that supernatural strength. I used to be able to lift the back end of a carriage; now, carrying in Miss Hisselpenny's hatboxes gave me heart palpitations."

Alexia snorted. "You should see the hats inside."

"I'd forgotten how to shave," continued the first with a little laugh.

Felicity gasped and Ivy blushed. Bringing up a gentleman's toilette at the table—imagine being so indiscreet!

"Cubs," barked Lady Kingair, "that is by far enough of that."

"Aye, my lady," bobbed the three gentlemen, who were all two or three times her age. They had probably seen her grow up.

The table fell silent.

"So, are you all *aging*?" Lady Maccon wanted to know. She was blunt, but then, that was part of her charm. The earl looked to his great-great-great-granddaughter. It must drive Sidheag batty that she could not order Alexia, a guest, to be silent.

No one answered Lady Maccon. But the pack's collective worried expression spoke volumes. They were back to being entirely human, or as human as creatures who had once partially died could get. *Mortal* was perhaps a better word for it. It meant they could finish dying now, just like any other daylight mundane. Of course, Lord Maccon was in the same situation.

Lady Maccon chewed a small bite of hare. "I commend you for not panicking. But I am curious—why not ask for medical assistance while in London? Or perhaps seek out BUR to make inquiries? You did come through London with the rest of the regiments."

The pack looked to Lord Maccon to rescue them from his wife. Lord Maccon's expression said it all: they were at her mercy, and he was enjoying witnessing the carnage. Still, she needn't have asked. She was perfectly well aware of the fact that most supernatural creatures mistrusted modern doctors, and this pack would hardly seek out the London BUR offices with Lord Maccon in charge. Of course, they would want to get out of London as quickly as possible, retreat to the safety of their home den, hiding their shame with tails between their legs—proverbially, of course, as this was no longer literally possible. No tails to be seen.

Much to the pack's relief, the next course arrived, veal and ham pie with a side of beet and cauliflower mash. Lady Maccon waved her fork about expressively and asked, "So, how did it happen? Did you eat some polluted curry or something while you were over in India?"

"You must excuse my wife," said Lord Maccon with a grin. "She is a bit of a gesticulator, all that Italian blood."

Awkward silence persisted.

"Are you all ill? My husband thinks you have a plague. Will you be infecting him in addition to yourselves?"

Lady Maccon turned to look pointedly at the earl sitting next to her. "I am not entirely sure how I would feel about that."

"Thank you for your concern, wife."

The Gamma (what had her husband called him? Oh yes, Lachlan) said jokingly, "Come off it, Conall. You canna expect sympathy from a curse-breaker, even if you did wed her."

"I heard of this phenomenon," piped up Madame Lefoux, turning her attention to their conversation. "It did not extend to my neighborhood, so I did not experience it firsthand; nevertheless, I am convinced there must be a logical scientific explanation."

"Scientists!" muttered Dubh. Two of his fellow pack members nodded in agreement.

"Why do you people keep calling Alexia a curse-breaker?" wondered Ivy.

"Precisely. Isn't she simply a curse?" said Felicity unhelpfully.

"Sister, you say the sweetest things," replied Lady Maccon.

Felicity gave her a dour look.

The pack Gamma seized this as an opportunity to change the subject. "Speaking of which, I was under the impression that Lady Maccon's former name was Tarabotti. But you are a Miss Loontwill."

"Oh"—Felicity smiled charmingly—"we have different fathers."

"Ah, I see." The Gamma frowned. "Oh, I *see*. *That* Tarabotti."

He looked at Alexia with newfound interest. "I should never have thought *he* would marry."

The Beta also looked at Lady Maccon curiously. "Indeed, and to produce offspring. Civic duty, I suppose."

"You knew my father?" Lady Maccon was suddenly intrigued, and, it must be admitted, distracted from her course of inquiry.

The two werewolves exchanged a look. "Not personally. We knew *of* him, of course. Quite the traveler."

Felicity said with a sniff, "Mama always said she could never remember why she leg-shackled herself to an Italian. She claimed it was a marriage of convenience, although I understand he was very good-looking. It did not last, of course. He died, just after Alexia was born. Such a terribly embarrassing thing to do, simply to up and die like that. Goes to show, Italians cannot be trusted. Mama was well rid of him. She married Papa shortly thereafter."

Lady Maccon turned to look hard at her husband. "Did *you* know my father too?" she asked him in a low voice to keep things private.

"Not as such."

"At some point, husband of mine, we must have a discussion, you and I, about the proper methods of fully transferring information. I am tired of feeling consistently behind the times."

"Except that, wife, I have two centuries on you. I can hardly tell you everything I have learned and about everyone I have met during all those years."

"Do not trouble me with such weak excuses," she hissed.

While they were arguing, the suppertime conversation moved on without them. Madame Lefoux began explaining that she felt the aethographic transmitter's crystalline valve resonator's magnetic conduction might be out of alignment. Compounded, of course, by the implausibility ratio of transference during inclement weather.

No one, except the bespectacled claviger, was able to follow a word of her explanation, but everyone was nodding sagely as though they did. Even Ivy, who had the look of a slightly panicked dormouse on her round face, pretended interest.

Tunstell solicitously passed Miss Hisselpenny the plate of potato fritters, but Ivy ignored him.

"Oh, thank you, Mr. Tunstell," said Felicity, reaching across to take one as though he had offered them to her.

Ivy huffed.

Tunstell, apparently frustrated by Miss Hisselpenny's continued rejection, turned in Miss Loontwill's direction, and began chatting with her about the recent influx of automated eyelash-curling implements imported from Portugal.

Ivy was more annoyed by this and turned away from the redhead to join in the werewolves' discussion on a possible hunting outing the next morning. Not that Miss Hisselpenny knew a whit about guns or hunting, but dearth of knowledge on a subject had never yet kept Ivy from waxing poetical upon it.

"I believe there is considerable range in the bang of most guns," she said sagely.

"Uh . . ." The gentlemen about her drifted in confusion.

Ah, Ivy, thought Alexia happily, *spreading a verbal fog wherever she goes.*

"Since we can go out during the day, we might as well take advantage and get a little dawn shooting in for old times' sake," said Dubh finally, ignoring Miss Hissel-penny's comment.

"Is Dubh his given name or surname?" Alexia asked her husband.

"Good question," he replied. "Hundred and fifty years I have had to put up with that blighter and he never told me the which way of it. I dinna know much about his past before Kingair. Came in as a loner, back in the early seventeen hundreds. Bit of a troublemaker."

"Ah, and you wouldn't know anything about secrecy or troublemaking, would you, husband?"

"Touché, wife."

The dinner drew to a close, and eventually the ladies left the gentlemen to their drinks.

Lady Maccon had never much supported the vampire-derived tradition of after-dinner gender segregation. After all, what had begun as an honor to the hive queen's superiority and need for privacy now felt like a belittling of the feminine ability to imbibe quality alcohol. Still, Alexia recognized the opportunity for what it was and made an effort to fraternize with Lady Kingair.

"You are fully human, yet you seem to act as female Alpha. How is that?" she asked, settling herself on the dusty settee and sipping a small sherry.

"They lack leadership, and I'm the only one left." The Scotswoman was blunt to the point of rudeness.

"Do you enjoy leading?" Alexia was genuinely curious.

"It'd work a mite better if I were a werewolf proper."

Lady Maccon was surprised. "Would you really be willing to try? It's such a grave risk for the gentler sex."

"Aye. But yon husband of yers didna care for my

wishes." Left unsaid was the fact that Conall's was the only opinion that mattered. Only an Alpha capable of Anubis Form could breed more werewolves. Alexia had never witnessed a metamorphosis, but she had read the scientific papers on the subject. Something about soul reclamation needing both forms at once.

"He thinks you would die in the attempt. And it would be at his hand. Well, at his teeth."

The woman sipped her own sherry and nodded. Suddenly she looked every bit of her forty years and then some.

"And I the last of his mortal line," said Sidheag Maccon.

"Oh." Alexia nodded. "I see. And he would have to give you the full bite. It is a heavy burden you ask of him, to end his last mortal holding. Is that why he left the pack?"

"You think I drove him out with my asking? You dinna ken the truth of it?"

"Obviously not."

"Then it isna my place to be telling you. You married the blighter; you should be asking him."

"You think I have not tried?"

"Cagey old cuss, my gramps, that's for pure certain. Tell me something, Lady Maccon, why *did* you cleave to him? 'Cause he's seated right proper in an earldom? 'Cause he heads up BUR and they watchdog your kind? What could one such as you gain from such a union?"

It was clear what the Lady of Kingair thought. She saw Alexia as nothing more than some kind of pariah who had married Lord Maccon out of either social or pecuniary avarice.

"You know," replied Lady Maccon, not playing into her trap, "I ask myself that question daily."

"It ain't natural, a blending like that."

Alexia looked over to ensure that the other ladies were out of earshot. Madame Lefoux and Ivy were engaged in complaining about long-distance travel in the mild manner of those who had thoroughly enjoyed the experience. Felicity stood on the far side of the room, looking out into the rainy night.

"Of course it is not natural. How could it be natural when neither of us are?" Lady Maccon sniffed.

"I canna make you out, curse-breaker," replied Sidheag.

"It is really very simple. I am just like you, only without a soul."

Lady Kingair leaned forward. Those familiar tawny eyes of hers were set in an equally familiar frown. "I was raised by the *pack,* child. 'Twas always intended I become Alpha female and lead them, whether he changed me or not. You merely married into the role."

"And in that you have the advantage over me. But then again, instead of adapting, I am simply retraining *my* pack to accept my ways."

A half-smile appeared on Sidheag's dour face. "I wager Major Channing is cracked over your presence."

Alexia laughed.

Just when Lady Maccon felt like she might be gaining ground with Lady Kingair, an enormous crash reverberated against the wall nearest the dining chamber.

The ladies all exchanged startled looks. Madame Lefoux and Lady Maccon immediately leaped to their feet and went swiftly back toward the supper room. Lady

Kingair was but a few steps behind, and all three burst through to find Lord Maccon and the Kingair Beta, Dubh, grappling fiercely on top of the massive table, rolling about among the remnants of what once had been a most excellent brandy and plate of sticky meringues. The other members of the pack, the Kingair clavigers in residence, and Tunstell had arranged themselves well out of the way and seemed to be viewing the fisticuffs in the manner of sportsmen at the races.

Tunstell was running a commentary. "Oh, nice uppercut from Lord Maccon there, and, oh, did Dubh *kick*? Bad form, terribly bad form."

Alexia paused, regarding the two large Scotsman rolling about among the sticky powder of crushed meringue.

"Lachlan, report!" barked Lady Kingair over the racket. "What's going on?"

The Gamma, who Alexia had thought of as rather sympathetic up until that point, shrugged. "It needs getting out right to the open, mistress. You know how we like to settle things."

The woman shook her head, gray-streaked plait flying back and forth. "We settle things by teeth and claw, na fist and flesh. This isna our way. This isna pack protocol!"

Lachlan shrugged again. "Having na teeth possible, this be the next best option. You canna stop it, mistress, challenge was issued. We all witnessed the wording of it."

The other pack members nodded gravely.

Dubh landed a good right punch to Lord Maccon's chin, sending him flying backward.

Lady Kingair stepped hastily to one side to avoid a silver platter as it skidded off the table toward her.

"Oh my goodness!" came Ivy's voice from the doorway. "I do believe they are actually skirmishing!"

Tunstell immediately sprang into action. "This is not a thing a lady should witness, Miss Hisselpenny," he exclaimed, rushing over and shepherding her out of the room.

"But . . ." came Ivy's voice.

Lady Maccon smiled proudly at the fact that the redhead hadn't considered her sensibilities. Madame Lefoux, noting that Felicity still stood watching with wide, interested eyes, gave Alexia a look and left the room, shutting the door behind her and sweeping Felicity in her wake.

Lord Maccon slammed into Dubh's stomach with his head, propelling the werewolf backward into the wall. The whole room shook at the impact.

Now, thought Alexia maliciously, *Kingair will have to remodel.*

"At least take the disagreement outside!" yelled Lady Kingair.

There was blood everywhere, as well as spilled brandy, broken glass, and crushed meringues.

"For goodness' sake," said Lady Maccon, exasperated, "don't they realize that as humans, they could seriously injure one another if they carry on like this? They do not have the supernatural strength to take those kinds of blows, nor the supernatural healing to recover from them."

Both men rolled to the side and fell off the tabletop with a loud thud.

Good Lord, thought Lady Maccon, noting that a good

deal of the blood seemed to be emerging from her husband's nose, *I do hope Conall has brought a spare cravat.*

She was not particularly worried, for she had little doubt in her husband's pugilistic skills. He boxed regularly at Whites, and he was *her* chosen mate. Of course, he would win the fight, but still, the disarray being generated was unacceptable. Things could not be allowed to continue much longer. Imagine, the poor Kingair staff, having to clean up such a mess.

With that thought, Lady Maccon whirled about and went purposefully to fetch her parasol.

She need not have bothered. By the time she returned, numbing darts loaded and parasol ready to fire, both men were slumped in opposite corners of the room. Dubh was clutching his head and coughing in sharp painful little gasps, and Lord Maccon was listing to one side, blood dribbling out of his nose and one eye nearly swollen shut.

"Well don't you two look a picture," Alexia said, resting her parasol against the wall and crouching down to examine Conall's face with gentle fingers. "Nothing a spot of vinegar won't put to rights." She turned to one of the clavigers. "Run and get me some cider vinegar, my good man." Lord Maccon looked at her over the top of his cravat, which he was now holding to his nose. Ah well, the cravat was ruined already.

"Didna ken you cared, wife," he grumbled, but leaned in against her gentle ministrations nevertheless.

So as not to seem too sympathetic, Alexia began vigorously brushing off the meringue crumbs covering his jacket.

At the same time, she looked over at the Kingair Beta

and said, "Settle the issue to your mutual satisfaction, did you, gentlemen?"

Dubh gave her a deadpan expression that still managed to indicate a certain profound level of deep disgust in her very existence, let alone her question. Alexia only shook her head at such petulance.

The Kingair claviger returned bearing a flask of cider vinegar. Lady Maccon immediately began to copiously douse her husband about the face and neck with it.

"Ouch! Steady on, that stings!"

Dubh made to rise.

Lord Maccon instantly struggled to his feet. He would have to, Alexia surmised, to maintain dominance. Or it could be that he was trying to get away from her vinegar-riddled attentions.

"I know it stings," she said. "Not nice to have to heal the old-fashioned way, now, is it, my brave table warrior? Perhaps you will pause to consider next time before you commence fighting in a confined space. I mean really, look at this room." She tutted. "You both should be thoroughly ashamed of yourselves."

"Nothing has been settled," Dubh said, returning hastily to his slumped position on the carpeted floor. He appeared to have gotten the worse end of things. One of his arms looked broken, and there was a nasty gash in his left cheek.

However, Lady Maccon's brisk application of vinegar seemed to have shattered everyone else's collective inertia, for they began bustling around the fallen Beta, splinting up his arm and tending to his wounds.

"You still abandoned us." Dubh sounded like a petulant child.

"You all know *exactly* why I left," Lord Maccon growled.

"Uh," said Alexia timidly, raising a questioning hand, "I do not."

Everyone ignored her.

"You couldna control the pack," Dubh accused.

Everyone present in the room gasped. Except Alexia, who did not comprehend the gravity of the insult and was occupied trying to pick the last of the meringue off her husband's dinner jacket.

"That isna fair," said Lachlan, not moving from his stance. Unsure of his allegiance, the Gamma simply stayed away from both Conall and Dubh.

"*You* betrayed *me*." Lord Maccon did not yell, but the words carried and, even though he could not change to wolf form, there was wolf anger in them.

"And you pay us back in kind? The emptiness you left, was that fair?"

"There is naught fair about pack protocol. You and I both know that; there is simply protocol. And there was none to cover what you did. It was entirely unprecedented. So I was cursed with the dubious pleasure of having to make it up myself. Abandonment seemed to be the best solution, since I didna want to spend another night in your presence."

Alexia looked over at Lachlan. The Gamma had tears in his eyes.

"Besides"—Lord Maccon's voice softened—"Niall was a perfectly good Alpha alternative. He led you well, I hear. He married my progeny. You were tame enough for decades under his dominance."

Lady Kingair finally spoke. Her voice was oddly soft.

"Niall was my mate, and I pure loved him. He was a brilliant tactician and a good soldier, but he wasna a true Alpha."

"Are you saying he wasna dominant enough? I heard naught of lack of discipline. Whenever I ran a recognizance on Kingair, you all seemed to be perfectly content." Conall's voice was soft.

"So you did check up on us, did you, old wolf?" Lady Kingair looked hurt at that rather than relieved.

"Of course I did. You *were* once my pack."

The Beta looked up from where he still lay on the floor. "You left us weak, Conall, and you knew it. Niall had na Anubis Form, and the pack couldna procreate. Clavigers abandoned us as a result, the local loners rebelled, and we didn't have an Alpha fighting for the integrity of the pack."

Lady Maccon glanced at her husband. His face was carved in stone, relentless. Or what little she could see behind the puffy eye and bloodstained cravat seemed that way.

"You betrayed me," he repeated, as though that settled the matter. Which, in Conall's world, it probably did. He valued few things more than loyalty.

Alexia decided to make her presence known. "What is the point of recriminations? Nothing can be done about it now, since none of you can change into any form at all, Anubis or otherwise. No new wolves can be made, no new Alpha found, no challenge battles fought. Why argue over what was when we are immersed in what isn't?"

Lord Maccon looked down at her. "So speaks my practical Alexia. Now do you understand why I married her?"

Lady Kingair said snidely, "A desperate, if ineffectual, attempt at control?"

"Oooh, she has claws. Are you positive you never bit

her to change, husband? She has the temper of a werewolf." Alexia could be just as snide as the next person.

The Gamma stepped forward, looking at Lady Maccon. "Our apologies, my lady, and you a newly arrived guest among us. We must truly seem the barbarians you English take us for. 'Tis only that na Alpha these many moons is making us nervous."

"Oh, and here I thought your behavior sprang from the whole not-being-able-to-change-shape quandary," she quipped back sharply.

He grinned. "Well, that too."

"Werewolves without pack leaders tend to get into trouble?" Lady Maccon wondered.

No one said anything.

"I don't suppose you are going to tell us what trouble you got into overseas?" Alexia tried to look as though she wasn't avidly interested, taking her husband's arm casually.

Silence.

"Well, I think we have all had enough excitement for one evening. Since you have been human these many months, I assume you are keeping daylight hours?"

A nod from Lady Kingair.

"In that case"—Lady Maccon straightened her dress—"Conall and I shall bid you good night."

"We shall?" Lord Maccon looked dubious.

"Good night," said his wife firmly to the pack and clavigers. Grabbing her parasol in one hand and her husband's arm in the other, she practically dragged the earl from the room.

Lord Maccon lumbered obediently after her.

The room they left behind was filled with half-thoughtful, half-amused faces.

"What are you about, wife?" Conall asked as soon as they were upstairs and out of everyone's earshot.

His wife plastered herself up against him and kissed him fiercely.

"Ouch," he said when they pulled apart, although he had participated with gusto. "Busted lip."

"Oh, look what you did to my dress!" Lady Maccon glared down at the blood now decorating the white satin trim.

Lord Maccon refrained from pointing out that she had initiated the kiss.

"You are an impossible man," continued his ladylove, swatting him on one of the few undamaged portions of his body. "You could have been killed in such a fight, do you realize?"

"Oh, phooey." Lord Maccon waved a dismissive hand in the air. "For a Beta, Dubh is not a verra good fighter even in wolf form. He is hardly likely to be any more capable as a human."

"He is *still* a trained soldier." She was not going to let this rest.

"Have you forgotten, wife, that so am I?"

"*You* are out of practice. Woolsey Pack Alpha has not been on campaign in years."

"Are you saying I'm getting old? I'll show you old." He swept her up like some exaggerated Latin lover and carried her into their bedchamber.

Angelique, who was engaged in some sort of tidying of the wardrobe, quickly made herself scarce.

"Stop trying to distract me," said Alexia several moments later. During which time her husband had managed to divest her of a good percentage of her clothing.

"Me, distract you? You are the one who dragged me off and up here right when things were getting interesting."

"They are not going to tell us what is going on no matter how hard we push," said Alexia, unbuttoning his shirt and hissing in concern at the array of harsh red marks destined to become rather spectacular bruises by the morning. "We are simply going to have to figure this out for ourselves."

He paused in kissing a little path along her collarbone and looked at her suspiciously. "You have a plan."

"Yes, I do, and the first part of it involves you telling me exactly what happened twenty years ago to make you leave. No." She stopped his wandering hand. "Stop that. And the second part involves you going to sleep. You are going to hurt in places your little supernatural soul forgot it could hurt in."

He flopped back on the pillows. There was no reasoning with his wife when she got like this. "And the third part of the plan?"

"That is for me to know and you not to know."

He let out a lusty sigh. "I hate it when you do that."

She waggled a finger at him as though he were a schoolboy. "Uh-uh, you just miscalculated, husband. I hold all the high cards right now."

He grinned. "Is that how this works?"

"You have been married before, remember? You should know."

He turned on his side toward her, wincing at the pain this caused. She lay back against the pillows, and he ran one large hand over her stomach and chest. "You are perfectly correct, of course; that is exactly how this works." Then he made his tawny eyes wide and batted his eyelashes at her, pleading. Alexia had learned that expression from Ivy and had employed it effectively on her husband during their, for lack of a better word, courtship. Little did she know how persuasively it could be applied in the opposite direction.

"Are you going to at least see me settled?" he murmured, nibbling her neck, his voice gravelly.

"I might be persuaded. You would, of course, have to be very very nice to me."

Conall agreed to be nice, in the best nonverbal way possible.

Afterward, he lay staring fixedly up at the ceiling and told her why he had left the Kingair Pack. He told her all of it, from what it was like for them, as both werewolves and Scotsmen, at the beginning of Queen Victoria's rule, to the assassination attempt on the queen planned by the then Kingair Beta, his old and trusted friend, without his knowledge.

He did not once look at her while he talked. Instead his eyes remained fixed on the stained and smudged molding of the ceiling above them.

"They were all in on it. Every last one of them—pack and clavigers. And not a one told me. Oh, not because I was all that loyal to the queen; surely you know packs and hives better than that by now. Our loyalty to a daylight ruler is never unreserved. No, they lied to me because I was loyal to the cause, always have been."

"What cause?" wondered his wife. She held his big hand in both of hers as she lay curled toward him, but otherwise she did not touch him.

"Acceptance. Can you imagine what would have happened if they had succeeded? A Scottish pack, attached to one of the best Highland regiments, multiple campaigns served in the British Army, killing Queen Victoria. It would have thrown over the whole government, but not only that, it would have taken us back to the Dark Ages. Those daylight conservatives who have always been against integration would call it a nationally supported supernatural plot, the church would regain its foothold on British soil, and we would be back to the Inquisition quicker than you could shake a tail."

"Husband"—Alexia was mildly startled, but only because she'd never given Conall's political views much consideration—"you are a progressive!"

"Damn straight! I couldna believe *my pack* would put all werewolves into such a position. And for what? Old resentments and Scottish pride? A weak alliance with Irish dissidents? And the worst of it was, not a one had told me of the plot. Not even Lachlan."

"Then how did you find out about it in the end?"

He huffed in disgust. "I caught them mixing the poison. Poison, mind you! Poison has no place on pack grounds or in pack business. It isna an honest way to kill anyone, let alone a monarch."

Alexia suppressed a smile. This would appear to be the aspect of the conspiracy that upset him the most.

"We werewolves are not known for our subtlety. I had realized they were plotting something for weeks. When I found the poison, I forced a confession out of Lachlan."

"And you ended up having to fight and kill your own Beta over it. Then what, you simply took off for London, leaving them without leadership?"

He finally turned and looked at her, propping himself on his elbow. Seeing no judgment or accusation in her eyes, he relaxed slightly. "There is no pack protocol to cover this kind of situation. A large-scale betrayal of an Alpha with no qualified reason or ready replacement. Led by my own Beta." His eyes were agonized. "My *Beta*! They deserved to be without metamorphosis. I could have killed them all, and not a one would have objected, least of all the dewan, save that they were not plotting against me; they were plotting against a daylight queen."

He looked to her and his eyes were sad.

She tried to distill the story down into one manageable chunk. "So your leaving was a point of pride, honor, and politics?"

"Essentially."

"I suppose it could have been worse." She smoothed away the frown creasing his forehead.

"They could have succeeded."

"You realize, as muhjah, I am forced to ask: will they try again, do you think? After two decades? Could that explain the mysterious weapon?"

"Werewolves have long memories."

"In the interest of Queen Victoria's safety, is there a way for us to provide a surety against this?"

He sighed softly. "I dinna know."

"And that's why you came back? If it's true, you'll have to kill them all, won't you, sundowner?"

He turned away from her words, his broad back stiff, but he did not deny them.

CHAPTER TEN

Aether Transmissions

Using the information Lord Akeldama had provided, and with the assistance of a personable young man the vampire referred to only as Biffy, Professor Lyall set up an operation. "Ambrose has been meeting with various members of the incoming regiments," Lord Akeldama had informed him over an aged scotch—a warm fire in the grate and a plump calico cat on his knee. "At first I thought it was *simply* opiates or some other form of illegal trade, but now I believe it to be something more sinister. The hive is not only employing its vampire contacts—it's approaching any common soldier. Even the ill-dressed. It's *horrible*." The vampire gave a delicate little shudder. "I cannot discern what it is they are buying up so greedily. You want to find out what Westminster is up to? Tap into those werewolf military connections of yours, *darling,* and set up an offer. Biffy can take you to the preferred venue."

And so it was, on the information provided by a rove vampire, that Professor Lyall now sat in a very seedy pub, the Pickled Crumpet, accompanied by a spectacularly well-dressed drone and Major Channing. A few wobbly tables away sat one of Major Channing's most trusted soldiers, clutching several suspicious packages and looking nervous.

Professor Lyall slouched down and nursed his beer. He hated beer, a vile common beverage.

Major Channing was twitchy. He shifted long legs, jostling the table and sloshing their drinks.

"Stop that," his Beta instructed. "No one's come yet. Be patient."

Major Channing only glared at him.

Biffy offered them a pinch of snuff. Both werewolves declined in thinly veiled horror. Imagine mucking about with one's sense of smell! Such a vampiric kind of affectation.

Some while later, with Professor Lyall's beer barely touched but Major Channing on his third pint, the vampire entered the pub.

He was a tall, exceedingly comely individual, who looked exactly as a novelist might describe a vampire—sinister and pensive with an aquiline nose and unfathomable eyes. Professor Lyall sipped his beer in salute. He had to give Lord Ambrose tribute—the man put on an excellent show. Top marks for dramatic flair.

Lord Ambrose made his way straight to the soldier's table and sat down without introduction. The tavern was loud enough to make an auditory disruptor unnecessary, and even Lyall and Channing with their supernatural hearing caught only about one word in ten.

The exchange moved quite rapidly and culminated in the soldier showing Lord Ambrose his collection of goods. The vampire looked each one over, then shook his head violently and stood to leave.

The soldier stood as well, leaning forward to ask a question.

Lord Ambrose clearly took offense, for he lashed out with supernatural speed, striking the man across the face so fast even a soldier's reflexes stood him in poor stead.

Major Channing immediately jumped to his feet, his chair crashing back as he surged forward. Professor Lyall grabbed his wrist, halting his protective instinct. Channing all too often thought of his soldiers as pack.

The vampire's head swiveled around, focusing in on their little band. He hissed through his teeth, the tips of both fangs visible over thin lips. Then with a swirl of long burgundy greatcoat, he swept majestically from the inn.

Professor Lyall, who had never done anything majestically in all his life, faintly envied the man.

The young soldier came over to them, a harsh red welt about the side of his mouth.

"I'll murder the liverless bastard," swore Major Channing, making as if to follow Lord Ambrose out into the street.

"Stop." Professor Lyall's hand tightened on the Gamma's arm. "Burt here is perfectly fine. Aren't you, Burt?"

Burt spat out a bit of blood but nodded. "Dealt with worse at sea."

Biffy picked his snuffbox off the table and tucked it into a coat pocket. "So"—the young man gestured for the soldier to pull up a chair and join them—"what did he say? What are they looking for?"

"It's the weirdest thing. Artifacts."

"What?"

The soldier bit his bottom lip. "Yeah, *Egyptian* artifacts. But not objects as we might have thought. Not a weapon as such. That's why he was so angry with my offerings. Thems is looking for scrolls. Scrolls with a certain image on 'em."

"Hieroglyphic?"

Burt nodded.

"What image, did he say?"

"Seems they're quite desperate, 'cause it was pretty indiscreet of him to tell me, but, yeah, he said. Something called an ankh, only they want it broken. You know, in the picture, like the symbol was cut in half."

Professor Lyall and Biffy looked at one another. "Interesting," they both said at the same time.

"I wager the edict keepers have some kind of record of the symbol." Biffy, of course, had some knowledge of vampire information sources.

"Which means," Lyall said thoughtfully, "this has happened before."

Alexia left her husband soundly asleep. After centuries as an immortal, he had forgotten how a mortal body seeks succor in slumber when it has injuries to deal with. Despite the excitement, the night was young and most of the rest of the castle was still awake.

She nearly ran full tilt into a rapidly scuttling Ivy in the hallway. Miss Hisselpenny had a fierce frown decorating her normally amiable face.

"Good Lord, Ivy, what an expression." Lady Maccon leaned casually on her parasol. The way things were progressing this evening, she was unwilling to part with the accessory.

"Oh, Alexia. I do not mean to be forward, but I really must venture: I simply loathe Mr. Tunstell."

"Ivy!"

"Well, I mean to say, well, really! He is so very impossible. I was given to understand that his affection for me was secure. And one little objection and he switches allegiance quite flippantly. One might even call him flighty! To bill and coo around another female so soon after I went to such prodigious lengths to break his heart. It gives him the countenance of a, well, a vacillating butterfly!"

Lady Maccon was arrested trying to imagine a cooing butterfly. "Really, I thought you were still quite enamored of him, despite rejecting his suit."

"How *could* you think such a thing? I positively detest him. I am in full agreement with myself on this. He is nothing more than a billing-cooing *vacillator*! And I shall have nothing more to do with a person of such weakened character."

Lady Maccon was not quite certain how to converse with Miss Hisselpenny when she was in such a mood. She was accustomed to Ivy-overset and Ivy-chatterbox, but Ivy-full-of-wrath was a new creature altogether. She opted for the fallback position. "You are clearly in need of a fortifying cup of tea, my dear. Shall we go and see if we can hunt one down? Even the Scots must stock some form of libation."

Miss Hisselpenny took a deep breath. "Yes, I think you may be right. Excellent notion."

Lady Maccon solicitously shepherded her friend down

the stairs and into one of the smaller drawing rooms, where they ran into two clavigers. The young gentlemen were more than eager to hunt down the requisite tea, see to Miss Hisselpenny's every whim, and generally prove to the ladies that all good manners had not fled the Highlands along with its complement of trousers. As a result, Ivy forgave them their kilts. Lady Maccon left her friend to their stimulating accents and tender care and went in search of Madame Lefoux and the broken aethographor, hoping for a peek at its functional component parts.

It took her some time to track the massive machine down. Castle Kingair was a real castle, with none of Woolsey's practical notions on conservation of space and gridlike layout. It was very large, with a propensity for confusing itself with additional rooms, towers, and gratuitous staircases. Lady Maccon was logical in her approach (which may have been her mistake). She surmised that the aethographor must be located in one of the many castle turrets, but *which one* proved to be the difficulty. There was a decided overabundance of towers. Very concerned with defensibility, the Scots. It took a good deal of time to climb the winding steps to each turret. She knew she was in the right area, however, when she heard the cursing. In French, of course, and not words that she was familiar with, naturally, but she was in no doubt as to their profane nature. Madame Lefoux appeared to be experiencing some form of inconvenience.

When she finally attained the room, Alexia came face-to-face, or as is were, face-to-bottom, with yet another good reason for the lady inventor to don trousers. Madame Lefoux was on her back, half underneath the apparatus, only her legs and backside visible. Had she been in skirts, it would have been a most indelicate position.

Kingair's aethographic transmitter was raised up on little legs above the stone floor of the castle. It looked somewhat like two attached privy houses with footstool feet. Everything was brightly lit with gas lamps, as the pack had clearly spared no expense on this room. It was also clean.

Lady Maccon craned her neck to see into the darkened interior of the chamber that Madame Lefoux worked under. It appeared that the transmitting mechanicals were the ones being problematical. The Frenchwoman had with her a hatbox that appeared to be no hatbox at all but a cleverly disguised toolkit. Lady Maccon instantly coveted one herself—so much less *obvious* than a dispatch case.

The bespectacled claviger, with the ever-present expression of panic, crouched nearby, passing the inventor, one after another, a string of exciting-looking tools.

"The magnetomotor modulating adjustor, if you please," Madame Lefoux would say, and a long, sticklike object with a corkscrew of copper at one end and a glass tube full of an illuminated liquid at the other was passed over. Shortly after, there would emit another curse, the tool would be passed back to the claviger, and a new one called for.

"Goodness gracious," exclaimed Alexia. "What *are* you doing?"

There came the sound of a thump, Madame Lefoux's legs jerked, and further cursing ensued. Moments later, the Frenchwoman wormed her way out and stood up, rubbing her head. The action only added to a vast collection of grease smudges covering her pretty face.

"Ah, Lady Maccon, how lovely. I did wonder when you would track us down."

"I was unavoidably delayed by husbands and Ivys," explained Alexia.

"These things, regrettably, are bound to occur when one is married and befriended." Madame Lefoux was sympathetic.

Lady Maccon leaned forward and, using her parasol as a prop, tried to see underneath the contraption. Her corset made this action mostly impossible, so she turned back to the Frenchwoman. "Have you determined the nature of the problem?"

"Well, it is definitely the transmitting chamber that is malfunctioning. The receiving room seems fully operational. It is hard to tell without an actual transmission of some kind."

Alexia looked to the claviger for confirmation, and the young man nodded. He did not appear to have much to say for himself, but he was eager to help. The best kind of person, felt Alexia.

"Well," said Lady Maccon, "what time is it?"

The young gentleman took out a small pocket watch and flipped it open. "Half past ten."

Lady Maccon turned to Madame Lefoux. "If you can get it ready by eleven, we can try to raise Lord Akeldama on his aethographor. Remember, he gave me the codes, a valve frequensor, *and* an eleven o'clock time slot for open-scan transmission."

"But if he doesna have our resonance, what good is that? He willna be able to receive." The claviger snapped his watch closed and stashed it once more in his waist-coat pocket.

"Ah," Madame Lefoux jumped in, "he has a multi-adaptive model that does not operate using crystalline compatibility protocol. All he need do is scan for a transmission to his frequency during the allotted time. We can receive back because Lady Maccon *does* have the appropriate valve component."

The claviger looked even more surprised than usual.

"I understand they are dear friends." Madame Lefoux appeared to feel this would explain everything.

Alexia smiled. "On the evening of my wedding, I held his hand so he could watch the sunset."

The claviger looked confused. Again, more confused than usual (his was a difficult face for expressing the full range of human emotion).

Madame Lefoux explained, "Lord Akeldama is a vampire."

The young man gasped. "He trusted you with his life?"

Lady Maccon nodded. "So trusting me with a crystalline valve, however technologically vital, is no very great thing by comparison."

Madame Lefoux shrugged. "I do not know about that, my lady. I mean to say, one's life is one thing; one's technology is an entirely different matter."

"Nevertheless, I can provide you the means to test this aethographor's effectiveness, once it has been repaired."

The claviger gave her a look of burgeoning respect. "Efficient female, aren't you, Lady Maccon?"

Alexia was not certain whether she should be pleased or offended by the statement, so she chose to ignore it.

"So, I had better get to it, hadn't I?" Madame Lefoux turned and crawled back under the transmitter, returning to her tinkering.

Muffled words emanated a few moments later.

"What was that?"

Madame Lefoux's head reappeared. "I said, would you like to inscribe a message to Lord Akeldama while you are waiting?"

"Superb idea." Lady Maccon turned to the claviger. "Would you mind finding me a blank scroll, a stylus, and some acid?"

The young man jumped to oblige. While she waited for the supplies, Alexia poked about looking for the pack's valve frequensor library. Who did Kingair communicate with? Why had they bothered to invest in the aethographor at all? She found the crystalline valves in a small set of unlocked drawers off to one side. There were only three, but they were all entirely unlabeled and without any other identification.

"What are you doing, Lady Maccon?" The claviger came up behind her, looking suspicious (an expression entirely unsuited to his face).

"Just pondering why a Scottish pack would need an aethographor," replied Alexia. She was never one to dissemble when forthrightness could keep others off guard.

"Mmm," the young man replied, noncommittal. He handed her a metal scroll, a small vial of acid, and a stylus.

Lady Maccon set herself up in one corner of the room, tongue sticking out slightly as she attempted to be as neat as possible inscribing one letter into each grid square on the scroll. Her penmanship had never won her any school awards, and she wanted to make it as clear as possible.

The message read, "Testing Scots. Please reply."

She removed Lord Akeldama's crystalline valve from the secret pocket of her parasol, carefully using her copious skirts to shroud her movements so the claviger could not see where it was hidden.

Madame Lefoux was still puttering, so Lady Maccon entertained herself by exploring the receiving room, the part of the aethographor on which Madame Lefoux was not working. She tested her own memory on the parts. They were, in general, larger and less streamlined than on Lord Akeldama's transmitter, but they were in the same place: filter to eliminate ambient noise, dial for amplifying incoming signals, and two pieces of glass with black particulate between.

Madame Lefoux surprised Alexia with a gentle touch on her arm.

"We are almost ready. It is five minutes until eleven. Shall we set the machine to transmit?"

"Will I be allowed to watch?"

"Of course."

The three of them crammed into the tiny transmitting room, which, like the receiving room, was packed with machinery that looked like Lord Akeldama's—except that the gadgetry was more tangled, something Alexia had not thought possible, and the dials and switches were more numerous.

Madame Lefoux smoothed out and slotted Alexia's metal scroll into the special frame. Alexia placed Lord Akeldama's valve into the resonator cradle. After confirming the time, Madame Lefoux pulled down on a large knob-ended switch and engaged the aetheric convector, activating the chemical wash. The etched letters began to phosphoresce. The two small hydrodine engines spun to life, generating opposing aetheroelectric impulses, and the two needles raced across the slate. Sparking brightly whenever they were exposed to one another through the letters, transmission commenced. Alexia worried about the rain causing delay, but she had faith that Lord Akeldama's improved technology was capable of greater sensitivity and could cut though climatic interference.

"Testing . . . Scots . . . please . . . reply" sped invisibly outward.

And leagues to the south, at the top of a posh town house, a well-trained vampire drone, dressed like a candied orange peel, who looked as though his gravest concern was whether winter cravats permitted paisley or not, sat up straight and began recording an incoming transmission. The source was unknown, but he had been told to sweep on broad receiving at eleven o'clock for several nights straight. He took down the message and then noted the transmission coordination frequency and the time before dashing off to find his master.

"It is hard to know for certain, but I believe everything went smoothly." Madame Lefoux switched off the transmitter, the little hydrodine engines spinning quietly down. "Of course, we will not know if communication has been established until we receive an answering transmission."

The claviger said, "Your contact will have to determine the correct frequency from the incoming message so that he can dial it in from his end, without a companion valve frequensor. How long will such an endeavor take?"

"No way to know," replied the Frenchwoman. "Could be quite rapid. We had best go turn the receiving room on."

So they let themselves into the other chamber and lit the silent little steam engine located under the instrument board. Then came a long quarter of an hour simply sitting, as quietly as possible, waiting.

"I think we will give it just a few more minutes," Madame Lefoux whispered. Even her whisper caused the magnetic resonator coils to shake slightly.

The claviger frowned at her and went to retune the ambient noise filtration component.

Then, with no warning at all, Lord Akeldama's message slowly began to appear between the two pieces of glass on the receiver. The small hydraulic arm with its mounted magnet began painstakingly moving back and forth, shifting the magnetic particulate one letter at a time.

The claviger, whose name Alexia still did not know, began carefully and quietly copying down the incoming letters on a soft piece of washed canvas using a stylographic pen. Lady Maccon and Madame Lefoux held their collective breaths and tried not to move. Silence was vital. After each letter was complete, the arm reset itself and the glass shook softly, erasing the previous letter and preparing for the next.

Eventually, the arm stopped moving. They waited a few more minutes, and when Alexia went to speak, the claviger held up his hand autocratically. Only when he had switched everything off did he nod, allowing them to talk. Lady Maccon realized why he had charge of the aethographor. The Scots were a silent, dour lot, but he seemed to have the least to say of any of them.

"Well? Read out the message," she demanded.

He cleared his throat and, blushing slightly, read out, " 'Got you. Scots taste good?' "

Lady Maccon laughed. Lord Akeldama must have misread her message. Instead of "testing Scots," he had read "tasting Scots." "Regardless of the reply, we know that this transmitter is working. And I can gossip with Lord Akeldama."

The claviger looked offended. "An aethographor isna intended for *gossip,* Lady Maccon!"

"Tell that to Lord Akeldama."

Madame Lefoux's dimples appeared.

"Could we send him one more message to be certain as to the efficaciousness of the transmitting room?" Lady Maccon asked hopefully.

The claviger sighed. He was reluctant to agree but was apparently also unwilling to resist the request of a guest. He wandered off and returned with another metal scroll.

Alexia inscribed, "Spy here?"

From what she could recall, Lord Akeldama's newer model had the ability to overhear other transmissions, if it knew where to look.

Minutes later in the other room, the reply came. "Not mine. Probably chatty bats."

While the other two looked confused, Alexia only nodded. Lord Akeldama thought that any spy would belong to the vampires. Knowing her friend, he would now take it upon himself to start monitoring the Westminster Hive and nearby roves. She could just imagine him rubbing pink-gloved hands together, thrilled with the challenge. With a smile, she removed Lord Akeldama's valve and, when the claviger was not looking, stashed it back in her trusty parasol.

Lady Maccon was exhausted by the time she sought her bed. It was not a small bed by any means, yet her husband seemed to be occupying the entirety of it. He was sprawled, snoring softly, wrapped every which way in a ragged and much-abused (clearly throughout its long and not very successful life) coverlet.

Alexia climbed in and applied a tried-and-true technique she had developed over the last few months. She braced herself against the headboard and used her legs to push him as much to one side as possible, clearing sufficient space for her to worm her way down before he took to sprawling once more. She supposed he had spent decades, even centuries, sleeping alone; it would take some time to retrain him. In the meantime, she was developing some decent thigh muscles from her nightly ritual. The earl was no lightweight.

Conall growled at her slightly but seemed pleased enough to find her next to him once she snuggled against his side. He rolled toward her, nuzzled the back of her neck, and wrapped a heavy arm about her waist.

She tugged hard at the coverlet, which would not budge, and settled for arranging the earl's arm about her instead of the blanket. As a supernatural creature, Conall was supposed to be cold most of the time, but Alexia never felt it. Whenever she touched him, he was mortal, and his mortal body seemed to run at temperatures something akin to a high-end steam boiler. It was nice to be able to sleep touching him for once, with no worries she might cause him to age.

And on that note, Lady Maccon drifted off.

She awoke still warm. But her husband's affection, or possibly his hidden murderous tendencies, had shoved her so far toward the edge of the bed that she was partly suspended in midair. Without his arm about her waist, she would most certainly have tumbled off the side. Her nightgown was, of course, gone. How did he always manage to do that? The nuzzling at the back of her neck had turned into nibbles.

She cracked an eyelid: it was just about dawn, or the gray and depressing Highland winter version of dawn. Kingair heralded the day with a sad, reluctant spit of light, which in no way encouraged one to spring swiftly from the bed and trip lightly the morning dew. Not that Alexia was any kind of springer or tripper first thing on normal occasions.

Conall's nibbles turned into slightly more insistent bites. He was fond of a bite here or there. Sometimes Alexia was given to wonder if, had she not been a preternatural, he would not have actually eaten a chunk of her once in a while. There was something in the way his eyes came over yellow and hungry when he was in an amorous mood. She had ceased fighting the fact that she loved Conall, but that did not stop her from being practical about his requirements. Baser instincts were baser instincts, after all, and, her touch aside, he was still a werewolf. On occasions like this, she had reason to be glad her own powers kept his teeth nice and square. Although, of course, the way things stood in Kingair, had she been in full possession of a soul, she still would not have had to worry.

He turned his attention to her ear.

"Stop that. Angelique will be in presently to see me dressed."

"Bother her."

"For goodness' sake, Conall. Think of her delicate sensibilities."

"Your maid is a prude," was her husband's grumbled reply. He did not leave off his romantic attentions. Instead he moved his arm to better facilitate his notion of acceptable morning activities. Unfortunately, he neglected to realize his arm was all that was holding his wife in the bed.

With an undignified squawk, Alexia tumbled to the floor.

"Good Lord, woman, what'd you do *that* for?" her husband asked in profound confusion.

Lady Maccon checked to see that everything was unbroken and then stood, angrier than a hornet. She was just about to sting her husband into oblivion with the sharper side of her already-sharp tongue when she remembered that she was naked. At that same moment, she came to the sudden realization of exactly how cold a stone castle could get during a Highland winter. Cursing her husband a blue streak, she jerked the covers off of him and launched herself at him, burrowing into his warmth.

Seeing how this put her naked body plastered on top of him, Lord Maccon had no objection. Except that his wife was still annoyed and was now wide awake and twitchy, and he was aching something awful from his fight the night before.

"I am going to find out what is going on with this pack of yours today if it is the last thing I do," she said, swatting at his hands when they attempted to make interesting forays. "The longer I spend lazing about in bed, the less time I have to investigate."

"I wasna planning on being lazy," came the growl.

Lady Maccon decided that, in the interest of economy, she would have to face the cold, or her husband would carry on about this for hours. When he took it into his head to do a thing, he liked to see it done properly.

"It will have to wait until this evening," she said, extracting herself from his embrace. In a swift movement, she rolled off of him to one side, spinning the coverlet around herself. She part rolled, part hopped off the edge of the bed to her feet and shuffled across the floor toward her pelisse. This left her poor husband naked on the bed behind her. He was less disturbed by the cold, for he simply propped himself up on a pillow, folded his hands behind his head, and watched her out of heavy-lidded eyes.

Which was the scene poor Angelique came in upon— her mistress wrapped in a blanket like a large upended sausage roll, and her master sprawled naked for all the world to see. The maid had been living among werewolves, and in the presence of Lord and Lady Maccon, long enough not to have this bother her overmuch. She squeaked, winced, averted her eyes, and carried the basin of washing water over to the little stand provided.

Lady Maccon hid a smile. Poor Angelique. To come from the world of hives into the chaos that was pack life must be disconcerting. After all, no one was more civilized than the vampires, and no one less civilized than werewolves. Alexia wondered if vampires ever even made it to bed sport; they were so busy being polite to one another. At least the werewolves lived large: loud and messy, but also large.

She thanked the maid and took pity on her, sending her off to find tea. Then she quickly dropped the blanket to wash.

Conall lumbered off the bed and came over to see if he could "help" with her ablutions. His assistance caused some giggling, and a lot of splashing, and a certain degree of wetness that was not necessarily water related. But she did manage to be safely enshrouded in her pelisse and to see him shoved off into his dressing chamber and under the tender ministrations of Tunstell's waistcoat choices before Angelique reappeared.

She sipped tea while the maid picked out a perfectly serviceable tweed day dress and underthings. She pulled these on in an apologetic silence, with not even a token complaint, figuring they had already put the poor woman's finer feelings through the wringer that morning.

She huffed a little as the corset went on. Angelique was merciless. Soon enough Alexia was seated, docile and dressed, while the Frenchwoman did her hair.

Angelique asked, "So, ze machine, iz it fixed?"

Alexia gave her a suspicious look through the mirror. "Yes, we believe so. But I wouldn't be too excited; Madame Lefoux shows no inclination to depart anytime soon."

Angelique made no reply.

Alexia was positively aquiver with the need to know the history between the two women but resigned herself to the fact that French caginess beat out British stubbornness, in this at least. So she sat in silence while the maid finished her work.

"Tell him this is good enough," came her husband's roar.

Lady Maccon stood and turned around.

Conall came striding in, trailed by the long-suffering Tunstell.

Lady Maccon looked at her husband with a critical eye.

"Your shirt is untucked, your cravat has no finish, and your collar is bent at one side." She stood and began fussing with his rumpled clothing.

"I dinna ken why I bother; you always side with him." Conall submitted to her ministrations with ill grace.

"Did you know your accent has gotten stronger since we arrived in Scotland?"

That got her a dour look. Lady Maccon rolled her eyes at Tunstell over Conall's shoulder and gestured with her head that he could leave.

"*We* didna arrive in Scotland. *I* arrived; *you* followed." He ran a finger under his high collar.

"Stop that—you'll dirty the white."

"Have I mentioned recently how loathsome I find the current fashions?"

"Take it up with the vampires; they set the trends."

"Hence the high collars," he grumbled. "I and mine, however, have no need to hide our necks."

"No," quipped his wife, "simply your personalities." She stepped back, brushing down the shawl collar of his waistcoat. "There. Very handsome."

Her large supernatural husband looked shy at that. "You think so?"

"Stop fishing for compliments and go get your jacket. I am positively starving."

He pulled her against him and administered a long, deep, and distracting kiss. "You are always hungry, wife."

"Mmm." She could not take umbrage with a true statement. "So are you. Simply for different things."

They were only slightly late for breakfast.

Most of the rest of the house was not yet up. Lady Kingair was there—Alexia wondered if the woman slept—and two clavigers, but none of the Kingair Pack. Of course, Ivy and Felicity were still abed. They kept London hours, even in the country, and could not be expected to appear until midmorning. Tunstell, Lady Maccon suspected, would find things to occupy himself until the ladies came down.

The castle put on a decent breakfast, for the middle of nowhere. There were cold cuts of pork, venison, and woodcock; potted shrimp; fried wild mushrooms; sliced pears; boiled eggs and toast; as well as a nice collection of fruit preserves. Lady Maccon helped herself, then settled down to tuck in.

Lady Kingair, who was eating a bowl of unseasoned porridge and a piece of plain toast, gave Alexia's loaded plate a telling look. Alexia, who had never let the opinions of others sway her overmuch, especially where food was concerned, merely chewed loudly and with appreciative gusto.

Her husband shook his head at her antics, but as he himself sported a plate piled nearly twice as high as his wife's, he could not cast aspersions.

"If you are back to being human," Lady Maccon said after a pause, "you will get rotund eating like that."

"I shall have to take up some sort of abrasively atrocious athletic sport."

"You could go in for the hunt," suggested Alexia. "Tallyho and view halloo."

Werewolves, as a general rule, were not big on riding. Precious few horses were willing to carry a wolf on their back, even if he did look temporarily human. Driving a team was about as close as most werewolves could get. Since they could run faster in wolf form than a horse anyway, this fact did not tend to trouble the packs much. Except, of course, those men who had enjoyed riding before their metamorphosis.

Lord Maccon was not one of those men. "Foxhunting? I should think not," he said, gnawing on a bit of pork. "Foxes are practically cousins; wouldna sit well with the family, if you take my meaning."

"Oh, but how dashing you would look in shiny boots and one of those flashy red jackets."

"I was contemplating boxing or possibly lawn tennis."

Lady Maccon stifled a giggle by stuffing her face with a forkful of mushroom. The very idea of *her* husband prancing around all in white with a little netted baton in his hand. She swallowed. "Those sound like lovely ideas, dear," she said, deadpan, eyes bright and dancing. "Have you considered golf? Highly suited to your heritage and sense of style."

Conall glared at her, but there was a bit of a smile playing about his lips. "Now, now, wife, there's no cause for blatant insult."

Alexia was not certain whether she was insulting him

by suggesting golf or insulting golf by suggesting he was its ideal participant.

Lady Kingair watched this byplay with both fascination and repugnance. "Goodness, I had heard it said that yours was a love match, but I couldna countenance it."

Lady Maccon huffed. "Why else would any woman marry him?"

"Or her," agreed Lord Maccon.

Something caught Alexia's attention out of the corner of one eye. Something small and moving near the door to the room. Taken with curiosity, she stood, arresting the table conversation, and went to investigate.

Upon closer examination, she squealed in a most un-Alexia-like manner and jumped away in horror. Lord Maccon leaped to her rescue.

Lady Maccon looked at her great-great-whatever-daughter-in-law. "Cockroaches!" she accused, horrified out of any politeness that dictated she not mention the filthiness of the abode. "Why does your castle have *cockroaches*?"

Lord Maccon, with great presence of mind, removed his shoe and went to crush the offending insect. He paused, examined it for a split second, and then squished it flat.

Lady Kingair turned to one of the clavigers. "How did that get in here?"

"Canna keep them confined, my lady. They seem to be breeding, they do."

"Then summon an exterminator."

The young man glanced furtively in Lord and Lady Maccon's direction. "Would he ken how to deal with"—a pause—"this particular type?"

"Only one way to find out. Hie yourself into town immediately."

"Very good, madam."

Alexia returned to the dining table, but her appetite had deserted her. She made to rise shortly thereafter.

Lord Maccon inhaled a few last bites and then took off after his wife, catching up to her in the hallway.

"That was not a cockroach, was it?" she asked.

"Aye. It wasna."

"Well?"

He shrugged, his big hands spread wide in confusion. "Strangely colored, all shiny."

"Oh, thank you for that."

"Why bother? 'Tis dead now."

"Point taken, husband. So, what are we planning for today?"

He nibbled a fingertip thoughtfully. "You know, I thought we might discern exactly why the supernatural isna working properly here."

"Oh, darling, what a unique and original idea."

He paused. The subject of Kingair's little affliction of humanity seemed not to actually be foremost in his mind. "Red jacket and shiny boots, you say?"

Lady Maccon looked at her husband, confused for a moment. Where was he going with this line of reasoning? "Boots are causing the illness?"

"No," he grumbled, shamefaced, "on me."

"Ah!" She grinned hugely. "I believe I might have mentioned something to that effect."

"Anything else?"

The grin widened. "Actually, I was envisioning

boots, jacket, and nothing else at all. Mmm, perhaps just boots."

He swallowed, nervous.

She turned to him, upping the odds. "If you were to make this fashion event happen, I might be open to a little negotiating about which of us will be doing the riding."

Lord Maccon, werewolf of some two hundred years, blushed beet red at that. "I am eternally grateful you have not taken up gambling, my dear."

She wormed herself into his arms and raised her lips to be kissed. "Give me time."

CHAPTER ELEVEN

Chief Sundowner

That afternoon, Lord and Lady Maccon decided to take a walk. The rain had let up slightly, and it looked to be turning into a passable day, if not precisely pleasant. Lady Maccon decided she was in the country and could relax her standards slightly, so did not change into a walking dress, instead simply slipping on practical shoes.

Unfortunately for Lord and Lady Maccon, Miss Loontwill and Miss Hisselpenny decided to join them. This occasioned a wait while both ladies changed, but since Tunstell had made himself scarce, there was less competition than there might otherwise have been in this endeavor. Alexia was beginning to think they wouldn't get out of the house before teatime when both girls appeared sporting parasols and bonnets. This reminded Alexia to get her own parasol, causing yet another delay. Really, mobilizing an entire fleet for a great naval battle would probably have been easier.

Finally they set forth, but no sooner had they attained

the small copse on the southern end of the grounds than they came across the Kingair Gamma, Lachlan, and Beta, Dubh, having some sort of heated argument in low, angry voices.

"Destroy it all," the Gamma was saying. "We canna continue ta live like this."

"Not until we ken to which and why."

The two men spotted the approaching party and fell silent.

Politeness dictated they join the larger group, and, with Felicity and Ivy's assistance, Alexia actually managed to get some semblance of polite conversation going. Both men were reluctant to say much at the best of times, and, clearly, the pack was under a gag order. However, such orders did not take into account the success with which sharp determination and frivolity could loosen the tongue.

"I know you gentlemen were on the front lines in India. How brave you must be, to fight primitives like that." Miss Hisselpenny widened her eyes and looked at the two men, hoping for tales of heroic bravery.

"Not much fighting left to do out there anymore. Simply some minor pacification of the locals," objected Lord Maccon.

Dubh gave him a dirty look. "And how would you know?"

"Oh, but what's it really like?" asked Ivy. "We get the stories in the papers now and again, but no real feel for the place."

"Hotter than hell's—"

Miss Hisselpenny gasped in anticipation of lewd talk. Dubh civilized himself. "Well, hot."

"And the food doesna taste verra good," added Lachlan.

"Really?" That interested Alexia. Food always interested Alexia. "How perfectly ghastly."

"Even Egypt was better."

"Oh." Miss Hisselpenny's eyes went wide. "You were in Egypt too?"

"Of course they were in Egypt," Felicity said snidely. "Everyone knows it is one of the main ports for the empire these days. I have a passionate interest in the military, you know? I heard that most regiments have to stop over there."

"Oh, do they?" Ivy blinked, trying to comprehend the geographic reason behind this.

"And how did you find Egypt?" asked Alexia politely.

"Also hot," snapped Dubh.

"Seems to me most places would be, compared to Scotland," Lady Maccon snapped back.

"*You* chose to visit *us*," he reminded her.

"And you chose to go to Egypt." Alexia was not one to back down from a verbal battle.

"Not entirely. Pack service to Queen Victoria is mandatory." The conversation was getting tense.

"But it does not have to take the form of military service."

"We are not loners to slink about the homeland with tails twixt our legs." Dubh actually looked to Lord Maccon for assistance in dealing with his irascible wife. The earl merely winked at him.

Help came from an unlooked-for source. "I hear Egypt

has some very nice, old"—Ivy was trying to keep matters civil—"stuff."

"Antiquities," added Felicity, proud of herself for knowing the word.

In a desperate attempt to keep Lady Maccon and the Beta from killing one another, Lachlan said, "We picked up quite a collection while we were there."

Dubh growled at his pack mate.

"Isn't that illegal?" Lord Maccon wondered softly in his BUR voice. No one paid him any attention, except for his wife, who pinched him.

She said, "Oh, really? What kind of artifacts?"

"A few bits of jewelry and some statuary to add to the pack vault and, of course, a couple of mummies."

Ivy gasped. "Real live mummies?"

Felicity snorted. "I should hope they are not alive." But even she seemed excited by the idea of mummies in residence. Alexia supposed that, in her sister's world, such things were considered glamorous.

Lady Maccon said, pressing her advantage, "We should have a mummy-unwrapping party. They are all the rage in London."

"Well, we shouldna want to be thought backward," said Lady Kingair's abrasive voice. She had come upon them all unnoticed, looking gray and severe. Lord Maccon, Lachlan, and Dubh all started upon hearing her speak. They were accustomed to having their supernatural sense of smell tell them when anyone approached, no matter how stealthily.

Sidheag turned to the Gamma. "Lachlan, get the clavigers to arrange it."

"Are you certain, my lady?" he questioned.

"We could do with a bit of fun. We wouldna want to disappoint the visiting ladies, now, would we? We are in possession of the mummies. Might as well unwrap them. We were after the amulets anyway."

"Oh, how thrilling," said Miss Hisselpenny, practically bouncing in her excitement.

"Which mummy, my lady?" asked Lachlan.

"The smaller one, with the more nondescript coverings."

"As you say." The Gamma hurried off to arrange for the event.

"Oh, I shall find this so very diverting," crowed Felicity. "You know Elsie Flinders-Pooke was lording it over me just last week that she had been to an unwrapping. Imagine what she will say when I tell her I experienced one in a haunted castle in the Scottish Highlands."

"How do you know Kingair is haunted?"

"I know because, obviously, it *must* be haunted. You could not possibly convince me otherwise. No ghosts have appeared since we arrived, but that is no proof to the contrary," Felicity defended her future tall tale.

"Delighted we could provide you with some significant social coup," sneered Lady Kingair.

"Your pleasure, I'm sure," replied Felicity.

"My sister is a woman of mean understanding," explained Lady Maccon apologetically.

"And what are you?" asked Sidheag.

"Oh, I am simply mean."

"And here I was, thinking you were the sister with the understanding."

"Not just yet. Give me time."

They turned around and headed back toward the castle. Lord Maccon moved to draw his wife back slightly so they could converse privately.

"You believe one of the artifacts to be a humanization weapon?"

She nodded.

"But how would we know which one?"

"You may have to come allover BUR on the Kingair Pack and simply confiscate all their collected antiquities as illegal imports."

"And then what? See them all incinerated?"

Lady Maccon frowned. She fancied herself a bit of a scholar and was not generally in favor of wanton destruction. "I had not thought to take things quite so far."

"It would be a terrible destruction, and I should be opposed, save that we canna simply have these things wandering around the empire. Imagine if they fell into the wrong hands?"

"Such as the Hypocras Club?" Lady Maccon shuddered to even think it.

"Or the vampires." No matter how integrated the two became into civilized society, werewolves and vampires would never really trust one another.

Lady Maccon stopped suddenly. Her husband got four long strides ahead before he realized she had paused. She was staring thoughtfully up into the aether, twirling the deadly parasol about her head.

"I have just remembered something," Alexia said when he returned to her side.

"Oh, that explains everything. How foolish of me to think you could walk and remember at the same time."

She stuck her tongue out at him but began drifting toward the house once more. He slowed to match her pace. "That bug, the one that scared me at breakfast. It was not a cockroach at all. It was a scarab beetle. From Egypt. It must have something to do with the artifacts they brought back."

Lord Maccon's lip curled. "Yuck."

They had fallen some distance behind the rest of the party. The others were busy entering the castle just as someone else emerged. There was a pause while they all politely greeted one another, and then the new figure headed purposefully in the direction of Lord and Lady Maccon.

The figure rapidly resolved itself into the personage of Madame Lefoux.

Alexia waved a "how do you do" at the Frenchwoman. She was wearing her beautiful morning coat of dove-gray, striped trousers, a black satin waistcoat, and a royal-blue cravat. It made for a pretty picture, the Kingair castle—mist-shrouded and gray in the background—and the attractive woman, as improperly dressed as she may be, hurrying toward them. Until Madame Lefoux neared enough for them to realize she was also wearing something else: a concerned expression.

"I am glad I 'ave found you two." Her accent was unusually strong. She sounded almost as bad as Angelique. "Ze most extraordinary thing, Lady Maccon. I waz looking for you just now to let you know, we went to check on the aethographor; then I saw—"

The most tremendous clap resounded through the Scottish air. Alexia felt certain she could see the mist shake with the noise. Madame Lefoux, her face changing from worry to surprise, stopped midsentence and mid-

step and tumbled forward, as limp as overcooked pasta.
A bloom of red appeared on one immaculate gray lapel.

Lord Maccon caught the inventor before she could fall
completely to the ground and carefully lowered her there
instead. He held his hand briefly before her mouth to see
if she was breathing. "She is still alive." Alexia quickly
pulled her shawl from about her shoulders and handed it
to him to use as a bandage. No sense in his spoiling the
last of his good cravats.

Alexia looked up at the castle, scoping the battlements
for a glint of sun on a rifle barrel, but there were too
many battlements and there was too little sun. The sharp-
shooter, whoever he might be, was not visible.

"Get down this instant, woman," ordered her husband,
grabbing her by one skirt ruffle and yanking her down
next to the fallen Frenchwoman. The ruffle ripped. "We
dinna know if the shooter was aiming at her or at us," he
growled.

"Where's your precious pack? Shouldn't they be high-
tailing it to our rescue?"

"How do you ken it isna them shooting?" her husband
wondered.

"Good point." Lady Maccon shifted her open parasol
defensively so that it shielded them as much as possible
from sight of the castle.

Another shot rang out. It hit the ground next to them,
splattering turf and small pebbles.

"Next time," grumbled the earl, "I shall pay extra and
have that thing made with metal shielding."

"Oh, that will be tremendously practical for hot summer afternoons. Come on, we need to find cover," hissed

his wife. "I shall leave the parasol propped here as a diversion."

"Break for that hedge?" suggested Conall, looking over to their right, where a little berm covered in wild roses seemed to be the Kingair formal garden hedge substitute.

Alexia nodded.

Lord Maccon hoisted the Frenchwoman over one shoulder easily. He might no longer have superhuman strength, but he was still strong.

They dashed toward the berm.

Another shot rang forth.

Only then did they hear yelling. Alexia peeked around the rosebush. Members of the pack poured out of the castle, looking about for the source of the shooting. Several yelled and pointed up. Clavigers and pack reentered the castle at a run.

Lord and Lady Maccon stayed hidden until they were convinced that no one would be taking any more shots at them. Then they emerged from behind the bushes. Lord Maccon carried Madame Lefoux, and Lady Maccon retrieved her parasol.

Upon attaining the house, it was found that Madame Lefoux was in no serious medical danger but had simply fainted from the wound, her shoulder badly gouged by the bullet.

Ivy appeared. "Oh dear, has something untoward ensued? Everyone is gesticulating." Upon catching sight of the comatose form of Madame Lefoux, she added, "Has she come over nonsensical?" At the sight of the blood, Ivy became rather breathless and looked near to fainting herself. Nevertheless, she trailed them into the back parlor, unhelpfully offering to help and interrupting, as they lowered Madame Lefoux to the small settee, with, "She hasn't caught a slight fatality, has she?"

"What happened?" demanded Lady Kingair, ignoring Ivy and Felicity, who had also entered the room.

"Someone seems to have decided to dispose of Madame Lefoux," Lady Maccon said, bustling about ordering bandages and vinegar. Alexia believed that a generous application of cider vinegar could cure most ills, except, of course, for those bacterial disorders that required bicarbonate of soda.

Felicity decided to immediately absent herself from any possible associated danger via proximity to Madame Lefoux. Which, as it absented everyone else from her, was no bad thing.

Only Lady Kingair had the wherewithal to respond. "Good Lord, why? She's naught more than a two-bit French inventor."

Alexia thought she saw the Frenchwoman twitch at that. Was Madame Lefoux shamming? Alexia leaned in on the pretext of checking bandages. She caught a whiff of vanilla, mixed with the coppery smell of blood this time instead of mechanical oil. The inventor remained absolutely still under Alexia's gentle ministrations. Not even her eyelids moved. If she was shamming, she was very, very good at it.

Lady Maccon glanced toward the door and thought she caught a flicker of servant black. Angelique's white, horrified face peeked around the corner. Before Alexia could summon her in, the maid disappeared.

"An excellent question. Perhaps she will be so kind as to tell us once she has awakened," Lady Maccon said, once more watching Madame Lefoux's face. No reaction to that statement.

Unfortunately for everyone's curiosity, Madame Lefoux did not awaken, or did not allow herself to be awakened, for the entirety of the rest of the afternoon. Despite the assiduous attentions of Lord and Lady Maccon, half the Kingair Pack, and several clavigers, her eyes remained stubbornly shut.

Lady Maccon took her tea in the sickroom, hoping the smell of baked goods would awaken Madame Lefoux. All that resulted was that Lady Kingair came to join her. Alexia had settled into not liking this relation of her husband's, but she had not the constitution that would allow for anything to interfere with her consumption of tea.

"Has our patient awakened yet?" inquired Lady Kingair.

"She remains dramatically abed." Alexia frowned into her cup. "I do hope nothing is seriously wrong with her. Should we call a doctor, do you think?"

"I've seen and tended to much worse on the battlefield."

"You go with the regiment?"

"I may not be a werewolf, but I'm Alpha female for this pack. My place is with them, even if I dinna fight alongside."

Alexia selected a scone from the tea tray and plopped a dollop of cream and marmalade on top of it. "Did you side with the pack when they betrayed my husband?" she asked in forced casualness.

"He told you about it."

Lady Maccon nodded and ate a bite of scone.

"I was just sixteen when he left, away at finishing school. I didna have a say in the pack's choices."

"And now?"

"Now? Now I ken they all behaved like fools. You dinna piss upwind."

Alexia winced at the vulgarity of the statement.

Sidheag sipped her tea, relishing the effect of her barracks language on her guest. "Queen Victoria might not chase the tails of a werewolf agenda, but she isna bleeding to the vampire fang either. She's no Henry or Elizabeth to be throwing her support full tilt behind the supernatural cause, but she hasna been as bad as we'd feared either. Perhaps she doesna watch the scientists as careful as she might, and she sure plays us close and fast, but I dinna think she is the worst monarch we could be having."

Lady Maccon wondered if Sidheag was attempting to guarantee the pack's safety or if the woman was talking truth. "Do you consider yourself a progressive, then, like my husband?"

"I'm saying, everyone handled the incident poorly. An Alpha abandoning his pack is extreme. Conall ought to have killed all the ringleaders, not just the Beta, and restructured. I love this pack, and to leave it leaderless and turn to a *London* pack instead is worse than death. It was a national embarrassment, what your husband did." Lady Kingair leaned forward, eyes fierce. She was close enough for Alexia to see that her graying hair, pulled tightly back into a braid, was frizzing slightly in the humid air.

"I thought he left them Niall?"

"Na. I brought Niall back with me. He was naught more than a loner I met abroad. Handsome and dashing, just what all schoolroom misses want in a husband.

I thought I'd be bringing him home to meet the pack and gramps, get permission, and post the bans. Only to find the old wolf gone and the pack in shambles."

"You took on the responsibility of leadership?"

Sidheag sipped her tea. "Niall was an excellent soldier and a good husband, but he'd have made a better Beta. He took on Alpha for my sake." She rubbed at her eyes with two fingers. "He was a good man, and a good wolf, and he did his best. I willna speak against him."

Alexia knew enough about herself to realize she couldn't have taken on leadership like that so young, and she considered herself a capable person. No wonder Sidheag was bitter.

"And now?"

"Now we're even worse off. Niall killed in battle and no one able enough to take Alpha role, let alone be Alpha in truth. And I'm knowing full well Gramps willna come back to us. Marrying you cemented that. We've lost him for good."

Lady Maccon sighed. "Regardless, you need to trust him. You should take your concerns to him and talk this out. He will see reason. I know he will. And he will help you find a solution."

Lady Kingair put her cup down with a sharp clatter. "There is only one solution. And he willna take it. I have written and asked every year for the last decade, and time is running out."

"What is that?"

"He needs to see me changed."

Lady Maccon sat back, puffing out her cheeks. "But that is so very perilous. I do not have the statistics on hand, but aren't the odds completely against a woman surviving the metamorphosis bite?"

Lady Kingair shrugged. "No one has tried in hundreds of years. 'Tis one of the ways packs beat out hives. At least we dinna need females to sustain ourselves."

"Yes, but vampires still manage to survive longer—less fighting. Even if you do survive the bite, you're setting yourself up to Alpha for the rest of your life."

"Hang the danger!" Sidheag Maccon practically yelled. Alexia thought the woman had never looked more like Conall. Her eyes also turned toward yellow when she was overset with extreme emotion.

"And you want Conall to do this for you? Risk killing off the last of his living relatives?"

"For me, for the pack. I'm na having any bairns at my age. He willna be able to continue the Maccon line through me. He's needing to move on from that. He owes Kingair some kind of salvation."

"You'll likely die." Lady Maccon poured herself another spot of tea. "You have held this pack together as a human."

"And what happens after I die of old age? Better to take the risk now."

Alexia was silent. Finally she said, "Oddly enough, I agree with your assessment."

Lady Kingair stopped drinking her tea and simply clutched the saucer for a long moment, fingertips white with tension. "Would *you* talk to him for me?"

"You want me to involve myself in Kingair's problems? Is that wise? Couldn't you simply go to another pack's Alpha for the bite?"

"Never!" There went that stiff werewolf pride, or was

it Scottish pride? Difficult to tell the difference sometimes.

Alexia sighed. "I will discuss it with him, but it is
a moot point: Conall cannot bite you or anyone else to
change, as he cannot take Anubis Form. Until we find out
why this pack is changeless, nothing else can happen. No
Alpha challenge, no metamorphosis."

Lady Kingair nodded, relaxing her grip enough to sip
at her tea once more.

Alexia noted that the woman did not crook her finger
properly. What kind of finishing school had she been sent
to, where they did not teach the basics of teacup holding?
She cocked her head. "Is this humanization plague some
kind of foolish self-flagellation? Do you want to take the
rest of the pack with you into mortality because my husband will not bite you to metamorphosis?"

Lady Kingair's tawny eyes, so much like Conall's, narrowed at that. "It isna my fault," she practically yelled.
"Dinna you understand? *We* canna tell you because we
dinna ken why this has happened to us. I dinna know.
None of us know. We dinna ken what's doing it!"

"So can I count on your support to figure it out?"
Alexia asked.

"What's it to you, Lady Maccon?"

Alexia backpedaled hurriedly. "I encourage my husband's BUR concerns. It keeps him out of household affairs. And I am interested in these things, as a new Alpha
of my own pack. If you have some kind of dangerous
disease, I should very much like to understand it fully
and prevent it from spreading."

"If he agrees to try for my metamorphosis, I'll agree
to help."

Knowing she couldn't make any such promise on her husband's behalf, Lady Maccon nevertheless said, "Done! Now, shall we finish our tea?"

They finished drinking in companionable discussion of the Women's Social and Political Union, whose stance both ladies supported but whose tactics and working-class routes neither was inclined to ally with publicly. Lady Maccon refrained from commenting that, from her more intimate knowledge of Queen Victoria's character, she could practically guarantee that lady's continued low opinion of the movement. She could not make such a statement, however, without revealing her own political position. Even an earl's wife would not be on such intimate terms with the queen, and she did not wish Lady Kingair to know that she was muhjah. Not yet.

Their pleasant conversation was interrupted by a knock at the parlor door.

At Lady Kingair's call, Tunstell's copious freckles came wandering in, attached to a somber-looking Tunstell.

"Lord Maccon sent me to sit with the patient, Lady Maccon."

Alexia nodded her understanding. Worried and unsure of whom to trust, Lord Maccon was placing Tunstell as a surety against further attacks on Madame Lefoux's person. Essentially, her husband was utilizing Tunstell's claviger training. Tunstell may look like a git of the first water, but he could handle werewolves in full-moon thrall. Of course, that meant both Ivy and Felicity were soon likely to take up residence in the sickroom as well. Poor Tunstell. Miss Hisselpenny was still convinced she did not want him, but she was equally convinced she must protect him from Felicity's wickedness. Lady Maccon felt that the presence of both women would provide a better defense than anything else. It was hard to get up to serious shenanigans under the enthusiastic interest of two perennially bored, unmarried ladies.

Eventually, however, it became necessary for everyone but Tunstell to leave the still-unconscious Frenchwoman and dress for dinner.

Upon attaining her chamber, Lady Maccon received her second major shock of the day. It was a good thing she was a woman of stalwart character. Someone had upended her room. Again. Probably looking for the dispatch case. Shoes and slippers were everywhere, and the bed had been torn apart; even the mattress was slashed open. Feathers coated flat surfaces like so much snow. Hatboxes lay broken, hats disemboweled, and the contents of Alexia's wardrobe lay strewn across the floor (a condition familiar to only the nightgowns).

Alexia propped her parasol safely to one side and took stock of the situation. The chaos was greater than it had been on board the dirigible, and the crisis was compounded shortly thereafter when Lord Maccon discovered the carnage.

"This is a gross outrage! First we are shot at, and now our rooms are ransacked," he roared.

"Does this kind of thing always happen around a pack without an Alpha?" wondered his wife, nosing about, trying to determine if anything significant was missing.

The earl grunted at her. "A terrible bother, leaderless packs."

"And messy." Lady Maccon picked her way delicately about the room. "I wonder if this was the information

Madame Lefoux had to impart before she was shot. She said something about trying to find me regarding the aethographor. Perhaps she disturbed the culprits in action when she came looking for me here." Alexia began to form three piles: things beyond salvation, items for Angelique to repair, and the undamaged.

"But why would someone shoot at her?"

"Perhaps she saw their faces?"

The earl pursed his well-formed lips. "It is possible. Come here, woman; stop your fussing. The dinner bell is about to go, and I'm hungry. We shall tidy later."

"Bossy britches," said his wife, but she did as she was bid. It wouldn't do to get into an argument with him on an empty stomach.

He helped her unbutton her dress, so well distracted by the day's proceedings that he only fluttered kisses down her spine and did not even nibble. "What do you believe they were looking for? Your dispatch case again?"

"Difficult to know. Could be someone else, I suppose. I mean, not the same miscreant as when I was floating." Alexia was confused. Initially, on board the dirigible, she had suspected Madame Lefoux, but that lady had been asleep and in company all day long. Unless the inventor managed it before she was shot at, this chaos must be attributed to someone else. A different spy with a different motive? Things certainly were getting complicated.

"What else might they be looking for? Did you bring something I should know about, husband?"

Lord Maccon said nothing, but when Alexia turned about and gave him the wifely eye of suspicion, he looked like a guilty sheepdog. He left off unbuttoning and went to the window. Throwing aside the shutters, he stuck his head far out, reached around, retrieved something, and returned to her side with a look of relief, carrying a small package wrapped in oiled leather.

"Conall," said his wife, "*what* is that?"

He unwrapped and showed her: a strange chubby little revolver with a square grip. He clicked open the chamber to display its armament: hardwood bullets inlaid with silver in a cagelike pattern and capped to take the powder explosion. Alexia wasn't big on guns, but she knew enough about the mechanics to realize this little creature was expensive to make, used only the most modern technology, and was capable of taking down either a vampire or a werewolf.

"A Galand Tue Tue. This is the Sundowner model," he explained.

Lady Maccon took her husband's face in her hands. His skin was rough with a day's growth of beard; she would have to remind him to shave, now that he was human all the time. "Husband, you are not here to kill someone, are you? I should hate to find out that you and I were working at cross purposes."

"Simply a precautionary measure, my love, I assure you."

She was not convinced. Her fingers tightened about his jaw. "When did you start carrying the deadliest supernatural weapon known to the British Empire as a *precaution*?"

"Professor Lyall had Tunstell bring it for me. He guessed I'd be mortal while I was here and thought I might want the added security."

Alexia let go of his face and watched as he wrapped the deadly little device back up and returned it to its hidey-hole just outside the window.

"How easy is that to use?" she asked, all innocence.

"Dinna even consider it, wife. You've got that parasol of yours."

She pouted. "You are no fun as a mortal."

"So," he said, deliberately changing the subject, "where did you hide your dispatch case, then?"

She grinned, pleased that he would not think her so feeble as to have kept it where it could be stolen. "In the least likely place, of course."

"Of course. And are you going to tell me where?"

She widened her large brown eyes at him, batting her eyelashes and attempting to look innocent.

"What is in it that someone might want?"

"That's the odd thing. I really have no idea. I took the smallest things out and stashed them in my parasol. So far as I can tell, there is nothing too valuable left: the royal seal; my notes and paperwork on this latest issue with the humanization plague, minus my personal journal, which got pinched; the codes to various aethographors; a stash of emergency tea; and a small bag of gingersnaps."

Her husband gave her his version of the *look*.

Lady Maccon defended herself. "You would not believe how long those Shadow Council meetings are prone to running, and being as the dewan and the potentate are supernatural, they don't seem to notice when it's teatime."

"Well I hardly think anyone is ransacking our rooms in a desperate bid to acquire gingersnaps."

"They are very *good* gingersnaps."

"I suppose it could be something other than the dispatch case?"

Lady Maccon shrugged. "This is useless speculation

for the time being. Here, help me on with this. Where is Angelique?"

In the absence of the maid, Lord Maccon buttoned his wife up into her dinner dress. It was a gray and cream affair with a multitude of pleated gathers all up the front and a long, rather demure ruffle at the hem. Alexia liked the gown, except that it had a cravatlike bow at the neck, and she wasn't entirely behind this latest fashion for incorporating masculine elements into women's garb. Then again, there was Madame Lefoux.

Which reminded her that, since Tunstell was on French-inventor guard detail, she would have to help her husband dress. It was a mild disaster: his cravat came out lopsided and his collar limp. Alexia was resigned. She had, after all, been a spinster most of her life, and cravat-tying was not a proficiency generally acquired by spinsters.

"Husband," she said as they finished their preparations and headed downstairs for dinner, "have you considered biting your many-times great-granddaughter to change?"

Lord Maccon stopped abruptly at the head of the staircase and growled, "How on God's green earth did that bloody woman persuade *you* to *her* cause?"

Alexia sighed. "It makes sense, and it is an elegant solution to Kingair's current problems. She is already acting like an Alpha; why not make it official?"

"It isna as simple as that, wife, and you verra well know it. And her chances of survival—"

"Are very slim. Yes, I am well aware of that."

"Not simply slim—they are beyond salvation. You are essentially suggesting that I kill the last living Maccon."

"But if she survived . . ."

"If."

Lady Maccon tilted her head. "Isn't it her risk to take?"

He remained silent and continued on down the massive staircase.

"You should think about it, Conall, as BUR, if nothing else. It is the most logical course of action."

He kept on walking. There was something about the set of his shoulders.

"Wait a moment." She was suddenly suspicious. "That was the reason you came back here all along, wasn't it? The family problem. You intend to fix the Kingair Pack? Despite the betrayal."

He shrugged.

"You wanted to see how Sidheag was handling things. Well?"

"There's this changeless issue," he prevaricated.

Alexia grinned. "Yes, well, apart from that. You must agree I have a point."

He turned to frown up at her. "I hate it when you come over all correct."

Alexia trotted down the staircase until they were nose to nose. She had to stand one step up from him for it to be so. She kissed him softly. "I know. But I am so very good at it."

CHAPTER TWELVE

The Great Unwrapping

They decided the mummy would be unwrapped, for the titillation of the ladies, just after dinner. Alexia was not convinced as to the cleverness of this plan. Knowing Miss Hisselpenny's constitution, if the mummy were gruesome enough, dinner might just be revisited. But it was believed that darkness and candlelight best suited such an illustrious event.

None of the ladies present had ever before been to a mummy-unwrapping party. Lady Maccon expressed some distress that Madame Lefoux and Tunstell would be missing the fun. Lord Maccon suggested that as he had little interest and he would go relieve Tunstell, thus allowing the claviger at least to participate. Tunstell, everyone knew, enjoyed drama.

Alexia looked sharply at Miss Hisselpenny, but Ivy held herself composed and untroubled by the possibility of a redheaded thespian and naked mummy in the same room. Felicity licked her lips in anticipation, and Lady Maccon prepared herself for inevitable histrionics. But it was she, not Felicity or Ivy, who felt most uncomfortable in the presence of the ancient creature.

Truth be told, it was a rather sad-looking mummy. It resided in a not-very-big boxlike coffin that had only minimal hieroglyphic decorations upon it. Once removed from the coffin, the wrappings on the mummy were revealed to be minimally painted with one repeated motif: what looked to be an ankh, broken. The dead thing did not disgust or frighten Alexia in any way, and she had seen mummies before in museums without desultory effects. But there was something about this particular mummy that, simply put, repulsed her.

Lady Maccon was not given to bouts of sentimentality, so she did not think her reaction an emotional one. No, she was being literally repulsed, in the scientific definition of the word. It was as though she and the mummy both had some kind of magnetic field, and they were the same charge, with forces violently repelling one another.

The actual unwrapping seemed to take an exceptionally long time. Who knew there would be so dreadfully many bandages? They also kept breaking. Every time an amulet was uncovered, the whole operation stopped and people gasped in delight. As more and more of the mummy was revealed, Alexia found herself instinctively backing toward the door of the room, until she was at the fringe of the crowd, standing on tiptoe to witness the proceedings.

Being soulless, Alexia had never given death much consideration. After all, for preternaturals like her, death was the end—she had nothing whatsoever to look forward to. In BUR's special documentation vaults, an inquisition pamphlet lamented the fact that preternaturals, the church's last best weapon against the supernatural threat, were also the only human beings who could never be saved. What Alexia felt, most of the time, was indifference to her own mortality. This was the result of an ingrained practicality that was also due to her soullessness. But there was something about this mummy that troubled her even as it repulsed: the poor, sad, wrinkled thing.

Finally they worked their way up to his head, exposing a perfectly preserved skull with dark brown skin and some small portion of hair still adhered to it. Amulets were removed from ears, nose, throat, and eyes, revealing the empty eye sockets and slightly gaping mouth. Several scarab beetles crawled out of the exposed orifices, plopped to the floor, and skittered about. At which both Felicity and Ivy, who had until that moment remained only mildly hysterical, fainted.

Tunstell caught Miss Hisselpenny, clutching her close to his breast and murmuring her given name in tones of marked distress. Lachlan caught Miss Loontwill and was nowhere near as affectionate about it. Two sets of expensive skirts draped themselves artistically in ruffled disarray. Two sets of bosoms heaved in heart-palpitating distress.

The evening's entertainment was pronounced a definitive success.

The gentlemen, marshaled into action by Lady Kingair's barked commands, carried the two young ladies into a sitting room down the hall. There the ladies were duly revived with smelling salts, and rosewater was patted across the brow.

Alexia was left alone with the unfortunate mummy, unwitting cause of all the excitement. Even the scarab beetles had scuttled off. She cocked her head to one side, resisting the insistent push, which seemed even worse now that there was only the two of them. It was as though the very air were trying to drive her from the room. Alexia narrowed her eyes at the mummy, something niggling the back of her brain. Whatever it was, she could not recall it. Turning away, still thinking hard, she made her way into the other room.

Only to find Tunstell kissing Miss Hisselpenny, who was apparently wide awake and participating with gusto. Right there in front of everyone.

"Well, I say!" said Alexia. She had not thought Ivy possessed that degree of gumption. Apparently, she was finding Tunstell's kisses less damp than she had previously.

Felicity blinked awake, probably desirous to see what had pulled everyone's attention so thoroughly away from her own prostrate form. She caught sight of the embrace and gasped, joining Alexia in amazement. "Why, Mr. Tunstell, what *are* you doing?"

"That should be perfectly clear, even to you, Miss Loontwill," Lady Kingair snapped, not nearly so scandalized as she ought.

"Well," said Alexia, "I take it you are feeling more the thing?"

No one answered her. Ivy was still occupied with kissing Tunstell. It appeared there might even be tongue involved at this juncture. And Felicity was still occupied watching them with all the good-humored interest of an irritated chicken.

The touching scene was broken by Lord Maccon's fantastically loud yell, which welled suddenly forth from the downstairs front parlor. It was not one of his angry yells either. Lady Maccon would hardly have bestirred herself for one of those. No, this yell sounded like pain.

Alexia was out the door and galloping pell-mell down the staircase, heedless of the very real danger to her delicate apparel, waving her parasol about madly.

She crashed into the parlor door, which refused to budge. Something heavy was blocking it. She heaved against it desperately, finally shoving it open far enough to find that it was her husband's fallen body that blocked her entrance.

She bent over him, checking for injuries. She could find none on his back, so with prodigious effort, she rolled him over, checking his front. He was breathing slowly and laboriously, as though drugged.

Alexia paused, frowning suspiciously at her parasol, lying near her at the ready. *The tip opens and emits a poisoned dart equipped with a numbing agent,* she heard Madame Lefoux's voice say in her head. How easy, then, would it be to create a sleeping agent? A quick glance about the room showed Madame Lefoux was still unconscious but otherwise undamaged.

Lady Kingair, Dubh, and Lachlan appeared at the door. Lady Maccon held up a hand indicating she was not to be disturbed and stripped her husband bare to the waist, examining him more closely, not for injuries but for . . . aha!

"There it is." A small puncture wound just below his left shoulder.

She pushed her way through the crowd at the door and

yelled up the stairs, "Tunstell, you revolting blighter!" In Woolsey Castle, such affectionate terminology for the claviger meant for him to come quickly, and come armed. Lord Maccon's idea.

She turned back into the room and marched over to the prone form of Madame Lefoux. "If this is your fault," she hissed to the still-apparently-comatose woman, "I shall see you hanged as a spy; you see if I don't." Heedless of the others listening and watching in avid interest, she added, "And you know very well I have the power to do so."

Madame Lefoux lay as still as death.

Tunstell muscled his way into the room and immediately bent over his fallen master, reaching to check his breath.

"He is alive."

"Barely," replied Alexia. "Where did you—"

"What has happened?" interrupted Lady Kingair impatiently.

"He has been put to sleep, some kind of poisoned dart. Tincture of valerian perhaps," explained Lady Maccon without looking up.

"Goodness, how remarkable."

"Woman's weapon, poison." Dubh sniffed.

"I beg your pardon!" replied Lady Maccon. "None of that, or you shall meet the blunt end of *my* preferred weapon, and let me assure you, it isn't poison."

Dubh wisely beat a retreat to avoid offending the lady further.

"You will have to leave off your tender ministrations of Miss Hisselpenny's delicate constitution for the moment, Tunstell." Lady Maccon stood and strode purposefully to the door. "If you will excuse us," she said to the assembled Kingair Pack. Then she shut them firmly out of their own front parlor. Terribly rude, of course, but sometimes circumstances required rudeness, and there was simply nothing else for it. Luckily, under such circumstances, Alexia Maccon was always equal to the task.

She proceeded on to another unpardonably rude offense. Leaving Tunstell to see her husband comfortable—which he did by dragging the earl's massive frame over to another small couch, then folding him onto it before covering him with a large plaid blanket—Lady Maccon marched over and began stripping Madame Lefoux of her garments.

Tunstell did not ask, only turned his head away and tried not to look.

Alexia did this carefully, feeling about and checking every layer and fold for hidden gadgets and possible weapons. The Frenchwoman did not stir, although Alexia could have sworn the woman's breath quickened. By the end, Alexia had a fine pile of objects, some of them familiar: a pair of glassicals, an aether transponder cable, an encephalic valve, but most of them unknown to her. She knew Madame Lefoux normally boasted a dart emitter, because she'd said she used it during the fight on board the dirigible. But none of the objects in the pile looked to be such a device, even disguised as something else. Had it been stolen? Or had Madame Lefoux used it on Conall and then contrived to hide it somewhere else?

Lady Maccon slid her hands under the sleeping woman. Nothing there. Then she tucked them down Madame Lefoux's side where it rested against the back of the settee. Still nothing. Then she looked under and behind the couch. If the inventor had hidden it, she had done so quite thoroughly.

With a sigh, Lady Maccon set about putting the Frenchwoman's clothing back together again. It was odd to think, but she had never before seen another woman's naked body until now. She must admit Madame Lefoux did have a rather nice one. Not so well endowed as Alexia's own, of course, but trim and tidy with neat small breasts. It was a good thing the inventor opted for masculine garb, she reflected, as it was much easier to manage. Once the task was completed, Lady Maccon's hands were trembling slightly—from embarrassment, of course.

"Keep a close eye on her, Tunstell. I shall return directly." With that, Lady Maccon stood and marched out of the room, shutting the door behind her and ignoring the Kingair Pack, still milling about confusedly in the vestibule. She went immediately upstairs and inside her bedchamber. Angelique was already there, rummaging about.

"Out," she said to the maid.

Angelique bobbed a curtsy and scurried away.

Lady Maccon went directly to the window and, standing on tiptoe, reached around for Conall's precious little oiled leather package. It was well beyond her reach, stashed behind a jutting brick. Impatient, she balanced on the sill precariously, bemoaning her overly skirted state, bustle squeezing up tight against the side of the window. Despite the hazardous position, she managed to grab hold of the package without mishap.

Unwrapping the little weapon, she stashed it under her ridiculous lace cap, nested among her copious dark curls, and marched on to Ivy's room to retrieve her dispatch case.

Ivy was lying in half-faint, half-flutter on her bed.

"Oh, Alexia, thank goodness. What am I to do? This is such a terrible crisis of apex proportions. Such palpitations of the heart. Did you see? Oh, of course you saw. He kissed me, right there in public. I am *ruined*!" She sat up. "Yet I love him." She flopped back. "Yet I am ruined. Oh, woe is me."

"Did you actually just utter the phrase 'woe is me'? I'm just going to, uh, check on those socks."

Miss Hisselpenny was not to be distracted from her majestic problems. The removal of the dispatch case, not to mention her friend's militant expression, went unnoticed.

"He told me he would love me forever."

Lady Maccon flipped through the various stacks of papers and rolls of parchments inside her case, looking for her muhjah letter of marque. Where had she put the bedamned thing?

"He said that this was the true, the one, the only."

Lady Maccon gave a noncommittal murmur at that. What else could one say to such folderol?

Miss Hisselpenny, unconcerned by a lack of response, continued to bemoan her fate. "And I love him. I really and truly do. You could never understand this type of love, Alexia. Not such true love as ours. Marrying for practical gain is all very well and good, but this . . . this is the real thing."

Lacy Maccon tilted her head in sham surprise. "Is that what I did?"

Ivy continued without acknowledgment. "But we cannot possibly marry."

Alexia continued to rummage. "Mmm, no, I see that."

That made Miss Hisselpenny sit up and look daggers down at her friend. "Really, Alexia, you are not being even remotely helpful."

Lady Maccon remembered she had transferred her most important papers to her parasol after the first break-in and quickly snapped the dispatch case shut, locked it, and tucked it back behind Ivy's stack of hatboxes.

"Ivy, my dear, I am terribly sympathetic to your plight. Honestly, I am, most sincerely. But you must excuse me. Necessity demands I handle a situation downstairs rather hurriedly."

Miss Hisselpenny flopped back onto the bed, hand to her head. "Oh, what kind of friend are you, Alexia Maccon? Here I lie, in crisis and abject suffering. This is the worst evening of my whole life, you realize? And *you* care only for your husband's lucky socks!" She flipped over and buried her head in the pillow.

Alexia departed the room before Ivy could come up with further histrionics.

Most of the pack still stood outside the parlor door, looking confused. Alexia glared at them with her best Lady Maccon glare, opened the door, and shut it once more in their faces.

She handed the gun to Tunstell, who took it but swallowed nervously.

"You know what this is?"

He nodded. "Tue Tue Sundowner. But why would I

need it? There are no vampires here, or werewolves for that matter. Not with the way things currently stand."

"They are not going to stand like this for much longer, not if I have anything to say about it. Poison does not work on a werewolf, and I intend to see my husband wide awake sooner than it would take for that stuff, whatever it may be, to run its course through a human system. Besides, that deadly little gun will work just as well on daylight folk. Are you authorized to use it?"

Tunstell shook his head slowly. His freckles stood out starkly on his white face.

"Well, you are now."

Tunstell looked like he would like to argue the point. Sundowner was a BUR position. Technically the muhjah had no real say in the matter. But his mistress was looking dreadfully belligerent, and he had no wish to try her patience.

She pointed an autocratic finger at him. "No one is to come in or out of this room. *No one,* Tunstell. No staff, no pack, no claviger, not even Miss Hisselpenny. Speaking of which, I really must insist you refrain from embracing her in public. It is most discomforting to watch." Her nose wrinkled slightly.

Tunstell flushed at that, his freckles fading under the red, but he kept to the main point. "What are you going to do now, my lady?"

Lady Maccon glanced up at the grandfather clock ticking sonorously in the corner of the room. "Send an aetherogram, and soon. This is all getting terribly out of hand."

"To whom?"

She shook her head, hair falling down now that she

wore no cap. "Just you do your job, Tunstell, and let me do mine. I will want to know immediately if either of them awaken or worsen. Understood?"

The redhead nodded.

She scooped up the large pile of Madame Lefoux's gadgets, stuffing them into her lace cap as a kind of bag. Her hair was loose about her face, but sometimes one must sacrifice appearance to cope with trying circumstances. Grasping the cap of booty in one hand and her parasol in the other, she exited the parlor, pulling the door firmly closed with her foot.

"I am afraid I must inform you, Lady Kingair, that no one is to go in or out of that room, including yourself, for the foreseeable future. I have left Tunstell exceedingly well armed and with strict instructions to fire on any who attempt to enter. You would not want to test his obedience to me, now, would you?"

"Under whose authority have you done this? The earl's?" Lady Kingair was shocked.

"My husband has become"—Alexia paused—"indisposed at the moment. So, no, this is no longer a BUR matter. I have taken it under my own jurisdiction. I have tolerated this shilly-shallying and hedging of yours long enough. I have pandered to your pack problems and your pack ways, but *this* is outside of enough. I want this plague of humanization lifted, and I want it lifted now. I will not have anyone else shot at, or attacked, or spied upon, or any further rooms ransacked. Things are getting far too messy, and I cannot abide a mess."

"Temper, Lady Maccon, temper," remonstrated Lady Kingair.

Alexia narrowed her eyes.

"Why should we do what you say?" Dubh was militant.

Alexia shoved the letter of marque under the Beta's nose. He left off his grumbling, and the oddest expression suffused his wide, angry face.

Lady Kingair grabbed the paperwork and held it up to the indifferent light of a nearby oil lamp. Satisfied, she passed it on to Lachlan, who appeared the least surprised by its contents.

"I take it you were not informed of my appointment?"

Sidheag gave her a hard look. "I take it you didna marry Lord Maccon purely for love?"

"Oh, the political position was a surprise advantage, I assure you."

"And one that wouldna have been given to a spinster."

"So you know the queen's disposition sufficiently to predict that at least?" Alexia took her marque back and tucked it carefully down the front of her bodice. It would not do for the pack to be made aware of her parasol's hidden pockets.

"Muhjah has been vacant for generations. Why you? Why now?" Dubh was looking less angry and more thoughtful than Alexia had yet seen him. Perhaps there was brain behind all that brawn and bluster.

"*She* did offer it to your father," Lachlan pointed out.

"I had heard something to that effect. I understand he turned it down."

"Oh no, no." Lachlan gave a little half-smile. "We filibustered."

"The werewolves?"

"The werewolves and the vampires and one or two ghosts as well."

"What *is* it with you people and my father?"

At that Dubh snorted. "How much time do you have?"

The grandfather clock, locked in the room with Tunstell and his two comatose charges, tolled a quarter 'til.

"Apparently, not enough. I take it you accept the letter as authentic?"

Lady Kingair was looking at Alexia as though a good number of her previous questions about one Lady Maccon had now all been answered. "We will accept it, and we will defer to your authority in this." She gestured to the closed parlor door. "For the time being," she added, so as not to lose face in front of the pack.

Lady Maccon knew this was as good as she was going to get, so, in characteristic fashion, she took it and asked for more. "Very good. Next I will need to compose and send a message on your aethographor. While I am doing that, if you would please collect all the artifacts you brought back from Egypt into one room. I should very much like to peruse them as soon as my message has been sent. If I cannot determine which artifact is most likely causing the humanity problem, I shall have my husband removed to Glasgow, where he should return to supernatural and recover with no ill effects." With that, she headed up to the top of the castle and the aethographor.

She was in for a prodigious surprise. For what should she find on the floor of the aethographor room but the comatose form of the bemused claviger who was caretaker of the machine and every single valve frequensor in Kingair's library broken to smithereens. The place was littered with glittering crystalline shards.

"Oh dear, I knew they ought to have been locked

away." Lady Maccon checked the claviger, who was still
breathing and as fast asleep as her husband, and then
picked her way through the wreckage.

The apparatus itself was undamaged. Which made
Alexia wonder; if the objective in destroying the valve
frequensors was to prevent outside communication,
why not take down the aethographor itself? It was,
after all, an awfully delicate gadget easily and quickly
disabled. Why smash all the valves instead? Unless,
of course, the culprit wanted continued access to the
aethographor.

Alexia rushed into the transmitting chamber, hoping that the fallen claviger had disturbed the vandal in
the act. It looked like he had, for there, still sitting in
the emitter cradle, was a unrolled scroll of metal with a
burned-through message clearly visible upon it. And it
was *not* the message she had sent to Lord Akeldama the
evening before. Oh no, this message was in French!

Lady Maccon was not quite as good at reading French
as she should have been, so it took her long precious moments to translate the burned-through metal.

"Weapon here but unknown," it said.

Lady Maccon was disgruntled that the bloody thing
did not read like an old-fashioned ink-and-paper letter,
with a "dear so-and-so" and a "sincerely, so-and-so,"
thus revealing all to her without fuss. Who had Madame
Lefoux sent the message to? When had the message
been sent—just before she was shot, or earlier? Was it
really the inventor who had also destroyed the valve frequensors? Lady Maccon could not believe that wanton
destruction of technology was Madame Lefoux's style.
The woman adored all gadgetry; it would be against her

nature to destroy it with such abandon. And, regardless of all else, what *had* she been trying to tell them right before she was shot?

With a start, Alexia realized it was getting on toward eleven o'clock, and she had best etch her message and prepare it to send right away. Currently, the only concrete action she could think to take was consultation with Lord Akeldama. She did not have the valves to contact the Crown or BUR, so the outrageous vampire would have to do.

Her message read simply, "Floote check library: Egypt, humanization weapon? BUR send agents to Kingair."

It was a long message for the aethographor to handle, but it was the shortest she could formulate. Lady Maccon hoped she could remember the pattern of movements the young claviger had used the evening before. She was generally good about such things, but she might have missed a button or two. Still, there was nothing for it but to try.

The tiny transmitting room was much less crowded with only one person. She extracted Lord Akeldama's valve from her parasol and placed it carefully into the resonator cradle. She slotted the inscribed metal into the frame and pulled down the switch that activated the aetheric convector and chemical wash. The etched letters burned away, and the hydrodine engines spun to life. It was easier than she had thought. The director of the Crown's aethographic transmitter said one needed special schooling and certification to run the complicated apparatus—little liar.

The two needles raced across the slate, sparking as

they met. Alexia sat in perfect silence throughout the
transmission, and when it was finished, she removed the
slate from the cradle. She wouldn't want to be so careless
as the spy had been.

Lady Maccon bustled into the other chamber, which
proved far more difficult to operate. No matter how many
knobs she twiddled or cogs she turned, she could not get
the ambient noise down far enough to receive. Luckily,
Lord Akeldama took his sweet time replying. She had
nearly half an hour to get the receiving chamber quiet.
She did not manage to get it down nearly so low as the
claviger had, but it was eventually quiet enough.

Lord Akeldama's response began to appear inside
the black magnetic particulates between the two pieces
of glass, one letter at a time. Trying to breathe quietly,
Alexia copied down the message. It was short, cryptic,
and totally unhelpful.

"Preternaturals always cremated," was all it said. Then
there was some kind of image, a circle on top of a cross.
Some kind of code? That was rich! Blast Lord Akeldama
for being coy at a time like this!

Alexia waited another half an hour, past midnight, for
any additional communication, and when nothing further materialized, she turned the aethographor off and
left in a huff.

The house was abuzz. In the main drawing room
across from the front parlor, in which remained Tunstell
and his charges, a cheery fire burned in the fireplace and
maids and footmen bustled about setting out artifacts.

"Good gracious, you did do a little shopping in Alexandria, now, didn't you?"

Lady Kingair looked up from the small mummy she

was arranging carefully on a side table. It appeared to
have started life as some kind of animal, perhaps of the
feline persuasion? "We do what we must. The regimental
pay isna adequate to cover Kingair's upkeep. Why should
we not collect?"

Lady Maccon began looking through all the artifacts,
not quite certain what she was looking for. There were
little wooden statues of people, necklaces of turquoise
and lapis, strange stone jars with animal-head lids, and
amulets. All of them were relatively small except for
two mummies, both still properly clothed. These were
more impressive than the one they had unwrapped. They
resided inside curvy, beautifully painted coffins, the
surfaces of which were covered in colorful images and
hieroglyphics. Cautiously, Alexia moved toward them
but felt no overwhelming repulsion. None of the artifacts,
mummies included, seemed any different from those she
had seen on display in the halls of the Royal Society or,
indeed, in the Museum of Antiquities.

She looked suspiciously at Lady Kingair. "Are there
no others?"

"Only the entertainment mummy we unwrapped, still
upstairs."

Lady Maccon frowned. "Did they all come from the
same seller? Were they all looted from the same tomb?
Did he say?"

Lady Kingair took offense. "They are *all* legal. I have
the paperwork."

Alexia sucked her teeth. "I am certain you do. But I
understand very well how the antiquities system works in
Egypt these days."

Sidheag looked like she would like to take umbrage at that, but Alexia continued. "Regardless, their origins?"

Frowning, Lady Kingair said, "All different places."

Lady Maccon sighed. "I will want to see the other mummy again in just a moment, but first . . ." Her stomach went queasy at the very idea. It was so uncomfortable, to be in the same room with that thing. She turned to look at the rest of the Kingair Pack, who were milling about looking unsure of themselves, large men in skirts with scruffy faces and lost expressions. For a moment Alexia softened. Then she remembered her husband, comatose in another room. "None of you purchased anything privately that you are not telling me about? Things will go dreadfully ill for you if you did"—she looked directly at Dubh—"and I find out later."

No one stepped forward.

Lady Maccon turned back to Sidheag. "Very well, then, I shall take one more look at that mummy. Now, if you would be so kind."

Lady Kingair led the way up the stairs, but once there, Alexia did not follow her into the room. Instead she stood at the door, looking intently at the thing. It pushed against her, so that she had to fight a strange urge to turn and run. But she resisted, staring at the withered dark brown skin, almost black, shrunken down to hug those old bones. Its mouth was slightly open, bottom teeth visible, gray and worn. She could even see its eyelids, half-lidded, over the empty eye sockets. Its arms were crossed over its chest as though it were trying to hold itself together against death, clutching its soul inward.

Its soul.

"Of course," Alexia gasped. "How could I have been so blind?"

Lady Kingair looked to her sharply.

"I have been thinking all along that it was an ancient weapon, and Conall that it was some plague your pack caught and brought back with you from Egypt. But, no, it is simply *this* mummy."

"What? How could a mummy do such a thing?"

Resisting the terrible pushing sensation, Lady Maccon strode into the room and picked up a piece of the mummy's discarded bandage, pointing to the image depicted on it. An ankh, broken in half. Like the circle on top of a cross in Lord Akeldama's aethographic message, only fractured.

"This is not a symbol of death, nor of the afterlife. That is the name"—she paused—"or perhaps the title, of the person the mummy was in life. Do you not see? The ankh is the symbol for eternal life, and here it is shown broken. Only one creature can end eternal life."

Sidheag gasped, one hand to her lips, and then she slowly lowered it and pointed to Lady Maccon. "A cursebreaker. You."

Alexia smiled a tight little smile. She looked to the dead thing sadly. "Some long-ago ancestor, perhaps?" Despite herself she began to back away from it once more, the very air about the creature driving her away.

She looked to Lady Kingair, already knowing her answer. "Do you feel that?"

"Do I feel what, Lady Maccon?"

"I thought as much. Only I *would* notice." She frowned again, mind racing. "Lady Kingair, do you know anything about preternaturals?"

"Only the basics. I should know more, were I a werewolf, for the howlers would have told me the stories that, as a human, I am not allowed to hear."

Alexia ignored the bitterness in the older woman's voice. "Who, then, is the oldest of the Kingair Pack?" She had never missed Professor Lyall more. He would have known. Of course he would. He was probably the one who told Lord Akeldama.

"Lachlan," Lady Kingair answered promptly.

"I must speak with him directly." Alexia whirled away, almost bumping into her maid, who stood behind her in the hallway.

"Madame." Angelique's eyes were wide and her cheeks pink. "Your room, what haz 'appened?"

"Not again!"

Lady Maccon dashed to her bedchamber, but it looked the same as when she had last left it. "Oh, this is nothing, Angelique. I simply forgot to tell you about it. Please see it is tidied."

Angelique stood forlornly among the carnage and watched her mistress rush back downstairs. Lady Kingair followed sedately after.

"Mr. Lachlan," Alexia called, and that earnest gentleman appeared in the vestibule, a look of concern on his pleasant face. "A private word if you would be so kind."

She led the Gamma and Lady Kingair across the hall into a tight huddle away from the other pack members.

"This may come as a strange question, but please answer to the best of your knowledge."

"Of course, Lady Maccon. Your wish is my command."

"I am muhjah." She grinned. "My command is your command."

"Just so." He inclined his head.

"What happens to us when we die?"

"A philosophical conversation, Lady Maccon? Is now the time?"

She shook her head, impatient. "No, not us here. I mean to say we as in preternaturals. What happens to preternaturals when we die?"

Lachlan frowned. "I have not known very many of your kind, rare as they fortunately are."

Alexia bit her lip. Lord Akeldama's message said preternaturals were cremated. What would happen if one was not? What would happen if the body was never allowed to decompose? Ghosts displayed, in their very nature, the fact that excess soul was tethered to the body. As long as the body could be preserved, the ghost would stick around—undead and progressively more insane, but around. Surely the ancient Egyptians would have discovered this for themselves through the process of mummification? It might even be the reason they mummified. Was there something about *not* having a soul that was also connected to the body? Perhaps soul-sucking abilities were coupled to a preternatural's skin. After all, it was through her touch that Alexia managed to negate supernatural power.

She gasped and, for the first time in her stalwart life, actually felt near to fainting. The implications were endless and terrifying. The dead bodies of preternaturals could be turned into weapons against the supernatural. Preternatural mummies, like the one below, could be divided up and transported about the empire, or even turned into a powder and made into a poison! A *humanity* poison. She frowned. Such a drug might pass through the body after digestive processing, but still, for a time, a werewolf or vampire would be mortal.

Lachlan and Lady Kingair remained silent, staring at Alexia. It was almost as though they could see the gears and cogs in her head moving. Only one question remained to be answered: why was she repelled by the mummy? She asked Lachlan, "What happens when two preternaturals meet?"

"Oh, they dinna. Not even their own bairns. You never met your father?" Lachlan paused. "Course, he wouldna been the type. But, regardless, they simply dinna. Preternaturals canna stand to share the same air as one another. 'Tis naught personal, simply unbearable, so they tend to avoid the same social circles." He paused. "Are you saying somehow yon dead mummy is doing all this?"

"Maybe death expands our soulless abilities so they no longer require touch. Just as a ghost's excess soul can move outward from its body to the limits of its tether." Alexia looked at them both. "It would explain the mass exorcism within a specific radius."

"And the fact that this pack cannot change." Lady Kingair was nodding.

"Mass curse-breaking." Lachlan frowned.

Just then they heard the murmur of voices from behind the locked door near them. The parlor door clicked open, and Tunstell stuck his red head out. He started back upon seeing the three of them standing so close.

"Mistress," he said, "Madame Lefoux has awakened."

Alexia followed him inside, turning to Lady Kingair and Lachlan before shutting the door. "I need hardly tell you how dangerous the information we just discussed."

Both looked appropriately grave. Behind them, the rest of the pack emerged from the artifact room, curious at Tunstell's appearance.

"Please do not tell the rest of your pack," Alexia asked, but it sounded like a command.

They nodded and she shut the door.

CHAPTER THIRTEEN

———

The Latest Fashion from France

Tunstell was bent over the inventor, helping her to sit upright on the small settee, when Alexia entered. Madame Lefoux was looking groggy, but her eyes were open. They focused on Alexia as she walked into the room, and the Frenchwoman gave a slow smile—there were the dimples.

"My husband," asked Lady Maccon, issuing forth her own brief upturn of the lips, "has his condition changed also?" She went to Conall's side, a mountain of a man on the tiny little couch. Its bowed, claw-foot legs looked like they were buckling under his weight. She reached down to touch his face: slightly scruffy. She had *told* him he needed a shave. But his eyelids remained closed, ridiculously long eyelashes flat against his cheek. Such a waste of good eyelashes. She'd said only last month how much she resented him for them. He'd laughed and tickled her neck with them.

Her reminiscences were interrupted, not by Tunstell's voice answering her question, but by Madame Lefoux's slightly accented musical one. It was a little dry and croaky from lack of water.

"He will not regain his senses for some time, I am afraid. Not if he was disabled by one of the new sleeping darts."

Lady Maccon went over to her. "What was it, Madame Lefoux? What happened? What were you trying to tell us this morning? Who shot at you?" Her voice became very cold. "Who shot my husband?" She was confident she knew the answer, but she wanted Madame Lefoux to be the one to tell her. It was time the inventor chose a side.

The inventor swallowed. "Please do not be angry with her, Lady Maccon. She does not do it intentionally, you understand? I am convinced she doesn't. She is simply a little thoughtless—that is all. She has a good heart, under it all. I know she has.

"I found the aethographor, all those beautiful valves smashed to bits. How could she do such a thing? How could anyone?" There were tears now leaking out of those green eyes. "She went too far with that, and then when I came to tell you, instead I found her searching your room. That was when I knew it had gotten out of hand. She must have been looking for your crystalline valve, the one she knew you had, the one for Lord Akeldama's transmitter. To destroy it as well. Such destruction. I never knew she was capable. To push someone off a ship is one thing, but to destroy such perfectly functional beauty as a crystalline valve frequensor—what kind of monster does that?"

Well, that certainly told Alexia where Madame Lefoux's priorities lay.

"Who is Angelique working for? The vampires?"

Madame Lefoux, having talked herself out, nodded.

Lady Maccon swore, using words her husband would have been proud of.

Tunstell was shocked. He blushed.

"I suspected she was a spy, of course, but I did not think she would become an active agent. She did such lovely things with my hair."

Madame Lefoux tilted her head as though she could understand perfectly.

"What is she after? Why has she been doing this?"

The Frenchwoman shook her head. With her top hat off and her cravat untied, she looked almost feminine, most unlike herself. Softer. Alexia was not certain she liked it. "I can only suggest—the same thing you are after, muhjah. The humanization weapon."

Lady Maccon swore again. "And, of course, Angelique was standing just there. Right behind me in the hallway when I figured out what it was."

Madame Lefoux's eyes widened.

But it was Tunstell who said, voice full of awe, "You figured it out?"

"Of course I did. Where have you been?" Lady Maccon immediately headed toward the door. "Tunstell, my orders stand."

"But, mistress, you need—"

"They stand!"

"I do not think she wants to kill anyone but me," Madame Lefoux called after her. "I really do not. Please, my lady, do not do anything . . . terminal."

Lady Maccon whirled back at the door and bared her teeth, looking for all the world like a bit of a werewolf herself.

"She shot my husband, madame," she said.

Outside, where the Kingair Pack should have still stood, was only silence. Silence and a whole mess of plaid-skirted, large, sleeping bodies—quite the grand collapse.

Lady Maccon closed her eyes and took a long, annoyed breath. Really, must she do everything herself?

Gripping her parasol firmly, she armed the numbing spike, her finger hovering over the dart-ejection button, and charged up the stairs toward the mummy room. Unless she missed her guess, Angelique would try to get the creature out and on the road, probably by carriage, and back to her masters.

She missed her guess. The moment she opened the door to the room, it became patently clear the mummy was still in residence and Angelique was not.

Lady Maccon frowned. "What?"

She tapped the tip of her parasol on the floor in annoyance. Of course! A vampire spy's priority would be the transfer of information. It was the thing vampires valued most. Alexia changed her grip on the parasol and hurtled up too many staircases for her corset-clad self, arriving, panting, at the aethographic transmitter room.

Without even bothering to see if it was in use, she aimed her parasol and pulled down on the appropriate lotus leaf in the handle, activating the magnetic disruptor emitter. For just one moment everything stopped.

Then Alexia rushed forward and into the transmitting room of the apparatus.

Angelique was already standing up from the station. The little arms of the spark emitters were stopped midmessage. The French maid looked directly at Lady Maccon and, without pause, dashed toward her.

Alexia deflected the charge, but the girl's intention obviously had not been to attack, for she simply shoved Alexia to one side and leaped from the room. Lady Maccon fell back against a tangle of gadgetry on one wall of the chamber, lost her balance, and hit the floor hard, landing on her side.

She floundered among skirts, bustle, and petticoats, trying to regain her footing. As soon as she had, she raced to the transmitter cradle and grabbed out the metal scroll. Only three-quarters had burned through. Was it enough? Had her blast stopped the transmission, or did the vampires now have access to possibly the most dangerous information both about and to preternaturals?

With no time to check, Lady Maccon thrust the slate to one side, whirled about, and dashed after Angelique, convinced that now the young woman would be after the mummy.

This time she was correct.

"Angelique, stop!"

Alexia saw her from the landing above, struggling with the corpse of the long-dead preternatural, half carrying, half dragging the gruesome thing down the first set of stairs toward the front door of the castle.

"Alexia? What is going on?" Ivy Hisselpenny emerged from her room, cheeks blotchy and tearstained.

Lady Maccon took aim with her parasol, through the mahogany railing of the banister, and fired a numbing dart at her maid.

The French girl twisted, holding the mummy up as a shield. The dart hit and hung half inside of wrinkled brown skin thousands of years old. Alexia pounded down the next set of stairs.

Angelique pulled the mummy across her back so that it could protect her as she ran, but her progress was hampered by the awkwardness of having to carry the creature.

Lady Maccon paused on the staircase and took aim once more.

Miss Hisselpenny appeared in Alexia's line of view, standing on the landing above the first staircase, looking down at Angelique, entirely blocking Alexia's chance at a second shot.

"Ivy, move!"

"Goodness, Alexia, what is your maid up to? Is she *wearing* a mummy?"

"Yes, it is the latest Paris fashion, didn't you know?" replied Lady Maccon before, quite rudely, shoving her friend out of the way.

Miss Hisselpenny squeaked in outrage.

Alexia took aim and shot again. This time the dart missed entirely. She swore. She would have to get in some target practice if she were to continue this line of work. The parasol carried only a two-dart armament, so she increased her speed and went for the old-fashioned option.

"Really, Alexia, language. You sound like a fishmonger's wife!" said Miss Hisselpenny. "What is going on? Did your parasol just *emit* something? How untoward of it. I must be seeing things. It must be my deep love for Mr. Tunstell clouding my vision."

Lady Maccon entirely ignored her dear friend. The power of the mummy to repel her notwithstanding, she charged down the staircase, parasol at the ready. "Stay out of the way, Ivy," she ordered.

Angelique stumbled over the fallen form of one of the pack members.

"Just you stop right there," yelled Lady Maccon in her best muhjah voice.

French maid and mummy were almost at the door when Lady Maccon pounced, prodding Angelique viciously with the tip of the parasol.

Angelique froze, turning her head toward her former mistress. Her big violet eyes were wide.

Lady Maccon gave her a tight little smile. "Now, then, my dear, one lump or two?" Before the girl could answer her, she hauled her arm back and bashed Angelique as hard as she could over the head.

The maid and the mummy both fell.

"Apparently, just one is sufficient."

At the top of the stairs, Miss Hisselpenny gave a little cry of alarm and then clapped her hand to her mouth. "Alexia," she hissed, "how could you possibly behave so forcefully? With a parasol! To your own maid. It simply is not the thing to discipline one's staff so barbarically! I mean to say, your hair always looked perfectly well done to me."

Lady Maccon ignored her and kicked the mummy out of the way.

Ivy gasped again. "What are you doing? That is an ancient artifact. You love those old things!"

Lady Maccon could have done without the commentary. She had no time for historical scruples. The blasted mummy was causing too many problems and, if left intact, would become a logistical nightmare. There was no way it could be allowed to exist. Hang the scientific consequences.

She checked Angelique's breathing. The spy was still alive.

The best thing to do, Lady Maccon decided, was eliminate the mummy. Everything else could be dealt with subsequently.

Resisting the intense pushing sensation that urged her to get as far away from the awful thing as possible, Alexia dragged the mummy out onto the massive stone blocks that formed the front stoop of the castle. No sense in putting anyone else in danger.

Madame Lefoux had not designed the parasol to emit anything particularly toxic to preternaturals, if there existed such a substance, but Alexia was confident sufficient application of acid could destroy most anything.

She opened the parasol and flipped it so she was holding the spike. Just to be on the safe side, she turned the tiny dial above the magnetic disruption emitter all the way to the third click. The parasol's six ribs opened, and a fine mist clouded over the mummy, drenching dehydrated skin and old bone. She swayed the parasol back and forth, to be sure the liquid covered the entire body, and then propped it over the mummy's torso and backed away, leaving mummy and parasol alone together. The pungent aroma of burning acid permeated the air, and Alexia moved even farther away. Then came an odor like nothing she had ever smelled before: the final death of ancient bones, a mix of musty attic, and coppery blood.

The repelling sensation emitted by the mummy began to decrease. The creature itself was gradually disintegrating, turning into a lumpy puddle of brown mush, irregular bits of bone and skin sticking out. It was no longer recognizable as human.

The parasol kept spraying, the stone steps becoming pitted.

Behind Alexia, inside Kingair Castle, at the top of the grand staircase, Ivy Hisselpenny screamed.

On the other side of the British isle, in a hired, unmarked cab outside what looked to be a quite innocent, if expensive, town house in a discreetly fashionable neighborhood near Regent's Park, Professor Randolph Lyall and Major Channing Channing of the Chesterfield Channings sat and waited. It was a dangerous place for two werewolves to be, just outside the Westminster Hive. Doubly dangerous in that they were not there in any official capacity. If this got back to BUR, Lyall was tolerably certain he would be out of a job and the major cashiered.

They both practically jumped out of their skins, a true skill for a werewolf, when the cab door crashed open and a body tumbled inside.

"Drive!"

Major Channing banged on the roof of the cab with his pistol and the hack jumped forward. The horse's hooves emitted a shockingly loud clatter in the London night air.

"Well?" questioned Channing, impatient.

Lyall reached down to help the young man regain his feet and his dignity.

Biffy tossed back the black velvet cape that had fallen askew during his mad dash to safety. Lyall was at a loss to know how a cape could be of assistance when breaking and entering, but Biffy had insisted. "Dressing the part," he had said, "is *never* optional."

Professor Lyall grinned at the youngster. He really was a rather good-looking gentleman. Whatever else one might say about Lord Akeldama, and one might say a lot, he had excellent taste in drones. "So, how did it go?"

"Oh, they have one, all right. Right up near the roof. A slightly older model than my master's, but it looked to be in good working order."

A good-looking and *effective* gentleman.

"And?" Professor Lyall quirked an eyebrow.

"Let us simply say, for the time being, that it is most likely not as useful as it was a little while ago."

Major Channing looked at Biffy suspiciously. "What did you do?"

"Well, you see, there was this pot of tea, simply sitting there . . ." He trailed off.

"Useful thing, tea," commented Lyall thoughtfully.

Biffy grinned at him.

It was not one of Ivy's normal breathy, about-to-faint sort of screams. It was a scream of real terror, and it caused Lady Maccon to abandon her parasol to its acidic work and rush back inside, alone.

The scream's assertiveness had attracted the attention of others as well. Tunstell and a wobbly-looking Madame Lefoux both emerged from the downstairs parlor, despite Alexia's orders to the contrary.

"What are you doing?" she yelled at them. "Get back in there this instant!"

But their collective attention was entirely held elsewhere. It was fixed on the landing above, where Angelique stood close behind Miss Hisselpenny, a deadly looking knife held to that young lady's throat.

"Miss Hisselpenny!" yelled Tunstell, his face suffused with horror. And then, abandoning all decency and decorum, "Ivy!"

At the same time Madame Lefoux yelled, "Angelique, no!"

Everyone charged toward the stairs. Angelique dragged Ivy back with her toward the room that had once housed the mummy.

"Stay back or she will die," said the maid in her native tongue, hand steady and eyes hard.

Tunstell, not understanding, drew the Tue Tue and pointed it at the maid. Madame Lefoux pulled down on his arm. She proved surprisingly strong for one so recently injured. "You'll hit the hostage."

"Angelique, this is madness," said Lady Maccon, trying to be reasonable. "I have destroyed the evidence. Soon the pack will be awake and recovered. Whatever drug you gave them will not last once they reclaim their supernatural state. It cannot possibly be long now. You simply will not be able to escape."

Angelique continued to move backward, dragging the hapless Miss Hisselpenny with her. "Zen I have nothing to lose, non?" She continued into the room.

As soon as she was out of sight, Lady Maccon and Tunstell both dashed up the stairs after her. Madame Lefoux tried to follow, but her progress was much slower. She was clutching at her wounded shoulder and breathing with difficulty.

"I need her alive," Alexia panted at Tunstell. "I have questions."

Tunstell tucked the Tue Tue into his breeches and nodded.

They attained the room at about the same time. They found Angelique, still armed, directing Ivy to open the shutters to the far window. Alexia bitterly regretted her lack of parasol. Really, she would have to chain the bloody thing to her side. Every time she did not have it, she found herself in grave need of its services. Before Angelique caught sight of them, Tunstell ducked down and to one side, using the various furnishings about the room to shield himself from the maid's view.

While he approached in secret, making his way cautiously about the room, Lady Maccon took it upon herself to distract the spy. It was not easy; Tunstell was not what one could describe as subtle. His flaming red hair bobbed up with each pointed and articulated footstep, as though he were some cloaked Gothic villain creeping across a stage. Melodramatic fat-head. It was a good thing the room was darkened, lit by only one gas lamp in the far corner.

"Angelique," Lady Maccon called.

Angelique turned, jerking roughly at Miss Hisselpenny with her free hand, the other still clutching the wicked-looking knife at Ivy's neck. "Hurry up," she growled at Miss Hisselpenny. "You"—she jerked her chin at Alexia—"stay back and let me see your hands."

Lady Maccon waved her empty hands about, and Angelique nodded, clearly pleased by the lack of weaponry. Alexia privately urged Ivy to faint. It would make matters much easier. Ivy remained stubbornly conscious and distraught. She never did faint when it was actually warranted.

"Why, Angelique?" Lady Maccon asked, genuinely

curious, not to mention eager to keep the maid's attention off of the blatantly skulking Tunstell.

The French girl smiled, her face even more beautiful. Her large eyes shone in the light of the gas lamp. "Because she asked me to. Because she promised she would try."

"She. *She* who?"

"Who do you think?" Angelique practically snapped back.

Lady Maccon caught a whiff of vanilla scent, and then a soft voice spoke from her side. Madame Lefoux leaned weakly against the doorjamb next to her. "Countess Nadasdy."

Lady Maccon frowned and bit at her lip, confused. She continued to speak to Angelique, only half acknowledging the inventor's presence. "But I thought your former master was a rove. I thought you were at the Westminster Hive under sufferance."

Angelique prodded at Ivy again, this time using the tip of the knife. Ivy squeaked and fumbled with the latch of the shutters, finally managing to throw them back. The castle was old, with no glass in its windows. Cool, wet night air rushed into the room.

"You think too much, my lady," sneered the spy.

Tunstell, having finally made his way about the room, sprang forward at that moment, launching himself at the Frenchwoman. For the first time in their acquaintance, Alexia felt he was finally showing some of the grace and dexterity one would expect in a soon-to-be werewolf. Of course, it could all be showmanship, but it was impressive nevertheless.

Miss Hisselpenny, seeing who it was who had come to

her rescue, screamed and fainted, collapsing to one side of the open window.

Finally, thought Alexia.

Angelique reeled around, brandishing the knife.

Tunstell and the maid grappled. Angelique struck out at the claviger with a wicked slash, training and practice behind the movement. He ducked, deflecting the blade with his shoulder. A bloody gash appeared on the meat of his upper arm.

Lady Maccon jerked forward to go to Tunstell's aid, but Madame Lefoux held her back. Her foot came down with a sad little crunch noise, and Alexia tore her gaze away from the grappling forms to see what had caused it. *Ugh!* The floor was littered with dead scarab beetles.

The claviger was unsurprisingly stronger than Angelique. She was a delicate little thing, and he was built on the larger end of the scale, as both werewolves and stage directors preferred. What he lacked in technique, he more than made up for in brawn. He came up out of the crouch, twisting to push his uninjured shoulder to the maid's gut. With a scream of anger, the woman fell backward out the window. This was probably not quite what she had originally intended upon opening it, if the rope ladder was any indication. She let forth a long, high scream that ended in a crunchy kind of thud.

Madame Lefoux screamed herself and left off holding back Lady Maccon. The two dashed over to look out the window.

Below, Angelique lay in a crumpled heap. Probably not the landing she had intended either.

"Did you miss the part where I said I needed her alive?"

Tunstell's face was white. "Then she isn't? I killed her."

"No, she flew off into the aether. Of course you killed her, you—"

Tunstell forestalled his mistress's wrath by fainting into a freckled heap.

Alexia turned her ire on Madame Lefoux. The inventor was staring, white-faced, down at the fallen maid.

"Why did you hold me back?"

Madame Lefoux opened her mouth, and a sound like stampeding elephants halted whatever she had been about to say.

The members of the Kingair Pack appeared around the open doorway. They were minus their human companions, as the clavigers and Lady Kingair still labored under the effects of Angelique's sleep drug. The fact that they were up and about indicated that the mummy must have finally and completely dissolved.

"Move, you mongrels," growled a vehement voice behind them. Just as quickly as they had appeared, the pack disappeared, and Lord Conall Maccon strode into the room.

"Oh, good," said his wife, "you are awake. What took you so long?"

"Hello, my dear. What have you done now?"

"Be so kind as to leave off insulting me, and see to Ivy and Tunstell, would you, please? They may both require vinegar. Oh, and keep an eye on Madame Lefoux. I have a body to check on."

Noting his wife's general demeanor and expression, the earl did not question her dictates.

"I take it the body is that of your maid?"

"How did you know?" Lady Maccon was understandably peeved. After all, she had only just figured this all out. How dare her own husband be a step ahead of her?

"She shot me, remember?" he replied with a sniff.

"Yes, well, I had better check."

"Are we hoping for dead or alive?"

Lady Maccon sucked her teeth. "Mmm, dead would make for less paperwork. But alive would make for fewer questions."

He waved a hand flippantly. "Carry on, my dear."

"Oh, really, Conall. As if it were your idea," said his wife, annoyed but already trotting out the door.

"And I chose to marry that one," commented her husband to the assembled werewolves in resigned affection.

"I heard that," Lady Maccon said without pausing.

She made her way quickly back down the stairs. She was certainly getting her exercise today. She picked her way through the still-slumbering clavigers and out the front door. She took the opportunity to check the mummy, which was no more than a pile of brown slush. The parasol was no longer emitting its deadly mist, obviously having used up its supply. She would have to see about a tune-up, as she had already used much of its complement of weaponry. She closed it with a snap and took it with her around the side of the castle to where the crumpled form of Angelique lay, unmoving on the damp castle green.

Lady Maccon poked at her with the tip of the parasol from some distance. When that elicited no reaction, she bent to examine the fallen woman closer. Without a doubt, Angelique's was not a condition that could be cured through the application of vinegar. The French girl's head listed far to one side, her neck broken by the fall.

Lady Maccon sighed, stood, and was just about to poodle off, when the air all about the body shivered, as heat will ripple the air about a fire.

Alexia had never before witnessed an unbirth. As with normal births, they were generally considered a little crass and unmentionable in polite society, but there was no doubt about what was happening to Angelique. For there before Lady Maccon appeared the faint shimmering form of her dead maid.

"So, you might have survived Countess Nadasdy's bite in the end."

The ghost looked at her. For a long moment, as though adjusting to her new state of existence—or nonexistence as it were. She simply floated there, the leftover part of Angelique's soul.

"I always knew I could have been something more," replied Formerly Angelique. "But you had to stop me. Zey told me you were dangerous. I thought it was because zey feared you, feared what you were and what you could produce. But now I realized zey feared *who* you are az well. Your lack of soul, it haz affected your character. You are not only preternatural, you also think differently az a result."

"I suppose I might," replied Alexia. "But it is hard for me to know with any certainty, having only ever experienced my own thoughts."

The ghost floated, hovering just over her body. For some time she would be tethered close, unable to stretch her limits until her flesh began to erode away. Only then, doomed to deterioration as the connection to the body became weaker and weaker, would she be able to venture farther away, at the same time dissolving into poltergeis and madness. It was not a nice way to enter the afterlife.

The Frenchwoman looked at her former mistress. "Will you be preserving my body, or letting me go mad, or will you exorcise me now?"

"Choices, choices," said Lady Maccon rather harshly. "Which would *you* prefer?"

The ghost did not hesitate. "I should like to go now. BUR will persuade me to spy, and I should not wish to work against either my hive or my country. And I could not stand to run mad."

"So, you do have some scruples."

It was hard to tell, but it seemed as though the specter smiled at that. Ghosts were never more than passing solid; one scientific hypothesis was that they were the physical representation of the mind's memory of itself. "More zan you will ever know," said Formerly Angelique.

"And if I exorcise you, what will you give me in return?" Alexia, preternatural, wanted to know.

Formerly Angelique sighed, although she no longer had lungs with which to sigh or air with which to emit sound. Lady Maccon spared a thought to wonder how ghosts managed to talk.

"You are curious, I suppose. A bargain. I will answer you ten questions az honest az I am able. Zen, you will set me to die."

"Why did you do all of this?" Lady Maccon asked immediately, and without hesitation: the easiest and most important question first.

Formerly Angelique held up ten ghostly fingers and ticked one down. "Because ze comtesse offered me ze bite. Who does not want eternal life?" A pause. "Aside from Genevieve."

"Why were you trying to kill me?"

"I waz never trying to kill you. I waz always after Genevieve. I waz not very good at it. Ze fall, in ze air, and ze shootings, zat was for her. You were an inconvenience; she iz ze danger."

"And the poison?"

Formerly Angelique now had three fingers bent. "Zat was not me. I am thinking, my lady, zat someone else wants you dead. And your fourth question?"

"Do you believe it is Madame Lefoux trying to kill me?"

"I think not, but it iz hard to tell with Genevieve. She iz, how do you say? Ze smart one. But should she want you dead, it would be your body lying there, not mine."

"So why do *you* wish our little inventor dead?"

"Your fifth question, my lady, and you waste it on Genevieve? She 'az something of mine. She insisted on giving it back or telling the world."

"What could be so horrible?"

"It would have ruined my life. Ze comtesse, she insists, no family. She will not bite to change if there iz children—part of vampire edict. A lesser regulation but the comtesse 'az always played hive politics close. And seeing how Lady Kingair complicates your husband's life, I begin to understand why the rule waz in place."

Lady Maccon put all things together. She knew those violet eyes had been familiar. "Madame Lefoux's son, Quesnel. He is not her child, is he? He is yours."

"A mistake that no longer matters." Another finger went down. Three questions left.

"Madame Lefoux was on board the dirigible tracking you, not me! Was she blackmailing you?"

"Yez, either I take up my maternal duty or she'd tell the countess. I could not have that, you understand? When I had worked so hard for immortality."

Alexia blushed, grateful for the cool night air. "You two were . . ."

The ghost gave a kind of shrug, the gesture, still so casual, even in specter form. "Of course, for many years."

Lady Maccon felt her face go even hotter, erotic images flashing through her brain: Madame Lefoux's dark head next to Angelique's blond one. A pretty picture the two of them would have made, like something out of a naughty postcard. "Well, I say, how extraordinarily French."

The ghost laughed. "Hardly that. How do you think I caught Comtesse Nadasdy's interest? Not with ze hairdressing skills, let me assure you, my lady."

Alexia had seen something of the kind in her father's collection, but she had never imagined it might be based on anything more than masculine wistfulness or performances put on to titillate a john's palate. That two women might do such things voluntarily with one another and do so with some degree of romantic love. Was this possible?

She did not realize she had voiced this last question aloud.

The ghost snorted. "All I can say iz, I am certain she loved me, at one time."

Lady Maccon began to see much more in the inventor's actions and comments over the past week than she had originally. "You are a hard little thing, aren't you, Angelique?"

"What a waste of your last question, my lady. We all become what we are taught to be. You are not so hard as you would like. What will that husband of yours say, when he finds out?"

"Finds out what?"

"Oh, you really do not know? I thought you were play-acting." The ghost laughed, a genuine laugh, harsh and directed at the confusion and future misery of another.

"What? What do I not know?"

"Oh no, I have fulfilled my half of the bargain. Ten questions, fairly answered."

Alexia sighed. It was true. She reached forward, albeit reluctantly, to perform her very first exorcism. Odd that the government had known of her preternatural state for her whole life, had recorded her in the BUR Files of Secrecy and Import as the only preternatural in all of London, yet never used her in her kind's most common capacity—that of exorcist. Odd, too, that her first use of this ability should be at a ghost's request, in the Highlands of Scotland. And odd, last of all, that it should be so dreadfully easy.

She simply laid her hand upon Angelique's broken body, performing the literal application of the term *laying the body to rest*. As quick as that, the ghostly form disappeared, tethers broken, and all excess soul was terminated. With no living body to call it back when Alexia raised her hands, it was gone forever: complete and total disanimus. The soul could never return, as it did with werewolves and vampires. With the body dead, such a return was fatal. Poor Angelique, she might have been immortal, had she made different choices.

Lady Maccon found a very strange scene when she made her way back inside the castle and up the stairs into the mummy room. Tunstell was awake, his shoulder and upper arm bandaged with a red-checked handkerchief of Ivy's origination, and he was busy applying a good deal of excellent brandy to his mouth as a curative addendum. Miss Hisselpenny was kneeling next to him, cooing unhelpfully, having recovered her senses, at least enough to attain wakefulness, if not actual sense.

"Oh, Mr. Tunstell, how exceedingly brave you were, coming to my rescue like that. So heroic," she was saying. "Imagine if it got known that I had been knifed by a maid, a *French* maid, no less? Had I died, I should *never* have lived it down! How can I possibly thank you enough?"

Madame Lefoux stood next to Lord Maccon, looking composed, if a little drawn about the eyes and mouth, her dimples secured away for the time being. Alexia could not interpret this expression. She was not yet confident in the inventor's trustworthiness. Madame Lefoux had entertained some considerable vested interest in the proceedings from the start. Not to mention that suspicious octopus tattoo. If nothing else, Alexia's experience with the bedeviled scientists of the Hypocras Club had taught her not to trust octopuses.

She strode up to the Frenchwoman and said, "Angelique has had her say. It is time, Madame Lefoux, for you to do the same. What did you really want—simply Angelique or something more? Who was trying to poison me on board the dirigible?" Without pause, she turned her attention onto Tunstell, eyeing his wound critically. "Did he get vinegar put on that?"

"Had?" Madame Lefoux asked, apparently grappling with only one of the many words Lady Maccon had uttered. "Did you say *had*? Is she dead, then?"

"Angelique?"

Teeth nibbling fretfully at her bottom lip, the Frenchwoman nodded.

"Quite."

Madame Lefoux did the most curious thing. She opened her green eyes wide, as though in surprise. And then, when that did not seem to help, turned her dark head aside and began to cry.

Lady Maccon envied her the skill of crying with aplomb. She herself went allover splotchy, but Madame Lefoux seemed to be able to execute the emotional state with minimal fuss: no gulps, no sniffles, just silent fat tears falling down her cheeks and dripping off her chin. It seemed all the more painfully sad, immersed in unnatural silence.

Lady Maccon, never one to be moved by sentiment, cast her hands up to heaven. "Oh, by glory, what now?"

"I ken, wife, now is the time for us all to be a tad more forthcoming with one another," said Conall. He was a softer touch. He steered both Alexia and Madame Lefoux away from the scene of battle (and Ivy and Tunstell, who were now making horrible kissy noises at one another) to a different part of the room.

"Oh dear." Lady Maccon glared at Lord Maccon. "You said 'us all.' Were you involved as well, my darling husband? Have you, perhaps, been less forthcoming than you should with your loving wife?"

Lord Maccon sighed. "Why must you always be so difficult, woman?"

Lady Maccon said nothing, simply crossed her arms over her ample bosom and stared pointedly at him.

"Madame Lefoux was working for me," he admitted, his voice so low it was almost a growl. "I asked her to keep an eye on you while I was away."

"And you did not tell me?"

"Well, you know how you get."

"I most certainly do. Really, Conall, imagine assigning a BUR agent to track me, as though I were a fox in the hunt. That is simply the living end! How could you?"

"Oh, she isn't BUR. We've known each other a long time. I asked her as a friend, not an employee."

Alexia frowned. She wasn't sure how she felt about *that.* "How long a time and how good a friend?"

Madame Lefoux gave a watery little smile.

Lord Maccon looked genuinely surprised. "Really, wife, you are not usually given to such denseness. I dinna fit Madame Lefoux's preferences."

"Ah, any more than I fit Lord Akeldama's?"

Lord Maccon, who was prone to getting a mite jealous of the effete vampire and resented the man's close relationship with Alexia, nodded his understanding. "Verra well, I take your point, wife."

"Admittedly," interjected Madame Lefoux, her voice soft and tear-strained, "I was also interested in contacting Angelique, and she *is* Lady Maccon's maid."

"You had your own agenda," accused Lord Maccon, looking with suspicion at the Frenchwoman.

"Who doesn't?" wondered Lady Maccon. "Angelique

told me you used to be intimate and that Quesnel is hers, not yours."

"When did she tell you this, before she died?" wondered Lord Maccon.

Alexia patted his arm. "No, dear, after."

Madame Lefoux brightened considerably. "She is a ghost?"

Lady Maccon waggled her fingertips about. "Not anymore."

The inventor gasped, what appeared to have been a strange kind of hope quickly followed by a return to sadness. "You exorcised her? How cruel."

"She asked, and we struck a bargain. I am sorry. I did not think to take your feelings into account."

"These days, no one seems to." The inventor sounded bitter.

"There is no need to wallow," replied Lady Maccon, who did not approve of maudlin humors.

"Really, Alexia, why such sharpness with the woman? She is overset."

Lady Maccon looked more closely into Madame Lefoux's face. "I believe there may be cause. You are not so sad over lost love as you are over a lost past. Is that not so, madame?"

Madame Lefoux's face lost a modicum of its grief, and her eyes narrowed, sharpening on Alexia. "We were together for a long time, but you are right. I did want her back—not for me but for Quesnel. I thought perhaps a son would ground her in the daylight world. She changed so very much after she became a drone. They tapped into the hardness Quesnel and I had once managed to temper."

Alexia nodded. "I deduced as much."

Lord Maccon looked at his wife appreciatively. "Good Lord, woman, how could you have possibly known that?"

"Well"—Lady Maccon grinned—"Madame Lefoux here did play a bit of the coquette with me while we were traveling. I do not think she was entirely shamming."

Madame Lefoux flashed a sudden smile. "I did not know you were even aware."

Alexia arched both eyebrows. "I was not until recently; hindsight can be most illuminating."

Lord Maccon glowered at the Frenchwoman. "You were flirting with *my wife*!" he roared.

Madame Lefoux straightened her spine and looked up at him. "No need to raise your hackles and get territorial, old wolf. You find her attractive—why shouldn't I?"

Lord Maccon actually sputtered.

"Nothing happened," corroborated Alexia, smiling broadly.

Madame Lefoux added, "Not that I wouldn't like—"

Lord Maccon growled and loomed even more menacingly in Madame Lefoux's direction. The inventor rolled her eyes at his posturing.

Alexia's grin widened. It was rare to have someone else around brave enough to tease the earl. She shot a quick glance in the Frenchwoman's direction. At least, she thought they were teasing. Just to be on the safe side, she hastily switched topics. "This is all very flattering, but could we return to the subject at hand? If Madame Lefoux was on board the dirigible to keep an eye on me and to blackmail Angelique with parental duties, then it was not she who tried to poison me and got Tunstell instead. And I now know it was not Angelique either."

"Poison! You didna tell me about a poisoning, wife! You only mentioned the fall." Lord Maccon began to vibrate with suppressed anger. His eyes had turned feral, solid yellow now instead of tawny brown. Wolf eyes.

"Yes, well, the fall *was* Angelique."

"Dinna change the subject, you impossible woman!"

Lady Maccon switched to defending herself. "Well, I did suppose Tunstell would have told you. He took the brunt of the incident, after all. And he is your claviger. Normally he tells you everything. Regardless"—she turned back to Madame Lefoux—"*you* are after the humanization weapon as well, aren't you?"

Madame Lefoux smiled again. "How did you guess?"

"Someone keeps trying to break into or steal my dispatch case. Since you knew about the parasol and all its secret pockets, I figured it had to be you, not Angelique. And what could you possibly want with it except my records as muhjah on the London humanization and the dewan and potentate's findings?" She paused, her head cocked to one side. "Would you mind stopping now? It is most aggravating. There is nothing of import in the case, you do realize?"

"But I am still eager to know where you hid it."

"Mmm, ask Ivy about lucky special socks."

Lord Maccon gave his wife a funny look.

Madame Lefoux ignored that bizarre statement and moved on. "You did figure it out in the end, didn't you? The source of the humanization? You must have, because"—she gestured to Lord Maccon's wolf eyes—"it seems to have been reversed."

Lady Maccon nodded. "Of course I did."

"Yes, I thought you might. That was the real reason I followed you."

Lord Maccon sighed. "Really, Madame Lefoux, why not wait until BUR had it cleared and simply ask what had happened?"

The inventor gave him a hard look. "When has BUR, or the Crown for that matter, ever shared such information openly with anyone? Let alone a French scientist? Even as a friend, you would never tell me the truth of it."

Lord Maccon looked like he would rather not comment on that statement. "Were you, like Angelique, being paid by the Westminster vampires to find this information out?" he asked, looking resigned.

Madame Lefoux said nothing.

Alexia felt rather smug at this point. It was rare for her to be able to put one over on her husband. "Conall, you mean to say you did not know? Madame Lefoux is not really working for you. She is not working for the hives either. She is working for the Hypocras Club."

"What! That canna be possible."

"Oh yes, it can. I saw the tattoo."

"No, really it is not," Lord Maccon and Madame Lefoux said at the same time.

"Trust me, my dear, we saw to it that the entire operation was disbanded," added the earl.

"That explains why you turned so cold toward me all of a sudden," said Madame Lefoux. "You saw my tattoo and jumped to conclusions."

Lady Maccon nodded.

"Tattoo, what tattoo?" Lord Maccon growled. He was looking ever more annoyed.

Madame Lefoux yanked down her collar, which was easy without her cravat, exposing the telltale mark upon her neck.

"Ah, my dear, I see the source of the confusion." The earl seemed suddenly much calmer, rather than launching into violence over the octopus as Alexia had expected.

He took his wife's hand softly in his large paw. "The Hypocras was a militant branch of the OBO. Madame Lefoux is a member in good standing. Are you not?"

The inventor gave a little half-smile and nodded.

"And what, pray tell, is the OBO?" Lady Maccon yanked her hand out of her husband's patronizing grip.

"The Order of the Brass Octopus, a secret society of scientists and inventors."

Lady Maccon glared at the earl. "And you did not think to tell me about this?"

He shrugged. "It is meant to be *secret*."

"We really must work on our communication. Perhaps if you were not so constantly interested in other forms of intimacy, I might actually have access to the information I need to survive with my temper intact!" Alexia poked at him with a sharp finger. "More talk, less bed sport."

Lord Maccon looked alarmed. "Fine, I shall make time to discuss these things with you."

She narrowed her eyes.

"I promise."

She whirled about to look at Madame Lefoux, who was unsuccessfully trying to hide her amusement at Lord Maccon's discomfort.

"And this Order of the Brass Octopus, what are its policies?"

"Secret."

A hard look met that remark.

"In all honesty, we do agree with the Hypocras Club to a certain degree: that the supernatural must be monitored, that there should be checks in place. I am sorry, my lord, but it is true. Supernaturals continue to tamper with the world, particularly the vampires. You get greedy. Look at the Roman Empire."

The earl snorted but was not particularly offended. "As though the daylight folk have done so well: never forget, your lot boasts the Inquisition."

Madame Lefoux turned to Alexia, trying to explain. Her green eyes were oddly desperate, as though this, of all things, was terribly important. "You, as a preternatural, must understand. You are the living representation of the counterbalance theorem in action. You are supposed to be on *our* side."

Alexia did understand. Having worked alongside the dewan and the potentate for several months, she could comprehend this desperate need the scientists felt to constantly monitor the supernatural set. She wasn't yet quite certain which side she came down on, but she said firmly, "You understand Conall has my loyalty? Well, him and the queen."

The Frenchwoman nodded. "And now that you know my allegiances, will you tell me what caused the mass negation of the supernatural?"

"You want to harness it into an invention of some kind, don't you?"

Madame Lefoux looked arch. "I am convinced there

is a market. How about it, Lord Maccon? Imagine what I could do for a sundowner, with the ability to turn vampires and werewolves mortal. Or, Lady Maccon, what new gadget I might install in your parasol? Think of the control we could have over supernaturals."

Lord Maccon gave the inventor a long, hard look. "I didna realize you were a radical, Madame Lefoux. When did that happen?"

Lady Maccon decided then and there not to tell the inventor about the mummy. "I am sorry, madame, but it would be best if I kept this to myself. I have removed the cause, obviously"—she gestured to the pack, still hovering hopefully in the doorway—"with the help of your excellent parasol, but I am thinking this is knowledge best kept out of the public domain."

"You are a hard woman, Lady Maccon," replied the inventor, frowning. "But you do realize, we *will* figure it out eventually."

"Not if I have anything to do with it. Although it may be too late. I believe our little spy may have managed to get the word out to the Westminster Hive despite my precautions," said Lady Maccon, suddenly remembering the aethographic transmitter and Angelique's message.

She turned and strode toward the door. Madame Lefoux and Lord Maccon followed.

"No." She looked at the inventor. "I am sorry, Madame Lefoux. It is not that I do not like you. It is simply that I do not trust you. Please remain here. Oh, and give me back my journal."

The inventor looked confused. "I did not take it."

"But I thought you said . . ."

"I looked for the dispatch case, but it was not me who broke into your room on board the dirigible."

"Then who did?"

"The same person who tried to poison you, I suppose."

Alexia threw her hands up. "I don't have time for this." And with that, she led her husband from the room at a brisk trot.

CHAPTER FOURTEEN

Changes

Lord Maccon checked the hall. It was empty, the pack having filed into the mummy room or gone to collect Angelique's body. Seeing no one around to forestall his action, the earl slammed his wife up against the wall, pressing the full length of his body against hers.

"Ooomph," said his wife. "Not now."

He nuzzled in at her neck, kissing and licking her softly just below her ear. "Just a moment," he said. "I need a small reminder that you are here, you are whole, and you are mine."

"Well, the first two should be patently obvious, and the last one is always in question," replied his lady unhelpfully. But she wrapped her arms about his neck and pressed against him despite all protestations to the contrary.

He resorted, as always, to action over words and sealed his lips atop hers, stopping that wicked tongue.

Alexia, who had, until that moment, managed to remain rather pulled together and tidy, despite all of her dashing about the castle, cast herself into a willing state of hopeless disarray. There was really nothing else to do when Conall was in one of these moods but enjoy it. Her husband drove his hands into her hair, tilting her head to the correct angle for ravishment. Ah well, at least he was good at it.

Alexia sacrificed herself on the altar of wifely duty, enjoying every minute of it, of course, but still determined to pull him back and get on to the aethographor.

Her determination notwithstanding, it was several long moments before he finally raised his head.

"Right," he said, as though he had just finished a refreshing beverage. "Shall we continue on, then?"

"What?" Alexia asked, dazed, trying to recall what they had been about before he started kissing her.

"The transmitter, remember?"

"Oh yes, right." She swatted him out of habit. "Why did you want to go and distract me like that? I was quite in my element and everything."

Conall laughed. "Someone has to keep you off balance; otherwise you'll end up ruling the empire. Or at least ordering it into wretched submission."

"Ha-ha, very funny." She started down the hallway at a brisk trot, bustle waggling suggestively back and forth. Halfway down, she paused and looked back at him over one shoulder coquettishly. "Oh, Conall, *do* get a move on."

Lord Maccon growled but lumbered after her.

She stopped again, cocking her head. "What is that preposterous noise?"

"Opera."

"Really? I should never have guessed."

"I believe Tunstell is serenading Miss Hisselpenny."

"Good heavens! Poor Ivy. Ah well." She started onward again.

As they wound their way up through the castle toward the top turret where the aethographor resided, Alexia explained her theory that the now-destroyed mummy had once been a preternatural, that, after death, it had turned into some strange sort of soul-sucking weapon of mass disintegration. And that Angelique, believing the same, had tried to steal the mummy. Probably to get it into the hands of the Westminster Hive and Countess Nadasdy's pet scientists.

"If Angelique did manage to reveal all to the hive, no possible good can come of it. We might as well tell Madame Lefoux; at least she will use the knowledge to make weapons for our side."

Lord Maccon looked at his wife oddly. "Are there sides?"

"It would appear to be that way."

Lord Maccon sighed, his face worn with care, if not the passage of time. Alexia realized she was gripping his hand tightly and had thus brought him back into mortal state. She let go. He probably needed to be a werewolf right now, tapping into his reserves of supernatural strength.

He grumbled. "The last thing we need is a competition over weaponry based on dead preternaturals. I shall issue standing orders that all soulless are to be cremated after death. Covertly, of course." He looked to his wife, for once not angry, simply concerned. "They would all be after you and those of your kind dotted about the empire. Not only that, but you would also be more valuable dead if they knew that mummification worked as a preservation technique for your power."

"Luckily," Alexia said, "no one knows how the ancients conducted mummification. It gives us some time. And perhaps the transmission did not go through. I did manage to blast the aethographor with my magnetic disruption emitter."

She retrieved Angelique's metal scroll from where she had stashed it. It was not reassuring. The spy's message was burned completely through, and the track marks from the spark readers were evident across most of it.

Lady Maccon swore an impressive blue streak. The earl gave her a look that was half disapproval, half respect.

"I take it the message was sent on successfully?"

She passed the slate over to him. It read simply, "Dead mummy is soul-sucker." Not so many words in the end, but enough to complicate her life considerably in the future.

"Well, that has gone and torn it," was Lady Maccon's first cogent sentence.

"How can we be certain it went through to the other side?"

Alexia picked up a faceted crystalline valve, completely intact, from where it rested in the resonator cradle. "This must belong to the Westminster Hive." She tucked it into her parasol, in the pocket next to the one for Lord Akeldama's valve.

Then, with a thoughtful frown, she pulled that one out and examined it, twisting it this way and that in her gloved hand. What had Lord Akeldama's message said when they were testing Madame Lefoux's repairs?

Something about rats? Oh no, no, it had been bats. Old-fashioned slang for the vampire community. If Lord Akeldama was monitoring the Westminster Hive, as she'd thought at the time, would he, too, have received the transmission about the mummy? Would him knowing be any worse or better?

Only one way to find out. Try sending him a message and see if he responded.

It was well past her arranged transmission time, of course, but Lord Akeldama's was the kind of apparatus that, if it was on and directed toward the appropriate frequency, would receive whatever was sent. If he *had* intercepted something significant, he would be expecting Alexia to contact him.

Instructing her husband to please stay as silent as possible, with a glare that indicated real consequences should he misbehave, Alexia went to work. She was getting quite adept at running the aethographor. She etched in her message as quickly as possible. Fitting Lord Akeldama's valve into the cradle and the slate into its holder and activating the machine to transmit was much less difficult this time. Her message consisted of two things: "?" and "Alexia."

As soon as the transmission was complete, she went into the receiving chamber. Her husband merely continued to stand outside the aethographor, arms crossed, watching his wife's frilly form. She scuttled about, twiddling various dials and flipping large, important-looking switches. He might approve of her bluestocking tendencies, but he would never understand them. Back at BUR, he had people to run his aethographor for him.

Lady Maccon appeared to have things well in hand,

however, as a message began to appear, letter by letter, in the magnetic particulate. As quietly as possible, she copied it down. It was rather longer than any transmission she had received before. It took a good deal of time to come in and even longer for her to determine where the breaks were between words and how it should read. When she finally managed it, Lady Maccon began to laugh. "My *petal*." The italics were visible even across the length of England. "Westminster's toy had tea issues. Thank Biffy and Lyall. Toodle pip. A."

"Fantastic!" said Lady Maccon, grinning.

"What?" Her husband's head looked in at the door to the receiving chamber.

"My favorite vampire, with the help of your illustrious Beta, managed to get his fangs into the Westminster Hive's transmitter. Angelique's last message never made it through."

Lord Maccon frowned darkly. "Randolph was working *with* Lord Akeldama?"

Lady Maccon patted his arm. "Well, he is far more accepting than you about these things."

The frown increased. "Clearly." A pause. "Well, then, let me just . . ." Her husband, still holding the slate with Angelique's message on it, twisted the dangerous thing around itself, his muscles expanding impressively, and then crushed the scroll together until all that remained was a crumpled metal ball. "We had better melt it down as well," he said, "just to be on the safe side." He looked to his wife. "Does anyone else know?"

"About the mummy?" She bit her lip in thought. "Lachlan and Sidheag. Possibly Lord Akeldama and

Professor Lyall. And Ivy, but only in that way Ivy knows things."

"Which is to say, not with any real cogency?"

"Exactly."

They smiled at each other and, after Alexia shut down the machine, made their way leisurely back downstairs.

"Miss Hisselpenny has eloped."

After the general chaos of the night before, everyone had retired to their respective beds. Those still affected by Angelique's sleep drug were carried up by the pack. Then most of them, werewolves driven once more by antisun instincts and everyone else through pure exhaustion, slept the day away.

When Alexia came down for her first meal of the day, right about teatime, the sun had just set. It was as though her old pattern of nighttime living had miraculously transplanted itself to the Scottish Highlands.

The Kingair Pack sat about munching down fried kippers at the rate of knots, all looking brighter and bushier of tail, seeing as they now could go back to having tails. Even Lady Kingair seemed in slightly better spirits. She certainly relished delivering the news that Tunstell and Ivy had set out for Gretna Green sometime that morning, while everyone was still abed.

"What?" barked Lady Maccon, genuinely surprised. Ivy was silly, but was she really *that* silly?

Felicity, whom Alexia had, it must be admitted, entirely forgotten about in the chaos of the night before, looked up from her meal. "Why, yes, sister. She left you a note, with me of course."

"Did she, by George?" Alexia snatched the scribbled missive from her sister's pink-gloved hand.

Felicity grinned, enjoying Alexia's discomfort. "Miss Hisselpenny was awfully distraught when she composed it. I noticed no less than ten exclamation marks."

"And why, pray tell, would she leave it with you?" Alexia sat down and served herself a small portion of haggis.

Felicity shrugged, biting into a pickled onion. "I was the only one keeping respectable hours?"

Alexia was instantly suspicious. "Felicity, did you encourage them in any way into this rash course of action?"

"Who, me?" Her sister blinked wide eyes at her. "I never."

Lady Maccon was confident that if Felicity had helped, she had done so out of malice. She rubbed at her face with one hand. "Miss Hisselpenny will be ruined."

Felicity grinned. "Yes, yes, she will. I knew no good could possibly come of their association. I never liked Mr. Tunstell. I never even thought to look in his direction."

Lady Maccon gritted her teeth and opened Ivy's message.

All about the dining table, fascinated eyes watched her and less fascinated jaws masticated even more kipper.

Dearest Alexia, the message read. *Oh, please absolve me of this guilt I already feel squishing on my very soul!* Lady Maccon huffed, trying not to laugh. *My troubled heart weeps!* Oh dear, Ivy was getting flowery. *My bones ache with the sin that I am about to commit. Oh, why must I have bones? I have lost myself to this transplant-*

ing love. You could not possibly understand how this feels! Yet try to comprehend, dearest Alexia, I am like a delicate bloom. Marriage without love is all very well for people like you, but I should wilt and wither. I need a man possessed of a poet's soul! I am simply not so stoic as you. I cannot stand to be apart from him one moment longer! The caboose of my love has derailed, and I must sacrifice all for the man I adore! Please do not judge me harshly! It was all for love! ~ Ivy.

Lady Maccon passed the missive to her husband. Several lines in, he began to guffaw.

His wife, eyes twinkling, said unhelpfully, "Husband, this is a serious matter. There are derailed cabooses to consider. You have lost your valet, for one, not to mention a promising claviger for the Woolsey Pack."

Lord Maccon wiped his eyes with the back of his hand. "Ah Tunstell, the nitwit, he was never a very good claviger. I was having doubts about him anyhow."

Lady Maccon took Ivy's note back from him. "But we must feel sorry for poor Captain Featherstonehaugh."

Lord Maccon shrugged. "Must we? He has had a lucky escape, if you ask me. Imagine having to look at those hats for the rest of one's life."

"Conall." His wife slapped his arm in reprimand.

"Well," Lord Maccon said truculently.

"You realize, husband, this puts us in an exceptionally embarrassing position? Ivy was in my charge. We shall have to inform her parents of this sad affair."

Lord Maccon shrugged. "The newlyweds will probably make it back to London before we do."

"You believe they are headed there after Gretna Green?"

"Well, Tunstell is hardly likely to give up the stage. Besides, all of his possessions are at Woolsey."

Lady Maccon sighed. "Poor Ivy."

"Why poor Ivy?"

"Well, my dear, you must admit, she has come rather down in the world."

Lord Maccon waggled his eyebrows. "I always thought your friend had a flair for the dramatic, *my dear*."

Alexia winced. "You suppose she will join him in treading the boards?"

Lord Maccon shrugged.

Felicity, who had been avidly listening in to their conversation, slapped her fork down on her empty plate with a clank. "Well, I *say*! You mean she will not be completely ruined?"

Lord Maccon only smiled.

"You know, husband"—Lady Maccon glanced at her sister—"I think you may be right. She might make for a passing good actress. She certainly has the looks for it."

Felicity stood up from the table and marched out of the room.

Lord and Lady Maccon exchanged grins.

Alexia figured this was as good a time as any. "Husband," she said, casually helping herself to another small portion of haggis and assiduously avoiding the kippers. Her stomach was still feeling a little queasy, having never really recovered from the dratted dirigible experience, but a body had to eat.

"Aye?" Conall loaded his plate down with mounds of various dead critters.

"We will be departing presently, will we not?"

"Aye."

"I *ken* it is time you bit Lady Kingair, then," she stated baldly into the quiet munching of the dinner table.

The pack was immediately in an uproar, everyone talking at once.

"You canna change a woman," objected Dubh.

"She's the only Alpha we got left," added Lachlan, as though Alpha were a cut of meat to be acquired at the butcher.

Lady Kingair did not say anything, looking pale but resolute.

Alexia, rather boldly, took her husband's chin in one gloved hand, turning him mortal and turning him toward her.

"You need to do this, regardless of your pack laws and your werewolf pride. Take my counsel in this matter; remember, you married me for my good sense."

He grumbled but did not jerk his head away. "I married you for your body and to stop that mouth of yours. Look where that's got me."

"Aw, Conall, what a sweet thing to say." Lady Maccon rolled her eyes and then kissed him swiftly, on the lips, right there in front of the whole dinner table.

It was the surest way to silence a pack—scandalize them all. Even Conall was left speechless, with his mouth hanging slightly open.

"Good news, Lady Kingair," said Alexia. "My husband has agreed to change you."

The Kingair Beta laughed, breaking the dumbfounded hush. "I'm guessing she *is* a proper Alpha for all she was born a curse-breaker. Never thought I'd see you line up short to the petticoats, old wolf."

Lord Maccon stood up slowly and leaned forward,

staring across at Dubh. "Want to try me again, pup? I can beat you down just as soundly in wolf form as I could in human."

Dubh quickly turned to one side, baring his neck. Apparently he agreed with the earl in this matter.

Lord Maccon made his way over to where Lady Kingair sat, still and straight in her chair at the head of the table. "You certain about this, lass? You ken 'tis probably death that's facing you?"

"We need an Alpha, Gramps." She looked to him. "Kingair canna survive much longer without one. I be the only option we've got left, and at least I'm Maccon. You owe the pack."

Lord Maccon's voice was a low rumble. "I dinna owe this pack anything. But you, lass, you're the last of my line. And it's time I took your wishes into consideration."

Lady Kingair sighed softly. "Finally."

Conall nodded once more. Then he changed. Not entirely. There was no full breaking of bone, no complete melting from one form to the next, and no shifting of hair into fur—except about his head. Only there did Lord Maccon transform: his nose elongating, his ears expanding upward, and his eyes shifting from brown to full yellow and lupine. The rest of him remained fully human-looking.

"Goodness me!" exclaimed Lady Maccon. "Are you going to do it right here, right now?" She swallowed. "At the dinner table?"

No one responded. They all stopped eating—a serious business, indeed, to put a Scotsman off his food. Pack and claviger alike became still and focused, staring hard at Lord Maccon. It was as though, by sheer strength of will, they could all see this metamorphosis through to a successful conclusion. Either that, or they were about to regurgitate their meals.

Then Lord Conall Maccon proceeded to eat his great-great-great-granddaughter.

There was really no other way of putting it.

Alexia watched in wide-eyed horror as her husband, wearing the head of a wolf, began to bite down on Lady Kingair's neck and then kept on chomping. Never before had she thought to behold such a thing.

And he was doing it right there, supper dishes not yet cleared away. The blood leaking down from Lady Kingair's throat seeped into the lace collar and silk bodice of her dress, a dark spreading stain.

The Earl of Woolsey savaged Sidheag Maccon. Not one of the pack stepped in to save her. Sidheag flailed against the full bite. Instinct would not deny such a reaction. She clawed and hit at Conall, but he remained unmoved and unhurt, his werewolf strength easily outmatching her pathetic human struggles. He simply clamped those big hands about her shoulders—and they were still simply hands, without claws—and kept on biting. His long white teeth ripped through skin and muscle right down to the bone. Blood covered his muzzle, clotting the fur there.

Lady Maccon could not pull her eyes away from the gruesome sight. There seemed to be blood everywhere, and the copper smell of it battled against the scent of haggis and fried kipper. She was beginning to discern the inner workings of the woman's neck, as though this were some kind of horrific tableside anatomy lesson. Sidheag stopped struggling, her eyes rolling far back, showing almost all the whites. Her head, barely still attached to the rest of her body, lolled dangerously far to one side.

Then, in some farcical mockery of death, out came Conall's big pink tongue, and like an excessively friendly dog, he began licking over all the flesh he had just butchered. And he kept on licking, covering Sidheag's face and her partly open mouth, spreading lupine saliva about Lady Kingair's gaping wounds.

I am never going to be able to perform my wifely duty with that man ever again, thought Alexia, her eyes wide and fixed on the repulsive sight. Then, entirely unexpectedly and without even knowing it was about to happen, she actually fainted. A real honest-to-goodness faint, right there, face forward into her half-eaten haggis.

Lady Maccon blinked awake to her husband's worried, looming face. "Conall," she said, "please do not take this the wrong way. But that may have been the most disgusting thing I have ever seen in my life."

"Have you ever attended the birthing of a human child?"

"No, of course not. Don't be vulgar."

"Well, perhaps you had best wait to pass judgment, then."

"Well?" Alexia levered herself up slightly and glanced about. She appeared to have been carried into one of the drawing rooms and put to rest upon a brocade settee of considerable age.

"Well what?"

"Did it work? Did the metamorphosis work? Is she going to survive?"

Lord Maccon sat back slightly on his haunches. "A

remarkable thing, a full Alpha female. Rare even in our oral histories. Boudica was an Alpha, did you know?"

"Conall!"

The head of a wolf came into Alexia's line of vision. It was not one she was personally familiar with: a craggy, rangy creature, graying about the muzzle but muscled and fit despite evident signs of age. Lady Maccon struggled to prop herself farther up onto the pillows.

The wolf's neck was covered in blood, the fur matted with a dark red crust, but otherwise it showed no injury. As though the blood were not her own. Which, technically, as she had now become supernatural, it might not be anymore.

Sidheag Maccon lolled a tongue out at Alexia. Alexia wondered how the wolf would respond to a scratch about the ears and decided, given the dignity of the woman when mortal, not to risk such an approach.

She looked at her husband. At least he seemed to have changed his shirt and washed his face during her mental absence. "I take it it worked?"

He grinned hugely. "My first successful change in years, and a female Alpha at that. The howlers will cry it to the winds."

"Somebody's proud of himself."

"Except that I should have remembered how distressing metamorphosis is to outsiders. I am sorry, my dear. I didna mean to upset you."

"Oh pish tosh, it wasn't that! I'm hardly one to be overcome by a bit of blood. It was simply a little dizzy spell."

Lord Maccon shifted forward against her and ran a large hand down the side of her face. "Alexia, you have been entirely comatose for well over an hour. I had to send for smelling salts."

Madame Lefoux came around the side of the couch and crouched down next to Alexia as well. "You had us very worried, my lady."

"So what happened?"

"You fainted," accused Lord Maccon, as though she had committed some egregious crime against him personally.

"No, with the metamorphosis. What did I miss?"

"Well," said Madame Lefoux, "it was all very exciting. There was this crash of thunder and a bright blue light and then—"

"Don't be ridiculous," snapped Lord Maccon. "You sound like a novel."

Madame Lefoux sighed. "Very well, Sidheag started to convulse and then collapsed to the floor, dead. Everyone stood around staring at her body, until all of a sudden, she began spontaneously changing into a wolf. She screamed a lot—I understand the first change is the worst. Then we realized you had collapsed. Lord Maccon threw a conniption fit, and we ended up here."

Lady Maccon turned accusing eyes to her husband. "You didn't, and on your granddaughter's metamorphosis day!"

"You fainted!" he said again, disgruntled.

"Stuff and nonsense," replied his wife sharply. "I never faint." A bit of her old color was returning. Really, who would have suspected she could turn quite that ashen?

"There was that one incident, in the library, when you killed the vampire."

"I was shamming and you knew it."

"How about that time we visited the museum after hours and I trapped you in a corner behind the Elgin Marbles?"

Lady Maccon rolled her eyes. "That was an entirely different kind of passing out."

Conall crowed. "My point exactly! Just now, you actually, positively, did faint. You never do that kind of thing; you're not that kind of female. What's wrong with you? Are you ill? I *forbid* you to be ill, wife."

"Oh, really. Stop fussing. There is absolutely nothing wrong with me. I'm just a tad off-kilter, have been since the dirigible ride." Alexia pushed herself more upright, trying to smooth her skirts and ignore her husband's still-stroking hand.

"Someone could have poisoned you again."

Alexia shook her head decisively. "As it wasn't Angelique who tried before, and it wasn't Madame Lefoux who stole my journal, and both occurred on board the dirigible, I believe the perpetrator never followed us to Kingair. Call it a preternatural hunch. No, I'm not being poisoned, husband. I'm just a little bit weak, that's all."

Madame Lefoux snorted, looking back and forth between the two of them as though they were both batty. She said, "She is just a little bit pregnant is what she is."

"What!" Lord Maccon's exclamation was echoed by Alexia. Lady Maccon stopped smoothing out her skirts, and Lord Maccon stopped smoothing out his wife's face.

The French inventor looked at them, genuinely amazed. "You did not know? Neither of you knew?"

Lord Maccon recoiled away from his wife, violently, jerking to stand upright, arms stiff by his sides.

Alexia glared at Madame Lefoux. "Don't talk piffle, madame. I cannot possibly be pregnant. That is not scientifically feasible."

Madame Lefoux dimpled. "I was with Angelique during her confinement. You show every possible sign of a delicate condition—nausea, weakness, increased girth."

"What!" Lady Maccon was genuinely shocked. True, she had been slightly sick to her stomach and unreasonably off some foods, but was it really possible? She supposed she might be in an indelicate condition. The scientists could be wrong, after all; there didn't exist very many soulless females, and none of them were married to werewolves.

She turned a suddenly grinning face to her husband. "You know what this means? I am not a bad dirigible floater! It was being pregnant that made me ill on board. Fantastic."

But her husband was not reacting in quite the manner anticipated. He was clearly angry, and not the sort of angry that made him bluster about, or shout, or change form, or any of those normal Lord Macconish kinds of things. He was quietly, white-faced, shivering angry. And it was terribly, terribly frightening.

"*How?*" he barked at his wife, backing away from her as though she were infected with some terrible disease.

"What do you mean, how? The *how* should be perfectly obvious, even to you, you impossible man!" Alexia shot back, becoming angry herself. Shouldn't he be delighted? This was evidently a scientific miracle. Wasn't it?

"We only *call* it 'being human' when I touch you, for lack of a better term. I'm still dead, or mostly dead. Have been for hundreds of years. No supernatural creature has ever produced an offspring. *Ever.* It simply isna possible."

"You believe this can't be your child?"

"Now, hold on there, my lord, don't be hasty." Madame Lefoux tried to intervene, placing one small hand on Lord Maccon's arm.

He shook her off with a snarl.

"Of course it's your child, you pollock!" Now Alexia was livid. If she hadn't still been feeling weak, she would have stood and marched about the room. As it was, she groped for her parasol. Maybe whacking her husband atop his thick skull would drive some sense into him.

"Thousands of years of history and experience would seem to suggest you are lying, wife."

Lady Maccon sputtered in offense at that. She was so overset she couldn't even find the words, a remarkably novel experience for her.

"Who was he?" Conall wanted to know. "What daylight-dependent dishtowel did you fornicate with? One of my clavigers? One of Akeldama's poodle-faking drones? Is that why you're always visiting him? Or just some milk-curling mortal blowhard?"

Then he began calling her things, names and words, dirtier and harsher than she had ever heard before—let alone been called—and Alexia had encountered more than her fair share of profanity over the past year. They were horrible, cruel things, and she could comprehend the meanings of most, despite her lack of familiarity with the terminology.

Conall had committed many a violent act around Alexia during their association, not the least of which was savage a woman into metamorphosis at the supper table, but Alexia had never been actually afraid of him before.

She was afraid of him now. He did not move toward her—in fact, he'd backed farther away toward the door—but his hands were fisted white at his thighs, his eyes had changed to wolf yellow, and his canines were long and extended. She was immeasurably grateful when Madame Lefoux physically interposed herself between Alexia and the earl's verbal tirade. As though, somehow, the inventor could provide a barrier to his horrible words.

He stayed there, on the other side of the room, yelling at Alexia. It was as though he'd placed the distance between them, not because he didn't want to come at her and tear her apart, but because he really thought he might. His eyes were such a pale yellow they were almost white. Alexia had never seen them that color before. And, despite the filthy words coming out of his mouth, those eyes were agonized and bereft.

"But I didn't," Alexia tried to say. "I wouldn't. I'd never do those things. I am no adulteress. How could you even think? I would never." But her protestations of innocence only seemed to injure him. Eventually, his big, good-natured face crumpled slightly about the mouth and nose, drawing down into lines of pain, as though he might actually cry. He strode from the room, slamming the door behind him.

The silence he left behind was palpable.

Lady Kingair had, during the chaos, managed to change back into human form. She came around the front of the couch and stood a moment before Alexia, entirely naked, shielded only by her long gray-brown hair, loose over her shoulders and chest.

"You will understand, *Lady* Maccon," she said, eyes cold, "if I ask you to leave Kingair territory at once. Lord Maccon may have abandoned us once, but he is still pack. And pack protects its own."

"But," Alexia whispered, "it is his child. I swear it. I was never with anyone else."

Sidheag only stared at her, hard. "Come now, Lady Maccon. Shouldna you come up with a better story than that? 'Tis na possible. Werewolves canna breed children. Never have done, never will do." Then she turned and left the room.

Alexia turned to Madame Lefoux, shock written all over her face. "He really believes I was unfaithful." She herself had reflected recently how much Conall valued loyalty.

Madame Lefoux nodded. "I'm afraid it is a belief most will share." Her expression sympathetic, she placed a small hand on Alexia's shoulder and squeezed.

"I wasn't, I swear I wasn't."

The Frenchwoman winced. "I believe that, Lady Maccon. But I will be in the minority."

"Why would you trust me when even my husband does not?" Alexia looked down at her own stomach and then rested shaking hands upon it.

"Because I know how very little we understand about preternaturals."

"You are interested in studying me, aren't you, Madame Lefoux?"

"You are a remarkable creature, Alexia."

Alexia widened her eyes, trying not to cry, her mind still vibrating with Conall's words. "Then how is this possible?" She pressed hard against her stomach with both hands, as though asking the tiny creature inside to explain itself to her.

"I imagine that is something we had best figure out. Come on, let's get you out of this place."

The Frenchwoman helped Alexia to stand and supported her weight out into the hallway. She was surprisingly strong for such a delicate-looking creature, probably all that lifting of heavy machinery.

They ran into Felicity, looking remarkably somber.

"Sister, there was the most awful to-do," she said as soon as she saw them. "I believe your husband just smashed one of the hall tables into a thousand pieces with his fist." She cocked her head. "It *was* an astonishingly ugly table, but still, one could always give it to the deserving poor, couldn't one?"

"We must pack and leave immediately," said Madame Lefoux, keeping one arm supportively about Alexia's waist.

"Good Lord, why?"

"Your sister is pregnant, and Lord Maccon has cast her out."

Felicity frowned. "Well, *that* does not follow."

Madame Lefoux had clearly had enough. "Quickly, girl, run off and gather your things together. We must quit Kingair directly."

Three-quarters of an hour later, a borrowed Kingair carriage sped away toward the nearest train station. The horses were fresh and made good time, even in the slush and mud.

Alexia, still overcome with the most profound shock, opened the small window above the carriage door and poked her head out into the rushing wind.

"Sister, come away from the window. That will wreak havoc with your hair. And, really, your hair doesn't need the excuse," Felicity jawed on. Alexia ignored her, so Felicity looked to the Frenchwoman. "What *is* she doing?"

Madame Lefoux gave a sad little grimace of a smile—no dimples. "Listening." She put a gentle hand on Alexia's back, rubbing it softly. Alexia did not appear to notice.

"For what?"

"Howling, running wolves."

And Alexia was listening, but there was only the damp quiet of a Scottish night.

extras

orbit

meet the author

Ms. Carriger began writing in order to cope with being raised in obscurity by an expatriate Brit and an incurable curmudgeon. She escaped small-town life and inadvertently acquired several degrees in Higher Learning. Ms. Carriger then traveled the historic cities of Europe, subsisting entirely on biscuits secreted in her handbag. She now resides in the Colonies, surrounded by a harem of Armenian lovers, where she insists on tea imported directly from London. She is fond of teeny-tiny hats and tropical fruit. Find out more about Ms. Carriger at www.gailcarriger.com.

introducing

If you enjoyed CHANGELESS,
look out for

BLAMELESS

The Parasol Protectorate: Book the Third

by Gail Carriger

H ow much longer, Mama, must we tolerate this gross
humiliation?"

Lady Alexia Maccon paused before entering the
breakfast room. Cutting through the comfortable sounds
of chinking teacups and scrunching toast came her sister's nondulcet tones. In an unsurprising morning duet
of well-practiced whining, Felicity's voice was soon followed by Evylin's.

"Yes, mumsy darling, such a scandal under our roof.
We really shouldn't be expected to put up with it any
longer."

Felicity championed the cause once more. "This is

ruining our chances"—crunch, crunch—"beyond all
recuperation. It isn't to be borne. It really isn't."

Alexia made a show of checking her appearance in the
hall mirror, hoping to overhear more. Much to her con-
sternation, the Loontwills' new butler, Swilkins, came
through with a tray of kippers. He gave her a disapprov-
ing glare that said much on his opinion of a young lady
caught eavesdropping on her own family. Eavesdropping
was, by rights, a butler's proprietary art form.

"Good morning, Lady Maccon," he said loudly
enough for the family to hear even through their chatting and clattering. "You received several messages this
morning." He handed Alexia two folded and sealed letters and then waited pointedly for her to precede him into
the breakfast room.

Alexia hid her annoyance and flounced in. "Good
morning, dearest family."

Said family responded reluctantly to her pleasant
greeting.

As she made her way carefully to the only empty chair,
four pairs of blue eyes watched her progress with an air
of condemnation. Well, three pairs: the Right Honorable
Squire Loontwill seemed entirely taken with the correct
cracking of his soft-boiled egg. This involved the application of an ingenious little device, rather like a handheld
sideways guillotine, that nipped the tip off the egg in perfect, chipless circularity. Thus happily engrossed, he did
not bother to attend to the arrival of his stepdaughter.

Alexia carefully poured herself a glass of barley water
and took a piece of toast from the rack, no butter, trying
to ignore the smoky smell of breakfast. It had once been
her favorite meal; now it invariably curdled her stomach.

So far the infant-inconvenience—as she'd taken to thinking of it—was proving itself far more tiresome than one would have thought possible, considering it was years away from either speech or action.

Mrs. Loontwill looked with manifold approval at her daughter's meager selection. "I shall be comforted," she said to the table at large, "by the fact that our poor dear Alexia is practically wasting away for want of her husband's affection. Such fine feelings of sentimentality." She clearly perceived Alexia's breakfast-starvation tactics as symptoms of a superior bout of wallowing.

Alexia gave her mother an annoyed glance. Since the infant-inconvenience had already brought with it a small amount of weight added to Alexia's already substantial figure, she was several stone away from "wasting." Nor was she of a personality inclined toward wallowing. In addition, she resented the fact that Lord Maccon might be perceived as having anything whatsoever to do with the fact—aside from the obvious, of which her family was as yet unaware—that she was off her food. She opened her mouth to correct her mother in this regard, but Felicity interrupted her.

"Oh, Mama, I hardly think Alexia is the type to die of a broken heart."

"Nor is she the type to be gastronomically challenged," shot back Mrs. Loontwill.

"I, on the other hand," interjected Evylin, helping herself to a plateful of kipper, "may jolly well do both."

"Language, Evy darling, please." Mrs. Loontwill snapped a piece of toast in half in her distress.

The youngest Miss Loontwill rounded on Alexia, pointing a forkful of eggs at her accusingly. "Captain

Featherstonehaugh has thrown me over! How do you like that? We received a note only this morning."

"Captain Featherstonehaugh?" Alexia muttered to herself. "I thought he was engaged to Ivy and you were engaged to someone else. How confusing."

"No no, Evy's engaged to him now. Or, was. How long have you been staying with us? Do pay attention, Alexia dear." Mrs. Loontwill admonished.

Evylin sighed dramatically. "And the dress is already bought and everything. I shall have to have it entirely made over."

"He did have very nice eyebrows," consoled Mrs. Loontwill.

"Exactly," crowed Evylin. "Where will I find another pair of eyebrows like that? Crushed, I tell you, Alexia. I am absolutely crushed. And it's all *your* fault."

Evylin, it must be noted, did not actually look nearly so bothered as one rightly ought over the loss of a fiancé, especially one reputed to possess such heights of eyebrow superiority. She stuffed the eggs into her mouth and chewed methodically. She had taken it into her head recently that chewing every bite of food twenty times over would keep her slender. What it did was keep her at the dinner table longer than anyone else.

"He cited philosophical differences, but we all know why he really broke things off." Felicity waved a gold-edged note at Alexia—a note that clearly contained the good captain's deepest regrets—a note that, from the stains about its person, had received the concerted attention of everyone at the breakfast table, including the kippers.

"I agree." Alexia calmly sipped her barley water.

"Philosophical differences? That cannot possibly be true. You don't actually have a philosophy about anything. Do you, Evylin dear?"

"So you admit responsibility?" Evylin was moved to swallow her eggs early so that she could launch the attack once more. She tossed her blond curls, only one or two shades removed from the color of her eggs.

"Certainly not. I never even met the man."

"But it is still *your* fault. Abandoning your husband like that, staying with us instead of him. It is outrageous. People. Are. Talking." Evylin emphasized her words by stabbing ruthlessly at a sausage.

"People do tend to talk. I believe it is generally considered one of the better modes of communication."

"Oh, why must you be so impossible? Mama, do something about her." Evylin delegated her mother as responsible for Alexia's good conduct, gave up on the sausage, and went back to her eggs.

"You hardly seem very cut up about it." Alexia watched as her sister chewed away.

"Oh, I assure you, poor Evy is deeply effected. Shockingly overwrought, even." Mrs. Loontwill came to her daughter's defense.

"Surely you mean *affected*?" Alexia was not above a barb or two where her family was concerned.

At the end of the table, Squire Loontwill, the only one likely to understand a literary joke, chuckled softly.

"Herbert," his wife reprimanded immediately, "don't encourage her to be pert. Most unattractive quality in a married lady, pertness." She turned back to Alexia. Mrs. Loontwill's face, that of a pretty woman who had aged without realizing it, screwed itself up into a grimace

Alexia supposed was meant to simulate motherly concern. Instead she looked like a Pekinese with digestive complaints. "Is that what the estrangement with *him* is over, Alexia? You weren't . . . brainy . . . with *him,* were you, dear?" Mrs. Loontwill had refrained from referring to Lord Maccon by name ever since her daughter's marriage, as if by doing so she might hold on to the fact that Alexia *had* married—a condition believed by most to be highly unlikely right up until the fateful event—without having to remember *what* she had married. A peer of the realm, it was true, and one of Her Majesty's finest, to be certain, but also a werewolf. It hadn't helped that Lord Maccon loathed Mrs. Loontwill and didn't mind who knew it—including Mrs. Loontwill. Why, Alexia remembered, once he had even . . . She stopped herself from further thought of her husband, squashing down ruthlessly on the small smile attempting to creep up at the memory.

"It seems clear to me," interjected Felicity with an air of finality, "that your presence here, Alexia, has somehow overset Evy's engagement. Even you cannot argue your way out of that, sister dear."

Felicity and Evylin were Alexia's younger half sisters by birth and were entirely unrelated to her if one took into account any other factors. They were short, blond, and slender, while Alexia was tall, dark, and, quite frankly, not so very slender. They were inclined to giggle, waste hours over the fashion papers, and don the color pink. Alexia was not. Lady Maccon was known throughout London for her intellectual prowess, patronage of the scientific community, and biting wit. Felicity and Evylin were known for their puffed sleeves. The world, as a result, was generally a better place when the three were not living together under the same roof.

"And we all know how considered and unbiased your opinion is on the matter, Felicity." Alexia's tone was unruffled.

Felicity picked up the scandal section of the *Ladies Daily Chirrup,* clearly indicating she wanted nothing more to do with the conversation.

Mrs. Loontwill drove courageously on. "Surely, Alexia, darling, it is high time you returned home to Woolsey? I mean to say, you've been with us nearly a week, and, of course, we do love having you, but *he* is rumored to be back from Scotland now."

"Who is?"

"Well, uh, Lord Maccon."

"Bully for him."

"Alexia! What a shocking thing to say!"

Evylin interjected, "No one has seen him in town, of course, but they say he returned to Woolsey yesterday."

"Who says?"

Felicity rattled the gossip section of the paper explanatorily.

"Oh, *they.*"

"He must be pining for you, my dear." Mrs. Loontwill resumed the attack. "Pining away, miserable for want of your . . ." She flailed.

"For want of my *what,* Mama?"

"Uh, scintillating companionship."

Alexia snorted, actually snorted, at the dining table. Conall may enjoy her bluntness, but if he missed anything, she doubted her wit was at the top of the lot. Lord Maccon was a werewolf of hearty appetites, to say the least. What he would miss most about his wife was located substantially lower down than her tongue. An image of her husband's face momentarily broke her resolve. That look in his eyes the last time they saw each other—so betrayed. But what he believed of her, the fact that he doubted her in such a way, was inexcusable. How dare he leave her remembering some lost-puppy look simply to toy with her sympathies! Alexia Maccon made herself relive the things he had said to her, right then and there. She was *never* going to go back to that—her mind grappled for a description—that *antitruster*! Apparently her mind had rejected all options and come up with a new word as recompense.

Lady Alexia Maccon was the type of woman who, if thrown into a briar patch, would start to tidy it up by stripping off all the thorns. She had, in fact, over the past three days and throughout the course of an inexcusably foul train journey back from Scotland, come to terms with her husband's rejection of both her and their child. This had involved exactly twelve tears, about twelve hundred unpleasant words—said at high volume to anyone who would listen—concerning Lord Maccon's ancestry back several generations, and finally had ended in icy outrage. Alexia was used to defending herself for having done something wrong, but defending herself when completely innocent made for an entirely different, and far more frustrating, experience. Not even Bogglington's Best Darjeeling succeeded in soothing her temper. And if tea wasn't good enough, well, what *was* a lady to do? Simmering softly in the deepest of angers had been her only solution. After days of such simmering, Lady Maccon was quite tender about the edges. Her family ought to have recognized the signs.

Felicity snapped the paper closed suddenly, her face an uncharacteristic red color.

"Oh dear." Mrs. Loontwill fanned herself with a place setting. "What *now*?"

Squire Loontwill looked resignedly up and then back down at his egg.

"Nothing." Felicity hastily tried to shove the paper under her plate.

Evylin was having none of it. She reached over, snatched it away, and began scanning through it, looking for whatever juicy tittle-tattle had so disturbed her sister.

Felicity nibbled on a scone and looked guiltily at Alexia.

Alexia had a sudden sinking feeling in the pit of her stomach. It did not mix well with her already-unsettled interior. She finished the barley water with some difficulty and sat back in her chair, waiting for the next round of recriminations.

"Oh gosh!" Evylin seemed to have found the troublesome passage. She read it out for all to hear. " 'London was flabbergasted earlier this week when news reached this reporter's ears that Lady Maccon, previously Alexia Tarabotti, daughter of Mrs. Loontwill, sister to Felicity and Evylin, and stepdaughter to the Honorable Squire Loontwill, had quit her husband's house after returning from Scotland without said husband. Speculation as to the reason has been ample, ranging from suspicions as to Lady Maccon's intimate relationship with the rove vampire Lord Akeldama to suspected family differences hinted at by the Misses Loontwills'—oh, look, Felicity, they mentioned us twice!—'and certain lower-class social acquaintances. Lady Maccon cut quite a fashionable swath through London society after her marriage'—la, la, la, ah, here it picks up again—'but it has been revealed by sources intimately connected to the noble couple that Lady Maccon is, in fact, in a most delicate condition. Given Lord Maccon's age, supernatural inclination, and legally recognized postnecrosis status, it must be assumed that Lady Maccon has been *indiscreet*. While we await physical confirmation, all signs point to the Scandal of the Century.' "

Everyone looked at Alexia and began talking at once.